VOYAGE OF THE GRAY WOLVES

"A stunning page-turner that grabs the reader and never lets go!"

—Joe Buff, author of *Crush Depth*, *Tidal Rip*, and *Straits of Power*

"A slam-bang confrontation on the high seas. A great read!"

—Chet Cunningham, author of *Hell Wouldn't Stop: The Battle of Wake Island in World War II*

"Steven Wilson takes us on a taut, suspenseful, engaging and frightening saltwater thriller to the secret, dangerous undersea horrors of WWII submarining, where his war machines are as deeply soulful—and as realistically lethal—as his combat-weary yet inspired characters. No submarine fiction fan's bookcase is complete without Wilson's *Voyage of the Gray Wolves*. Bravo zulu and good hunting, Steven."

—Michael DiMercurio, author of *Emergency Deep* and *Terminal Run*

"Wow! What great, page-turning action and captivating characters. Wilson will keep you enthralled and on the edge of your seat."

—David E. Meadows, author of the *Sixth Fleet* and *Joint Task Force* series

"A fine adventure nov
McLean; once you pick

—Tom
and

BOOK YOUR PLACE ON OUR WEBSITE AND MAKE THE READING CONNECTION!

We've created a customized website just for our very special readers, where you can get the inside scoop on everything that's going on with Zebra, Pinnacle and Kensington books.

When you come online, you'll have the exciting opportunity to:

- View covers of upcoming books
- Read sample chapters
- Learn about our future publishing schedule (listed by publication month *and author*)
- Find out when your favorite authors will be visiting a city near you
- Search for and order backlist books from our online catalog
- Check out author bios and background information
- Send e-mail to your favorite authors
- Meet the Kensington staff online
- Join us in weekly chats with authors, readers and other guests
- Get writing guidelines
- AND MUCH MORE!

Visit our website at
http://www.kensingtonbooks.com

VOYAGE
OF THE
GRAY
WOLVES

Steven M. Wilson

PINNACLE BOOKS
Kensington Publishing Corp.
http://www.kensingtonbooks.com

Chapter I

Holy Island, the Irish Sea, October 1978

Edwin Land, Royal Navy Retired, opened the door of his modest cottage and saw a white-haired man in a navy peacoat standing before him.

"You're the American chap?" he said, trying to recall the name. "Coleman?"

"Close. Cole," the American said, holding out his hand and flashing a broad grin. "Jordan Cole. Thanks for taking the time to see me, Commander."

"Oh, let's dispense with all of that nonsense. Please call me Land. Everyone does. Rank and titles no longer suit old men." He motioned Cole in and gestured to a dilapidated wing chair. "She doesn't look like much but she's the best seat in the house. Hang your coat on that peg if you like. Tea's brewing. I don't have any coffee. Nor hot chocolate. Plugs me up anyway." Land disappeared from the tiny sitting room.

Cole heard the sound of dishes. He looked around. There were three bookshelves along one wall. A quick glance revealed that they were filled with books that all had something to do with sailing or the sea. A small table against another wall blossomed with dozens of photographs, some black and white, and some color. Some of the black and white were of very long ago—

earnest young men in uniform standing on the deck of a destroyer. Cole smiled in remembrance. He once knew a young man like that.

"Well, here we are," Land said. "Nice and comforting on a day like this. Blustery, isn't it? Why I choose to retire here, I shall never know. I suppose it's the solitude."

Cole took a cup. "You were hard to find. I had to go through your solicitor."

"Yes," Land said. He took a sip of tea. "You're writing a book?"

"A series of books for the Naval Institute," Cole said. "A record of the naval actions in the Atlantic. I wanted to start with U-boats. Your name came up and here I am."

"All the way from America? You must be desperate, old boy."

Cole chuckled. "No. I was already here doing research at the Imperial War Museum."

"So you thought you'd pop over and spend the afternoon talking with an old sailor?"

Cole smiled, looking into his cup of tea. "One old sailor to another, I guess."

"Atlantic or Pacific?"

"Atlantic," Cole said.

"Jolly good. You and I will have something to talk about. No soft winds and palm trees for North Atlantic sailors. No, indeed. You saw action, then?"

"Yes. I was on a plane that went down in the North Atlantic. A British destroyer picked me up. It was Fire-something-or-other."

"Not *Firedancer*?"

"That's it," Cole said. "If I ever see those guys again, I'll buy them a beer."

Land raised his teacup. "Here sits one of 'those

guys,' before your very eyes. I was number one on old *Firedancer.* Fancy that for a coincidence. I remember you now. You were a pretty sad sight indeed when we took you in. Forty-one, wasn't it?"

"Yes," Cole said. "I remember your captain most of all."

"George Hardy," Land said with a knowing smile. "One does not easily forget George Hardy when one has had the pleasure. Is that why you've come to see me?"

No," Cole said. "Not exactly." He pulled out a pad and pen. "Did you hear about the plane going down?"

"The airliner? Bloody awful mess. People blowing up innocent women and children. Made me sick just to think about it and I've seen plenty enough to make me sick during the war, but that was war, you understand, not murder. Well, getting tied up in a tizzy at my age won't help. It's the world today, I suppose." He glanced at Cole. "Sorry about going on like that. Ask your questions, Mr. Cole, and I shall do my best to answer them."

"Okay. You see, when divers were sent down to locate the plane's black box—"

"The radio locator beacon."

"Yes. About 150 miles north-northwest of here. They unexpectedly stumbled upon a wreck. A U-boat. They couldn't figure out what it was at first."

Land rose slowly, a look of stunned disbelief on his face, and made his way to a window. "So that one's come back, has she?" He stood, silently, watching two fishing boats with outstretched yardarms burdened with bundles of black nets sail lazily across the sea. They lolled on the rolling waves, each arm in turn beckoning. Land crossed his arms in resignation and said without turning back, "Like nothing they'd ever seen?"

Cole closed the pad and laid it on his lap. "Yes."

Land turned. "A Type XXI?"

Cole nodded. "I saw the sonar charts and photographs. I couldn't get much because examining the boat wasn't their primary mission. But from what I know of them—yes, a Type XXI."

Land smiled at Cole and returned to his chair. "You know, Mr. Cole, the official story about the Type XXI is that only two of those wonderful vessels went on war patrol and both were forced to return because of mechanical difficulties."

"That's what I hear, Mr. Land, but I've been in this man's navy long enough to have a healthy skepticism for the official side of any story. But I'd like to hear your side."

"My side? Oh, my side!" Land laughed fully. "If only Georgie were here. He'd set you straight on what 'my side' of the story was. By God, I could hear the bloody bastard now. 'My aunt's pajamas, Number One, you can't tell your left from your right, let alone port from starboard. Stand there and try not to bump into me.' By God, people called him a madman and they were probably right."

Cole smiled, waiting.

"Yes," Land said, remembering the past of gray clouds, vague shapes, and dead friends. "She was a Type XXI, all right, the boat that was found. I know it for certain because I know where we sank her. God, she was fast! And dangerous. And big! She could have been as big as our Kelly Class, if not larger. I can tell you, I was frightened more than once when we went up against her. Hardy wouldn't let go—the chase, I mean—he wouldn't give up on it."

"Yeah," Cole said, "I know how that is."

Land studied Cole closely and found that he liked this tall American. He had a seaman's face and the harsh black eyes of a fighter. But he was unhurried and thoughtful as well. There were strong veins running across the ropelike tendons of his hands, but his fingers were gentle, slender as if he were a man forced to live in two worlds—warrior and artist. There was within him, Land decided, a great many locked vaults, each containing some secret notion of the man, perhaps even unknown to him. He would not have many friends, none close, that was certain, and love would come only on his terms; it would be half love, something always held back, something always denied to his lover. He was and had always been a lonely man.

"Do you want to know all about this beastie, Mr. Cole?"

"Yes, I do, Mr. Land."

Land slapped the arms of his chair, sending dust boiling into the light of the evening sun. He went to the liquor cabinet and pulled out two glasses and a bottle of scotch. He filled each glass equally, set the bottle on the floor, and handed a glass to Cole. Land held his out.

"A toast. 'To sturdy ships and the good men who sail them.'" They touched glasses and downed the liquid. "Now, Mr. Cole, let's talk about the ghosts of men and ships."

Chapter 2

The blue-green waters of the Bay of Kiel bubbled into life as the rust-streaked conning tower of U-686 rose slowly out of the sea like a battered wreck called to life. Her low hull, the wooden deck glistening with algae, settled uncertainly into the rolling waves. She was not comfortable upon the sea. Better the quiet darkness below the waves, the place of safety.

The conning tower hatch flew open and the lookouts scrambled up the ladder. They quickly took their positions and scanned the cloud-mottled blue sky for danger. Behind them came Oberleutnant Guenter Kern, taking his place on the bridge. He threw a pair of binoculars to his eyes, searching for enemy aircraft. A sand-colored beard covered his face, and a formless white cap was pushed back off his forehead. His worn, gray leather coat hung loosely on his thin frame as he swept the horizon. His pale green eyes saw nothing but a haze that blurred the line between sea and sky and the dark shapes of distant islands that rode high above the soft waves of the bay.

He lowered the glasses and called down the hatch, "Gunners up. Ventilate the boat."

Kern's face was haggard, deep lines cut in his pale skin. His eyes were bloodshot. He rubbed his face roughly, trying to drive the fatigue away.

Kern watched as his gunners quickly moved to the 3.7cm automatic and the two double-barreled 2cm antiaircraft guns on the upper and lower gun decks. The men called the area aft of the bridge their "wintergarten." Here they snatched a few minutes to smoke their cigarettes and breathe air that did not stink of fuel and mold. It was a luxury to have the sun beat down on their faces, to taste the salt air, to smell the sea, to have the vast expanses of ocean and sky fill their vision. The one true luxury of the U-boat: three minutes in paradise as the men hurriedly smoked cigarettes while the next shift waited impatiently at the bottom of the ladder. Three minutes. If they were lucky.

The gunners readied the guns and waited nervously, their bearded faces upturned, blinking in the unaccustomed brightness. Kern watched them. They were experts at what they did, trained to the point that they functioned automatically. Not dullards or machines, far from it: U-boatmen who had survived five years of asdic—the relentless pinging as the British or Americans sent out underwater signals, trying to find them. And when they did, wabos, depth charges, innocently floating down to cave in their hull and kill them in an instant.

Oberleutnant Kern watched as the gunners trained their weapons, the barrels sweeping the sky in readiness.

Just like the pitiful remnant of a U-boat they sailed in, Kern's crew was worn out. Where red undercoating showed through the U-boat's gray battle paint in streaks from weeks at sea and too little time in dry dock, the puffy, red-ringed eyes of the crew betrayed men who had little sleep, and too much terror.

What do I say to men like that? Kern thought. *Do I ignore them for being seconds too slow in manning the gun because there isn't an ounce of strength left in any of them? Or, do I chastise them because those seconds allow an enemy plane to dive out of the sun? I know what it is like to have your heart beat through your chest when the fliebos, the bombs, land beside the boat. I know the terror of being caught on the surface when the only hope is a crash dive.*

"Don't be an ass, Kern," he whispered to himself. "This is no time to daydream."

He rubbed his eyes again and swept the skies, looking for enemy planes. He hated the bees—they were fast and ruthless and dove out of a blinding sun to kill him.

"Oberleutnant?"

Kern looked down to see Teddy Hartmann's pale face.

"Yes, Teddy?"

"The passengers are complaining, sir. Especially the generals and the silver stripes." The executive officer used the slang term for naval base officers. "They demand to be allowed on deck."

I should let them on deck, Kern thought, *and then take the boat down under them.* Instead he said, "Please give the passengers my compliments, but tell them it is impossible. Enemy planes make it so."

"I told them that, sir. They say that the smell is killing them."

"Tell them I said no, Teddy," Kern said. "If anyone gives you any trouble, place him under arrest."

Hartmann's eyes questioned Kern.

"Handcuff him to a pipe, Teddy. If we have any handcuffs on board."

"Yes, sir." Hartmann saluted, and disappeared in the darkness. Suddenly his head reappeared. "It's Frick, sir. He says that the diesels are ready. The propeller packing is still leaking, but the pumps are handling it. At least we've got that under control."

"Very well, Teddy. Both ahead one-third, steady on course. What about the electric motors?"

"No, sir," the exec said. "Nothing yet."

"All right," Kern said. "But tell Frick I don't want to be caught out here by the bees. If he wants to see his whores again, he'd better get them working."

"Yes, sir." Hartmann tossed a salute. "That should speed him up."

Kern returned to the horizon. Let the generals and staff officers complain. They got a taste of what it was like to live and fight a real war. U-686 was a warship, not a taxi. No, Kern thought, today she was a dilapidated lifeboat.

Kern had been ordered to take twenty-one high-ranking army and navy officers from Brest to Kiel by Flotilla Commander Kapitaen Winter. "There is nothing more that you can do here," Winter had said, handing him a sealed envelope. "The army wants to save their own, and so the Kriegsmarine. It is your duty to get them to safety. Take no unnecessary chances, Kern. Here is a list of those that will travel with you. Any questions?"

Kern knew that there was nothing more to be said—the city was lost. It was strange, he thought, this feeling of doom. It was not the sharp feeling of the fear of being hunted, nor the overpowering terror that gripped him when the boat falls uncontrollably to the ocean floor: it was a quiet acceptance of the end. Like a snow squall traveling slowly across the waves, coming gradually with no menace to it. It was inevitable. The squall would come on and envelop the boat and in that instant you could not see anything. The flakes pelted his face and swirled over the bridge and there was nothing that he could do to stop it. It was, Kern thought, almost a relief that some part of this war had an end to it: and the end did not necessarily mean death.

"Kapitaen?" Teddy said, breaking Kern from his thoughts. "Message from Wit. Escort coming out. Should be within sight any moment. They also tell us to keep an eye out for enemy aircraft. As if we haven't thought of that."

"Thank them for the escort and their concern, Teddy," Kern said, turning his binoculars to starboard.

"There she is, sir," the starboard lookout called. "Looks like an E-boat."

Kern watched as the motor torpedo boat sheared through the water, the waves peeling back in graceful white arcs from her bow.

"Message from Wit," Hartmann suddenly called out. "'Under attack. Take all precautions.'"

The E-boat eased alongside. "Wit's under attack. Can you dive?" an officer shouted above the low rumble of the E-boat's engines.

"No," Kern said. "Our electric motors are finished and we have a serious leak aft."

"Follow me," the E-boat officer said. "If the Tommies show up, you're on your own."

"Aircraft off the port beam!" a lookout cried. "Three bees!" As U-686's antiaircraft guns swung in that direction, the E-boat kicked up a wake and it darted ahead of the U-boat, putting maneuvering distance between the two.

"Both ahead two-thirds," Kern said. "Prepare to

take evasive action. Teddy, tell Frick to give me all he's got."

Kern trained his binoculars in the direction of the aircraft. There were three distant specks, coming in low. Fighter-bombers. Twin-engined Mosquitoes. Very fast.

Suddenly the three aircraft split. "They're coming in from different directions," Kern called to the gunners. A Mosquito lined up aft and began its attack. Kern turned to see another line up on the port beam. The third waited at a distance. Kern watched as the 3.7cm cannon on the lower gun deck spun to sight on the plane to port. It began to fire.

Immediately the twin 2cm's on the upper gun deck joined in. The acrid smell of cordite burned Kern's nostrils as the wind picked up the gun smoke and flung it in his face. The antiaircraft guns stuttered dully as the fighters came on. The airplane rushing at the U-boat from astern suddenly pulled up, and a black shape detached itself from the underbelly of the plane.

"Hard a-port!" Kern shouted as he watched the bomb seem to hang in midair.

U-686 turned her bow into the rolling swells as the twin 2cm's tracked the fighter's climb. The bomb fell directly at U-686. "Turn, turn." Kern urged his boat in a ragged whisper. "Turn." U-686 heeled over as the bomb flashed past the stern and crashed into the water with a roar. A waterspout cascaded over the boat as she swung back to even keel, drenching Kern and the gun crews with ice-cold water. He turned his attention to the attacker off the port beam. It was coming in low, too low for a bombing attack. They were going to be strafed.

"Aircraft dead ahead!" the lookout called. The third fighter.

"Both guns, concentrate on the fighter to port," Kern shouted to the gun crews.

Suddenly the plane's nose began to twinkle brightly and small waterspouts danced rapidly across the water toward the U-boat. Kern could turn the boat stern-on to the fighter, he knew, but if he did that he would show his beam to the plane just beginning its bombing run. He could dodge a bomb, he thought.

"Teddy!" he shouted down the hatch. "Both engines full at my command."

Hartmann's face appeared in the hatch.

"Kapitaen, we can't—"

Kern cut him off. "At my command, Teddy."

Kern saw the bomb released.

"Both ahead full!" he shouted. "Hard a-starboard!"

U-686 jumped ahead and heeled over, throwing Kern against the bridge shield.

The plane's machine guns churned the water into a frothy path as it cut just astern of the boat. U-686's guns followed it, pumping round after round into the air. Kern saw black smoke spurt from the fighter. A hit. He turned quickly to see the bomb explode twenty meters from the port bow. He was soaked again as U-686 ran through the column of water.

He rubbed the water from his eyes, frantically trying to locate the planes. He saw them at a distance, speeding away from the boat. A thin trail of smoke followed them.

"Both engines back to one-third. Damage report," Kern called down to Teddy. And then to his gun crews he said, "Very good, men. You got some of that one. Any injuries?"

"None, sir," the gun captain returned quickly. "But it was close."

Close, Kern thought. *Every action has been close since we left Brest.*

"The leak has increased, Kapitaen," Teddy said. "Chief requests permission to shut down starboard diesel, and run on port diesel only."

"Permission granted. Resume course to Wit."

"Oh, and, Kapitaen?" Hartmann added with a smile. "The generals say that if you don't let them up this instant, they will prefer charges against every officer on U-686. Should I place them all under arrest, sir?"

"You're enjoying this too much, Hartmann. Send them up. At least they can be sick over the side of the boat."

"You may get the Iron Cross for letting them puke in the fresh air, Kapitaen."

Kern smiled as the E-boat appeared and took station off the boat's bow. The torpedo boat matched its speed to that of the U-boat, and they headed toward Wit. They had sailed for nearly an hour when Kern noticed it. A black smudge dirtied the sky on the horizon, directly over the Kriegsmarine base. *We're not the only ones,* Kern thought. *It looks like someone else is in the Devil's Shovel.*

The crew stood silently on deck, watching the wreckage slowly glide past them as U-686 sailed into Wit. There was so little movement onshore that for an instant Kern thought the base had been abandoned. Debris covered the surface of the oily water and soot floated through the air like black snowflakes. Huge fires, their roar so deafening that they sounded like hundreds of continuous explosions, sent columns of thick smoke thousands of feet into the sky. The sun shone faintly through the smoke and the scene before Kern was of a melancholy, gray landscape. The charred rubble of buildings lined the ways, and the huge crane that once towered over the vessels of the Kriegsmarine at the Tirpitz Pier lay crumpled in a mass of twisted metal. The boat sought out the U-boat jetty at the Taproots Pier.

The wail of sirens could be heard over the fires as fire engines and ambulances raced about. Kern felt sick to his stomach as he tried to pick familiar landmarks out of the building fronts that stared at him with hollow eyes. Wit was destroyed.

No one spoke as a tug approached to take U-686 in tow. Kern ordered the engines shut down and the tug expertly guided the U-boat into position alongside the jetty. His eyes stung from the smoke that drifted over the boat. Tears slid down his cheeks. He wiped them away with his sleeve. It was the smoke that made him cry. It burned the inside of his nose and fouled his mouth so that he wished for a beer to wash the taste away.

Kern heard his name called and he looked down. The general officers and their aides were clustered on the deck, pale and wilted.

"Oberleutnant Kern," a major said. "I intend to register a complaint with your immediate superior."

Hartmann joined him on the bridge and said in a low voice: "Does he mean Churchill?"

"Behave yourself, Teddy," Kern returned. "What is the nature of your complaint?"

"I'll tell you what it is." A white-haired general in a vomit-stained uniform picked up the gauntlet. "You took unnecessary chances with the lives of important officers of the Wehrmacht. You put us in danger numerous times during the voyage, and you refused our requests to surface and allow some fresh air into that stifling pig boat of yours."

"My apologies, Herr General," Kern said. "But as you see I did manage to get you to your destination in one piece."

"That's beside the point," the major said. "You exceeded orders and placed these general officers at risk."

"We should have left them in Brest," Teddy said.

"Pardon me, gentlemen," Kern said as the tug worked U-686 into place, "but I have to dock my boat." He grabbed a megaphone and shouted instructions to the tug as she nestled along the U-boat's hull. The old-timer on the tug threw a friendly wave out of the wheelhouse when he was finished and took his boat off to other duties.

"Secure lines forward, secure lines aft," Kern called to the deck crew. "All right, Teddy. The boat is yours. I'll go make my report and deal with these soldiers. See how long it'll take the chief to get the boat in shape. I've got a feeling that we're going to be sent out again."

The generals and their staff jostled each other at the foot of the gangway like a flock of decrepit seagulls fighting for a piece of stale bread. The deck crew barely had time to secure the gangway before the army and shipyard naval officers frantically clambered up to the jetty. Kern jumped off of the lower gun platform and walked along the battered deck of the U-boat. Chunks of wooden decking were missing, and he noticed several large dents in the boat's tower. "Wabos," Kern said to no one and suddenly he was very tired. His legs seemed uncertain, and he felt as if he carried a huge weight across his shoulders. That feeling would go away, he knew. He would get his land legs, and sleep without worry would ease the burden until he felt refreshed enough to smile again. But each patrol made the smiles more difficult to come by, and they came sparingly, a commodity too precious to waste.

He climbed the gangway, hand trailing lightly over the rope railing, and stepped onto the pier. He was surrounded by destruction. To his left a fire crew poured water into a blazing building. It was a futile effort: the flames licked at the remnants of the building with impunity. Kern watched for a moment, lost in the scene. Streams of water turned into hissing, angry clouds of steam that joined with brown smoke to roll into a dirty blue sky.

How different it was the last time he was here, Kern thought. Then the ways had been lined with flotilla staff, a band, and off-duty nurses to welcome them back from a war patrol. There were the bright colors of the women's dresses, and the splashes of flowers that were thrown to the triumphant warriors as the boat docked. The overwhelming sense of victory carried them up the gangway into the crowd that surrounded and welcomed them with handshakes and praise. The first seaman to collect a kiss became a hero to his comrades, and Kern always stepped aside so that Teddy, or Frick, or one of the others was the first into the arms of a woman.

That was the signal for his men to laugh and joke with each other about shaving off their beards, and finding women and drink. When he heard his men's laughter, Kern relaxed. They were safe, far from the sea, from the wabos. All of it came to them as a just reward under a smiling sun that swept the chill of the

Atlantic from their bones, and the clean air that burned the stench of the U-boat from their nostrils. When they had set sail for their new bases in occupied France two years ago, more of the same. More music, flowers, cheering crowds, pretty women; more white handkerchiefs waved above the crowds like fluttering doves bidding them farewell—safe voyage.

It was all gone. Nothing remained but the memory that had become as faded as the gray leather jacket that he wore.

Kern felt someone approach him. He turned to see a kriegsmarine leutnant standing at attention. Kern noticed how clean the officer's uniform was, and how young the man looked.

"Oberleutnant Kern?" the officer said.

"Yes. I am Oberleutnant Kern," Kern replied. His words sounded dull against the youthful vigor of the leutnant's. He stood a little straighter and forced strength into his voice. "What is it?" he said sharply.

The young officer saluted and handed Kern a sealed envelope. Kern took it and examined it. It bore the seal of Kriegsmarine Headquarters. He looked at the leutnant and said: "Excuse me." He turned, ripped open the flap, and pulled out a single page. He saw at once that it was addressed to him, but he had to read the sender's name twice. *By order of Grand Admiral Doenitz . . .* Kern stopped reading. The Lion. *What does the Lion want with me?* he thought. He continued to read.

. . . to report to Kriegsmarine Headquarters at Koralle immediately. Utmost secrecy is required. It was signed Vice Admiral Eberhardt Godt. An image of the big man with dark features came to Kern's mind. He remembered Godt standing next to the slim, impassive

Doenitz at Lorient as the grand admiral reviewed his sailors. When was that? Two, three years . . .

"When you are ready, Oberleutnant," the young officer said. "I have a car available." Kern looked at him. *Immediately* . . . the message said. That meant that Kern had no time to bathe and change. It wouldn't make any difference anyway. His uniform was aboard U-686. It smelled of diesel oil and mold.

"Yes. Let me inform my executive officer. He'll need to make my report."

"That will be taken care of, Oberleutnant," the officer said. He gestured to a waiting staff car. The driver stood with the rear door open. The engine was running. "If you please, sir?"

Kern looked at the backseat of the Mercedes. It beckoned to him seductively. *I can sleep there*, he thought as he got into the car. The door was shut behind him. He took a deep breath and closed his eyes.

He knew that the car was moving and occasionally he could feel the bump of travel, but the soft leather upholstery convinced him to forget everything but his last command of the day: sleep.

Chapter 3

Kriegsmarine Headquarters, Koralle, outside Bernau

Kern stood at attention and saluted as Vice Admiral Godt, Doenitz's chief of staff, entered the outer office.

"At ease, Kern," Godt said, returning the salute. "Rested after your journey, I hope."

"Yes, Vice Admiral," Kern said. He'd had time enough only for a quick bath, but submerging himself in the steaming water and letting the stink wash off him was wonderful. It gave him new life.

"The uniform nearly fits you, doesn't it?"

Kern looked down. His oil-soaked clothes had been taken away and replaced by a new uniform. It hung on his thin frame. "Very nearly, Vice Admiral."

"Good. Ready for a bite to eat? The grand admiral wishes you to dine with him. Don't get your hopes up, Kern. His table is as spartan as ever. After you've dined with the grand admiral, I'll see that a real supper is brought to you. Come."

Kern followed Vice Admiral Godt into Doenitz's office. A large desk occupied the center of the room, just in front of a fireplace. One wall was covered with maps marking U-boat positions and convoy routes. Kern noticed a flurry of small black ribbons pinned to the map.

Across the room from the wall maps, high windows allowed the fading sunlight to stream over a large table set with china and crystal. At the end of the table stood Grand Admiral Karl Doenitz. A large black cloth covered one wall.

"Kern," he said. "How are you?"

Kern stopped and saluted. "Very well, Grand Admiral."

"Good. Good. Godt, have them brought in, will you? Sit, Kern. Sit. I know how young men eat."

Doenitz signaled for the meal as Godt directed orderlies carrying two large easels into the room. They ate quickly, talking of the old days of U-boats. Doenitz and Kern were careful not to mention of the names of captains who had been lost, including the grand admiral's two sons. "May God protect the German submariners," was Doenitz's motto, and yet to Kern it sometimes seemed if God had abandoned the men who sailed in U-boats.

After they had finished their meal, the dishes were cleared away.

"How did you find the Skagerrak?" Doenitz asked Kern. The narrow passage between Norway and Denmark was a death trap to U-boats returning to Wit.

"Difficult, sir. I didn't breathe until we reached the Kattegat and the Great Belt."

"None of it's fit for a U-boat, Kern. How many did you have on the boat?"

"Seventy-two men."

"Seventy-two? Do you hear that, Godt?" Doenitz asked, and then he said: "How was it?"

Kern frowned in remembrance. "They picked us up coming out of Brest. We left at night, of course. We went down to a hundred meters and stayed there. Destroyers found us about two hours later." He could hear the thin ping of the enemy asdic searching for them as he spoke. "Four destroyers, standard pattern. I lost count after sixty wabos. They kept us down about fourteen hours."

"Fourteen?"

"Yes. The men did well. The enemy was gone when we surfaced and so we ran on diesels for four hours, recharging the batteries. Three destroyers came back and brought bees. We were down only seven hours though."

"What is the condition of your boat?"

"The starboard engine is knocked off her mount. Starboard propeller packing is blown and the shaft is bent. Eight serious leaks. Two dozen smaller ones."

"How many times?" Godt asked.

"Sir?"

"How many times were you attacked?"

"Counting the bay, eighteen times, sir."

"Eighteen," Doenitz echoed, glancing at Godt. "Well, Kern, we've got more trouble for you."

The vice admiral pushed his chair aside and walked to one of the two easels covered with a black cloth. "What I am about to reveal to you is for your eyes only. *Geheime Kommandosache*—top-secret level," he said to Kern. "Share it with no one."

"Show him," Doenitz ordered.

Godt flipped back the cover of the first easel. On it was an engineer's drawing.

"*Raketen Tauch-Geschoss*," he said. "Rocket-propelled underwater missiles. RGTs for short. Missiles to be launched by U-boats. Submerged. We can attack and destroy the enemy, unseen."

Kern stared at the diagram on the board. Godt's words were lost to him—a dull monotone of unintelligible sounds. Something else had his interest. "May I?" he asked.

"Of course," Doenitz said. "Get as close as you like."

Kern approached the board. It showed two missiles positioned horizontally, side by side, atop a platform within a housing attached to the deck of a U-boat, aft of the long, low slab of a conning tower. Kern felt his heart beat rapidly. It was not the rockets that held his attention. It was the U-boat. He had never seen anything like her—she must be one of the new boats. He looked to Doenitz expectantly.

"Is this . . . ?"

"The other easel, Guenter," the grand admiral said. "Lift the cloth."

Kern did as he was told. There, in more detail, was the new boat. From its blunt, squared-off bow along its clean deck to the stern that dropped away to reveal a set of large screws, it was the vessel that he'd commanded only in his dreams.

There were no deck guns or antiaircraft guns to clutter the deck, or periscope housings or railings to spoil the lines of the conning tower that was balanced perfectly amidships. No wintergarten, he thought, no place for the men to smoke their cigarettes on balmy summer nights. She looked fast. He imagined her sleek form slicing through the waters in pursuit of a convoy. There was a deadly elegance about her, he thought, the kind reserved for birds of prey. She was dangerous. He smiled to himself. And she captured his heart.

He noticed two conical shapes, situated on top of, and on either end of, the conning tower. Gun barrels projected from them.

Kern turned to Godt. "Turrets? Are these antiaircraft guns in turrets?"

"Of course."

"He's never seen a Type XXI before," Doenitz said to Godt. "What do you think, Kern? Is she something that you can take to sea?"

"Yes, Herr Grand Admiral," Kern managed. He barely heard the question. *Look at her! Look at this remarkable creature.* His eyes ravaged the drawing, taking in every line.

"The Type XXI Elektro boat, Kern. Sixteen knots on the surface, seventeen knots submerged. An overall length of nearly eighty meters, and capable of diving to 280 meters. She displaces 2,100 tons with a range of 22,000 miles. They can stay down for two months. What are you in now? A VII F?"

"Yes," Kern answered, thinking of U-686. Her diesel engines were worn out and her batteries barely held a charge, and her electrical system threw sparks like fireworks when the wabos knocked her about. If she gave seven knots on the surface and four underwater, Kern and her crew considered themselves lucky. She needed to go in for a complete overhaul and Kern half agreed with the crew that it would take a month just to wash the stink out of her. She needed a rest. He felt ashamed that U-686 was quickly replaced in his heart by this beautiful ship. Like a courtesan and a faithful whore, he thought. How soon could one replace the other in a man's affection?

"The Type XXIs are true submarines," Doenitz said. "They're as close to fish as we can make them. They won't have the Walter turbines but they will still be fast enough. Six tubes instead of four. She can carry twenty-three torpedoes. Even with twelve TMC mines you can carry fourteen eels. Hydraulically loaded. All those eels to send into the hull of a fat American tanker." He looked troubled. "One day of course."

"When will they be ready, Herr Vice Admiral?" Kern asked. He could not take his eyes from the drawing. What a wondrous machine.

"Yours is ready now, Kern."

Kern turned to see Doenitz beaming like a father who has just given his son a gift.

"Mine, Grand Admiral?" Kern asked.

"U-3535, Kern. Blohm and Voss Builders. Now, Godt." He waved at the vice admiral. "Continue before we have to place poor Kern on the casualty list."

"My apologies, Grand Admiral," Kern said. He was behaving like a first-year cadet.

"But we are not talking of only one boat, Kern," Godt continued. "You're to lead a flotilla of Type XXI boats. Fifteen such Elektro U-boats, each boat armed with RGTs."

Kern tried to listen carefully, but he grew impatient. RGTs again. *Attack with rockets fired from underwater and not torpedoes? Why? With the new torpedoes we can sink anything we shoot at. Give us those instead of those bloody rockets.*

"Your unit will be called the first Special Flotilla," Godt continued. "And you'll have your work cut out for you. You must train fifteen crews for these new boats, Kern. The men must be proficient in the operation of this Elektro boat, and the RGTs."

"You are hereby promoted to the rank of kapitaen-leutnant. We can't have the first Special Flotilla commanded by a mere oberleutnant," Doenitz said.

"Thank you, Herr Grand Admiral," Kern said. "If I may ask, sir, how much time do I have to train?"

Kern noticed Godt quickly glance at Doenitz. The grand admiral stood and walked to his desk. He took a moment before saying: "We have to move quickly, Kern. You're to be ready for sea by mid-October."

Kern stiffened. Less than four months? Was the Lion mad? He was afraid the despair that he felt registered on his face.

"Yes. I know," the grand admiral said. "Too little time. But you can do it, Kern. We've lost our French ports, so we will operate from Norway. We have a site picked out for your training base. It's sufficiently secluded that you will have little trouble with the natives. Like all of Norway, it's under low cloud cover most of the year. Godt has issued orders to send what complete U-boat crews we have available, and we're supplementing those men with officer candidates from Flensburg, and able seamen from other Kriegsmarine duty. We can't give you much in the way of accommodations. You know how things are."

"Yes, Grand Admiral. Your pardon," Kern said, "but with just two RGTs on each boat, we can, under the best of circumstances, launch just thirty rockets." The statement was obvious—the question was: was it enough for what the grand admiral had in mind?

Godt was about to answer, when Doenitz spoke. "I'm sure Kapitaenleutnant Kern was only curious about the explosive payload of these rockets. Weren't you, Kern?"

The look at the grand admiral's face left no doubt that Kern was to answer in the affirmative.

"Yes, Grand Admiral," he said. "It is as you say."

"One thousand, eight hundred, sixty pounds," Godt said. "TNT. Ametol if we have it."

"Fifteen boats, thirty rockets. Thirty tons. Entirely sufficient," Doenitz said, ending the discussion.

"Yes, sir," Kern said. Sufficient for what? What were those strange things doing on the back of these superb machines?

"The estimated range of the RGT," Godt continued,

"is one hundred kilometers. That is under ideal launch conditions."

Kern was shocked. *Sixty miles? How can we see our targets? And how do we aim them? What about the guidance system? Are we to just shoot them into the air and pray that they fall on the target?* But he said nothing.

"You'll leave directly from here for Norway," Godt said. "We're hiding you in the wilderness, if you will. The village that we have appropriated is called Evanger, in Bokn Fiord. I'll see that you have transportation. The crew from U-686 will meet you when you pick up your boat. Your other crews should arrive at Evanger shortly after you get there. We have to send the men to you as we can, Kern."

"The other boats, Herr Vice Admiral? When can I expect the other boats?"

"The Ministry of Armament promises that we will have our other boats immediately," Doenitz said. "Precaution has to be taken in construction of the boats, you understand. The boats are built in eight sections, and then the sections are assembled at a shipyard. When the bulk of the construction is completed at the yards, the boats are dispersed to other areas for final work. That, of course, complicates matters, but it can't be helped. Better to have to wait a little longer and get the boats than to have them destroyed on the way. You shall have them the minute they are completed. You will combine the boats' sea trials with your crews' training to save time. You'll have that yellow training stripe off those boats in no time, Kern."

"Yes, Herr Grand Admiral."

"Vice Admiral Godt has your orders prepared. You will be informed of your target immediately before you set sail. Godt?"

The vice admiral handed a thick folder to Kern.

Across its cover was stamped *Operationbefehl Greif.* Operation Griffin.

"Do you know the animal, Kern?" Doenitz asked.

"A mythical creature, Herr Grand Admiral," Kern ventured.

"Yes," Doenitz said. "Half eagle, half lion."

"Yes, sir," Kern said, wondering if his boat was to be a hybrid as well. Rockets on U-boats—the idea distressed him.

"Any questions?"

"I'd like two seagoing tugs, sir. And a tender with a machine shop."

"Of course. You'll have them and base support. Other questions?"

"The targets, sir?"

"In time, Kern." Doenitz rose. "You should be on your way. Despite what Goring says about the Luftwaffe's control of the skies, it is best to travel at night. Keep me informed of your progress. Daily reports, you understand."

"Yes, Herr Grand Admiral."

"Pick up your orders at the adjutant's desk. Dismissed."

Kern saluted and turned to go when Doenitz spoke. "Guenter?"

Kern stopped. There was a gentleness in the grand admiral's voice that Kern had never heard before.

"This mission is critical to Germany's future and to the Kriegsmarine," Doenitz said.

Kern noticed for the first time that the Lion's skin was ashen and his features drawn and worn. "You see the cloth on the wall. It covers our situation map. It is filled with black flags. Black flags. U-boat losses, Kern. In 1940—twenty-two boats. In 1941 it was thirt-five. The following year, ninety-six. Last year, 237 U-boats. You must not fail, Kern. This mission . . ." The old man hesitated. "What you will accomplish could prevent Germany's ruin. Train hard. Drive your men. Drive yourself, and when the time comes and your targets are announced, be ready."

"Yes, Grand Admiral. We'll be ready."

"Very well. Dismissed."

The vice admiral watched Doenitz gather himself and walk to the charts on the far wall after Kern left. "How many times must I send my young submariners out, Godt? They are disappearing and all that I offer is more danger. More death."

"There is always hope, Herr Grand Admiral," Godt said. "Kern is a veteran. His men are well trained. He is lucky."

Doenitz turned with a grim smile. "Lucky? I may have given him the mission that sends him to his death. Lucky."

"He is a submariner—"

"Yes, yes." Doenitz waved the words away. "So? What news about the RGTs?"

"Bad news, I am afraid. Difficulties have arisen, Grand Admiral."

Doenitz exploded. "Difficulties? Who does not suffer difficulties at this point! Shall I go myself and make them work? Difficulties do not concern me. Will they be ready in time?"

"Grand Admiral," Godt said, "I don't know what to tell you. I have spoken to the White Coats every day. I was present at four tests. One of the RGTs launched successfully but traveled no farther than fifteen kilometers before crashing. Two traveled less than that and one failed to launch."

"From what depth?"

"Three fathoms."

"Three fathoms? From a U-boat?"

"The test bed was not attached to a U-boat. It was secured on a concrete sled pushed into the water."

"That is their idea of a test? Three fathoms won't keep the sun's rays off a U-boat's back," Doenitz said. "Press them, Godt—make their lives a living hell until they succeed. Everything—everything—depends on the RGTs. Kern will get them to their destination, but it will do no good if those wonder weapons fail. You tell them, Godt—I will not send that boy on a suicide mission. I've done that too often." He turned and studied the huge map of the Atlantic, the tiny black flags stark and unforgiving. "God help German submariners. God help Germany."

Kern took the sealed envelope from the adjutant, gathered his cap and navy greatcoat, and followed the man down a set of stairs and out into a courtyard. An oberbootsmannsmaat held the door of a gray staff car open for him. Kern judged that it had been a while since the chief petty officer had been to sea from the way his uniform coat stretched over his belly. He returned the chief's salute and slid into the backseat.

"My name is Erhinger, sir," the chief said. "I'll be your driver. These are for you, sir." He handed Kern a paper bag.

"What is this?"

"Sandwiches, sir. Compliments of Vice Admiral Godt. I have a thermos full of coffee up here if you would like some. I'm afraid it's only ersatz coffee, but it'll wash the sandwiches down."

Kern nodded, taking the bag. This must be the dinner that Godt promised. He put the bag on the seat beside him. He had the envelope opened and the first two pages read before he realized that the car was speeding down the highway. He thought of asking the chief where they were headed, but decided otherwise. Godt would have all of that taken care of, Kern thought, better to familiarize himself with his orders. The file added detail to what Kern learned in the meeting. Fifteen Type XXI boats would assemble at Evanger, a small fishing village at the end of Bokn Fiord. The village had been cleared of its inhabitants two weeks ago. He pulled a sheet of paper out of the pile and studied it. It was an inventory of the buildings. Two dozen residences, a community hall, a large building used to store and repair fishing nets, a school, and assorted outbuildings. No electricity. *I'll need generators,* Kern thought, *until the tender arrives. I don't want to run cables from my boats to power the base.* Evanger. Not very appealing, certainly not Lorient or Brest. He paged through the document. The orders reminded Kern that he would train his crews and be ready for sea no later than 15 October 1944. Ready for what? he thought. *What do I attack? Whales?* He forced himself to concentrate on the information. He chose the RGTs first, glancing through the packet.

They were awkward-looking things, pencils with stubby wings aft: just a shade over seventeen meters in length and two meters across. They were to be carried, two rockets to a boat, in a canister situated aft of the conning tower. The canisters would open like clamshells, and the rockets would be fired from a control panel located in the electric motor room. Kern shook his head. Those barns destroyed the long, clean lines of the boats. *We will not get our sixteeen knots with those things dragging through the water,* Kern thought. What a travesty, to build such lovely machines and then add these deformities.

"I don't know anything about rockets," Kern said.

"What was that, sir?" the driver asked.

"Nothing, Chief," Kern said. It all looked simple enough. Of course, Kern thought, there were a hundred things that could go wrong before they set sail, and while they were at sea, a thousand things. How would the RGTs and their canister travel underwater? It would be insane to take these things to the target just to have them fail. *What about torpedoes? How many will I be able to carry?* Kern thought. *The extra weight of the rockets and their canister means that I have to cut weight. From where? The only logical or possible place would be the torpedo payload. I can sink merchantmen and tankers with torpedoes, but I don't know what I can do with rockets.* He began leafing through the material, again. He was hungry to learn about his boats.

No, no, he told himself, *be systematic.* He reassembled the packet and laid it carefully on the seat next to him. He picked up the first page and began reading. Full darkness soon overcame the car and his hand sought out the overhead light above his left shoulder. He suddenly remembered the blackout curtains. He pulled them shut before switching on the light.

They were forced to stop and seek shelter from enemy aircraft throughout the journey. Four hours and seven stops later he was finished reading. *Rest a bit,* he told himself, *and read it again.*

Kern sat back in the seat and watched the driver maneuver in and out of a column of horse-drawn artillery, the eyes of the gaunt animals glowing ghostlike in the dim light of the blackout headlamps. He'd read enough, he decided, his eyes were tired. Better to save himself for what was ahead. He saw the broad neck of his driver.

"How long have you been in?" Kern asked the chief.

"Since the first war, sir. But not in U-boats like you; cruisers for me."

"I've never been on a cruiser," Kern said. "Nothing but U-boats and tenders. Before the war I used to sail."

"I've never been sailing, sir."

"You should," Kern said. "My family had a cottage on Lake Constance. Every summer my father would teach me something new about sailing. He wanted to be in the navy but grandfather wouldn't let him. Father was determined that I become a sailor."

"My father was a blacksmith," Erhinger said. "I became a sailor when I ran away from home."

"Have you ever been to Lake Constance?"

"No, sir."

"Go sometime," Kern said. "When the war is over. You'd enjoy yourself." He settled back in his seat and picked up the materials again. After a moment he put the papers down and thought of Lake Constance. The sky seemed so blue over the lake, a sharp, vibrant color that was unnatural. Full white clouds rushed across the sky and sometimes he would race their reflection in the water.

He remembered the cold water slapping over the bow, and his father sitting so rigidly in the stern, as if he was holding on to the moment with every ounce of his strength. His father was not a good sailor, he did not have a true sailor's natural feel for the wind and the waves, and he fought his boat, trying to force it to do what he wanted. Kern, as a boy, learned that was not what a sailor did.

Old Erwin's face came to mind. Guide the boat, the old sailor who cared for the rental boats told him. Don't force the boat, guide it. A boat is like a racehorse, full of spirit and will. Kern listened for hours to

Erwin, as the old man's gnarled fingers flew over bits of rope, making seaman's knots. Young Kern watched in amazement.

Take these home and study how they are made, Erwin told the boy. It was important to know as much as you could about the sea and sailing. Sailing on a lake is nothing, the old man said to Kern. Once you see the ocean, you'll never be able to sail on a lake again. The sea does that to a person. She reaches in and takes your heart and doesn't give it back until she's done with you. She is a ruthless mistress, the old man said. Remember that. Remember that it is you and your ship against the sea. The only way you can win is to respect the sea, and trust your ship.

Kern enjoyed the short summers at the lake, his solitary voyages at the helm of his little craft—the dreams of sailing the oceans that came to him under the warmth of a bright sun—the images of ships and harbors that formed high above him in the clouds, the soft hum of lines, and the gentle tug of the tiller as he swung her over. He feigned disinterest as he guided his boat past a staid cabin cruiser barely creasing the water, but secretly he felt superior. He was a sailor, and the rich man whose plump hand guided the cruiser was not.

His father, when his business permitted him, would sail with Kern, neither of them talking for hours, each deriving his own pleasure from the water. It was then that Kern felt his father was proud of him. Nothing was said, Kern never expected his father to compliment him, but there was a sense of pride in the way he watched Kern. That was enough. That was a gift. They sat side by side in the stern, watching the wind fill the sail, listening to the water hiss under the boat's bow, running across the water like a deer over a field. That was before his father lost his job—before everything changed.

Not so long ago, Kern thought as the car bumped along the road. Not many years at all. Fifteen, then on to the academy at Flensburg. That was the first time he had seen Doenitz, on the parade ground. The wind was pushing hard against the rigid square of ensigns drawn up to hear the Lion and Kern feared the breeze would snatch his cap at any moment. The admiral spoke briefly about duty and service to Germany, and then dismissed the cadets. Kern was disappointed with the dry speech and the Lion's monotone delivery. But he had no time to ponder on it: he was ordered off to Konigsberg immediately.

He had trained with two of his classmates in U-boats. Schreck and Paulssen. Their young faces appeared fleetingly in Kern's mind, the features decayed by time. Both dead now.

Eckstein. Oberleutnant Eckstein, Kern's first kapitaen. "Christ, they've saddled me with three ensigns this time!" he growled at the sight of the earnest young officers. "Well, God help us all, but God help you three most of all if you don't follow my orders exactly." He never let them rest. He had them do everything on the boat. Navigation, torpedoes, deck gun, diesels, E-motors, watch, helm: everything. Even when they crawled into their bunks and pulled the aluminum guardrail into position, dumb with fatigue, Eckstein expected them to study the boat's manuals.

Once Kern stood watch on the bridge with Eckstein on a foul day with a running sea and slate-gray sky. The icy spray seeped past the towel he had wrapped around his neck, and soaked his clothes, running down his pants to fill his boots. His teeth chattered and he fought to keep his binoculars cleared of the crusting of salt that covered everything. As the seas whipped the tower back and forth, battering him against the superstructure, he prayed that the steel belt that hooked him to the bridge would hold. He marveled at Eckstein's stoic acceptance of it all, as if the frigid seas that exploded against the tower and drenched them meant nothing, or that the putrid smells that filled the boat didn't exist. The raging dance of the surfaced boat in a force-eight storm as they tried to track a convoy was no more eventful to Eckstein than sailing a toy boat in a farm pond.

It was in dirty weather that Eckstein, leaning back against the bridge shield with his arms crossed and his white teeth flashing through his black beard, turned to Kern and said: "How do you like U-boats so far, Ensign Kern?" And Kern, trying desperately to keep his chattering teeth from biting the tip of his tongue off, and trying not to think of clothes that were always damp, and food that was always moldy, and air that always smelled of urine, to his own disgust replied, "Just fine, sir."

Eckstein's grin grew broader at Kern's lie, and he turned back to the wave-pierced horizon, laughing heartily at the great joke played on young ensigns by U-boat service.

Eckstein was dead. A Liberator had caught his injured boat on the surface as it raced for home and safety.

The car stopped with a jerk, waking Kern. He rubbed his eyes and looked around. It was dark, but he could tell he was at a military installation. He could smell the sea.

"Where are we, Ehinger?"

"Warnemunde, sir," Ehinger said in the darkness.

"There should have been someone here to meet you. I'll see about it."

"All right," Kern said. "I'm going to stretch."

Erhinger was out of the car and had the back door open before Kern realized it. It was certain that the chief knew how to keep his job.

Kern slipped on his greatcoat and walked a short distance from the car. It was misting, and the low lights there were ringed by iridescent haloes. He was surrounded by hammering and the ragged coughing of diesel engines. Occasionally a heavy truck passed, its tires hissing on the gravel. He heard something familiar—the sea breaking against a jetty. He followed the noise in the darkness, careful to mark the location of the car.

The sound of the waves increased as he walked down an incline. Ahead he could see the sharp blue-white bursts of welding and wondered why they were exposed in the darkness like that, when he noticed the vague outline of tarpaulins suspended over the workmen, shielding them from the sky. The brilliant sparks of the welders crackled sporadically, bouncing off the underside of the tarp to bathe the scene in man-made lightning, catching the indistinct likeness of men and metal forms. Long, thin, brown layers of welding smoke hung in the air, accompanied by the acrid smell of burning metal. It was unreal, the deep blackness and the stuttering harsh flashes of the arc welders. It seemed to Kern that he was witness to something evil, that within the darkness under the hand of the silent hunched forms, things were being made that would not stand the light of day.

Kern moved closer. Shapes began to emerge from the darkness as he walked out onto the jetty. Familiar shapes, but somehow different.

"Those are U-boats," Kern heard himself say. But they weren't Type VIIs. The conning tower was too large, and too long, and it had gun turrets at either end. Kern struggled to make out details in the flickering light of the welder's torch. He saw the broad band of yellow paint that ran the length of the conning tower; this boat was in training. Each flash tantalized him with an image, an edge, a curve, and the low line of the deck. The silent, gray shapes, unmoving in the darkness, tolerated the workmen who clambered over them. They were behemoths indifferent to the ministrations of midgets.

"Those are my boats," Kern said as the welder's lightning danced off the graceful curve of the conning tower. "They're working on my boats."

Chapter 4

Lieutenant Carlow poured himself a cup of tea, added a generous helping of milk, and took a chair next to Captain Sheen. There were about a dozen other officers seated around the table, trying to muster enough enthusiasm to begin the early morning briefing. A lieutenant with the face of a schoolboy stood next to several maps pinned on the wall and waited for a grizzled rating to pass out mimeographed sheets.

"Right," the schoolboy said while everyone shuffled through the materials. "First, Jerry has been very busy lately, moving U-boats about."

"That is because we sink them where they are now," a captain with a bulbous nose commented.

"Ah," the schoolboy said triumphantly. "But here is something different. He is sending some to Norway."

Sheen looked up. "Norway. How the devil do you know that?"

"Well, it's on a need-to-know basis, sir," the schoolboy said. "Very hush-hush and all. You understand. But our intelligence chaps tell us that the Jerries have a new kind of U-boat. Something much better than we have. One of several new types, in fact."

"Oh yes," Sheen said. "Very hush-hush. Did those chaps happen to give you more detail?"

"Just that they're going to Norway," the schoolboy said, missing Sheen's sarcasm. "Or they've left already. Radio traffic from Jerry gives us a very good idea where they are. Very good indeed."

"Oh, jolly good," Sheen said wryly. "Where are they?"

Carlow winced. Sheen was in a bad mood. That meant that Sheen's bad mood would translate into a bad day for Carlow.

"Well, we haven't pinpointed it exactly. But we are sure too. Radio traffic, you know. Jerry is very regular about demanding reports. We can find them that way. We should have it for you shortly. Then all that we need do is swoop in and take a few pictures. Catch Jerry asleep as it were."

Sheen scratched his ear and eyed Schoolboy. "You're Hostilities Only, aren't you?"

Schoolboy looked stunned. "Yes. But what has that . . ."

"Well," Sheen began, "our chaps swooping in is very dangerous because they have to swoop back out again. Jerry hates anyone swooping around his U-boat bases, don't you see, old boy? So before we send our blokes out armed with cameras in their planes and their cocks firmly planted between their legs—I'd like a little more information."

Carlow coughed delicately, pushing his hand over his mouth. Trust Sheen to liven up the briefing.

Schoolboy, red-faced, looked around the table for support. None was forthcoming. "Yes," he said. "Yes, sir. Of course. Type XXI and Type XXIII boats, sir. The Type XXI are the ones going to Norway. I'm afraid that we really don't have much about their capabilities. Details are a bit sketchy, in fact. The exact location of their base is yet to be determined, but I'm sure our intelligence boys will come through."

"Until then, I suppose," Sheen said, "we're to send our chaps up and down fiords trying to find them?"

"I'm afraid so, sir."

"Well," Sheen said, glancing at Carlow, "that shouldn't be too difficult. What do you think, Carlow, not more than several thousand fiords in Norway?"

Carlow had no idea how many fiords there were in Norway, but he wasn't about to admit that to Sheen. "I believe so, sir."

Sheen turned back to Schoolboy. "When your intelligence fellows dig up more information on these new U-boats and where Jerry has secreted them, I will be more than happy to send our blokes out to take their photographs. Until then, I haven't enough planes and not half enough crews, and I've got more than enough missions backlogged to keep everyone busy until 1955. Give me a bit more, will you, old boy, and I'll take it from there?"

Schoolboy nodded quickly. "I'll hop on that, sir."

Sheen's face broadened in a toothy grin. "Jolly good, old man."

Chapter 5

Aboard H.M.S. Firedancer, *St. George's Channel*

Captain George Percy Hardy, D.S.M., leaned against the windscreen on the bridge of His Majesty's destroyer *Firedancer*, looking astern.

"My aunt's pajamas, Number One! Look at the Tribal back there. She couldn't keep position if we nailed her in place. Pennants to *Punjabi*, Number One. Show her we're not asleep up here."

"Very well, sir," Lieutenant Land said with a smile. "*Punjabi*'s pennants, Signalman."

Hardy turned to Land with a look of disgust. "Three years chasing Jerry all over the North Sea, not to mention valuable service pulling the army's chestnuts out of the fire at Dunkirk, and now the fleet officers set me out here to rust like poor old *Firedancer*. Damned shame, Number One."

Hardy pushed past a sublieutenant and looked to port. "Well, *Fearless* and *Fury* are where they ought to be. Trust the Tribal to get lost."

Captain Hardy moved back to his original station, the sublieutenant quickly stepping aside. "So as I was saying, Number One, drawing is a matter of textures, do you understand? Take a tree for instance, you've got the bark to consider. Rough, very rough, so I go down lightly with the edge of my softest drawing pencil on a good-textured paper. Create my own bark. Now, shadowing is an art unto itself. Take B gun's barrel there. Do you see how the spray makes a sort of sheen right along the barrel? The trick is to shadow back off of that, to catch the roundness of its shape. Been drawing since well before Dartmouth, Number One, haven't got the hang of it yet."

A coxswain looked over at Signalman Brown. He'd seen Captain Hardy's work. Too right, he hadn't got the hang of it yet.

"What about you . . . what's your name again, Sublieutenant?"

"Barton, sir," the young man answered quickly.

"What sort of hobbies do you keep?"

The sublieutenant looked at Number One for help. Land's attention was on the binnacle, checking the course.

"Actually, none, sir."

"None! A man's got to have a hobby," Hardy said. "Keeps his interest up. Keeps the mind sharp, Barton. Get a hobby. Collect butterflies or some nonsense like that. What about it, Number One?"

"American movies," Land said. "Westerns, sir. Suggest ten to port, sir. Debris ahead."

"Ten to port, Quartermaster," Hardy said.

"Port ten, sir," came the reply. "Ten of port wheel on, sir."

"Shoot-em-ups, Number One? Never thought you were that type. I pictured you as an opera lover."

"No, sir."

Firedancer moved handily around the unidentifiable flotsam in the water. She was a Fame Class destroyer, built by Vickers-Armstrong in Newcastle in 1935, and for the past three years she had been Hardy's. As was the custom, his superiors knew him not by his given name but by the name of his command: Firedancer. Considering Hardy's scowling features and gravelly voice, his crew found it comical that he could be considered any kind of dancer.

Land liked Hardy. He was outspoken and gruff, and at times Georgie, the nickname that the crew gave him, was a bit eccentric. He was that, perhaps too much so to suit Their Lordships of the Admiralty, but he was a sailor and a fighter, and soon after he was given *Firedancer*, racked up two U-boat kills on the North Atlantic convoy run.

The crew loved Georgie even though he never let up on them, and what's more they respected and trusted Hardy. It was important to have confidence in the man who made the decisions on the bridge; he was the one who kept them alive.

"What do you think, Number One?" Hardy posed as he leaned over the windscreen, eyeing *Punjabi*. "Do you think old Doenitz is done?"

"No, sir," Land replied, glancing at the standard compass. "Steady on," he added to the quartermaster. He returned to the captain's question. "I think that there's still life left in the old boy's U-boats. He'll have them out here when he can."

"I wish he would," Hardy said. "Give me a chance to get back in the game."

"Escorting convoys is important work, sir."

"Escorting convoys is like herding sheep," Hardy replied. "It's a bloody nuisance to a fighting man. Cut me loose, Number One, and I'll go find what's left of the Admiral's U-boats. Give young Burton there, a taste of what it's like on the hunt." Hardy turned his attention to the sublieutenant. "How about it? Care to flush a U-boat and have at it, Burton?"

"Yes, sir," the sublieutenant replied hesitantly. "It's Barton, sir."

"What? Well, of course it is. Man should know his own name. Right, Number One?"

"Indeed, sir," Land agreed.

"Crafty bunch, those U-boat skippers. Bad business early on. Not enough escorts, too many U-boats. Most terrible sight I ever saw, Barton." Hardy laid his arm on the windscreen and rested his chin in the crook of his elbow. "Convoys in a night so black you couldn't see your own bow. One minute you're taking tea on the bridge, trying to keep yourself warm, the next minute a blossom of fire so bright that every ship's silhouette leaps out at you. Then the boom comes a second later and you know you're in for it. Wolf pack. Star shells flung high into the blackness, the sheep running frantically from the wolves. Ships' whistles piercing the night like the cries of the damned and the dying. Fear, pure terror. Escorts darting about looking for the bastards, and then, another huge light, another low boom. Ships calling for help. Off to starboard you see the bow of a freighter stuck straight up in the sky like a tombstone, bathed in the flames of a tanker on fire. You go in for the attack, the asdic pinging, searching for the bloody bastards. Searching. Depth charges churn up the black water into a phosphorescent cauldron, boiling up around the poor sods who managed to get off those ships only to have their insides blown out by their own chaps. All the while, merchantmen and tankers beating the seas to a white froth trying to get away. Men dying out there, Barton, men and ships pleading for help, but you can't give them any, your job's to find the U-boat and sink her. Fuel oil on the water, walls of flames. You manage to pick up a few survivors, wretches soaked in fuel oil, glistening black as midnight. Some of them swallowed the stuff. Poisoned. You lose three or four ships, and when the dawn comes you're stupid with fatigue. Battle stations all day. Snatch sleep when you can. The convoy tightens up, preparing for night. For another go at it. Out there, low in the water, waiting for the darkness—U-boats. Full night, it starts all over. Men and ships die. One week of it. One full week on the bridge with little sleep. Each morning rises on fewer ships, less men. Sixteen ships out of twenty-four. The sea swallowed them."

Hardy watched the crew of B gun, their white asbestos flash hoods and sleeves floating ghostlike in the darkness of the open turret. He said no more.

"Mr. Land, sir?" the call came over their voice pipe.

Land leaned over the pipe. "Land here."

"Message from Fleet Officer, sir. 'Proceed escort Convoy H-67.'"

"Very well. Reply, 'Message received. Proceeding as ordered.'" Land turned and called out a new course to their quartermaster. To the signalman he added, "Signal the course change to the others, Brown."

"For God's sake, make sure that *Punjabi* acknowledges," Hardy ordered. "They'll end up sailing right up Newfoundland Bay unless somebody caught them." He turned to see Barton scanning the horizon with his binoculars. "Right you are, Barton. Keep a close eye on everything. Mr. U-boat isn't done with us yet. He's still got teeth. Number One? What do you think about getting a piper on board *Firedancer*?"

"A piper, sir?"

"A piper! A piper, Number One. Bagpipes. Pipe us into battle. Get the blood stirred up."

Signalman Brown glanced at the coxswain. Old Georgie was at it again.

"Wonderful idea, sir. Shall I look into it?"

"No," Hardy growled. "Keep it to yourself. Their Lordships hear about that one and they'll think I've gone batty for sure."

"Believe I'll go below for a spot of tea before relieving you, sir," Number One said.

"Yes, yes. Good idea. Take Barton there with you. He looks a bit ragged to me."

Land motioned for the sublieutenant to follow.

They made their way to the ward room and found chairs around a small table covered with a white tablecloth.

"Tea?" Number One asked Barton.

"Yes, sir. Thank you, sir."

"Ross?" Land called into the wardroom galley. "Bring us some tea, will you? Bit early for a Horse's Neck, so I suppose tea will have to do. Now, how are you getting about, Barton? First time we've had a chance to chat. I wondered how things were with you."

"Fine, sir," Barton returned uncertainly.

Number One waited as Ross delivered the tea and went back to the galley. *Firedancer* shuddered a moment in a rough sea, and then fell back into her easy routine of riding the waves.

"Relax, Sublieutenant." Land smiled, pouring the tea. "This is not an inquisition. I save that for my real profession."

"Real profession, sir?"

"Barrister, Sublieutenant. When I'm not dashing around the North Atlantic, I'm addressing pompous old men dressed in robes and wearing silly wigs."

"I thought you were Active Service, sir."

"Regular navy? Heavens no, Sublieutenant. God help the Royal Navy if they had sailors like me in their midst. I'm Hostilities Only, Barton. Just like you. Like it aboard *Firedancer*, then?"

"Like it, sir? Yes, sir."

"Sublieutenant Barton," Land said. "If I had you on the stand I would have to propose to the jury that you weren't telling the whole truth. Out with it. A destroyer's too small for me not to know how unhappy you are. Don't worry about repercussions. We don't make anyone walk the plank around here. I don't even think that we could scratch up a plank if we wanted to. Now. Out with it."

Barton hesitated.

"All right," Land said. "I'll say it for you. You're not happy on *Firedancer* because she's a battered little cork that floats about the North Atlantic for no particular reason. You think her crew is insolent, her first officer is apathetic, and her captain, if not mad as a hatter, is certainly only a hairbreadth away."

The sublieutenant's mouth flew open. "No, sir. No, not at all, sir! I would never think that of you, sir. Or the crew. And the captain, no, sir. Not at all, sir."

"But you want off *Firedancer*?"

"Yes, sir. I was thinking about applying for the Fleet Air Arm, sir."

"They need men." Number One nodded in agreement. "I've seen the notices. I can't fault you for wanting advancement. I can't say that the Fleet Air Arm won't give you what you want. But I think you ought to give *Firedancer* a chance before you write us off entirely. You're doing good work as our gunnery officer, excellent work, in fact. The battle for the North Atlantic isn't over yet."

"Yes, sir. I know, sir, but—"

"Listen to me, Barton," Land began. "Because what I'm going to tell you is important. I started out with

Hardy on a corvette. He was the captain, of course, and I had just come aboard as a know-it-all sublieutenant. There wasn't a day went by on 477 that Hardy didn't find fault with everything that I did. To me it seemed that he was the most miserable human being that I ever encountered, and for some unknown reason he hated me. How I hated him, and how I hated corvette duty. We were on the Channel then, and if we weren't screening against U-boats and E-boats, we were plucking RAF chaps out of the drink. Hardy was after me every minute of every hour and every hour of every day. One day we were ordered in to Vlissingen. We were to work with two British and two French destroyers sent to rescue some of our boys cut off by the Germans. I've never seen such carnage and I hope to heaven I never in my life see anything like it again. It was hot from the moment we got there. We covered the destroyers as best we could. There were two corvettes. Us, of course, and 358. Well, 358 caught it right off, so did a French destroyer. Stukas. Seventeen hours of that madness. Smoke, shells, fire. Everything burning onshore.

"Gunfire so constant you would have thought a thunderstorm was in progress. I suppose one was, really. Everyone was hit. Every ship. We crowded into one of the docks and pulled some men off, ran them back out to the destroyers, and then went in again. We fought a running gun battle with three German tanks. That's something you're never trained for. Hardy on the bridge giving orders as calmly as if we were coming into Liverpool. Him and that damned silly hat of his. Back and forth we went, each time getting a little more shot up. Finally, we were told to head off. Four seventy-seven was a wreck, eight dead, thirteen wounded, but we did it. Here's the lesson, Barton. We did the job, did it well, and did it without thinking about anything but what we were trained to do. Hardy saw to that. When Hardy was given *Firedancer*, I asked to come along. He's eccentric; no one who knows him will deny that. But he's a fighter, Barton, and he leads men like he was born to it. When the chips are down, my money's on Hardy. You see, when I came to 477, I felt the same way you did. I'm sure when you caught sight of *Firedancer*, you wanted to turn right around and join the Royal Marines. She's tired, and her crew's worn out, and her captain marches to the tune of a different drummer; but she's the best in the flotilla, and the smartest I've ever seen in action. She runs on pride, Barton, and her men would no more think about letting themselves or their ship down than they would run from the Jerries."

"I know about the captain's record, sir," Barton said too quickly. "I know about *Firedancer* and her service in the North Atlantic. But, well, it's said that Captain Hardy is considered a bit of an odd duck by some at Derby House, and that he's sent out to keep an eye on the back door, and that he's not in anyone's way. Some of my friends on other ships, they've told me that at the Admiralty *Firedancer's* nickname is *Forgotten;* that once you're sent aboard her, you're just written off. I'm sorry, sir, but that's what I've been told and that's why I want a transfer." He sipped his tea. "Sometimes, she just seems so unmilitary."

"The King's Regulations and Admiralty Instructions," Number One said. "Well, there's no doubt that it may seem as if the K.R. and A.I. have been thrown overboard, but don't fall into that way of thinking, Barton. She's run by both, according to our own dear captain, and if he feels that something we did aboard *Firedancer* would receive Their Lordships Displeasure, he'd make our lives a living hell. My advice to you is to stay. Learn as much as you can, and do your job as best you can, and you will have received more in life's lessons than you could possibly garner in the Fleet Air Arm. As to the rest . . ." He stirred his tea thoughtfully. "I suppose those chair-bound sailors up at Derby House have their opinion about *Firedancer* and about Hardy, although I doubt that few of them have ever set foot on a ship. Look, Barton, you might as well get used to the fact that sometimes staff have little regard for what line is doing. Perhaps they simply don't care. Maybe that's being a bit harsh. So we're keeping an eye on the back door, are we? Well, maybe we are. But look here, Barton, if you were Jerry and wanted to get back into the game, would you come round to the front door or would you be sneaky about it and try to slip out the back?"

"Well, the back, sir," Barton answered reluctantly. "But from what I heard, Jerry's quite out of the picture. At least at sea. He has no surface ships, and his U-boats are practically wiped out. I don't want to wait out the war with no chance of seeing any action. I may be Hostilities Only, sir, but I want to get into it as much as anyone."

"I see." Land nodded. "Look. We've got some time in port for refit and resupply. After that, we're off to sea again, probably with two F-class and that reliable old Tribal. Hardy's blood's up, so he might have convinced the brass to cut us loose, maybe join up with a Hunter-Killer Group. I don't know. But I do know this; if there's a way to get us into action, Hardy will do it. My advice stands. Stick with us a bit longer and let's see where Hardy takes us. If we go out and don't find anything, I'll forward your request for transfer to the captain with my endorsement."

The sublieutenant thought for a moment. "All right, sir. I'll give it a go. I'll do my best to make sure of that. But I do hope that we see some action."

"I don't think you need worry about that, Barton," Land said. "Our captain has a habit of placing *Firedancer* where it's hottest. Keep a close watch on Hardy. The minute the Hat appears, and old Hardy orders number-three boiler lit off, it's Action Stations."

"The Hat, sir?"

"You'll know it when you see it, Barton. Now, why don't you see to your depth charge stores, and I'll go relieve our captain?"

Chapter 6

Evanger, Norway, July 1944

"Christ," Kern heard a crewman say. "What a
dump!"

Kern smiled as a chief petty officer took the seaman
to task for the opinion. The U-boatman was right, it
was a dump. Evanger looked to have been deserted
for months. From where Kern stood he could see a
dozen buildings, only two of which had more than
one story and none large enough to house the enlisted men of one U-boat, let alone fifteen crews. They
were ungainly wooden structures, low and foreboding, almost fragile, and they seemed hardly capable of
standing up to a Norwegian winter. The only color
was the sprays of wildflowers scattered indiscrimi-
nately around the town. It didn't seem right to Kern
that flowers bloomed along the edges of the buildings
when there were no people left to enjoy them.

A large barnlike structure stood close to the docks,
its twin doors thrown open to reveal a dark, cavernous
interior. Barren drying racks for fishing nets dotted
the hillside, their wood turned gray by the elements.
They looked like tombstones to Kern, but he shook
the thought from his mind, bad luck to think of such
things. A chief led the crew of U-3535 in unloading

their gear as Kern walked up the low hill that led to the village. He wondered what happened to the people who lived here. Men, women, and children here one day, and the next, when the cold sky sees the faint light of a Norwegian sun, they're gone. Doenitz was right about one thing—at least the weather was on their side; low formless clouds appeared to hang just out of reach above his head. They were like a weight pressing down on Kern, and suddenly he yearned to see the sun break through the clouds and bathe him in its warmth.

No, he thought, then the bees would come and the new Elektroboot that brought him to this haunted place would suffer the fate of so many of her older sisters. A gentle breeze tugged at curtains through the shattered glass windows of one of the unpainted buildings, like ghostly hands welcoming him to this strange place. The pine trees rustled gently as they murmured a greeting to the U-boat captain.

Teddy Hartmann was at his side. "There's got to be some kind of mistake," he said in a low voice. "This place is a dump."

"Well, Teddy, for the next few months it's home," Kern said. He could see the tall pines stretching over the tops of the low buildings. They came right to the edge of the village, binding the houses in an inexorable grip. A dirt road, its surface ribbed with rows of dried mud, led off into the forest. Godt couldn't have picked a more isolated place. "Have Frick begin working on the boat immediately. She's a beauty but she has more aches and pains than an old woman. Test the auxiliary machinery first. We're lucky at least that they managed the static testing for the diesel engines and main electric motors. I want them to know every mechanical and electrical system on that boat like they did the U-686. I don't want to hear anything about breakdowns or electrical shorts when we begin trim tests. Get her cleaned out. Those pigs from the shipyards left trash in her knee deep. Anyone not working on the boat had better be out here working on our new home."

"You needn't worry about the engineer, sir. I'd play the devil getting Frick and his crew out of that monster. I've never seen a man so excited over a boat. He was like a child at a carnival. I thought he would faint when he saw the control room."

Kern looked at U-3535. She was a gray behemoth next to the spindly pier. God, what a boat! She still had her yellow training stripe, and she desperately needed a new coat of paint, but she was beautiful. She looked sullen and dangerous; Kern glanced at his exec.

"But you're not excited at all, are you, Teddy?"

"Twice the depth of the old boats, lying at fifty meters to shoot eels that a computer has plotted for us? Excited, sir? There's wood over the bulkhead in the officers' mess. Wood! And did you see the freezer, sir? A freezer, of all things! My God, sir, she's a liner. Compared to this, U-686 looks like a dinosaur. To hell with Frick, you're going to have trouble keeping me out of that boat. . . ." Hartmann's voice trailed off. "What could we have done with boats like these two years ago? She's everything that we ever needed. She can slip by the Tommies' asdic and outpace the escorts submerged. I'm just sorry that the others never got to see her."

Kern nodded. The others—the men who lay dead at the bottom of the damned Atlantic. It did no good to think about dead men.

"So Frick is excited? He's got good reason to be.

She's his new mistress. I'll give Frick and his gang two weeks. When the RGTs get here they'll need to become expert in them as well. Have Chief Kerrl form a party and turn those buildings into livable quarters for the men. Did you find the officers a place to live, Teddy?"

"How about Paris?"

"When we get back, Teddy. I promise. Until then, this will have to do. Set up watches, and have men posted at the road. I don't think that we'll have any unexpected visitors, but you never know."

Kern looked across the black waters of the fiord. The dark, jagged mountains formed a wall that held up the massive gray clouds. Everywhere he looked he saw a sullen land, indifferent to his presence. This dreary place offered no welcome to him or his men. It was just another occupied territory.

"Have some men cut pine boughs to obscure the boat. Overcast or no overcast, I don't want any Tommies spotting us through a break in the clouds. Send to the Koralle that we've arrived. The Lion wants constant reports as usual." He squinted at the distant peaks. "Our signal may not get very far, but we'll have to make do. Run an antenna from the boat up one of those trees."

Hartmann studied the tree line. "But if the Koralle can pick up our signal, so can the Tommies."

"Orders, Teddy," Kern said. "The Lion's orders."

"What I wouldn't give for a U-boat pen over our heads right now," Hartmann said.

A seaman ran up from the dock.

"Message from the tugs, sir." He saluted Kern. "They've entered the mouth of the fiord and should be here in four hours."

"Very well. Return to your duties," Kern replied.

"What about the support facilities? When will they be set up? We'll need the machine shop and torpedo stores before we can do anything," Hartmann said.

"They're coming down from Trondheim. They ought to be here anytime. But never mind that now. I'll give you eight hours to get the place livable. That means everything, Teddy. Mess hall, latrines, everything. We won't have any electricity until the generators get here, so we have to make the best of the daylight." Kern peered into the overcast sky. "Such as it is. Don't let the men rest. Morale may be a problem. They've endured hardships before, but they've never been thrown into the wilderness. We'll start training tomorrow. We'll alternate classroom with sea trials. You set up the schedule. The other three boats at Warnemunde were close to completion. They should be joining us in the next twelve hours, if the schedule holds as planned. The others should come in directly after the first three. So far my flotilla consists of one boat and a tired crew."

"Our tender, Kapitaen?" Hartmann said. He never called Kern Kapitaen unless it was serious.

"I don't know where she is." Kern looked down the fiord, and then surveyed the surrounding hills and forest. His mind was on bees. "The only way for Tommy to line up on us is to come down the fiord. Even if he came over the mountains, he won't have time to set up for his bomb release." He stepped back and looked at the trees behind the buildings. "He doesn't have a chance coming this way. If we stay close inshore, he won't see us until he's well out in the fiord. He has to come down the fiord. Our guns can track him all the way. I'll send to Godt for an antiaircraft battery. We have excellent cover but Tommy won't be fooled for long."

"He never is," Teddy said. "With your permission, sir, I'll get started."

"Don't let up on them, Teddy. I don't want them to have time to think about how badly things are going or how rough they have it. Exercise first thing in the morning, barracks inspection after breakfast, anything you can think of to keep them alert and responsive. Keep after the men."

"Yes, sir," Teddy said. "By the way, congratulations on your promotion."

"Kapitaenleutnant of a one-boat flotilla," Kern mused to himself as Teddy sought out Frick. He watched his executive officer hail the chief and begin rounding up the crew. Hartmann would do things right. The men would listen to him. They'd grumble but they would do as he ordered. But that was not what bothered Kern. He expected the men to complain. That was natural. For two or three days, maybe a week or so, the men would complain about their barracks, the food, and the miserable condition of this abandoned fishing village. Even that would have little impact because the men would be too busy reveling in the power of U-3535. The crew had been as awed by the sight of the gray whale shouldering the wharf at Warnemunde as he had. It was good that they felt that way, Kern knew. Let them grow accustomed to the boat and her capabilities. Let them savor the newness of her. Let them itch to take her out and find some fat merchantman to send to the bottom, or better yet, an escort. Let them tell bold tales of what they could do with the boat, and boast about her ability to take on the Royal Navy and the American Navy as well. Let them jest with each other at mess and race to outperform their mates on sea trials. Kern expected that. But unless he could keep them so busy that they did not have time to think, the crew's morale would begin to disintegrate. It was inevitable. The crew would soon see how little support they had for their magnificent boat. The newness would gradually fade from her and mistakes in construction or problems with design would emerge like the petty faults of a beautiful woman, and the crew would see that under the paint and perfume was a weary whore. He had seen it before, and he knew the signs.

That was what Kern feared.

He was afraid that his beautiful boat would turn into a spiteful old hag that resented his demands and betrayed his orders, because she was worn out. He was afraid that he'd been sent to this rotten, cold place just to wait on promises that would never be fulfilled, until the end of the war overtook him. He was afraid that the well-dressed officers who sailed paper-covered desks in the Koralle would forget about the tiny base with its single U-boat at the end of a miserable fiord in Norway.

These fears had marched at Kern, one after another, as he stood on the bridge of his big new boat and tasted the spray that came up over the broad bow when they left Warnemunde. The questions had tugged at his mind as he called his lookouts down and prepared to dive, and they had followed him dutifully down the ladder and into the control room. They were at his shoulder as he had called for the periscope, and they had shared a cup of tea with him as he watched his crew become accustomed to U-3535.

I will drive the crew, work them, and force them to do what has to be done to perfection until they grow sick of seeing my face and wince at the sound of my voice. Let them have no time to consider how difficult things are. Deny yourself that time as well, Kern told himself.

I won't fail, Kern thought as he walked into the village. *Neither will my boat and my crew.* He had made that promise to himself as they sailed down the high throat of the fiord, parting the calm black water into silver strands that rolled toward the silent shores. *I won't fail.*

Kern walked into the village, taking his time to inspect Evanger. He poked his head into the tiny houses and empty buildings. He came across a large structure that must have been the village hall. He pushed open the door and stepped inside. It smelled of age and wood smoke. There was a battered counter along one wall and behind it a cabinet perforated by a dozen small boxes. Above it was a sign in Norwegian that looked official. A post office. In the center of the room were ten or fifteen chairs arranged loosely in rows, and in front of them was a desk with three chairs behind it. Something against the far wall caught Kern's attention. He moved closer, trying to keep his shadow from blocking what little light managed to filter in through the small windows. Tiny bits of dust danced in the beam of light, swirling in a thin band from the window to the floor.

He ran his fingers over the rough wood planking of the wall. Bullet holes, about chest high. He counted the holes: seven. They ran in an upward arch, splintering the boards. A machine pistol, he thought. He stepped back and looked down at his feet. He could barely make out the floorboards. He pushed the desk to one side, letting the feeble light spill across the floor. Dark stains. Blood. He knew that the dry wood probably soaked up much of it. Some fool resisted.

He looked back at the postal counter. Who was it? Who would be senseless enough to resist? The postmaster? Some unyielding old man who thought his minor position guaranteed immortality? Stupid. Why die for a few ugly buildings in the middle of nowhere?

He walked toward the doorway and bumped into a chair in the gloom. He cursed softly, wishing that he'd brought a flashlight.

Kern stepped into the street just to hear his name being called. He walked quickly down the road and saw Teddy talking to the driver of a large truck. Behind the first truck were several others. Kern didn't see the motorcycle and sidecar parked next to a building until a Kriegsmarine officer untangled himself from the sidecar and came over.

"Leutnant Edland, sir," the officer said, saluting. "Base support."

Kern returned the salute. "Welcome to Evanger, Leutnant. I trust that you have everything that we need."

"I doubt it, sir. I had to requisition quite a bit from Trondheim and Bergen. Unofficially, sir. I imagine Bergen is going to notice one of their generators missing very soon. We have torpedo stores, a mobile machine shop, most of what we need to set up an electrical shop, and medical supplies. But no doctor. Those are hard to come by, sir. We have a kitchen and a communications center. Well, a radio. We have the telegraph equipment but no wire."

"You wouldn't happen to have a milch cow in any of that, would you, Leutnant?"

"I beg your pardon, sir?"

"A milch cow. A U-tanker. I need fuel, Leutnant. I have no facilities here. Did anyone think to send fuel along?"

"No, Kapitaenleutnant."

Kern looked over the trucks waiting in line. "Teddy? Make some place for these people to set up." He turned back to the leutnant. "Things are very primitive, but we're only to be here for a short while.

See my executive officer about billeting. Get set up as soon as you can. I've found a town hall or something that I'll use as my quarters, but for the next several days I'll work out of my boat. I expect the other boats shortly. Get your radio set up right away. Did you hear anything about the RGTs?"

"The what, sir?"

"Never mind. Any questions? No? Good. He's all yours, Teddy. I'll be at the boat."

Kern walked down toward the pier. *Fuel,* he thought, *that is my priority.* He had nearly two hundred tons on U-3535, but he'd have to husband that pretty closely if the U-Tanker failed to show. *God,* he pleaded as he stepped on the pier, *give me what I need to do this. Help me serve the Fatherland. God help this German submariner.*

Chapter 7

Kern walked down the embankment toward the temporary wharf built for the U-boat tender *Lech*, a six-thousand-ton steamer that had survived the first war, and all of this war: for the present. Her broad sides were streams of orange rust alternating with camouflage paint that had long since faded to uselessness. Topside she had all workshops and welding stations, a factory sent to sea. She was in such poor shape that the men preferred to stay in their crude barracks ashore rather than in the dank surroundings of the "Wreck." She could provide oil, electricity, and supplies to U-3535, however, and for that reason Kern was relieved beyond measure to see her steam slowly up the fiord the day after the convoy of trucks arrived. A pair of veteran seagoing tugs nestled close to the larger ship.

"Now all we need is our other boats," he said to Hartmann in a burst of hope. "Just send our other boats and we'll have a chance. We've got our support, now we just need our boats."

They were on the way, Hartmann had said to Kern early that morning, handing him a decoded message.

"They've just entered the fiord."

"All of them, Teddy?" Kern asked, hurriedly reading the message. "Is it all of them?"

"They didn't say, sir," Hartmann replied. "But it has to be them. See? Look." He found the crucial portion. "All boats entering fiord now. Expect your position four hours."

"I can't believe it," Kern said with a grin. "What do you think about that, Teddy? The Lion did it! He got us our boats. By God, Teddy. We're going to do it! We're going to make the Americans and the Tommies wish that they had never tangled with the Kriegsmarine. Can you believe it? Finally, Teddy. Now the Tommies will feel the wrath of the Lion again. Let me know the minute the boats are sighted, do you understand? When they are, I want every man assembled onshore in formation. Let's show those fellows what a fine bunch they've joined."

Three hours later word came that the boats were just minutes away.

Kern walked down to the dock casually, he wanted to appear as calm as possible in front of the crew. Let them be reminded how cool Guenter "the Silent" was. He smiled to himself. *It's a good thing that they can't see my insides*, he thought. The men snapped to attention as Kern neared. Even the crew of the Wreck lined the sides in some semblance of order. The two tugs were nosed against her hull like pigs feeding from a sow.

"Have the men stand at ease, Teddy," Kern said as Hartmann handed him a pair of binoculars. Kern took them and scanned the throat of the fiord. He made out three distant shapes, black smudges against the gray haze of the mountain walls.

He turned to Hartmann. "Three?"

"That's all that I saw, sir," Hartmann replied. "But the haze obscures everything. The others could be right behind them. They are probably traveling in intervals."

"Yes," Kern agreed, looking through the binoculars again. "Yes, it wouldn't be safe to sail in a pack."

The three shapes grew larger, their features taking form, definition. Three boats, Type XXI. Behind them the flat water of the fiord was barren.

"There's no one behind them, Teddy," Kern said, hope melting away. He handed the binoculars to Hartmann. "See for yourself."

"Kapitaenleutnant," a petty officer shouted from the Wreck. "Message from the U-boats. One is damaged and requests assistance. Immediately."

"Engineering detail to me!" Kern ordered as he raced out over the pier. "Both tugs! Fire your boilers. Prepare to cast off." He could hear Frick and his men behind him as he ran up the Wreck's ladder and through her dark interior. He raced through the open gangway and down the ladder that led to the tugs, moored side by side next to the tender. Kern jumped on the deck of the first tug, followed by the engineering detail. "Send half your men over there, Frick," Kern ordered, pointing to the other tug. Turning to the tug's bridge, he called: "Ready to cast off?"

"Go ahead," the tug captain replied.

"All right, Frick," Kern shouted. His tug was inboard of Frick's; the other tug would have to go first.

"Cast off forward," Frick called. "Cast off aft."

The ropes were slipped and the little tug backed away from the Wreck until she had room to maneuver. She got under way enveloped in a cloud of her own black smoke.

"Let go forward," Kern ordered. "Let go aft." Kern's tug followed the first vessel, as Kern climbed up to the small bridge. "Steer to the boats," he said to the young coxswain. He looked to be no more than a boy.

"Yes, sir."

"Go ahead," the tug captain said to Kern. "I'm going to the engine room to get us some more power." He slapped the helmsman on the shoulder as he swung out to the ladder. "Rudy here knows enough to steer a straight course."

Kern squeezed into the small bridge and flicked the radio on. The dials glowed and the radio emitted a faint hum as the tubes warmed up. The tug pulled away from her mooring, building speed. Kern began spinning the dial to locate the U-boat's distress band. He clicked on the microphone.

"Tug to U-boat in distress, tug to U-boat in distress. What is your emergency? Over."

The radio buzzed loudly in reply.

"This is U-3780. We wish to declare an emergency."

Kern pushed the button. "This is Kern. Get on with it, what's your problem? Over."

The radio crackled, hissing at Kern. He tried again. "U-3780. This is Kern; we're on the way. What is your emergency? Over."

A voice came back, the words frantic, garbled by static. ". . . water . . . taking water . . . forward torpedo room . . . Do you hear me? U-3780 requests help."

"U-3780, this is Kern. We're on the way. Beach the boat. Do you understand? I order you to beach."

Kern looked out over the bow of the tug. Flick's tug was making better speed, but Kern could see that they were still two kilometers from the three boats. U-3780 was in the rear, and she was listing badly to port.

The engines of the two tugs banged loudly, the noise echoing across the water as it bounced off of the sheer rock cliffs. The black water foamed white and hissed under their blunt bows, rolling along their hulls.

"Engine room," Kern shouted into the voice tube. "More power."

"Engine room, aye."

But Kern knew it was no good. The boilers had been lit in both tugs in case of emergency, but these awkward vessels had not had time to build a full head of steam.

One of the XXI boats began to turn to port.

"Watch her, Helmsman," Kern said, as the U-boat swung in a graceful arch, heading back toward U-3780.

"Look, Captain," the helmsman said.

Kern watched in astonishment as the crew of U-3780 spilled out of her hatches and onto her narrow deck.

"U-3780," Kern shouted into the microphone. "This is Kern. Repeat, this is Kapitaenleutnant Kern. I order you to turn toward starboard and beach your boat."

The U-boat's list increased, and she was down by the bow. *She's losing headway,* Kern thought. *She'll never make it.* The other U-boat flashed past the tug and Kern watched as it turned to port astern of them. They were coming to the rescue of their sister as well. But they were too late.

Frick's tug nosed in on the port side of U-3780, just forward of the conning tower, trying to nudge the sinking U-boat toward shore.

Kern watched as U-boatmen clambered over the bow of the tug. All discipline was gone.

"Come up astern of her on the starboard side," Kern ordered the helmsman. "We'll try to push her tail out so that Frick can drive her straight into the shore."

"Can't we tie her off, sir?" Rudy asked.

"She's three times bigger than the tug, son," Kern said. "She'd pull us down with her."

There was no more room on Frick's tug, and the remainder of U-3780's crew gestured frantically for Kern's tug to come alongside and take them off. The tug was just turning when Kern saw U-3780 shudder. Her bow dipped and the huge stern, water running off her back in white torrents, rose inexorably above the cold water. Her slowly revolving propellers clawed futilely in the air for a moment, hoping to forestall her death, and then the boat disappeared beneath the waves. Air, oil, and flotsam boiled up in a cauldron of death to mark her grave.

"God in heaven," Rudy gasped.

"All stop!" Kern shouted into the voice tube. The tug's engines stopped immediately, but the momentum carried her toward the crewmen in the icy water. "Full reverse!" Kern cried. He could hear the men crying for help, frantically waving for him to rescue them. The tug stopped her forward momentum as Kern felt the propellers biting in the water. "All stop," he called and quickly climbed down the ladder to the tug's deck. Rudy joined him, and they began pulling men onto the tug's deck.

They're boys, Kern thought as he grabbed hold of outstretched hands and looked into terror-filled eyes. *They're nothing but boys.* He pulled them aboard and saw white faces, blue lips, and the eyes of men who had come close to death. They lay where they fell on the deck in wet, shivering bundles that stank of fuel oil and vomit. Low moans and muffed sobs were the only noise that any of them could manage.

Suddenly there were no more to be brought aboard. Bodies floated in the still waters between the two tugs.

The captain of the tug appeared and began distributing blankets to the trembling forms. *Boys,* Kern thought, *schoolboys.*

He waved at Frick. "Will you get those bodies?"

"Yes, sir," Frick called back.

Kern added, although he knew it would be of no use, "Stay here in case some of the others were able to escape. I'll send this tug back out to pick up your survivors."

"Understood," Frick said. "Kapitaen, how long do you want me to stay?"

Kern knew what he was saying. He was saying that the bottom of the fiord was well beyond any depth from which the crewmen could make a successful escape. He was saying that judging from this lot of frightened boys, she probably went down with her bulkhead hatches wide open. Kern looked at the water. Its surface was still, calmed by a heavy iridescent film of diesel oil and the inconsequential reminders of a U-boat's death. It was a pitiful memorial for U-boatmen.

"Better stay out for a couple of hours," Kern said, regretting the order. It was a foolish waste of the living, keeping a vigil for the dead. But he could not make himself order Frick in.

Frick waved his acknowledgment.

"Take us back to base," Kern ordered Rudy.

He stood on the deck watching the men huddle together, trying to keep warm.

"Where is your kapitaen?" he called out.

No one looked up.

"I said, where is your kapitaen? Your officers?"

One ashen face appeared, trembling uncontrollably.

"I am Ensign Steiner, sir." Black hair was matted to

the boy's forehead, and a red stream trickled down the side of his cheek.

"You're injured, Steiner."

The ensign touched his face and looked at the blood on his fingers in a daze.

"What happened, Ensign Steiner?"

"We came out from Kiel, sir. With the other two boats. Most of the men hadn't been in U-boats long, none over two months. They got terribly seasick, and Kapitaen Dozois . . ." Steiner rubbed his head and repeated the name again, as if it should have meant something. "Kapitaen Dozois didn't want to surface because of the Tommies. But the men complained because the smell in the boat was making them even sicker."

"What about your Schnorchel?" Kern asked. "Didn't you use your Schnorchel?"

"We couldn't, sir. It wasn't functioning properly. Kapitaen Dozois finally agreed to surface. When we did, the men went wild and climbed out on deck. We were trying to restore order when it happened. The Tommies came, sir. We managed to get most of the men below before we submerged." Steiner looked at Kern apologetically. "But we didn't get all of them, sir."

"I understand," Kern said. "Go on."

"Kapitaen Dozois gave the order to dive. It seemed like it took the longest time. Then the Tommies started to bomb us. It went on for hours. Some of the men went mad. We had to hold them down. The lights went out five or six times. The boat shook. I thought that I was going to die. After a while, the Tommies gave up and went away. We reformed with the other boats and came into the fiord. Then the forward torpedo room said that they were taking water.

They said the outer doors were sprung. Water started coming in. We didn't get the bulkhead door closed fast enough and the water got up in the boat. The pumps couldn't keep up with it. That's when some of the men began to abandon the boat. Then the rest of them went."

"What about Kapitaen Dozois?"

"Sir?"

"Where was Dozois?"

"In the control room," Steiner said with uncertainty.

"The exec?"

"The exec?" Steiner repeated. "I don't know what happened to him."

"All right, boy," Kern said. "Get some rest."

"Sir? Will they shoot me, sir? For not doing my duty?"

Kern looked down at the boy with the man's burden—something that he would carry for life. Steiner trembled uncontrollably, shaking tears from his eyes. Kern pulled the blanket around Steiner's neck.

"Rest, boy," he said. "No one's going to shoot you."

Kern walked back along the deck, picking his way through the pitiful forms, until he reached the base of the bridge. He looked up to see the rough face of the tug kapitaen looking down on him.

"Call the other tug," Kern ordered. "See if they have Kapitaen Dozois aboard, or the exec."

The tug kapitaen nodded. Kern made his way astern, looking back over the silent water that hid U-3780. The other two boats kept pace starboard of the tug, sleek gray whales moving effortlessly through the water. Kern watched the water roll under the stern of the tug, the ship's propellers turning the water over and over like a farmer's plow breaks the soil. *It's the same thing,* Kern thought. *Men ashore are buried in the soil, and sailors in the depths of the sea. That's all we do,* Kern thought, *plow the ocean's soil and bury our dead.*

When the tug reached the Wreck, Hartmann was there to meet Kern.

"I heard everything on the radio," the exec said. "Did you get everyone off?"

"No," Kern replied. "Not everyone. Get some dry clothes and food for those men. I'm going to my quarters. When those two boats tie off, have their kapitaens see me immediately. Understand?"

"Yes, sir," Hartmann said.

Kern was waiting when the two officers knocked and entered his quarters. They glanced nervously from Kern to his clerk, Bauer, who sat with an open notepad at the desk. Oberleutnant Wilhelm Gorlitz was a short man with a round face, and a worried air. Oberleutnant Peter Hickman was a big man with crude features and dark eyes. He studied Kern arrogantly. Kern took an immediate disliking to both of them.

"What happened in the Skagerrak, gentlemen?" he began.

"It was that fool Dozois—" Hickman began.

"You're addressing a superior office!" Kern snapped. "Act like it."

Both men stiffened to attention. Hickman's face turned red.

"We were ordered to travel submerged, sir," Hickman began again. "Kapitaen Dozois radioed that he had trouble with his Schnorchel."

"Who is senior kapitaen?" Kern asked.

"Dozois, sir," Gorlitz ventured.

"Proceed."

"I reminded Kapitaen Dozois of our orders, sir,"

Hickman said. "Nevertheless, Kapitaen Dozois decided to proceed on the surface once we were out of the Kattegat and into the Skagerrak. He was immediately picked up by the Tommies, sir, and bombed."

"My boat suffered some damage as well, Kapitaenleutnant," Gorlitz said, as if sympathy should be extended to him.

Hickman ignored him and continued the report. "The Tommies pounded him pretty hard, sir. He radioed about leaks in the forward torpedo room, and around the hydroplanes. There was nothing we could do, sir. I suggested to Kapitaen Dozois that we proceed to Evanger submerged. Run on the surface when we got to the fiord. Sir."

Kern said nothing.

"Kapitaen Dozois agreed," Hickman continued. "When we were running up the fiord, I noticed U-3780 listing. I attempted to make contact with Kapitaen Dozois. I couldn't. By that time, we saw the two tugs approaching."

"Yes," Gorlitz agreed softly. And then hurriedly added, "Sir."

"I see," Kern said. "Oberleutnant Hickman, how long have you had your boat?"

"Eight days, sir."

"Oberleutnant Gorlitz?"

"Five days, sir."

Days, instead of months. "Have either of you commanded a U-boat before?"

"No, sir," Hickman said, making it sound almost as if it were a point of pride with him.

"I was torpedo officer on the U-1220, sir," Gorlitz offered.

Kern folded his hands on his desk. "Your crews?

How many experienced U-boatmen do you have among your crews?"

"Twelve, I think," Gorlitz offered weakly.

Hickman straightened. "Eighteen of my men have seen action, sir. I myself was executive officer of U-994."

Kern looked up quickly. "That was Marksman's boat. Kessel was exec of U-994 when she went down. When were you the exec?"

The U-boat kapitaen's jaw tightened. "For three weeks, sir."

"What happened?"

Hickman glanced at the clerk sitting next to Kern.

"Quite right, Hickman," Kern said. "Dismissed, Bauer."

The seaman saluted and left.

Hickman continued. "Conduct unbecoming, sir. Difficulties with a woman."

"You won't have that trouble up here." Kern stood. "We've got two boats with undertrained and inexperienced crews. We have the remnants of another crew on our hands, but they're not going out again. I suppose neither of your boats have had sea trials?"

"No, sir," came the response from both men.

"U-3535 hasn't either. So we'll learn together. Since neither of you has combat command experience, I will train you myself. Make no mistake, gentlemen, our task is not an easy one and our mission will demand the utmost of everyone involved, especially the commanders. I will inform you of the exact nature of our mission when the time is right. Conduct a thorough inspection of your boats, top to bottom. Do that immediately. As you have found, the boats were delivered to us in less than fighting condition. Inspect everything. Make a list of the problem areas and the repairs needed. Frick is my engineering officer. I will see that he works with your engineering officers."

"Pardon, Kapitaenleutnant," Gorlitz said, "but do you have a medical officer? Some of my men are seasick."

"Oberleutnant Gorlitz," Kern said quietly, keeping his temper in check. "You may tell your men for me that they will have more than puking to complain about by the time I'm through with them. I have a medical orderly. He can bandage wounds and dispense aspirin. That is the extent of my medical facilities. Welcome to the outpost of the Reich, gentlemen. Don't expect feather pillows and silver spoons. And remember one thing. I expect every man to do more than his share to get these boats in order and ready for our mission. I will tolerate no malingers. The moment I see anyone on any boat becoming complacent, I will make the crew of that boat wish that they'd followed U-3780 to the bottom of the fiord. Is that understood?"

"Yes, sir," Hickman said. He was showing a talent for making the most ordinary words take on an insolent tone.

"Yes, sir," Gorlitz replied, standing so rigidly that Kern thought he would topple over.

"Very well, gentlemen," Kern said. "Dismissed."

Kern watched the two leave his makeshift headquarters. *What have they sent me? It's not enough the crews aren't trained and the officers are boys, now my kapitaens are incompetent.* He called his clerk in.

"Bauer, send this message to Koralle: 'Vice Admiral Godt. U-3712, U-3719 arrived. U-3780 sunk due to damages sustained in transit. Most of crew saved, Kapitaen Dozois and executive officer lost. Respectfully request estimated time arrival at this base of rest of

command. Request, respectfully, arrival date RGTs.'
Got it? Good. Sign it Kern and send it off. Have Hartmann and Frick see me immediately."

Bauer saluted and left Kern alone. The remains of
the crew from U-3780 would be fed and housed in the
old schoolhouse until they could be transported to
Trondheim, Kern thought. *They're more than useless—
they're a liability.*

There was a knock on the door, and Frick entered.
He'd let his reddish beard grow out and he looked
more like a Viking than an engineer.

"Yes, sir?" he said, saluting.

"How's your list coming along, Frick?" Kern asked.

"One problem at a time, Kaleu."

Kern smiled. Frick sometimes forgot himself and
used the shortened form of Kern's rank. Kern let it
go; it was a minor breach of discipline.

"Enough to keep us busy," Frick continued, "once
we got the boat cleaned out and in shape." He pulled
a list out of his tunic pocket and laid it on Kern's desk.

"The extender switch for the hydraulic periscope
system will be replaced. The surface control station
will have to be completely overhauled. The rudder
station and engine telegraphs are acting up. The control panels for both the GHG and the Nibelung SU
are shorting out. I've rewired them twice, myself. Still
working on that one. The hydraulics on the forward
hydroplanes are a mess. But we can fix that."

"Electric motors and diesels?"

"Operational. Both of them. Maybach Daimler-
Benz diesels, strong as iron. I'd stake my soul on
them. Torpedo-loading hydraulics, operational.
Pump cellar cleaned and ready. I've had to reglue the
Wesch mats on the Schnorchel head. Given time to

dry, they'll be all right. I hope they really do reduce the chances of Tommy picking up the head on radar."

"We'll find out soon enough."

"Yes," Frick agreed. "Both pressure oil pumps for the hydraulic system run hot."

"Maybe that's where your hydroplane problem is."

"No, sir. We checked that. The pumps are just running hot. I might have to break them down. Maybe the bearings."

Frick continued for the next three hours. There were dozens of problems with the big boat, and with each Kern felt an additional burden. *It wasn't always this difficult,* he thought. *The officers would come to me with problems and I would find a solution. Now the solutions seem just beyond my reach.*

"That's the worst of it," Frick said.

"Very well," Kern said, keeping the concern out of his voice. "I told Oberleutnant Gorlitz and Oberleutnant Hickman that I want them to begin inspection of their boats immediately. I'm sure that they received them in the same condition that we received U-3535. You're going to need to give them a hand, Frick. Both crews are inexperienced. I told them to expect you."

Frick grinned. "It'll be a pleasure, sir. The more I can get my hands into, the more I'll learn about these boats."

"I'm glad you feel that way, because I'm giving you exactly seven days to certify all three boats ready for service."

Frick's grin disappeared. "Seven days?"

"A week, Frick. You can do it. God made heaven and earth in only six."

"Yes, sir, but He had the manuals. I don't have half of the engineering manuals I need for these boats."

"I don't want to hear it, Frick. All I want to hear in seven days is that the boats are ready for service."

"Yes, sir." The engineer gathered up his notes and stuffed them into his coverall pocket. He saluted and left. Kern was about to look for Hartmann when the executive officer of U-3535 entered the office with Bauer. From the stricken look on Hartmann's face, Kern knew something was terribly wrong.

"What is it, Teddy?" Kern asked as Hartmann closed the door. "You're as white as a ghost."

"Bauer was sending your message to the Lion," Hartmann said, his voice trembling, "When we got this." He handed Kern the radio flimsy and added: "Bauer decoded it."

Kern took the paper and began to read. He felt as if someone had plunged a knife into his belly.

"My God! They've tried to kill Hitler."

Chapter 8

Harrow's Navy Club, Liverpool, England

Land slipped into the booth across from Hardy and signaled for a waiter. Hardy, his eyes bloodshot and vacant, looked up at *Firedancer*'s number one.

"Well? Is it true? Did they murder the old bastard?"

"No, sir," Land said, as the waiter arrived. "Scotch. Just a dash of soda." The waiter left. "He's still alive."

Hardy wiped his eyes and took a drink. "Leave it to the Germans. They can kill hundreds of thousands on the battlefield, but can't kill Hitler in the loo."

"A map room, I'm told, sir," Land said. "Someone planted a bomb in a map room. Adolf was wounded but survived."

Hardy watched as the waiter arrived with Land's drink. His eyes followed the glass to the other man's lips. "Damnable way to treat scotch, Number One. Contaminating it with soda."

Land smiled. "One of my many vices, sir. How are you getting on?"

"Oh, splendid, Mother."

"Sleeping well?"

"Not at all, as a matter of fact. And you?"

"Like a baby, sir."

"Here's to Morpheus," Hardy said, raising his glass.

"And the little bits of death he rewards us with each night." He finished his drink and searched the club crowded with blue uniforms for a waiter. Land studied Hardy. His eyes glistened and his skin was sallow and hung from his cheekbones. He thought Firedancer's hands were trembling a bit more than usual but he couldn't be sure. He looked old, worn out—as battered as his namesake. Hardy caught his look.

"Taking stock of the old wreck, Number One?"

"Not at all, sir. Admiring your stamina and clean lines."

Hardy's bushy eyebrows narrowed. "You *are* a barrister, aren't you, Number One? Diplomatic, polished, poised. You know just what to say at all times."

"Another vice, I'm afraid, sir. Comes with the silly little wig."

Hardy looked around. "Where is that damned waiter? Waiter! A man's dying of thirst over here!"

Heads turned to look in Hardy's direction. Land stood quickly. "I'll get it, sir. Scotch?"

"Just so," Hardy said. "And don't ruin it."

Land smiled and squeezed his way to the bar through the crowd of naval officers. An officer who looked vaguely familiar stepped aside to let him in.

"Tight again, is he?" the officer said.

Land said nothing. He motioned for a bartender.

"Jefferson," the officer said, holding out his hand. "*Belfast*. We've met before."

"Yes," Land said, embarrassed at not recognizing the man. He took the other man's hand.

"You're Land, aren't you? *Firedancer*?"

"Yes," Land said, trying to place the other officer's face. "Where—"

"Some damned boring party," Jefferson said, turning back to his drink. "I'm on leave. Came home to see my family. Saw them. Now I'm here. Is he on the rocks?" He motioned to Hardy.

"No. We've been out for a while. He's good as gold actually."

"Ah, well," Jefferson said, staring into his drink. "Jolly good to hear that. Jolly good. Can't stand to come in myself. Funny how things work out, isn't it? I can't wait to get back in, and when I do"—he downed his drink— "I spend my time in pubs. Your boy's the same way, isn't he?"

The bartender arrived and Land ordered a scotch straight up and another scotch and soda.

"Was it Sheila's party?" Land asked.

"What difference does it make whose bloody party it was?" Jefferson said.

"I suppose it doesn't."

"It was bloody boring, that's all I know."

Land drummed his fingers silently, waiting on the drinks.

"What are you going to do when it's all over?" Jefferson asked.

"What?"

"When the fun's over?"

Land looked at him. "That's a queer word to use, isn't it?"

"Is it?" Jefferson said. "You've got a cushy job to go home to, haven't you? I'm an accountant, But not just an accountant A very bad accountant. Before this business I was a bad accountant, and when it's all through I'll return to being a bad accountant. Dismal."

"Doesn't sound like a bad life," Land said. "I know plenty of good men who won't be coming back who would have settled for that."

"A philosopher, are you?"

"No."

"See here, Land. It's all about perspective, isn't it? Some men lead miserable lives. What is it that American writer chap said, 'lives of quiet desperation'? Give a fellow a chance to get out from under that, a chance to be somebody other than a bloke in a cheap suit, and it begins to mean something. You understand?"

"Yes," Land said. "I do."

"There you have it! So a bloke finds himself a part of something so big that he begins to feel big himself." Jefferson swirled the whiskey in his glass. "He begins to feel as if he's a part of something. Something worthwhile. Something important. I said fun and I bloody well mean fun. But it's bound to come to an end isn't it? Got to come to an end sometime, doesn't it? Everything goes back the way it was. Everything neatly in its place. Square pegs in square holes. Round pegs in round holes." Jefferson stared at his drink. "Everything back the way it was."

The drinks arrived and Land paid for them. "A pleasure," he said to Jefferson and returned to the booth.

"God's pajamas, Number One," Hardy said, reaching for the glass. "A man could die of thirst."

Land raised his glass for a toast, but Hardy was already drinking.

"Easy does it, sir."

Hardy set the glass down. "Who was that chap at the bar? Friend of yours?"

"An acquaintance."

"Another barrister?"

"No," Land said, lighting a cigarette. "An accountant."

Hardy shook his head. "Accountants and barristers at sea!"

Land smiled. "Frightening, isn't it, sir?"

Hardy was silent for a moment. Then he said: "Number One, I want to confess. Will you hear my confession?"

"I seem to have left my collar on board, sir."

"Well, hear it anyway. That's an order. You do still take orders, don't you?"

"Always, sir."

"Well then, hear my confession." Hardy cleared his throat and took a drink. A puzzled look crossed his face. "When are you happiest, Number One?"

"Is this part of your confession?"

Hardy gave him an exasperated look.

"I'm sorry, sir," Land said. "Please continue."

"At sea."

"I beg your pardon?"

"I'm happiest when I'm at sea, Number One. Put me on the bridge and I am in my element. Let me taste the salt in the air and feel the sting of the cold spray on my face and I am happy. Pluck me from *Firedancer* and drop me on terra firma and I am at my wits' end. I would even trade life on a country estate for shepherding idiotic merchant captains and those slow, fat cows of theirs."

"You're a sailor, sir. You belong at sea."

"Yes," Hardy said. He leaned back in the booth. "It's the endlessness of it, Number One. It beckons me, do you understand? A vast field of waves that roll on forever. A sky as overwhelming as the water that it lies on; clouds as big as mountains, sometimes so white that you can't look at them. You've seen it. The clouds are black with rain and wind, and the sky becomes green with hatred. Storms that take a man's breath and reason away and give him nothing in return except terror. Sunsets and sunrises that no one but poets could describe. Brilliant colors, Number One, right from God's pallet." A tiny smile appeared on Hardy's lips. "Silly of me, isn't it? Going on like this?"

"I don't think so, no, sir."

Hardy wiped his eyes. "My friends." He took a drink. "My friends who have gone up in rank—captain chairs and sail desks. They sit at windows overlooking the harbor and watch as ships steam out to sea—out into the vastness. Away they go, until they are nothing but gray slivers on the green sea. Poor bloody bastards— swivel chairs and pencil sharpeners. Not for me—not at all." He slammed the table with his fist. "I tell you, when we come in to reprovision . . ." Hardy stopped talking. "Am I boring you, Number One?" he asked in a low voice.

Land shook his head.

"I guess I'm in my cups. Getting maudlin on you."

Land waited for Hardy to continue. Firedancer looked haggard and he swayed a bit from the alcohol.

"It's funny, sir," Land said. "That fellow at the bar— Jefferson. In a way he was talking about the same thing that you are."

"The accountant?" Hardy said, piqued. "By God, now you're comparing me to an accountant!"

"Yes, sir. Perhaps not exactly. But it seems he's found a home in the navy. A place in war. Something that he'd rather not give up."

"The accountant," Hardy said again, but this time, thoughtfully. "Well, I suppose it happens the same way to different men."

"Maybe," Land said. "Maybe in some perverse way I shall miss all of this. Maybe the storms at sea and the abysmal discomfort of always being cold and wet and tired will disappear. What I'll have instead are my memories."

"You had better be careful, Number One," Hardy said, looking straight into his eyes. "Your memories will not let you sleep. You'll see the faces of the men you left to die, floating in the black water, because if you stopped to rescue them, your ship would be torpedoed. You won't miss those memories."

"Maybe I'm being a fool," Land said.

Hardy scratched the side of his head, dislodging a tuft of coarse gray hair that slipped over his ear. "No, you're not. You're being human. If you survive this the years will crush the bad memories into dust and the only thing that will remain is a faint longing to be on the bridge again, looking over the endless sea." Hardy snorted. "Goddamn me for being a sentimentalist! I ought to know better. "

Land studied Hardy for a moment. "I don't know, sir," he said with a grin. "I quite like the sentimental side in you."

The two remained silent for a moment.

"Do you know what the most beautiful piece of music in the world is?" Hardy asked.

"To me? Beethoven's Ninth Symphony."

"The most beautiful piece of music in the world, Number One, is a hymn."

"Which one?"

" 'Eternal Father, Strong to Save.' You've heard of it?"

"Yes, sir. Every good Episcopalian has."

"'Eternal Father, Strong to Save,'" Hardy said again. He lifted his glass. "Shall we toast those who are lost at sea?"

Land raised his glass. "To those lost at sea." They both drank. Number One studied Hardy for a moment before rising. "Gentlemen!" he called over the crowd. They turned to look at him. "'Eternal Father, Strong to Save!'" Land began singing, his voice soft but steady.

> "Eternal Father, strong to save,
> Whose arm hath bound the restless wave,
> Who bidd'st the mighty ocean deep . . ."

No one spoke or moved until a sublieutenant with a wispy moustache cleared his throat softly. He joined Land in a voice clear and unburdened. The two men managed a rough harmony.

> "Its own appointed limits keep;
> Oh, hear us when we cry to Thee."

People began standing. Others began to sing.

> "For those in peril on the sea!
> Most Holy Spirit! Who didst brood
> Upon the chaos dark and rude,
> And bid its angry tumult cease,"

Everyone was singing now, their voices strong and vital.

> "And give, for wild confusion, peace:
> Oh, hear us when we cry to Thee,
> For those in peril on the sea!"

Hardy stood now, and setting his glass down, joined in.

> "O Trinity of love and power!
> Our brethen shield in danger's hour;

From rock and tempest, fire and foe,
Protect them wheresoe'er they go;
Thus evermore shall rise to Thee
Glad hymns of praise from land and sea."

Chapter 9

Fleet Air Arm, Spotswoddie House

Captain Sheen eyed Carlow through half-closed eyes, his fingers locked together behind his head—a snake waiting for its prey to approach.

"Well?" he said, his voice raspy with fatigue.

"I think we've got them, sir," Carlow said dully. They'd been at it for the better part of three days, working with the intelligence teams to locate the German U-boat base in Norway. The radio traffic had been frequent enough to attempt a fix but not sustained enough to definitely locate the base. Finally, Carlow thought, things were working out.

"Well?" Sheen said again.

Carlow laid a map of Norway's coastline on Sheen's desk. There was an arc drawn in red pencil covering a good third of it.

"Those mountains are playing havoc with our triangulation," Carlow said. "But we've narrowed the location down to this area."

Sheen leaned forward, slumping in his chair, his large head suspended over the map in study. Carlow waited while the captain digested the information.

"How many fiords now?" Sheen asked without looking up.

"Still several hundred," Sheen said. "But every in-dication puts them about here." He pinned a portion of the coastline between his thumb and forefinger.

Sheen grunted and leaned back in his chair. "Are those U-boats that dangerous, Carlow?"

"Yes, sir. Our intelligence boys think that they are. They're faster than anything that we have and have a greater range than anything that Jerry has sent out before. Some fellows think that if the Jerries have enough of them, it could be the Battle of the Atlantic all over again."

Sheen ran his tongue over his lip in thought. It was a moment before he spoke. "Very well. Let's continue to monitor those bastards so that we can fix their lo-cation. Schedule reconnaissance flights. Maybe we'll find them through sheer dumb luck, because there's no other way to do it. Norway is either under cloud cover or fogged in ninety percent of the year, and un-less our chaps bump into them . . ."

Carlow waited for Sheen to finish, but the captain jerked his head toward the door instead. Carlow was dismissed—Sheen had said all that he was going to say. He was right. They were still far from precisely locating the U-boat base, and without that the airmen who were asked to fly into those treacherous fiords would have little chance of seeing anything. They could fly right over the enemy vessels and see nothing more than the heavy gray overcast beneath the air-craft.

What was it, Carlow thought as he walked back to his office with the map, a needle in a haystack? A nee-dle in a thousand haystacks? He was tired and his mind labored to find an analogy. In the end, as he picked up his telephone to contact Flight Operations, he simply let it go. Let the pilots figure it out.

Chapter 10

Bokn Fiord, Norway

Kapitaenleutnant Guenter Kern lifted his face to let the rain pummel him. Gray clouds covered the mountains and hid the tops of the trees. Raindrops danced frantically on the fiord's deep water, as sharp waves, edged in whitecaps, raced across its black surface. The Norwegian winds slid down off the mountainsides trying to steal his white cap, and throw open his worn, gray leather coat. Next to him stood the port lookout, and across from them in the other bridge opening stood the starboard lookout. Both the forward and aft antiaircraft turrets panned an empty sky, tracking imaginary targets.

Kern called into the voice tube over the rush of wind, "Kapitaen, engine room!" Frick's muffled voice came back through the tube.

"Frick here, Kapitaen."

"Are you ready, Frick?"

"Yes, sir."

"Good," Kern shouted as a gust of wind pushed him against the armored panels. "Teddy?" He called down to the surface control station below him. Hartmann's face appeared at the bottom of the ladder.

"Yes, sir?"

"We're going to try it again," he said. "Keep your eye on those damned revolution indicators. They've been reading twenty percent higher than Frick's. I don't know which to believe."

"Yes, sir."

The wind increased, viciously slapping waves against the U-boat's blunt bow. The spray spilled over the deck to be picked up by the gusting wind and thrown into the faces of the bridge watch. Kern wiped the water from his face.

"Teddy? Ahead both one-third!" he ordered.

He heard the ring of the engine telegraph, and the answering ring from the engine room. Suddenly, the big boat surged forward. Kern felt her vibrating through the soles of his rubber boots. He knew that Frick was frantically dancing from the starboard control station to the port control station in the engine compartment, his eyes covering every critical dial and gauge in a single sweep.

Kern breathed deeply the cold air, tasting the salt that had congealed in the corners of his mouth from the spray. He could feel the strength in his boat, feel her butt through the waves—carving a path through the water. True, this was not the ocean, but that did not matter—U-3535 was at play. This slim leg of water belonged to Kern and his boat.

That would come soon enough, and when it did this big whale would glide under the seas as if Neptune himself had made her. Kern was anxious about the tests, despite his words of caution to his officers and crew. These deep-water fiords with their treacherous currents and mountain walls were no place for sailors. The sea was where they belonged. It was where their boat belonged—in the cold depths of the vast ocean plain.

"Kapitaen, engine room!" he shouted into the tube. Frick hailed back.

"Well, Chief? Can I increase speed or not?"

"So far, so good, Kapitaen. Go ahead."

"So far, so good?" Kern grumbled to himself. "That doesn't sound reassuring. Hartmann! Both ahead, Hartmann! Both ahead two-thirds!"

He felt the boat trembling as she sped up. It was as if she were straining to hold her tremendous power in check. Kern noticed the lookouts grin at each other.

"Keep you eyes on the sky!" he ordered, but he knew that they were as excited as he was. She was like no other boat they had ever sailed on; she was a champion.

She sliced through the water, hungrily gobbling distance as if she were a racehorse. Kern glanced over to the brown walls of the mountains gliding past them. He felt himself smiling, and he wiped the spray from his face and beard. "Run," he urged the boat under his breath. "Run!"

"Hartmann! You call this speed?" he shouted. "All ahead both."

"Yes, sir. Permission to test the surface control rudder?"

"All right, Teddy," Kern said. "Starboard fifteen degrees."

"Yes, sir. All ahead both, starboard fifteen degrees."

U-3535 jumped ahead, shattering the waves that struck her bow into a million white droplets that hissed as the wind caught them and drove them the length of the boat. She swung easily to starboard, heeling as her big rudder bit into the water. It was Lake Constance, Kern thought. Dashing across the calm waters, her with the sails fat and straining at the sheets. He was lightning then, darting between the staid pleasure boats, laying the boat over on her side, hearing the sails snap with delight when they caught a fresh gust of wind. He was sailing again, and there was no more war.

Kern called two more course changes for U-3535, almost giddy at the way the big boat rolled in response to her rudder. All they needed was one boat like this against a convoy. Just one boat and to hell with the escorts! *If we only had her in '42. My God! We could have swept the seas!*

"Bridge? Engine room." It was Frick.

"Bridge. Kapitaen. What is it, Frick?"

"The starboard engine exhaust gas cooler and the Junker's compressor have both shut down. I recommend we reduce speed to ahead slow until I can figure out what the hell is the matter this time."

"All right," Kern said, exhilaration draining from him. "Reduce speed to both ahead slow." He felt the boat slow and saw the waves of her own wake wash over the stern and break away into nothing. Kern felt the dampness in his bones now, and he pulled his coat tightly against his throat. He looked up. The rain began to fall harder.

"Teddy?" he called down. "Let's take her in. Starboard thirty." Kern watched her bow swing slowly onto course, but there was no speed to kindle excitement. Now they were just course changes, not chances for the boat to show off. It was no wonder that men loved ships, Kern thought. *Look how they make men feel inside. Like kings,* he thought, as the base came into view. *When sailors are aboard ships they love, they feel like kings. On land, we are just men.*

U-3535 tied off on the starboard side of the Wreck, the other two boats off her port side. It was an awkward arrangement for the tender, but in case of an air strike there would just be one boat trapped inside instead of two.

"Teddy?" Kern said. "I'm going to the radio shack. Go and sit on Frick. I don't want any more disappointments when I take her out again."

"Do I have permission to flog him?"

"No," Kern said, stopping. "But if you two don't give me the boat I want when I want it, I will flog you."

Kern left Hartmann and Frick to their duties and walked to the radio shack. The young operator was just decoding a message when he walked in.

"It's for you, sir," the operator said, glancing over his shoulder. He was working quickly. He laid the pencil aside, folded the message, and handed it to Kern. It was the look on the young man's face that betrayed the contents of the message. Something was terribly wrong.

"What is it?" Kern said without opening the message.

"It's the other boats, sir. They aren't coming."

Kern felt his strength steal away. He unfolded the paper and read it.

Additional boats damaged or destroyed in ways. Unable to supply you as needed. Good luck. Doenitz.

It was very quiet in the radio shack. Kern could hear the shouts of sailors through the thin walls as they loaded practice torpedoes into the U-boats. Kern crumbled the message into a ball and pushed it into his pocket.

"No one is to know about this. Do you understand?"

The operator nodded weakly. "Yes, sir. Do you have a reply, sir?"

Kern thought for a moment before answering. "Send 'Message acknowledged, Kern.'"

He walked from the radio shack and sought out

Teddy. The executive officer was just coming up the hill when he saw Kern.

"What's the matter?" he asked.

"Is it that obvious?" Kern said.

"Yes. What is it?"

"We aren't getting any more boats, Teddy."

"What do you mean? Why not? What's happened to them?"

Kern shook his head. "The Tommies. Or the Americans, I don't know which. Our beautiful boats never got out of the harbor."

"Does . . . ?"

"No one knows but you and me. And Funker. I gave him orders. Now I'm giving you one. The men aren't to know. They can't know. Things are bad enough. Do you understand?"

"Yes. Yes, of course," Teddy said. "This doesn't give you much of a flotilla, does it?"

"See to the boat, Teddy. I'll be in my quarters." Kern looked over the small base as he walked up the incline, taking stock of what he did have. Leutnant Edland had proved to be a very capable officer, setting up a machine shop, mess hall, wireless center, and torpedo shed in a remarkably short period of time. Edland had run power lines from the tender to the base, and disconnected the ancient diesel generators that he had appropriated. Now the Wreck powered the base, and electricity wasn't a haphazard affair.

Several truck convoys had brought much-needed supplies and materials to the base, and a dilapidated coastal steamer showed up one morning with thirty-one T-5 torpedoes and forty-eight practice torpedoes. Kern had made sure that the T-5s were distributed between the Wreck and the torpedo shed onshore. In

case of attack he didn't want to take the chance of the
Wreck taking all of their torpedoes to the bottom of
the fiord. He had ordered the practice torpedoes divided among the three boats, with the surplus stowed
aboard the Wreck.

That was the best of it.

The worst of it was that Kern had gone out with the
other boats on training exercises. It was as he had expected: neither kapitaen was skilled beyond the most
rudimentary level of command. Their orders had
been delivered in an uncertain voice, and sometimes
countermanded almost as quickly as they were given.
Gorlitz had been the worst, and it was easy to see that
his inexperienced crew had no confidence in him, or
in themselves or their boat. Gorlitz had led his men as
if he expected rank alone to be sufficient reason for
them to follow his orders.

No, he didn't lead his men. It was rather that he
had performed the nominal duties of a U-boat kapitaen and then looked about in the hopes that
everyone else was doing what they were supposed to
do.

Hickman had been another story. His crew was
equally inexperienced, but his method of handling
them was based on intimidation. He was loud and arrogant, and more than once seemed on the verge of
striking seamen who did not respond to his commands as quickly as he thought they should. Kern had
seen his kind before—men whose limited abilities
were hidden by arrogance and brutality. He knew
kapitaens whose crews were beaten into submission,
but whose discipline disintegrated the moment that
they faced danger. Hickman badgered his men. He
bullied them, so that they understood to do their job

correctly meant that they would be left alone, and nothing else.

A happy boat is a good boat, Cremer had once told Kern. Maus had agreed as they shared a cup of tea for the last time at Lorient. Kern knew that the two renowned U-boat captins had been right, because in U-boats one man's mistake, no matter how minor, could instantly mean the death of everyone aboard. Give them discipline, Cremer had said, because it is a solid foundation upon which the men build their lives. They will anchor their performance to it, because it is the one consistency in this crazy war and it is the one thing, besides luck, that can bring them back from patrols. But make them realize that same discipline extends from the torpedo room to the engine room; that everyone, everyone will be as disciplined in their duty as the next man will.

That way, Maus had added as Allied bombs thundered in the distance and air raid sirens wailed, when the escorts have you pinned down they will not wonder if the man next to them is going to crack. Discipline makes your boat strong.

An ancient steward had tried to refill their cups with trembling hands when Maus sent him away. "Go to the air raid shelter, old man. I don't want you scalding my balls with hot tea."

Cremer had laughed and proposed a toast. "To scalded balls or death."

Kern remembered their conversation as he had watched Hickman bully his crew. *Cremer*, Kern thought, *yes, he's still alive.* But Maus? August Maus. Kern realized that he didn't know what had become of Maus. Dead? Captured? He didn't know.

So Kern had brought both Gorlitz and Hickman into his office, separately of course, and talked with them about their crews and their boats. Frick had gone over both boats with each boat's chief engineer, and after commenting that it would have been nice if the shipyards had completed the job, developed a list of scheduled maintenance. Both U-3712 and U-3719 had been delivered in much the same condition as U-3535: a hundred things wrong with them, and not half the manuals that were needed. Kern had listened patiently to Frick's complaints and then had said: "What are you going to do about it, Chief?" Frick had grumbled but set about doing what he had to do to right things mechanically. The crews and their kapitaens, those were Kern's responsibility. He had attacked that by having first Gorlitz's and then Hickman's crew train alongside U-3535's crew. It was dangerously crowded in the boat, of course, but it seemed the best way to handle the situation. Every station on the U-boat had two crewmen assigned to it, with two kapitaens in the control room.

Gorlitz had seemed pathetically grateful to have someone show him how to effectively handle a crew, but Kern knew that even with extensive training Gorlitz would never fully understand what a magnificent weapon he had at his disposal.

He should have been kept onshore, Kern had thought, safely barricaded behind forms and rubber stamps.

Hickman had been, as always, sullen. He had stood next to Kern as U-3535 went through her trials, and smoldered with the indignation of having to be shown what to do in front of his men. It couldn't be helped, Kern knew, better to be treated like a konfirmant, a kapitaen in training, than to lead an unprepared boat and an ill-trained crew out into the North Atlantic. The sea wouldn't be forgiving. She would send storms, and giant waves, and Tommies floating out of the sun to straddle you with fliebos, and if you dived safely you may find that some valve had failed and your boat turned against you.

It was a conspiracy, Kern had realized one day as he watched Gorlitz and his crew bring the boat to the surface after an unsatisfactory crash dive. *The Tommies and the North Atlantic have made a pact to kill me.* Having decided that, and sharing his theory with Hartmann over a quiet cup of tea one evening, Kern decided something else—*they're going to have a hell of a hard time doing it.*

Kern had just thrown himself onto the bunk in his office, behind the blanket serving as a curtain, when he heard the front door open and someone talking to his orderly.

"Well, tell him to get out of bed!" the voice commanded loudly. It sounded familiar.

Kern pulled the blanket aside and saw Oberleutnant Otto Shafer.

"Otto!" he cried, pushing himself out of the bunk.

"What are you doing in bed in the middle of the day?" Shafer asked, with a broad grin. "Get up! Show me the women and the wine you've got hidden away."

"How are you?" Kern asked, extending a hand to his old friend.

Shafer brushed aside the hand and threw both arms around Kern. "Alive! That's good enough for me. A kapitaenleutnant? The Lion must have been drunk. I saw your flotilla, Admiral! I'm impressed. Call the Lion and have me made an admiral, too."

Kern shook his head and laughed. Shafer had not lost any of his spirit. He did not enter a room; he captured it.

"Bauer," he said to his orderly. "Go and find something

to do so that I can talk to this madman alone." He offered Shafer a chair and searched behind the post office counter for a bottle of wine.

Shafer looked out the window. "Who did you piss off to be sent up here? It took me a day to find out where the hell you were, and now that I'm here I wonder why I wasted my time."

Kern pulled out the bottle and two glasses. The two men sat at the table, and Kern poured the drinks.

Shafer offered a toast. "To the service."

"To the service," Kern responded, and they downed their wine.

"What are you really doing here?" Kern asked as he poured more wine. "This is not exactly on the way to anyplace."

"I came to see you, my silent friend," Shafer answered. "But you're right about that. You and your tiny command are definitely out of the way. I've been transferred. I'm leaving beautiful Norway forever. I hope."

"Where are you going?" Kern asked. "Can you tell me?"

"I can tell you anything I want," Shafer replied. "I'm one of the chosen. You remember Rasch, don't you? Well, you're not the only one given a flotilla."

"What do you mean?"

"The Lion has placed Rasch in charge of the new See-Hund program. I'm to report to some little town outside of Neustadt." He glanced out the window. "If it's anything like this, I'm going to volunteer for the Eastern Front."

"See-Hund?"

Shafer gave Kern a skeptical look and poured another glass of wine. "Midget U-boats," he said. "Two-man U-boats that carry two torpedoes. Seals that are going to dash into the Channel and sink Allied ships before they can deliver more men and materials to the invasion. Well, what do you think? Fantastic, isn't it?"

Kern was stunned. Midget U-boats. The idea seemed ridiculous. It had to be a mistake, a code name for a project. Doenitz would not risk what was left of his kapitaens in fantastic schemes such as midget U-boats.

"Don't bother talking, friend," Shafer said. "That look says it all. It's the last wooden sword in our arsenal. Well, it's not my worry. It's Rasch's command; all I have to do is take orders. What about you? How did you luck on those beauties out there? Are they as good as everyone says they are? And what are you doing way the hell up here? The battles down where I'm headed, not here."

"Yes, they are as good as everyone says. Maybe better than anyone supposes. I can't tell you anything, Otto. It's all top secret. I'm surprised you even found me here."

"Top secret, my ass. I located you easily enough, so it can't be that top secret." Kern watched as his friend grew serious. "I tell you, Guenter, things are bad. Every time I look around, I see more of us missing. You can't take a boat out of the pens without a dozen bees showing up. It's death to attack a convoy. What am I saying? You know that. You know how things are."

"Yes, I do."

"You know about Hitler, of course?"

Kern nodded.

"What do you think about it?"

Kern was surprised by the question. "It was a despicable act. He is our fuehrer."

A sliver of a smile crossed Shafer's lips. "Yes, my sentiments exactly."

"You had better be careful what you say, Shafer," Kern said. "These are difficult times."

"Difficult times?" Otto laughed loudly. "The master of the understatement! Guenter, we always wondered what made you run. You're not a madman—that is reserved for me, thank you very much. You're not a zealot." Otto smiled and shook his head. "I've seen too many of those idiots come and go. Come on now, Guenter, Guenter the Silent, tell me what goes on in that mysterious mind of yours."

Kern chuckled. "You are a madman. Don't do anything mad with your See-Hunds."

"You'd better be damned careful wherever you go," Shafer said. "I'd hate to have to break in a new friend." He leaned closer, his eyes sparkling. "Tell me about them. Are they fast?"

Kern laughed. "Fast? It's like sailing. Submerged she can do eighteen knots for ninety minutes. She can do twelve to fourteen knots for ten hours. We've had her up to ten knots submerged and it's like she's standing still. Smooth, incredibly smooth. She has everything you'd ever want. She has a shower."

Shafer set his glass down on the table with a clunk. "A shower? In a U-boat? See here, Guenter, you won't be worth a damn after this. Next you'll want chambermaids and linen, and champagne before each watch."

"She is a wonder. She can run silently, I mean really run silently. She can dive to 280 meters. She's all that we ever wanted, Otto."

"Yes," Shafer offered wryly. "All that we ever wanted. But, Guenter, it's too late."

Kern said nothing.

"You and I both know the game's over," Shafer said. "Germany is caught between the Americans and the Russians. She's being squeezed to death, Guenter. It's only a matter of time. Those beautiful new boats out there, the See-Hunds, the new V-weapons—it's just too late. If things don't stop now, there will be nothing left of the Fatherland when the fighting stops."

"Since when did you begin to care about politics?" Kern asked.

"Politics be damned," Shafer said. "I'm talking about my skin. I'm a sailor. I take orders. I'll do my duty, and do it well. But that doesn't mean that I'm blind. I can see what's happening. Have you been to Berlin lately?"

"No," Kern admitted.

"No? Well, go and see for yourself. The city is destroyed. So are Hamburg and Dresden. And Frankfort. All destroyed. Yes, I'll do my duty. I'll take those little seals out and try to sink a six-thousand-ton freighter with my torpedoes. If I'm lucky, I'll come back and do it all over again. If I'm not . . ." He shrugged, leaving the sentence unfinished.

Kern asked: "Have you heard what's become of August Maus?"

Shafer looked up. "Maus?" He searched his memory. "Maus? No. I haven't. Why?"

"I was just thinking about him the other day. That's all."

Shafer downed his drink in one gulp. "If I see him, I'll tell him you were asking about him. Well, I'm off."

"So soon? You just got here."

"The See-Hunds wait for nobody. Besides that, I'm driving a stolen vehicle."

"What?"

"How else was I to make time to visit my old friend?

You know how transportation is. I wasn't given enough time to get to Neustadt as it was, let alone stop and visit an old friend. So I requisitioned a vehicle."

"Otto, you're mad. When the Lion finds out, he'll have your head."

"Well, he can't have it yet, it's promised to the Tommies." Tossing Kern a salute, he turned at the door. "Oh, by the way. If a Waffen SS major stops by looking for his staff car, just tell him it's on the way to Sweden."

"You're insane."

"Aren't we all? Well, Guenter the Silent, I hope your boats are everything that's promised, and that you come out of this madness alive. Good-bye until we see each other again."

Kern watched Shafer leave and get behind the wheel of a long, mud-covered staff car. It started with a roar and sped away, spitting clumps of mud from the rear tires.

Kern returned to his bunk, lay down, and drew the curtain shut. He wished Otto hadn't come to see him. It was as if his old friend had come to remind him of the inevitability of defeat.

He slid his arms under his head and closed his eyes. He thought that he was dozing, in that surreal half-sleep realm of gossamer dreams and fleeting images.

He was at Lake Constance, standing next to his father in the boathouse, waiting for a cloudburst to clear the lake. He had just graduated from Flensburg and was home on leave. His father stood, smaller than he had remembered, wearing a tie and sweater; he never saw his father without a tie, even when they sailed—calmly smoking a cigarette. They had spoken briefly of unimportant things; Kern knew that it was his father's manner to approach things slowly, cautiously, until he was firmly at ease confronting the subject.

"Guenter, there are several things that you must always remember," his father had begun as a soft rain tried unsuccessfully to get at them under the boathouse eves.

"Yes, Father," Kern had replied dutifully to show his father that he was listening but to show also that he was ready to accept his father's words.

"You are now in a position of responsibility," his father continued, looking over the lake. "You have accepted the challenge and now you must live up to it. Although I have no doubt that you will."

"Yes, Father."

"I was successfully employed at Heinz and Miller for twenty-eight years. I was responsible for the performance and well-being of 129 employees. But I was equally responsible to the company. You see this, don't you?"

"Yes, Father."

"Each one of those 129 men looked to me for guidance, for protection. They put their trust in me and I placed my trust in them. It is a bond, a covenant. I do my duty for the men, for the company, and because of it, for the Fatherland. I do not deviate from this, Guenter."

"I understand, Father."

Kern's father remained silent, scanning the waters as in the distance the sun broke through under dark clouds. "There will be many demands placed on you. You may become discouraged or confused. That is human nature. You must never allow yourself to relinquish your place in this hierarchy of duty—duty to your men, duty to the Kriegsmarine, duty to the Fatherland. If you are successful in one, you will be successful in all."

Then why were you let go, Father? After twenty-eight years of your life dedicated to the service of the company, why, one afternoon, were you dismissed? Was it fairness, honor, courage, stupidity, integrity—all of the things bundled together in a senseless gesture by a man so rigid in his beliefs that he sacrificed the well-being of his family for his principles?

Embezzlement—not by his father but by the son of Mr. Heinz—of Heinz and Miller. His father went to Mr. Heinz, who knew all too well that his son was stealing money from the company. Drop the matter, Mr. Heinz ordered Mr. Kern, but Mr. Kern refused to do so. There were the stockholders to consider and the employees to consider and finally, more than anything else, Mr. Kern knew that it was happening and that it was wrong. Wrong.

Twenty-eight years ended in an afternoon because Mr. Kern knew that it was wrong. And when Kern spoke to his father about it with the cigarette trembling in his father's hand but not from the cold wind at Lake Constance, his father looked at him with tears in his eyes and said: "Mr. Klein said, 'Come now. Let's forget all of this nonsense and write it off to youthful indiscretion.' I said to Mr. Klein, 'I cannot. What was I to do? What the boy was doing was wrong.'"

And Kern, to his own disgust and shame, had no answer to ease his father's pain. What his father said next was a warning that he had never forgotten: "Someday," his father said, his voice weak with defeat, "you may have to choose between what others tell you is wrong and what you know to be wrong. God grant you the wisdom to choose correctly."

Kern awoke with his arm thrown over his eyes. He

swung his legs off of the cot and flung the curtain back. His mouth was dry and tasted stale. He slid his hands into a bucket of cold water, drew up two palmfuls and threw it on his face. He shivered as the water rolled down his face and soaked the front of his uniform.

He walked to the window, thinking about what Shafer said. The game's over, it's just too late. Too late. "No," Kern heard himself say. "There's hope. As long as there's life, there's hope. The game's not over, and it's not too late." He saw Bauer trudging back up the low hill toward headquarters.

Kern jerked open the door.

"Bauer!" he called. His orderly snapped to attention. "Have the crews for all three boats assembled in thirty minutes. Tell them we're going out again. I didn't like the results of the drills, so we're going to do it again. You understand, Bauer? We'll do it over and over again until we get it right! Send to Godt again. Tell him that this is my third request for antiaircraft guns. We're sitting out here with nothing to protect us from aircraft but our U-boat batteries. Dismissed."

He slammed the door and went to his bunk. Slipping his feet into his boots, he knew what Bauer would do. He'd rush to Teddy and the other kapitaens and inform them of the orders. But he'd tell the crews about Kapitaenleutnant burning his ass about drills. The word would get out quickly that Kern was looking for blood.

"Let it," Kern said to himself, stamping his foot into the worn leather boot. "I'll burn Gorlitz's ass and that bully Hickman's as well if they don't do exactly what I want when I want it. Yes, and Teddy's, too." He stood and snatched his gray leather coat off the chair. "No, the game's not over yet. Not until I get another chance to throw the die."

Chapter 11

U-3535 slid neatly beneath the camouflage netting that extended from the shore, covering the Wreck and providing a canopy for the three U-boats. The complex rig of netting, rope, and cable was the product of Leutnant Edland's imagination and considerable engineering skills.

"It's not a concrete bunker, sir," Edland had told Kern. "But it's the best we could do."

Kern had taken the three boats out for crash dive practice. He and Hartmann watched from the starboard watch station on the bridge of U-3535 as first U-3712 and then U-3719 secured from surface running and dove into the fiord's depths. Kern studied the boats as Hartmann counted off the seconds on a stopwatch. It was a dangerous business, racing the clock to dive the boat, but how much more dangerous to be slow at in when a Sutherland was lining up to drop its fliebos? Neither boat had done particularly well, both taking about forty-five seconds to secure and disappear beneath the surface. After each dive, Kern and Hartmann looked at one another with an unspoken understanding: both kapitaens would have to do much better, much better. Kern took them in after five hours of drill. He was anxious to critique both boats' performance with Gorlitz and Hickman, and take them back out again for more drills. They would complain, of course, and his own crew would grumble about the drills, but Kern didn't care. Training was what the other two boats needed, constant drills so that the men could perform their duties in their sleep.

A U-boat crew normally got five months to train together. All Doenitz could give them was less than four and this in boats that were totally unknown to all of them. It wasn't long enough, but it was all that Kern had.

U-3535 slid in alongside U-3719, which was berthed next to U-3712, and tied off. Gangplanks were thrown from one boat to another and the men began to file over to the Wreck, the scene surreal under the mottled shadows of the camouflage netting. Kern met Gorlitz and Hickman on the deck of U-3712. The two kapitaens looked out of sorts to Kern, and he guessed that they were tired of the endless drills. Too bad.

"It's not good enough, gentlemen," he said to both kapitaens after the crews had gone. "If you don't get off the surface and down to twenty-five meters in twenty seconds, the Tommies will get you. From what I could see from my boat, you both need to clear the bridge of your lookouts faster."

"The men are tired, Kapitaenleutnant," Hickman said. "They complain all of the time."

"I don't care, Hickman," Kern snapped. "Would they rather be tired or dead? Twenty seconds; nothing else is acceptable."

"Kapitaenleutnant," Gorlitz began apologetically. That was his manner. "You have more experience in combat, of course, but I thought that with our Schnorchels, we would not need to surface. I was told that we could cruise at Schnorchel depth for weeks on end. Isn't this surface drill unnecessary?"

"Oberleutnant Gorlitz," Kern said. "Schnorchels are mechanical. Your Schnorchel, like everything else on your boats, has not been fully tested. You are right, I have combat experience, and I have found that in combat, mechanical things break down. You can count on your Schnorchel fouling, you can count on your depth gauges failing you, your electrical system short-circuiting, your hydraulics quitting, or your batteries failing. You can count on any one or all of these things happening to you at the worst possible time. When that happens, you must react with speed and with certainty because you have no time to think. You've heard of the expression 'He who hesitates is lost'? Well, it holds doubly true for the Atlantic. Keep this is mind, both of you. Don't let the Tommies catch you on the surface, but if they do, put enough distance between your boat and them so that you can dive safely. If they are close up on you and you try to dive, they will catch you with your ass hanging in the air. Remember that. First order of the day: don't ever let the bees catch you on the surface. There is no escape from them. We will drill, Oberleutnant Gorlitz, Oberleutnant Hickman, until your crews perform to my satisfaction. They must function like machines. They have not demonstrated that they can function as such, yet. Look to your boats, and see me in one hour. We will review your performance. In two hours we will take the boats out again for more drills. Dismissed."

He turned to Hartmann. "Our boat is no better than theirs, Teddy," he said sharply. His executive officer was shocked at Kern's tone, and for an instant the kapitaenleutnant was stunned at his own harshness. But only for an instant. "We can't expect to last five minutes out there at this rate."

"The men are worn out, Kaleu."

"I don't want to hear that. I don't want to hear any-thing from you but yes, sir, or no, sir. We have no time. We have no time. They will be ready for this mission, Hartmann, or I will leave you here and take them out myself."

Hartmann's face flushed red. "That is unfair. . . ."

"I don't give a damn about fair or your feelings," Kern said. "Do your job! You're a Kriegsmarine officer—act like it. If a job takes the men ten minutes, I want it done in five. If a man makes one mistake do not give him a chance to make a second."

Hartmann snapped to attention and threw a salute. "Yes, sir."

Kern felt himself calming. "Good," he said, his voice returning to normal. "Very good. Now we un-derstand each other." He returned his executive officer's salute and added: "Dismissed."

Kern brushed past his executive officer and made his way over the planks and up the gangway to the Wreck. He had tried to get two other kapitaens to re-place Gorlitz and Hickman, but Godt said there was none available. Make do, the vice admiral advised Kern, make do. Meanwhile Godt demanded that he be kept informed daily and that urgency was of the ut-most importance. *When will my demands be answered?* Kern thought.

This whole mission was make do, Kern thought an-grily, from the fifteen U-boats that were now three, to the materials and supplies that he had to beg for on a regular basis, to this old wreck of a tender that could barely keep herself afloat. Train the men. Drill them. Push them. Task them constantly so that they have no time to grumble about the lousy food, and the crowded houses turned into barracks.

When they were not in the boats, they were in the classroom set up in the torpedo shed, learning about their boats from officers who had no more experience with the wondrous machines than they. Maybe Shafer was right, maybe Germany was arming herself with wooden swords. Shafer. Kern wished that madman were here so that he could say what he really thought. He could not tell Hartmann. Kern was careful to hide his frustration from his executive officer. Suffer in silence, he constantly reminded himself. *Aren't you Guenter the Silent?* he added wryly as he climbed down the gangway ladder to the pier.

There was a Waffen SS corporal standing at attention.

"Kapitaenleutnant Kern?" the corporal said.

Kern stopped. "Who the devil are you?"

"Oberst Langsdorff wishes me to inform you that he would like to speak with you immediately, sir."

Kern looked past the corporal, up the hill. There were at least a dozen army trucks being unloaded by other SS.

"Langsdorff? Who's Langsdorff and what the hell is going on here?"

"If you will please follow me, Kapitaenleutnant?" the corporal said, walking up the hill. Kern followed him, trying to control his temper.

SS. He hated them and here they were. Why? What was going on? He fought to keep from exploding. Everything else and now this—now the SS.

The corporal led him to his own headquarters. Two SS sentries presented arms as Kern went up the stairs and threw open the door.

At a table against the wall near the window was a soldier installing a shortwave radio. Against the opposite wall was a large map of the area, with Evanger marked in red. At the table that Kern used as his desk were three SS officers studying a plan of the town. One of them, a man of medium height, with jet-black hair and blue eyes, noticed Kern standing in the doorway. Leutnant Edland was standing near the group with a stricken look on his face.

"Ah, Kapitaenleutnant Kern." The man straightened. "How good of you to come up. I'm Oberst Erich Langsdorff."

"Would you kindly explain to me, Oberst Langsdorff," Kern said, "what you are doing here, and who gave you permission to invade my office?"

"Invade?" Langsdorff laughed to the other SS officers. "Such a poor choice of words considering the situation in France, Kapitaenleutnant. Your Leutnant Edland here was kind enough to direct me to your headquarters. As for permission, why don't you allow me to explain?"

"I would appreciate that, Oberst Langsdorff," Kern replied tightly.

"First, introductions," Langsdorff said. "This is Hauptmann Klein, and Hauptmann Lossow, and that scholarly-looking fellow over at the map is Major Brandt. He looks harmless enough behind those thick glasses, but he is possessed of a keen intellect."

Kern nodded to the officers, and waited for the oberst to continue.

"We've met Leutnant Edland, of course," Langsdorff said. "But we haven't had the pleasure of meeting your other officers. I'm sure we will shortly. Now, as far as any permission goes, I am permitted in this office and on this base by order of Reichsfuehrer

Himmler himself, who directs my efforts at the express wish of the fuehrer."

"I have seen no such orders, nor have I been so informed by my superiors," Kern said.

"That is understandable. Communications are such that events often precede orders. That this is the case here I have no doubt, but we can manage."

"Oberst Langsdorff," Kern said. "I am a Kriegsmarine officer and this is a Kriegsmarine installation. As commander of this installation, I order you to remove your materials and yourselves from this office, immediately."

No one moved and the silence in the room was deafening.

"Kapitaenleutnant Kern," Langsdorff replied evenly, a kindly smile crossing his face. "You are a capable submariner and an excellent officer, which is why you were given this important mission. But, as I am sure you are aware, war is a fluid endeavor in which circumstances change radically at the drop of a hat. Let me restate what I have already said. By special directive of the fuehrer, Reichsfuehrer Himmler has ordered me to take over command of Operation Griffin. You will retain command of the U-boats, of course, I have no expertise with them, but the overall command of the project is mine. By order of the fuehrer. I hasten to add that such action was necessary purely because of the inability of the Kriegsmarine to properly support you, and under no circumstances is a reflection of your abilities."

When Langsdorff had stopped talking Kern felt everyone looking at him.

"May I see those orders, please?" he asked Langsdorff, his voice low with rage.

"Certainly," Langsdorff said, nodding to an orderly.

The orderly fished through a valise and pulled out an envelope. He handed it to Langsdorff, who removed a sheet of paper, unfolded it carefully, and handed it to Kern.

Kern took it from him, struggling to keep his hand from trembling. He read it carefully. He read it again. It was exactly as Langsdorff said. Kern noticed that the bottom of the paper carried the notice: *Copy forwarded to Grand Admiral Doenitz/Godt.*

Kern returned the order to Langsdorff.

"I can only imagine how awkward all of this must be for you, Kapitaenleutnant, a man of your experience, a decorated war hero, but we must not allow personal feelings to interfere with our duties. My staff and I are highly experienced at managing operations such as this, and we ourselves come with the necessary training to return this project to its original schedule, and to send you on your way. Think of us as providing you with the means to accomplish your mission. My men and I can relieve you of the responsibility of the camp and everything concerning the project except the training of your men."

"I will speak to Vice Admiral Godt about this," Kern said.

"Of course," Langsdorff said. "Until such time, permit me to show you what we have done to secure the base. I've two companies of Pioneers at my disposal and we've completely ringed the base, sealing it off from the outside—"

"Oberst Langsdorff," Kern broke in. "If you will pardon me, I need to confer with my officers. Leutnant Edland, would you accompany me, please?"

"Kapitaenleutnant Kern," Hauptmann Lossow said quickly. "We were just discussing the base layout with Leutnant Edland—"

Langsdorff stopped Lossow and then said: "We can meet with Leutnant Edland later. Gentlemen, shall we return to our work? There is one other thing, something that I must insist upon. The Kriegsmarine is notorious for its lack of radio discipline. After you send your message to Grand Admiral Doenitz I must ask you to refrain from any further transmissions. It makes no sense to help the enemy locate us by irresponsible radio communications, does it?"

"I know all about radio discipline," Kern said.

"Excellent. Then you will do as I ask, won't you?"

Kern glanced at Edland without answering. "Let's go," he said.

Kern walked out of the building and down the stairs with Edland on his heels. At a safe distance Kern turned to Edland.

"What the hell is going on in there?"

"Sir, I didn't have a chance," Edland said. "They just showed up and started taking over. By the time I found out who they were and what they were doing, it was too late to do anything. Oberst Langsdorff had me answering questions about the base, and you; about everything."

"Where are his men?"

"They've taken over the remaining houses as barracks. They've got checkpoints and sentries thrown all around the town. They have guards posted at the torpedo shed, the radio shack, everyplace. It's like we're prisoners. They've even got guards on the Wreck. I think they've got dossiers on all of the officers, too. I overheard that Major Brandt whisper something to the oberst about it."

Kern didn't hear him. He was thinking.

"You get over to the radio immediately, do you understand me? Send this to the Koralle, attention Godt.

'SS have taken over base and mission by order of the fuehrer, awaiting orders. I am prohibited from transmitting beyond this message.' Sign it Kern."

"What do you think will happen?" Edland asked.

"If I know the Lion, he'll fight this until there's no fight left in him. Until we hear from him or Godt, we'll continue training. Let's make sure our men keep away from the SS. I don't want any fights between our men and theirs. I want to assemble the officers and let them know what's happened. Have them meet me in the wardroom on the Wreck immediately."

"This is unbelievable," Edland said.

"You have your orders," Kern barked. "See to it." He watched Edland disappear toward the radio shack. Kern walked back to his boat. This was for higher powers to deal with; there was nothing he could do about it. Train the men, he told himself, get them ready to sail. The RGTs.

He'd meant to send to Godt to ask him about the readiness of the RGTs. He'd completely forgotten about the message. *I'll send it later,* he told himself; first he had to tell his men about the SS.

Oberst Langsdorff stood at the narrow window, looking out over the compound. He and his men had a lot of work to do. Kern might be a sailor but he was no manager of projects. That was obvious from the amateurish way his installation was set up. But it wasn't Kern's fault, Langsdorff knew. It was his superior's fault for not providing him with the necessary support. In Langsdorff's opinion the Kriegsmarine always operated haphazardly. Effort wasted on battleships that never left their moorings, U-boats that couldn't get close enough to convoys to sink ships, and modern submarines that were too complex to build; Langsdorff turned from the window. The Kriegsmarine was worse than the Luftwaffe, he decided; although neither one was as bad as the army.

Langsdorff felt good with his men around him. They could do anything, control any situation, and complete any mission. It was a matter of analytical thinking—of facts and figures and straightforward formulas that when properly applied rendered any problem moot. "I have absolute confidence in you and your men," Reichsfuehrer Himmler had told him, "and it is for that reason that I want you to go up to Norway and straighten out this Kriegsmarine fiasco. The fuehrer wishes it," Himmler added with a smile, "and so it shall be done."

It was a fantastic scheme, Langsdorff thought after reading the material, but it had possibilities. Real possibilities if it was properly handled. "I give it to you," the reichsfuehrer had told Langsdorff in the privacy of his office. "The vision of the Kriegsmarine is too limited. I have introduced a new component to the project," Himmler had said, "a means to bring much greater destruction to the Allies that as yet has never been realized. We will choke off England's greatest port, render it useless, and turn it into a wasteland. Every convoy from America will have to come through the Eastern Approaches, within range of our bombers and ships. The Allied armies in France will starve to death. You must make it work," Himmler added, his eyes seeming to float in the expanse of his thick glasses. "You must pay special attention to any act that hints of sedition or treason. We have cleansed the army of traitors. Now we must turn our attention to the Kriegsmarine. Let nothing impede you."

"Klein?" Langsdorff said. "Get me the files on Kern, Hartmann, Hickman, and Gorlitz. See that the sentries are properly posted and that no one enters or leaves the camp without my permission. I don't want any of those sailors sneaking off after women. Lossow, you have seventy-two hours to complete the rocket shed. Contact those idiots again and find out when we can expect the RGTs. I've had three different answers in as many days."

Klein handed him the folders. Langsdorff seated himself at the table and opened the folder marked Kern. "Now," he said to himself, "what about Guenter the Silent?"

Kern waited until the last of the officers had found a place to sit in the Wreck's tiny wardroom. They looked at him questioningly. He could read the alarm in their faces. All the way back to the Wreck he had tried to calm himself, but anger, like bile, kept rising in his throat until he was sure it would escape in a scream.

Even now, as he waited impatiently, his hands were clasped behind him firmly, to keep them from trembling in frustration. How he hated arrogance! How he hated the SS and how he hated anyone who discounted the courage and sacrifice of the U-boat service in such a cavalier fashion.

"All right," he said after the men arrived. "I will tell you this once, and you will listen. I have just been informed that this project is now under the control of the SS, by order of Adolf Hitler and Reichsfuehrer Himmler."

No one said anything; it was obvious to Kern that they found it best to let him continue. Perhaps they read his state of mind better than he did. He had no words left—they were driven from him by rage and frustration.

"Well?" Kern said. "Have you no questions?" He wanted someone to say something stupid, something that he could pounce on. Someone he could unload his frustration on. The voice in his head thundered: *Someone say something! Give me a chance to tear you to pieces!* He suddenly felt sick and weak inside. This was no way to act. He was acting like Hickman. He looked at the oberleutnant. He sat on the edge of a desk, his stupid face impassive. *He doesn't care,* Kern told himself. *He doesn't care who is giving the orders.* The officers of U-3712 and U-3719 remained silent. Oberleutnant Gorlitz finally allowed his hand to make its way into the air.

"Kapitaenleutnant?" Gorlitz said in his maddeningly deferential tone. "Why has the SS taken over the project?"

"I don't know, Gorlitz. That is for higher command to sort out."

Hickman spoke as if bored with the whole thing. "Have you heard about the rockets yet? Do we know when we are going to get them?"

Here was a perfect time to take Hickman to task for his insolence. And yet Kern didn't. He was simply too tired. Or maybe he too was shocked beyond sensibility. Instead he found his answer to be matter-of-fact, and without emotion.

"Nothing. Perhaps the SS can speed them on their way. I have, of course, sent immediately to Koralle for clarification of orders. I have seen the SS oberst's written orders, but I think it quite necessary for us to hear from the Lion. In the meantime, training goes on as scheduled. Oberleutnant Gorlitz, I understand that you are still having mechanical difficulties with U-3712?"

Gorlitz suddenly stiffened at the mention of his name.

"Yes, Kapitaenleutnant," he snapped as if on dress parade.

Kern saw Hickman smirk as Gorlitz recited the problems.

"We have difficulties with our hydraulic torpedo loaders, and none of the gauges in the pump cellar work. Also air compressor number three continues to malfunction."

Kern sought out Frick.

"Well, Frick? What can you do to help U-3712?"

"Working on it, sir," the engineering chief replied. "Those damned loaders are giving us trouble on all three boats, and I'm beginning to think that none of the gauges were properly calibrated before they were installed. I'll have to go back and look at the air compressor. It'll be the third time. It just runs hot. It may require replacement. And while we're on the subject, sir, we ought to run some trials on the M1H sonar and the GHG sound-detection apparatus."

"Schedule it with Hartmann," Kern said. It felt good, Kern realized, to be talking about U-boats. This was what he knew, not the politics of high command. He felt himself relaxed. "Oberleutnant Hickman? What about U-3719?"

Hickman shrugged in reply. "I've talked with Engineer Frick about it. He's the expert."

Kern's temper flared. "You're the kapitaen of your boat, Oberleutnant Hickman! I expect you to know what service your boat needs."

The room was silent as Kern watched Hickman ponder a response.

"Yes, Kapitaenleutnant. We are experiencing much the same troubles as U-3712. The Schnorchel apparatus doesn't work. The air intake has stuck open on two occasions on diving trials and we began taking water. The exhaust has stuck open once. The diesel air intake heads for surface running also do not operate properly. The electrical problems"—he shrugged—"continue." Hickman paused, looking around. "Frick knows the whole, sorry story."

"Frick?"

"Working on it, sir. We've removed the Schnorchel heads and we're trying to repair them in the Wreck's machine shop. U-3719's electrical system needs a complete overhaul, but since we can't do that we're tracking down the problems one at a time." Frick took nearly twenty minutes to detail the mechanical and electrical woes of the boat.

"Time to completion?"

"I can't give you that, sir."

"Why not? Can no one answer a simple question?"

"We don't have the manuals. I'm trying every short-cut I know, but she's a big boat. The other two, well, they're almost as bad."

"I see," Kern said, mulling over Frick's answer. It was not good, but there was probably nothing that could be done. The chief engineers on both U-3712 and U-3719 were inexperienced. That made Frick responsible for not only U-3535, but the other two boats as well.

"Keep me posted," Kern finally said.

"It would help if my crew was experienced," Gorlitz said to no one. He looked at Kern. "They are not properly trained. Perhaps if we had more experienced men."

"Make them into experienced U-boatmen," Kern

said bitterly. "You must lead them. You must train them. No one else can do it for you."

"I was only saying—" Gorlitz began.

"Kapitaenleutnant?" It was Hickman. "Whose orders do we take? Yours or the oberst's?"

Kern knew that the oberleutnant was challenging him. His tone, his look, the manner in which he had made those few words sound like an insult. He was a careful bully, approaching his fights with discretion.

Kern answered Hickman's arrogance with a grim smile. He saw Hickman's face redden.

"All of you . . ." the kapitaenleutnant said. "All of you are Kriegsmarine officers. Each of you has sworn an oath of loyalty to the fuehrer. Each of you realizes full well what the words *honor* and *duty* mean. The oberst's orders, and I have read them, say that the SS is in charge of this project. Those orders are so acknowledged. But every Kriegsmarine enlisted man and officer takes orders only from their naval superior. Understand me. You are sailors in service to the Reich. That service requires that your obedience be to the proper authority—your superior officer. Neither you nor your men are expected to take orders from SS personnel. God help anyone who fails to acknowledge me as senior naval officer at this post. We are in a difficult situation. That is nothing new. We are trained to handle difficult situations. You will return to your boats and tell your crews what has happened, but you will remind them what branch of the service they are in, and tell them bluntly: soldiers do not order sailors about."

Kern turned to Hickman. He felt rejuvenated. He was almost grateful to that bully for giving him an opportunity to feel like a kapitaenleutnant again.

"That answers your question, Oberleutnant Hickman, does it not?"

"Yes, Kapitaenleutnant," the oberleutnant said.

"Good," Kern said. "Return to your duties, except Frick and Hartmann. I want to see you two."

As the other officers filed out of the wardroom, Hartmann and Frick approached Kern. He massaged his eyes lightly with his fingertips, blinked several times to clear his vision, and then said: "Tell me everything about the condition of the three boats. Then tell me how you intend to remedy the situation."

Frick looked at Hartmann—it was obvious that he had something to say.

"What is it?" Kern said.

"I know that time is short, Kaleu," Hartmann said. "But the men are worn out. Can we stand down for twelve hours? Twelve hours would give them a chance to regain their strength. It would be better, I think."

"Stand down? Why? Because the men are tired?"

"Sir . . ."

"Maybe you're tired, Teddy. Is that it? Maybe you want to rest for twelve hours. You can't have twelve hours. No one can. I don't have twelve hours to give them, you, or me. Is that clear?"

"Yes, Kaleu," Hartmann said coolly. "I was thinking of the men and their efficiency. They are performing like robots. They are making mistakes."

"Your duty," Kern said slowly, "is to make sure that they do not make mistakes." He turned to Frick. "Fix the boats, Frick. I don't care how. Fix them. Do it quickly."

"Yes, Kaleu," Frick said in a subdued tone.

"I agree with Gorlitz about one thing," Hartmann said. "His men aren't experienced enough. Neither are Hickman's."

Kern stared at Hartmann. He felt as if his executive officer were defying him. As if Teddy were saying: *You're not doing enough.* Kern stood quickly and looked down at Hartmann. "You agree with Gorlitz?" he said, hoping that his tone cut into Hartmann.

"Yes."

Kern turned to Frick. "You?"

Frick shrugged and wiped his forehead with a grease-stained hand. "They're not getting any better."

"Yes," Kern said bitterly. "Do you have any suggestions? Either of you?"

"No," Hartmann said. Frick shook his head.

"No," Kern said, "I thought not." He stretched his neck to relieve the tightness in it and watched the overhead spin endlessly about, doing nothing more than moving the fetid air in the room about. The stale air churned endlessly as Kern searched for an answer in the whirling blades.

Kern dropped his head, resting his chin on his chest. "Assemble the crews," he said without looking at Hartmann.

"What?" Teddy said. "Everyone?"

Kern looked up quickly. "On the beach, every man and officer. Now."

Teddy and Frick left the wardroom and Kern followed them a few moments later. He could hear the shouts of the crews being assembled and the rumble as the men emptied the boats and ran through the Wreck, streaming out onto the narrow beach. They swirled around Kern as he walked up the hill and positioned himself to address the men.

Presently all three crews were drawn up. Kern felt Hartmann move next to him, waiting for orders. Kern shivered in the harsh wind that buffeted the men standing on the barren gravel beach and a voice warned him over and over: *Don't do it—think before you act.* There was nothing else to be done. He had no choice. He had no time. His officers and men were undertrained. Some worked hard to overcome this, some were hopelessly inadequate. Some—Kern studied the men standing at attention. He had no choice.

"The Fatherland expects every man to do his duty," he said, his voice carrying into the wind. He was struck by the darkness of the place, the dark figures of the crews, the dull gray water, the sunless sky. He dreaded his words, but he forced himself to speak with clarity and confidence. "You have all been working very hard." The words were stark and lifeless. Hollow with dishonesty. "But we have little time left and we need to accomplish a great deal." He looked over the men, trying to avoid the eyes of his crew. "We are going to reassign crew members." He saw Hartmann glance at him out of the corner of his eye. "I want one crew member from each department from U-3719 and U-3712 to assemble down the beach. Seamen only, no ratings or officers. Kapitaens, select your men now.

Hartmann was suddenly in front of him. "You can't do it, Kaleu. Not to our men. Don't do it."

Kern watched as Gorlitz and Hickman moved through their crews, pulling individuals out. He could not bring himself to look at Hartmann. "Select two men from each department, Teddy. No officers and ratings. Assign one to U-3719 and one to U-3712. Take their crew members into our crew as replacements."

"Don't you know what you're doing?" Hartmann pleaded. "You're destroying our crew. You're condemning our men to death."

"I am doing my duty," Kern said, his words stiff with anger. "Do as I order."

"This is madness," Hartmann said. "Don't do it, Guenter. For God's sake give our men at least a fighting chance to survive this war."

Kern felt himself trembling as he turned on Hartmann. "Do as I order, now."

"Why, for God's sake?"

"Because there is nothing else that I can do!" Kern exploded. "I have no time left to me." He stepped close to Hartmann, overwhelmed by rage at Hartmann's insolence and what he was forced to do. "Do as I order. Now, Leutnant Hartmann, or I will have you arrested and relieved of your position." Kern thought that he could see tears forming in Hartmann's eyes. He wished that he could cry as well.

"Yes, sir," Hartmann said grimly, stepping back and saluting. He turned and walked down the slope toward the men of U-3535.

Kern remained on the hill overlooking the beach, watching the men being sorted out.

"A very innovative approach," Langsdorff said from behind Kern. He walked up next to Kern and lit a cigarette, the smoke being whisked away in the breeze. "One that I don't think I would have thought of."

"It was necessary," Kern said.

"Oh, of course," Langsdorff said. "The necessities of command. One may not agree with what one has to do, but one does it." He scratched the side of his neck. "It's all about duty, isn't it?"

Kern said nothing.

"Kapitaen," Langsdorff said sympathetically, "I understand perfectly what must be done. The mission, the mission comes first no matter what." He swept the scene before him with his cigarette. "You were given little enough to begin with. You took them as far as they could be led. Or driven. So. Now you act with boldness. Now all three boats have a good chance of completing their mission. Not just U-3535. I commend you, sir. Innovation, daring. The experienced crew members support the inexperienced crew members. The Fatherland is proud of you."

Kern though of his father's words: duty to his crew, duty to the Kriegsmarine, duty to the Fatherland. If you are successful at one, you will be successful at all. Twenty-eight years. *Did that decision make you successful, Father?*

"Yes," Kern said dully. "I live for service to the Fatherland."

Chapter 12

The Koralle

Doenitz threw his cap on the desk. It sailed into a stack of papers, sending them flying into the air. They rustled to the carpet.

"He won't see me," he said angrily. "The fuehrer won't see me."

"Herr Grand Admiral," Godt began. "He doesn't suspect you—"

"Oh no," Doenitz said. "Nothing that confrontational. Oh no, Godt, our fuehrer is 'unavailable.' He sent his lackeys out to say that he was unavailable. That idiot Jodl just stood there like a magpie repeating, 'the fuehrer is unavailable at the moment.' So I said, 'When will he be available?' The idiot stammered, 'That is uncertain. Unavailable.' In all of my career, this is the first time that a commanding officer has refused to see me."

"Perhaps his injuries . . ."

"Injuries! He has no injuries. Haven't you seen the reports? The fuehrer is invincible. What would have killed lesser men simply made Adolf Hitler stronger. He is immortal, nothing can destroy our beloved fuehrer."

Godt picked up the papers surrounding Doenitz's

desk as the grand admiral made his way to the window overlooking the compound of Koralle.

"Two sons," Doenitz said, his voice drained of emotion. "I have given the Fatherland my two sons. I have given Germany my service and the lives of my two sons. To be treated like this . . ." He shook his head.

"I've put the morning reports on your desk," Godt said. "I'm afraid that they aren't very encouraging. Production is down twenty-eight percent on the See-Hunds, and the Walter boats' trials were inconclusive. It's the engines. I spoke to Rasch this morning. He is still very optimistic about See-Hund, although he says that he would have preferred a base with a few more accommodations. Of course, he was joking."

"What have you heard from Kern?" the grand admiral asked without turning.

The silence in the room finally forced Godt to speak. "Nothing since his last message. The SS controls his radio, I am sure."

Doenitz turned. "If he could speak he would ask if Himmler or I run the Kriegsmarine. A fair question, isn't it?"

"No, Herr Grand Admiral."

"You're a poor liar," Doenitz said, walking to his desk. "Read between the lines. I know what Kern thinks. He wonders if he is to take orders from the SS. What am I to tell him? Hitler will not see me, and if he will not see me I cannot get him to order Himmler to relinquish the project. It's not enough that we have to fight the Tommies and the Americans, old friend; now we have to fight our own high command."

"Guenter Kern is a very capable commander. He will do what is necessary until he receives further orders," Godt said.

"Yes, yes, yes." Doenitz waved away the vice admiral's

opinion. He sat down at his desk. "Kern will do all that he can. Meanwhile, I will try to get what U-boats I can out of that Mediterranean mousetrap and back into the Atlantic where they belong. Give Rasch what he asks for. If Operation Griffin is denied me, I must concentrate my efforts elsewhere. Get me Schnee. I want to hear from him about the Type XXIII tests. He was so impatient to test them; I will give him a chance to take the boats into battle. Let's see what he can do."

"Yes, sir. What response shall I send Kern?"

Doenitz removed his glasses and rubbed his eyes roughly with his fingertips. He put his glasses back on, picked up a report from his desk, and began to study it. "Sixty-seven percent of our boats are returning from their patrols. That is down another three percent from last month. That is unacceptable. Contact the Ministry of Armament and find out when we can expect more acoustic torpedoes. If we don't keep those escorts away, Godt, the Allies gobble us up three percent more each month until one hundred percent of our boats fail to return from patrol." He turned the page on the report and remained silent for a moment, then said: "Tell Kern that he is to follow that SS oberst's orders as if they were mine, until informed otherwise." He threw down the report and flipped the switch on his intercom.

"Bring tea," Doenitz ordered, "and make it strong."

Chapter 13

Over Bokn Fiord

Flight Lieutenant Allan Ball, RAF, tapped Pilot Officer Eric Lockhart on the shoulder.

"Don't you think we've gone far enough up this river?" he said into the intercom. His voice was barely audible over the roar of the plane's engines.

"It's not what I think, old boy," Lockhart replied. "It's what the hateful squadron leader will do to us if he doesn't think we've gone far enough up this river."

"It's not a river, sir. It's a fiord." Flight Sergeant Park's voice came from his position in the top turret of the Lockheed Hudson.

"Go back to sleep, Parky," Ball said.

"Can't, sir. You know how Jerry is about unwelcome guests."

"Let's go a bit farther," Lockhart said. "I'll slide over alongside the shore, and you get some pictures. There's a village coming up. Maybe Jerry's got another Tirpitz tied up there."

"I've seen more than my share of these bloody rivers," Ball said. "I thought our blokes had everything pinpointed."

"Well"—Lockhart tapping the altimeter with a

gloved knuckle—"they did until Jerry went to ground. No more radio transmissions. It's all dried up."

"So now we have to fly up and down these rivers until Kingdom Come?"

"Fiords, sir," Parky said.

"Shut up," Lockhart and Ball ordered in unison.

"Such is our burden," Lockhart said, looking out the side window. "To fly about until ordered to land."

They flew on in silence until Ball spoke again.

"Do you really think our squadron leader will be pleased if we brought back pictures of another Tirpitz?" Ball asked.

"I doubt it," Lockhart said. "Ready, cameras? Here we go."

The twin-engine aircraft dipped slightly to the right and kept a steady course along the shoreline. Inside its belly, the shutters of the plane's cameras began to snap rapidly.

"Ah, Kern," Langsdorff said, catching sight of the kapitaenleutnant as he walked up the hill. "I understand that your training has been going quite well."

"Satisfactorily," Kern replied, above the racket of the construction. Two companies of Pioneers were erecting flak towers in the woods, just on the edge of the village. Several buildings had been demolished at the other end of town to make way for two 88mm antiaircraft guns. Their long snouts pointed down the fiord, waiting for enemy aircraft. Behind the oberst, two squads of Pioneers were framing what Teddy had referred to as Fortress Langsdorff: the oberst's headquarters building.

Langsdorff motioned toward the gun platforms and towers. "We'll have those up in a very short time.

Just to the tops of the trees. If Tommy flies over again we can rake his belly with machine-gun fire."

"They'll know we're here when you do," Kern said. "I'd rather trust to the low ceiling."

"Of course they will but they won't know what we are. Your camouflage is excellent, and I had our vehicles well back in the trees. Perhaps they saw a few tents, some evidence of activity, but I wouldn't worry. With larger problems for the Allies to worry about, I doubt that we'll see more than a few reconnaissance flights. Just something to make sure that we stay small. We have nothing to draw their interest."

Kern looked toward the end of the village. "The gun emplacements? They mean that we have something to protect. That will interest them."

Langsdorff followed his gaze. The barrel of one of the 88s traversed the sky, and then disappeared behind the roof of a house.

"Two 88s won't attract anyone's attention, Kapitaenleutnant Kern. But if it would make you feel more secure, you could send some of your men over to give the gun crews suggestions on camouflage. I'm sure that they would be most amused."

"Do you have an air raid siren?" Kern asked, ignoring Langsdorff's remark.

"It's been mounted there, on the roof of that building."

Kern noted the bell-like shape of the siren pointing out, over the camp. "I suggest that we establish a spotter post, ten miles down the fiord. They can give us some warning of aircraft approaching. Enough for us to take the boats out away from the village."

"Away from the village?" Langsdorff said. "Your boats have four guns each. I should think that you would want to stay close to the village. A greater concentration of firepower."

"I have a healthy respect for Allied aircraft, Oberst Langsdorff," Kern said. "I prefer room to maneuver."

"So be it," Langsdorff said curtly.

"There is one other thing."

"Oh?" Langsdorff said, surveying the skeleton of his headquarters.

"There is a rumor going around camp that you plan to interrogate the men about their loyalty to the fuehrer? Is this true?"

"Rumors? You don't take stock in such, do you?"

Kern was tired. He had kept his crews training with little thought for time off. They needed rest; he needed rest. But there was none to be given even after combining crews and increasing their efficiency. His crew was still the best of the reconstituted three, but that meant very little. Their boat was still new to them, and it took time to learn. He didn't want anything to interfere with the training.

"I've found that most rumors are nothing more than that," Kern replied. "But it's not what I believe; it's what the crew believes. They believe that the SS plans an inquisition. Is it true?"

Langsdorff bristled. "I do not believe that I like your use of the word *inquisition*. That is totally unjustified. Any questioning that the SS does is necessary to uncover traitors. May I remind you that an attempt was recently made on our fuehrer's life, and that only through the grace of God did he survive uninjured?"

"So it's true? The men are to be questioned?"

"No," Oberst Langsdorff said. "Not the men. Only the officers. It is simply a formality. Nothing more."

"We all took the Fuehrer's Oath," Kern said. "Isn't that enough?"

"The assassins took the same oath to Adolf Hitler. You needn't worry about your precious training schedule. The interviews won't interfere."

"They won't interfere, because I won't allow them to take place," Kern said. "You'll have to be satisfied with my word that these men are loyal."

"Your word isn't enough, I'm afraid. The interviews will go forward as planned. Reichsfuehrer Himmler will support me in this, and that is all the authority that I need."

Kern knew that he couldn't win this battle. The oberst's authority was complete. There was nothing to be done but comply.

"I wish to be present," Kern said.

"I'll give your request consideration, Kapitaenleutnant."

Hauptmann Lossow approached Langsdorff and saluted.

"Oberst Langsdorff," he said, "I am happy to report that the White Coats are here with their rockets."

Langsdorff slapped his hands together. "There, you see, Kern? Things begin to happen once the SS arrives. They're here, are they, Lossow?"

"Yes, sir. Just entering the village now."

"Come, Kern," Langsdorff said. "Let us go and see what marvels German engineering has given us."

Kern watched Lossow and Langsdorff set off for the front gate. He was angry. Angry with Doenitz, disgusted with Godt, angry that the SS got everything that he had been pleading for since he arrived. Let the SS snap their fingers, and men and materials fall from the heavens. Now the officers were being questioned about their loyalty to the fuehrer. Kern couldn't decide whether they came as a result of orders, or if Langsdorff was merely playing God. He looked around. God in a wilderness. The workers raised a wall of Langsdorff headquarters with a shout, while others rushed in and nailed it in place. Langsdorff would be able to hold court in his new headquarters in three days.

Kern followed the SS officers. He was very tired. He hadn't been sleeping well and he had barely kept his temper in check. Twice he had taken Hartmann to task for minor infractions, and once he had found himself shouting at a helmsman. Shouting. He had never done that in his career. Too much training and too little sleep. An endless cycle where days melted into one another and hours were decades long. That was all he and the men did. The men were nearly stupid with fatigue at times. Well, perhaps the sight of the RGTs would instill some enthusiasm in them all. It would take something; he was drained. Sometimes he felt as if his muscles had turned to lead, and he began to wonder if his mind was growing stale as well. He could not allow himself to give in to his anger and frustration, or to let himself lapse into routine. He even thought about going to the SS surgeon that Langsdorff had brought with him. Maybe the doctor had some pills to keep him awake and focused. *I need a spark,* Kern told himself. *I need something to give me energy. I can't go on like this.*

"Kapitaenleutnant Kern?"

Hartmann came running up. He stopped and saluted, being very formal. Kern knew that Hartmann found his anger and impatience impossible to understand. Kern didn't care. He'd lost a good friend and alienated his men and he didn't care.

"Yes, Teddy?"

"The RGTs are here, sir," Hartmann said, standing at attention.

"Yes, I know," Kern said. "Come. We'll see them together."

"I beg your pardon, sir," Hartmann said. "I must return to the boat. I have other duties to perform."

Kern felt as if he had been slapped in the face. He tried to be friendly and look what that got him. "Very well, Exec," Kern snapped. "Go and do it."

Hartmann tossed a salute, turned, and left.

Kern walked to the front gate. He stopped when he saw the column of trucks pulling into the village. Langsdorff was conferring with an SS officer and two civilians. The civilians looked nervous and out of place among the uniforms. Scientists, Kern thought, Godt's White Coats.

"Here is Kapitaenleutnant Kern. Guenter 'the Silent,' I am told he is called," Oberst Langsdorff announced cordially. "He is the gentleman that will be delivering your gifts. Kapitaenleutnant Kern, may I present Professor Herman Mueller and Professor Hans Spengler?"

Kern noted that Spengler and Mueller looked like brothers. The same confused look, the same spectacles perched at the ends of their noses, and the same crumpled suits that hung on them like sacks. The only difference in the two was that Mueller was short and sported a wire-thin mustache.

"This is Hauptmann Kapp," Langsdorff continued, motioning to the aristocratic-looking officer standing next to him. "He is the column commander. These"—Langsdorff made a grand sweep with his hand—"are what you've been waiting for. The reason you've trained for so long."

Kern watched as the long, flatbed trailers rolled past in a haze of dust and into the compound. Even with them covered by weathered, canvas tarpaulins,

Kern could tell what they were. RGT canisters with rockets inside—the long, cumbersome structures that would sit on the backs of his boats. Despite their size, there was nothing exciting about them. They looked like long pipes and he hated the thought of what they would do to the fine lines of his boats.

"Will they work?" Kern shouted over the roar of the passing trucks.

Langsdorff reddened, and the two scientists looked at each other in confusion.

"Yes," Mueller said in a high voice. "Yes, of course they will work. We've tested them extensively."

"When can we see them?" Kern asked. "I want to have my men meet with you and your technicians immediately. We have a lot to learn about your rockets."

"Your pardon, Kapitaenleutnant," Oberst Langsdorff interrupted. "But security must be established. The RGTs will immediately be installed in their sheds."

"Yes," Mueller agreed. "We must inspect them. It's been a long journey."

"Quite so," Langsdorff agreed. "The RGTs are off-limits for the present. Neither you nor your officers will be granted access to the weapons until you have been cleared."

"Cleared? I am a kapitaenleutnant in the Kriegsmarine. My men are veterans of five years of war. Is this your damned loyalty again?"

"Loyalty, no," Langsdorff was quick to respond. "Security. The RGTs will be housed in the shed. Guards will be posted and access restricted to the civilian technicians and SS officers only. Under no circumstances will you or any of your men be allowed to approach the shed until you are authorized to do so."

"How can you deny—"

"I'm sure you realize the necessity for such actions," Langsdorff said. "All of Germany is depending on us. Precautions, no matter how distasteful, must be taken."

Kern turned to Mueller and said sharply: "When we are cleared, I want the technical manuals for these things immediately distributed to my men. My officers and I will meet with you, and you will train us in the operations of the RGTs and the launching system. You will be present when they are loaded on the backs of my boats, and you will go on training exercises with us."

"In a U-boat?" Mueller stammered. "Underwater? Oh. No. No, that can't be."

"Dr. Mueller," Kern said, "it will be. If my men are going to risk their lives launching your rockets, you're going to overcome your fears to train them."

"You must excuse Kapitaenleutnant Kern's abrupt tone," Langsdorff said. "He and his men have been training rigorously in preparation for the arrival of these weapons. He sometimes forgets his manners."

Kern smiled thinly at the group. "Yes. My manners. You see, gentlemen, I am a sailor. A U-boat kapitaen, not a soldier, or a scientist. My men hope that we can kill the enemy before they kill us. So you see, when someone gives us a new weapon, we are naturally skeptical. To maintain a healthy skepticism is what keeps us alive. That and luck. So please forgive my rudeness in asking if they work. I ask only because if they don't, it is the sailors who will pay the price, not the soldiers or the scientists. You understand what I expect of you, Dr. Mueller. See that you are prepared. I must see to my boats."

"He is an insolent bastard, isn't he?" Hauptmann Kapp said to Langsdorff as Kern walked away.

"Yes," Langsdorff said. "I will put him in his place, however. One must always be prepared to deal harshly with hotheads such as Kern. He thinks that the Kriegsmarine is the only service in the Reich. I must educate the man."

"Oberst, if you please?" Mueller said. "Who are those other men that travel with us? Those civilians?"

"Why?" Langsdorff asked coolly.

"I only ask, you see, that is, I don't mean to intrude, but they having nothing to do with the RGTs. And there is that large truck—"

Langsdorff cut him off. "Yes, I know that you don't mean to intrude. That is why you must hurry to your business."

Mueller looked from Langsdorff to Kapp. "Yes. Yes. Yes, I will." He trotted off, disappearing in the swirling dust thrown up by the trucks.

"By the way, Oberst," Kapp said. "I've managed to acquire some very fine cognac. Could I interest you in a glass?"

Oberst Langsdorff smiled. "By all means, Hauptmann." He took Kapp by the arm and guided him out of the hearing of others. "The special payload, you have it?"

"There," Kapp said. Two large trucks followed the others into the compound. A Volkswagen bearing four civilians followed the trucks.

"Who knows about this?" Langsdorff asked.

"The four scientists, of course, and you and me," Kapp replied.

"Let it remain so. No one else is to know. Especially Spengler and Mueller."

"What about Kern?"

"Kern is a troublemaker. I will not have him jeopardizing this mission."

"He'll need to know," Kapp said.

"When I decide the time is right," Langsdorff said. "Until then share this information with no one. The future of the Reich depends upon secrecy. This could be the start of a new offensive, Kapp. It could mean the end of the allies and the triumph of the Reich. "

Kern walked back to the Wreck. He made his way up the gangway strung along her rusting bulk, and onto her deck. He absentmindedly returned the salutes of the sailors, as he mounted the ladder that took him up the superstructure and into the tiny radio room just aft of the bridge.

The young seaman on duty saw Kern enter and, snapping to attention, knocked a message pad to the deck.

"Take down this message," Kern said.

"Sir," the stricken seaman said. "I have orders from Oberst Langsdorff."

"Now you have an order from me," Kern said quickly.

"Yes, Kapitaenleutnant," the sailor said, fumbling for a pencil. He bent down and picked up the pad, readying himself.

"Make to Vice Admiral Godt, the Koralle," Kern began. "'RGTs arrived this morning with civilians. Advised that the tests were successful. Will begin installation of RGTs on boats tomorrow, if possible. Unless measures are taken to clarify my position'"—Kern matched his speech to the pencil darting over the pad— "'I will have no recourse but to resign.'" The pencil faltered, and then continued. "Signed, Guenter Kern, kapitaenleutnant."

The sailor finished the sentence and looked up at Kern.

"Read it back to me," Kern said.

The sailor cleared his throat and began reading. Kern listened, and when the boy had finished, nodded his acceptance.

"Good. Encode it and send it off. I want to be notified the moment you receive an answer. Understand?"

"Yes, Kapitaenleutnant," the radio operator said, reaching for his codebook.

"Seaman?"

The young man looked up. "Yes, Kapitaenleutnant?"

"After the message is sent, destroy the flimsy and forget you sent it," Kern said. "If Langsdorff finds out tell him I held a pistol to your head."

The seaman blanched and croaked out, "Yes, sir."

Kern turned and left the radio room. As he made his way down the corridor, he glanced at his watch. Time to get aboard U-3535, he thought. Time for another drill.

SS Oberst Langsdorff was immaculately dressed, his raven-black hair combed back off of a high forehead. His skin was free of wrinkles. His blue eyes quickly searched the dispatch that he held in his hands, darting over the words. Kern finally realized whom the oberst reminded him of. There was an inn at Lake Constance, a modest establishment that had attained some status by virtue of longevity. It had survived the years with the aplomb of a dowager, and commanded the shore as completely as a matriarch leads her family. Most people who took a holiday at Lake Constance referred to it simply as the Inn, and it was considered as much a part of the lake as the deep blue waters that beckoned vacationers. The assistant manager at the Inn, a self-important man, ran his little world by a schedule of his own making. He took station in his small office near the front desk, and when one checked in, one could always see his back and rounded shoulders as he bent over his desk, hard at work. When he was summoned to the front desk, Kern remembered, he always stopped in his office doorway, straightened his jacket, and smoothed the hair on either side of his head with his palms.

It was the ritual by which he proclaimed himself a man of importance.

Langsdorff was the assistant manager, indisputable ruler of his immediate world.

The oberst finally looked up.

"I suppose you've heard?" he said tightly.

"About Paris?" Kern said. "Yes."

"Why did we not fight for it?" Langsdorff asked, obviously dismayed by the news. "Why did we simply abandon it? Declare it an open city?"

The oberst's arrogance was gone briefly, replaced by confusion. His world was changing too rapidly for him to comprehend, Kern thought. The mantle of superman had slipped from his shoulders.

"It would be a shame to see such a lovely city destroyed," Kern said.

Langsdorff's eyes flashed. "But what of Berlin? Look at our capital. Look at the destruction wrought by the British and the Americans. Tens of thousands of German civilians killed. Well? Why should the French escape the suffering that we Germans have endured?"

Kern said nothing. He knew that the SS officer did not understand the triumph of one beautiful city saved from the horrors of war, even if it belonged to the enemy. He was a man of distorted values who could not see that sometimes it was enough just to have a moment of humanity in an inhumane conflict.

Langsdorff made a great show of gathering the official dispatches together, wrapping himself in regulations, memoranda, and orders; reassembling the world that he knew.

"Berlin was just as beautiful as Paris," he said, straightening the bundle of papers on his desk and tapping the mass into order. "More so. More so. Frankfort and Cologne. Have you been to either since the war began? I think not, otherwise your comments would be entirely different."

"I've seen the destruction. I know what is happening."

Langsdorff set the papers to one side. "I hardly think so. You show remarkable restraint when it comes to holding the enemy accountable for killing Germans. For every German death we should kill twenty of the enemy. For every German city destroyed, we should destroy five of theirs. You hold the opinion that Paris should have escaped? I find that very troubling, Kapitaenleutnant."

"I'm accountable for my own share of destruction," Kern said, remembering the flaming hulks of merchant ships as they settled into the sea. Remembering the tiny black figures bobbing in the remorseless waves. Those were men dying out there. This was the enemy that Langsdorff held in contempt, and Kern would have given anything to feel as Langsdorff did. Those were enemy sailors silhouetted against the towering flames of a tanker—those were enemy ships sliding beneath the cold waters of the Atlantic, and that knowledge should have released Kern from regret. But it did not. "After a while," he continued, "you begin to hope that some of the world's beauty survives the war. If not Berlin, then perhaps Paris."

Langsdorff locked his fingers together, considering Kern's comments. Finally, he dropped his hands to his desk, a signal that he felt the conversation was useless. He pulled several files from the briefcase next to the desk.

"As you are aware, I have interviewed all of the officers under your command."

"Except me," Kern said.

"Yes. Except you." He flipped open a folder and began examining its contents. "You will be pleased to hear that I consider all of your officers to be loyal Germans."

"I expected as much," Kern said with a trace of sarcasm.

"Now." Oberst Langsdorff motioned for a clerk to join them. "For the purposes of this meeting, as you are well aware since you attended all of the previous interviews, we will record all that is said."

"Yes," Kern replied, watching the clerk ready a note pad and pencils. "I would like a copy of these notes."

Langsdorff smiled and nodded at the clerk. "Provide Kapitaenleutnant Kern with a copy of the meeting notes." He adjusted his tunic and leveled his blue eyes on Kern. "Let us begin."

It was the same as the dozen sessions that Langsdorff had conducted before. The oberst felt it necessary to question only the commissioned officers, believing that they were the ones most likely to prove disloyal, or as he explained to Kern, more likely to pursue the war with less zeal than required. He never said that he ques-

tioned an officer's loyalty, but Kern knew that this was
the case. The attack on the fuehrer had sent ripples
throughout the Reich, even into the wilderness of Norway, and the tiny base in Bokn Fiord.

Kern knew that there was a manhunt abroad, not
only for those who were truly guilty of conspiring to
kill the fuehrer but also those whose loyalty was in
question. What brings one's loyalty into question?
The wrong answer, an impolitic question, a lack of
enthusiasm—Kern felt the idea of conspiracy tight-
ening around his chest like a vise. At the center of
it, the SS, the Knights of the Silver Dagger.

Langsdorff behaved as he did during the previous
interviews. His manner was relaxed, almost friendly,
the questions about one's family, friends, and opin-
ions of the war phrased in a matter-of-fact fashion.
The only sound that filled the brief moments of silence between the questions and the answers was the
faint scratching of the clerk's pencil over the pad.
Langsdorff was composed, unhurried, and methodi-
cal. The oberst was cool but not cold, polished and
efficient but not unfriendly. There was no threat to
the man and Kern could see how easily others could
be lulled into a sense of well-being as the bureaucrat
shuffled papers and asked questions. Kern watched
him as he carefully crossed out each question on his
typed sheet after it had been dutifully answered. It
would be funny, Kern decided, if it weren't so tragic.

Germany fighting for her life, her warriors forced
to fight with unproven weapons on fantastic missions;
and yet her bureaucracy of distrust still functioned
flawlessly. Kern felt relieved that Paris had survived.
Her sanctity seemed a victory over the madness of a
war fought by clerks with clipboards.

After approximately two hours, Oberst Langsdorff drew a line through the last question.

"There we have it." He smiled at Kapitaenleutnant Kern as if everyone had a right to be satisfied. "I see no reason to doubt your loyalty to the Fatherland or the fuehrer, Kapitaenleutnant. Congratulations."

"Thank you," Kern said. He wanted to say something more, but he decided that anything he said would be useless.

"Kapitaenleutnant Kern," Langsdorff began. "I wonder if you have truly considered your situation?" He asked the question as he already knew the answer.

"My situation?"

"If you will permit me," Langsdorff said in a friendly tone, a man anxious to ingratiate himself. "I think that I can illuminate some points for you that will help you to understand exactly the true nature of circumstances surrounding your mission."

Kern nodded, knowing that the more he understood Langsdorff, the greater his chance of thwarting the man when the time came. Know your enemy, one of his instructors had told him, and you'll know your enemy's weakness.

"Good," Langsdorff said. "Have you not thought it strange that you were given an important mission for the Reich and yet you have not received the necessary supplies and weapons to carry out that mission?"

"I know of the difficulties faced by war production. The Fat Man can't keep a lid on Germany, so the Tommies and Americans bomb everything that moves."

"Reichsmarshall Goring is doing all that he can," Langsdorff said, but the words lacked conviction. Nobody saw much point in defending Goring anymore.

"I don't see Luftwaffe planes protecting us."

"Nevertheless, aircraft production is up," Langsdorff said quickly. "Eh? Did you know that, Kapitaenleutnant? There are difficulties in transportation, of course, rail lines and roads. But production is up. You have three U-boats riding at anchor out there. Where are your other twelve?"

"Destroyed by the enemy," Kern said.

A thin smile crept across the oberst's face. The smile of a privileged man. The look of a man who had important information.

"Not so, Kapitaenleutnant. They are ready and waiting at the yards, but not for this mission. Your grand admiral is saving them for another Battle of the Atlantic. You look surprised? Is that it? Or disappointed? Well, it's true. Is this not true that you begged for antiaircraft guns and received nothing? I arrive, call for the same guns, and they are delivered."

He was lying, Kern thought. Doenitz would not betray him. But the seed was planted and Kern grew disgusted with himself as he considered it. Doenitz could have withheld the boats and there would be no way for him to know for certain.

"Everyone knows," Kern said, keeping his temper, "that the SS is given priority."

"Everyone knows!" Langsdorff said, laughing. "What nonsense. But here is the proof of what I am about to tell you. You ask for guns and materials, and get crumbs. I ask, and get all that we need. Maybe your grand admiral does not want to waste his resources on a mission such as this."

"Are you suggesting that Grand Admiral Doenitz is withholding U-boats and supplies from me?"

"Perhaps," Langsdorff said. Suddenly he was coy. "Perhaps he does not believe, as our fuehrer believes, that this mission may turn the course of the war to Germany's advantage. I ask you only to consider the facts. You were promised fifteen boats, you have but three. I look at your U-boat commanders and their crews. A coward and a bully, Kern? Even after you split up the crews you do not have enough hardened veterans, as I'm sure that you are aware. Old men and boys for the most part, am I right? Perhaps Grand Admiral Doenitz sees this as a lost cause and therefore wishes to commit only as little as he can get by with. I take exception in the case of you and your crew, of course. I have the highest regard for you and your men. But see here, Kern: perhaps your grand admiral views this mission as nothing more than a nuisance, something to detract him from the real battle—the North Atlantic and the Channel. You know he is pushing for more new U-boats to attack the convoys. Did you know that he promised the fuehrer that his See-Hunds could sink a hundred thousand tons of Allied shipping?"

Kern took a deep breath. He wished he were at sea, far away from the insanity that had overwhelmed the Fatherland. At sea, one faces death, but the lines are clearly and fairly drawn; here . . . here it is like *Gulliver's Travels*, a land where small men with tiny minds rule.

"If it is as you say," Kern said slowly, finding his words. "That Grand Admiral Doenitz fails to commit resources to this mission because he does not believe it will be successful, there is nothing that I can do. He is my superior. But you, Oberst Langsdorff, you and the SS have ways of making men and materials appear. Therefore, does it not stand to reason that you can get me my twelve additional boats?"

"Oh, that's not possible," Langsdorff said.

"Why not? You made antiaircraft guns appear. The materials to build barracks and sheds."

"Those things are very little compared to U-boats. Even the SS has its limits."

"If Doenitz denies them to me, as you say, then all you need do is request them through Reichsfuehrer Himmler. If the grand admiral is not committed to this mission, then it is up to the SS to carry out the fuehrer's wishes. Do it. Send now and get me my other boats and crews."

"You misunderstood what I said," Langsdorff said. "Your admiral holds them. Not I. This is a Kriegsmarine operation as you so often point out."

"No," Kern replied. "I understand perfectly. I know what you imply, and I know why you imply it. Have you ever been to war, Oberst?"

Langsdorff straightened. It was evident that he was uncertain of Kern's question. "I have been an SS officer since 1938."

"No, no," Kern said. "No, I mean, have you ever been in combat? Seen men die, or faced death yourself?"

Kern watched Langsdorff compose his answer.

"I have served the Reich faithfully since 1938 in any capacity ordered by my superiors," the oberst said. "I am a proud member of the SS. You have no reason to question me on this matter."

Kern smiled at the answer, the wrinkles at the corners of his eyes growing deeper.

"Then your answer is no. I will tell you, Oberst Langsdorff, about war. It is a very brutal existence. In a U-boat, fifty-one men in a long tube, living in the stench of their own excrement and fear, waiting as unseen enemies feel for them in the darkness of a cold sea. Time? Time stops. Every instant is an eternity. Every feeling is multiplied fifty-fold, every sense becomes attuned, and every thought is of one thing—to live. To survive. It is as if the Fellow Upstairs is dealing cards with one card marked Death. He flips them, one at a time. If the game ends before Death is dealt, you go on to another game, maybe in an hour, or a day. Always the cards, always the waiting and watching. Perhaps, one time, the Death card is played."

"You're being melodramatic. . . ."

"No," Kern said. "No. After a while, in war, men begin to depend on one another for their existence. Each man holds other men's lives in his hands. You learn to count on what a man says. It becomes almost an instinct. You begin to trust other men with your life, because you are entrusted with theirs. Maybe it could be called a warrior's trust; I don't know. I'm not a poet. But I do know that when everything else is taken from you, that warrior's trust remains. I suppose there is no way for anyone who has not been in battle to understand it. That is not to say men who have seen battle are superior, it is just to explain that we see things differently. We are comrades who face a common end. Death. That brings us closer together, like a family. Brothers. Maybe that's it—brothers. From it comes the common bond of trust. If it is as you suggest, that the Lion denies me men and materials, then he has broken that trust."

"The same trust that you broke with your crew by reassigning them." Langsdorff smiled triumphantly. "What about your brotherhood now? Does any trust remain between you and your men now?"

Kern nodded, knowing that at least part of what Langsdorff accused him of was true. "I did what I felt I had to. I had no choice except one." He continued, "I don't think that the Lion is that kind of man." Then he added, because he could see that Langsdorff would never understand, "Are we done?"

"Yes," Langsdorff said. "Quite done."

The oberst stood and shook Kern's hand. Then he offered a Nazi salute and a crisp "Heil Hitler."

Kern responded with the traditional Kriegsmarine salute, fingertips to forehead.

"The navy has not yet adopted the party salute," Langsdorff observed.

"The Kriegsmarine is not a political party," Kern said. "I am a military officer. I gave a military salute."

"Perhaps that will change," Langsdorff said.

Kern was just reaching for his cap when he heard the shot. He and Langsdorff looked at each other. Kern bolted for the door, followed by the oberst and some of his staff. Kern saw several of his sailors running toward the RGT shed. Hartmann was among them.

"What's happened?" Kern called as he joined his exec.

"I don't know," Hartmann said. "I just heard the shot, and someone said they've shot one of our men."

"Who is shot?"

"I don't know, Kapitaenleutnant."

They ran up the long slope and around the house used as a U-boat barracks. They stopped in the clearing just below the camouflaged shed. There was a sailor laying facedown in the dirt, a dark stain of blood spilling out from his head. Kern approached the body in disbelief. Several nervous SS guards stood in front of the shed, their rifles pointed at his men.

Kern and Hartmann gently turned the sailor over. It was Bauer. One side of his head was a mass of tissue and brains. His lifeless eyes were half closed.

"They killed him," Kern heard a man behind him say. "They killed him for nothing."

Kern gently closed Bauer's eyes and stood, facing

the crowd of sailors. He had to swallow before he could find his voice.

"What happened?" he asked.

"It was a bet, sir," a man Kern recognized as a petty officer from U-3712 said. "Bauer bet some of the men that he would be the first sailor to see the rockets. He wasn't trying to do anything but see what they looked like. That's all."

Kern turned to a young SS guard. The guard immediately snapped to attention.

"Did you shoot this boy?" Kern demanded.

"What of it?" Langsdorff said.

Kern turned to see the oberst push his way through the crowd.

Kern pointed to the body. "He killed one of my men."

"He followed orders," Langsdorff said quickly. "He did what he should have done."

"He killed Bauer in cold blood. There was no reason to shoot him."

"I ordered that no one approach the shed. You heard my orders. My men were under strict orders to prevent anyone, anyone from approaching the shed."

The civilian scientists came out into the compound.

"That was no reason to shoot the boy!" Kern said. "He was curious. That's all."

"I gave my orders," Langsdorff said, "and that is the end of it. It is a shame that a sailor had to die, but there is nothing to be done about it now. If he had listened he would be alive to serve the Fatherland. As it is, at least now he can be a lesson to others."

Kern swung his fist, striking Langsdorff in the face. The oberst let out a cry of surprise, and stumbled back into the arms of two of his men. Kern heard the bolts of the soldiers' rifles send a round into the chamber.

He saw the weapons leveled at him as two SS officers pinned his arms.

Langsdorff shook his head to regain his senses. His cap had fallen off, and his dark hair hung over his eyes. He pushed it back with his hand and ordered a guard to retrieve his cap.

"You struck me," Oberst Langsdorff said to Kern, blood streaming from his nose. "I can have you arrested for that." He pulled a kerchief from his pocket to stem the blood.

"Your man killed this boy in cold blood. You're responsible for this."

"It was his own fault," Langsdorff spat, pressing the kerchief against his nose.

"Bastards!" one of the sailors shouted.

"Cover them," Major Brandt ordered.

The SS guards leveled their rifles at the crowd of sailors.

Langsdorff looked at Kern triumphantly. "Call off your men, or there will be more bloodshed. I mean it."

Kern looked over his shoulder at the crowd of sailors, and then back to the soldiers' rifles. He was about to answer when he was stopped by a voice.

"Oberst? If you please?"

It was Chief Engineer Frick.

Kern turned to see Frick, pointing back to the shoreline. Kern followed Frick's gaze down to the boats. The last of the four available antiaircraft turrets was just swinging into position, its guns aimed at the shed.

"I think that you had better let go of our kapitaen," Frick said.

"You will kill as many of your men as you do mine," Langsdorff said.

"We will kill no men," Frick said. "They are aimed at the shed. If you don't let go of our kapitaen, we might shoot the shit out of your rockets."

"Oh no!" Professor Mueller made his way forward. "You mustn't. Please don't. Gentlemen, I beg of you, please. There are no more. If you destroy these we cannot build replacements. Please. Can't you settle this another way?"

Langsdorff looked at Kern. "This is treason."

"What of it, Oberst? According to you, all you have to do is snap your fingers and more rockets will appear. Go ahead. Arrest me. You can get more boats and crews." He nodded to the shed. "Maybe more rockets."

"Gentlemen?" Mueller tried again. "Can't we just forget this dreadful incident and go on? We're so close to readiness. Days, in fact. I beg of you. For the sake of Germany."

Langsdorff pulled the kerchief away from his face. The bleeding had stopped. "For the sake of Germany, yes," he said, studying the stained handkerchief. He forced a smile.

"You're quite right, Professor. For the sake of Germany. Kapitaenleutnant Kern, I deeply regret this incident. The death of one of your men was unfortunate. I will immediately countermand my orders." To the SS officers who held Kern he ordered: "Release him."

The SS officers stood back.

"We need access to the rockets," Kern said.

Langsdorff smiled thinly. "Of course. But for officers only, eh? Is that satisfactory? You want more? For the officers and those men directly responsible for the operation of the weapons."

Kern nodded. "That is acceptable. I'll take full

responsibility for their behavior and for the security of the rockets when they are in my care."

"Good," Langsdorff said, wiping the blood away from his mouth.

"Is this the first time that you've shed blood for the Fatherland?" Kern asked.

Langsdorff dabbed his lip again, anger and humiliation flashing in his eyes. "We've settled everything here, haven't we? You're satisfied with the arrangement, Kern?"

"Yes," Kern said, "I accept your apology. As Professor Mueller says, for the sake of Germany. I will order the men not involved with the rockets to keep away from the shed."

Hauptmann Lossow stepped forward. "Herr Oberst, he struck you. He should be arrested."

"For the sake of Germany," Kern reminded Langsdorff.

"This incident is closed!" Langsdorff ordered. "Return to your duties!"

Kern ordered four men to take Bauer's body back to the boat. "We'll bury him in the fiord," he told Hartmann. "It's not the ocean but it's the least that we can do for the boy. Order the men to stay away from the shed. Again. I don't want anyone else killed."

Hartmann nodded and followed the seamen bearing the body, back down the hill.

"Frick!" Kern called. The chief disengaged himself from the group and returned to Kern, throwing a salute.

"Never mind that nonsense," the kapitaenleutnant ordered. "What the devil do you think you were doing?"

"Defending my kaleu," Frick said.

"That would have been a hell of a mess. There's no

telling how many men would have been killed if those guns had fired. Not to mention the damage to the rockets. Did you think of that?"

"Oh yes," Frick said.

"And?"

"Well, If the kapitaen had looked, he would have noticed all of our gunners up here, sir."

"Who the hell is manning the guns?"

"My mechanics, sir."

"Your mechanics! They aren't trained on those guns. Jesus, it's worse than I thought! They could have killed the lot of us."

"Oh no, sir," Frick said. "There was really nothing to worry about—the guns aren't loaded."

Kapitaenleutnant Kern stepped up to the sailor. "Chief Engineer Frick, loaded or not, your men were likely to hit the trees, the shed, Langsdorff's men, my men, and the ground even if they fired straight up into the air. If I didn't need you, I'd have you arrested."

"Yes, Kapitaenleutnant," Frick said, unconcerned.

"Return to your duties."

The chief engineer saluted and walked back to his boat, whistling.

Kern looked at the dark stain at his feet. Blood. Bauer's blood. *Strange,* he thought, *how it stains the earth black. At sea, it turns the water bright red, but then it mingles with the ocean and disappears. There will be much more spilled by submariners before this is over.* He turned to see the SS guard who shot Bauer standing his post. Tears were streaming down his young face.

"You'll have to learn to live with it, boy," Kern said softly. "We all have to learn to live with the memories of the men that we kill."

Chapter 14

Evanger, Norway

"Come. Come, Kapitaenleutnant Kern," Mueller said happily, waving Kern into the RGT shed. Hartmann followed Kern as they walked into the low building. The RGTs, minus their canisters, were still mounted on their platforms atop the low trailers, the long rockets gleaming under the rows of lights suspended above each truck.

Professor Spengler stood to one side, beaming.

"I spoke to Herr Oberst this morning," Mueller said excitedly. "He authorized me to begin training your men. He is a gentleman, Herr Oberst."

Spengler approached, clicked his heels with a stiff bow, and smiled broadly. "How wonderful of you gentlemen to visit us."

Hartmann looked at Kern in disbelief. "It's like they've invited us to tea," he whispered.

Mueller walked closely behind them as they viewed the RGTs. He began talking immediately.

"We weren't quite sure how they would take the journey. They are delicate instruments, after all. We've been fortunate in that the last several flight tests have gone exceedingly well, wouldn't you agree, Professor Spengler?"

"Yes, well. Well indeed, Professor Mueller. These haven't been tested, of course. That is to say that we have conducted static tests, but these vehicles have never been flight tested. To do so would to destroy them."

"The engines were always of concern to us, but we adapted the rocket engines used in the V-project to our purpose," Mueller said.

"They were very difficult to come by," Spengler added.

"Yes, they were," Mueller said. "But they have performed beautifully. The guidance system is always of concern. Very touchy."

"Always."

"Yes, so we've made every effort to strengthen the housing surrounding the internal gyroscopes," Mueller said.

"There are no external gyroscopes, I take it?" Kern said dryly.

"Oh no. No," Spengler said seriously. "Why would one want external gyroscopes on rockets? Internal refers of course to their location deep within the body of the rocket."

"An integral part of the Flight Guidance System," Mueller said.

"Gentlemen," Kern said, "I assure you that both my executive officer and I are astounded by the possibilities of these rockets. But my officers and chief engineers must be thoroughly trained in the operation of these weapons."

"Of course," Spengler said. "We're most anxious to begin training. Aren't we, Professor Mueller?"

"By all means."

"I think that you will be especially impressed by the RGTs' launching mechanism," Spengler offered proudly. "In fact, it is ingenious if I do say so myself. Smaller rockets will actually boost the RGTs off the rails to clear the surface of the water. At that point the main engines engage and propel the missiles to their destination. The missiles' speed, distance, and course are calculated and loaded into the missiles' guidance system. Beforehand, naturally."

"How are the engines that launch this thing engaged?" Hartmann asked.

"Oh, electrically, of course," Mueller said. "But here is another ingenious aspect. It is done by remote control. Radio signal from inside the submarine. There is no need to pierce the pressure hull of the submarine."

"Vice Admiral Godt was most insistent on that," Spengler said sourly. "He was rude, in fact."

"We submariners don't like holes in our pressure hulls," Kern said. "The firing mechanism?"

"Yes," Mueller said. "Entirely remote controlled. The transmitter will be located in the engine room. Simply transmit the appropriate code to the receiver located on the RGT, and the launching sequence begins. Booster rockets fire, followed by the main rockets. The rails are attached to the deck, and the rockets are locked into the rails with a slot track mechanism. It keeps the rocket from tumbling off the track while the submarine is in motion."

"What happens to the rails once the rockets are launched?" Hartmann asked.

"Oh, they must remain on the submarine," Spengler said. "We've made no allowances for them after launch. They really weigh very little."

"Aluminum," Mueller said. "Honeycomb construction that provides strength without adding additional weight."

"Ingenious," Spengler said.

"How are these raised into position?" Kern asked, studying the rails.

"Electric motors activated by radio control. Three minutes to extend."

"If the motors fail?" Kern asked.

"That is highly unlikely, Kapitaenleutnant. They've been tested thoroughly."

"Of course," Kern said. "But if they fail?"

"There is a contingency," Spengler said.

"That is to say," Mueller said, "it must be done manually."

Kern and Hartmann exchanged glances.

"Oh, it's all very easy, I assure you," Mueller said. "Two men on each rail can lift them into position by means of a crank and gear mechanism. We've tested it a number of times. It's possible, and not as difficult as one would think."

"Gentlemen," Kern said, "such an operation on the deck of a surfaced U-boat in the open seas would be difficult at any time, if not impossible. Add to that the fact that we must accomplish this operation within sight of enemy territory and most certainly in a heavily patrolled area. It is unacceptable."

"No, no," Mueller said. "It can be done. Look, there." He pointed to a box with a handle folded into position at the base of the rail, several feet from the rocket's tail fins. "See? Simply extend the crank handles and begin turning in a clockwise fashion. One mechanism for each rocket. The rails will be in position in twenty minutes."

"Twenty minutes!" Hartmann said.

"Professor Spengler, Professor Mueller," Kern tried again. "I don't think that you understand the nature of my concerns. The operation that you describe is extremely dangerous. Even if we were to have calm weather, we expose ourselves to enemy surface vessels and aircraft for twenty minutes. It will not do."

"No?" Mueller said to Spengler. The latter shrugged in confusion.

Kern turned to Hartmann. "Have four of the strongest men from each boat detailed for this assignment immediately. Do not mention the length of time that our friends here say that it takes to raise these rails into firing position. I will give them five minutes. Five minutes, Teddy. That is all."

"Yes, sir," Hartmann said.

"When will you make the replacement warheads available, Kapitaen?" Spengler asked.

Hartmann and Kern looked at one another. "What are you talking about?" Kern said. "We have no warheads here."

"How can that be?" Mueller asked. "We were told to expect them."

"What are those warheads?" Kern said, pointing at the nose of the RGT.

"Yes," Spengler said. "High explosives. But we were told to expect replacements."

"What's wrong with those?"

"Nothing. Absolutely nothing," Mueller said. "But . . . we were told to expect replacement warheads. I thought that you had them. I thought that you knew all about it."

"Langsdorff has something to do with this," Hartmann said to Kern.

"I'll see to it, gentlemen," Kern said to the scientists. "I shall need to establish a training schedule for my men. I shall also need access to the manuals for these weapons. That includes all electrical schematics, mechanical drawings, and maintenance instructions.

They will have to travel a very great distance underwater, and I would not be happy should they fail to work once we reach our targets."

"Fail to work?" Spengler said. "Why, of course they will work. They've been engineered to work perfectly. Fail to work? That's simply inconceivable."

"Inconceivable," Mueller agreed.

"Nevertheless," Kern said. He heard the door open and saw Hauptmann Lossow and three SS soldiers enter. "I have found such complex machines fail to function precisely at the wrong moment. When on patrol, our torpedoes are removed from their tubes and inspected every four days. It is that sort of attention to maintenance requirements that ensures our success."

"Kapitaenleutnant Kern?"

Kern turned to see Lossow saluting him. The soldiers stood behind him with their weapons at port.

"Hauptmann," Kern said. "You have orders for my arrest, no doubt?"

"No, sir," Hauptmann Lossow said. "My orders are to arrest Leutnant Hartmann."

Chapter 15

Fleet Air Arm, Spotswoddie House, England

Captain Sheen, RN, had just emerged from the washroom and was on his way back to his office in the photographic reconnaissance section when Lieutenant Carlow, Fleet Air Arm, asked him to step into the tiny photo identification room.

"Some of our RAF blokes flying over Norway took these," Carlow said, laying them on a light table.

Sheen maneuvered himself into position to see the photographs. "What am I looking for, Carlow?" he said brusquely. He had a lot to do, and he thought Carlow was a bit of an eccentric. Couldn't be helped though, not enough Active Service to go around, the Royal Navy had to rely on this load of Hostilities Only. Day sailors and sea lawyers, or worse. Damned poor way to run a war.

Carlow pushed his glasses up off the end of his nose and, using a pencil as his pointer, began his explanation. "This is a photograph of Bokn Fiord several miles from the village of Evanger. If you'll notice here, sir, the shoreline appears natural. See how the waves break here, and again here?"

"All right, Lieutenant. I see. Waves breaking on the shore. What of it?"

"Just bear with me a minute, sir, if you will." Carlow pushed the photograph aside and replaced it with another. "Now, here we have the village of Evanger."

Sheen leaned closer. "Eh? Something's going on there. What is it?"

"Yes, sir," Carlow replied. "Some new construction. Two flak towers. One here and here. As yet incomplete. Several new buildings. You can see them, sir. Not really very large but new, nevertheless."

"Yes, damn it, I can see them! I'm not blind, Carlow!"

"No, sir," the Lieutenant said, unfazed. "Now, taken by themselves, the buildings and their location are little enough to be concerned with. A bit off of the beaten path as it were. But look at the shoreline here, sir. The shadows are all wrong, and there are no waves breaking against the shore."

Sheen pulled the photograph closer. "Give me that glass," he ordered, pointing to a stereoscopic magnifying lens on the table next to the light board. Carlow quickly handed it to him and stood back. After a respectable period, he said: "What do you think, sir?"

Sheen straightened and laid the glass on the photograph. "Camouflage. Runs from the shore over that ship. Something's under it too, can't see what."

"Yes, sir. That's just what I thought."

Sheen skewered him with a glare. "Is that so? Well, Lieutenant, what do you think Jerry's got hiding under that netting?"

"I don't know, sir. I thought it was too small for a capital ship, sir. I've studied it, but I haven't got the foggiest, sir."

"Eh," Sheen said. "Me either, Lieutenant, but Jerry's not about to build flak towers for nothing. It's too small for a ship of any size except a U-boat. Maybe some E-boats. Although why Jerry has anything up that fiord is beyond me. But he wants to protect it, so that means it's important. If it's important to Jerry, it's important to us. A U-boat, maybe two. Those new boats they've been warning us about. That's my guess, but a guess is all it is. Did we find this by radio transmission?"

"No, sir," Carlow said. "By the time this sortie had been dispatched, the signals dried up."

"So it was with sheer dumb luck that one of our planes stumbled onto this?"

"Yes, sir. That's about right."

Sheen shook his head. "This business never fails to amaze me."

"Should we call for an air strike, sir?"

"Air strike? No. That's a damned mousetrap. The pilots would have a devil of a time getting in and back out. They'd have to come down the fiord to get a good shot at them. Too long under the guns. No. No air strike. I've got a better idea, Lieutenant."

"Better idea, sir?"

"Yes! Better idea, Carlow. That's why I'm the captain and you're the lieutenant." He gestured to the photograph. "I think some of our motor torpedo boat lads would like to have a go at this. Write that up and get it to me immediately."

"Yes, sir," Carlow said as Sheen turned to leave.

"Damned fine catch, Carlow," the captain threw back as he left. "Keep it up and you might be badgering young lieutenants in no time."

"Yes, sir," Carlow replied as Sheen disappeared. And then to himself he added, "I'd bloody well be happier badgering ill-tempered senior captains."

* * *

"Release him," Kern shouted. "Now!"

Langsdorff looked up from his desk. "That's impossible."

"Why has Hartmann been arrested? I'm the one who struck you."

Langsdorff stood and took a cup of tea from Lossow. The other soldiers in the office tried to look occupied.

"Kapitaenleutnant Kern, this has nothing whatsoever to do with our altercation," Langsdorff said, making his way to a stack of radio messages. "Leutnant Hartmann was arrested for an entirely different matter." He picked up a message, scanned it, and handed it back to a clerk. "Entirely different."

He was enjoying this, Kern thought—*he's reveling in my frustration. Maybe he knows that he has won, that there is nothing I can do.* The thought shot through Kern's mind like an electrical charge. *Maybe Hartmann is lost.* "I wish to know the reason that my executive officer has been arrested by the SS, Oberst Langsdorff."

"Of course, Kapitaenleutnant," Langsdorff said, holding out his hand to Hauptmann Klein. Klein handed a file to the oberst. "Leutnant Hartmann has been arrested for suspicion of treason."

"Treason! Are you mad?"

"Hartmann is the nephew of the vice mayor of Leipzig," Langsdorff said, flipping open the folder with one hand. He glanced at Kern. "Did you not know that, Kapitaenleutnant? No? Well, so he is. The mayor of Leipzig has been arrested for his part in the nefarious plot to kill the fuehrer. It was necessary to arrest the vice mayor also." Langsdorff made a show of reading the file. "For 'suspicion.' It's all very complicated, you realize, but we will soon get to the bottom of it."

"And Hartmann?" Kern asked. "Why was he arrested?"

"A precaution, of course," Langsdorff said, handing the folder back to Klein. "One never knows how deep or how far these sorts of things go. It's a vast seething web of deceit. But I'm sure that there's nothing to worry about. Regarding Hartmann, he seems an exemplary sort. A man of integrity."

"If there is nothing to worry about, then release him to me. I will be responsible for his loyalty."

"I cannot do that. I have direct orders from Reichsfuehrer Himmler, who was charged with the investigation by the fuehrer himself. After things are thoroughly investigated I am sure that your leutnant will be released in time to join you. Now, Kapitaenleutnant, let us talk about the RGTs. We can return to Hartmann. You've spoken to our scientists. What is the status of the weapons?"

Kern hesitated before speaking, his mind racing. He had to get Hartmann back. There was only one recourse open to him: get Doenitz involved. Send a message detailing what had happened to the grand admiral. But he was unsure what the result would be. The Lion had been suspiciously silent during the takeover of the project by the SS. The only messages that Kern had received in reply to his inquiries were from Godt, and they did nothing but urge Kern to practice patience. Patience! They had practiced patience, and now a sailor was dead and Hartmann arrested. The SS understood brute force only, but Kern knew that was not the way out of this mess. He was forced to play Langsdorff's game. For now. He focused on the RGTs.

"I will have my crews load them on the boats this afternoon," Kern finally said. He watched as a trace of a smile crossed Langsdorff's lips. *He thinks that he's won,* Kern realized. *But he hasn't.* "My torpedo men will be responsible for the maintenance of the missiles. They are being trained now. The launching mechanism seems to be relatively simple. My only concern is the condition of the rockets after prolonged exposure to seawater."

"Precisely," Langsdorff agreed, as if everything were forgotten, and they were now comrades-in-arms. "That was my question to those White Coats. They assure me that was taken into consideration in the design and construction of the weapons. Thirty days is what they told me. That is, the length of time that those weapons can survive underwater. What about firing them?"

"The guidance system does not allow us to aim the rockets with any certainty, or to make adjustments once the rockets are launched," Kern said. "The coordinates will be computed and transmitted to the rockets before we leave for the launch point. Those coordinates will be nothing more than the course. The distance will be determined by expenditure of fuel. When the fuel is expended they will drop from the sky."

Langsdorff gave the matter some thought. "Tell me, Kapitaenleutnant Kern, how will you . . ." He searched for the right word. "Uncase the rockets?"

"The canisters?" Kern said. "I plan to leave those behind."

"What?"

"They're designed to streamline and to protect the rockets," Kern said. "They're vented to allow access to seawater, so that there is no need to pressurize them. But my concern is that loaded with seawater, the things will be top-heavy and unwieldy. I will give up a few knots in speed due to the drag of the exposed rockets to maintain the boat's maneuverability. The Type XXI boats are big whales, Herr Oberst; they do not maneuver as quickly as the Type VII boats. The extra bulk of the canisters will hang on us like concrete blocks."

"Kapitaenleutnant, I think that this is something that the scientists should decide. It is their creation. I'm sure that they've taken that into consideration."

"They have not. They told me as much. Those canisters have to be opened manually. That's extra time in the open that could prove fatal. My chief engineer believes that he can strap the rockets to their launching rails. When we approach our target, we surface, cut the bands, raise the launching rails into position, submerge, and fire. This should take two minutes."

"But still," Langsdorff considered. "To leave them behind . . ."

"They're flimsy structures. There is the possibility that they will jam in the closed position during the voyage. We would have no way of opening them aside from blowing them open."

"Explosives?" Langsdorff considered the alternatives.

"We couldn't launch the rockets," Kern said, watching Langsdorff's face for any sign of comprehension. The oberst was concerned about the canisters now. Good—let him sweat.

"I know what it means, Kapitaenleutnant," Langsdorff snapped. "I am still not convinced, however, that leaving them behind is a solution. I've have to consider it."

You arrogant fool, Kern thought.

"Do those scientists know the targets?" Langsdorff asked.

"No," the kapitaenleutnant said. "They have supplied me with a series of tables that contain variables to launch by distance only. All we need is to locate our position and apply the calculations to launch the rockets. It's like shooting an eel except we can't see the target, and it isn't moving."

"An eel?"

"Torpedo."

"But with much greater impact. Much greater," Langsdorff said, smiling. "Think of it, Kern, we are inaugurating a new method of war. These weapons will truly mean victory for Germany."

Kern was amazed. Langsdorff really believed what he said. Six rockets transported on the backs of three untested U-boats, through waters patrolled by hundreds of enemy ships and planes. Victory for Germany? No. But maybe they would allow her to sue for an honorable peace.

"Oberst Langsdorff, what is this business about replacement warheads?"

Langsdorff opened his hands innocently. "Yes?"

Kern waited for an answer and finally Langsdorff continued.

"You have nothing to worry about, Kapitaenleutnant. Everything is in order. Those warheads that you speak of are simply new, more powerful warheads. The thinking was to find a way to increase damage and destruction to the enemy. You understand, don't you? You must have seen torpedoes improve over the past several years, no? It is the same thing, that's all."

Kern was not satisfied with the explanation. It was smooth and lacked detail but there was nothing that he could do now. He decided to return Langsdorff to the real question.

"Herr Oberst," he said. "The success of this mission

is critical to the well-being of the Fatherland. It will require skill and planning, and a sailor's luck to succeed."

"Luck? I was told that German sailors make their own luck, Kapitaenleutnant. I have the utmost confidence in the performance of you and your men, and I look forward to the day when I can be among those who welcome you back to Germany after a successful mission. You will be a heroic son of the Fatherland, embraced by the fuehrer himself. It is an honor of which many dream but few realize. It will be yours, Kern, everything you want."

"Yes, Herr Oberst," Kern said, "I want my executive officer."

"But that's not possible, Kapitaenleutnant. As I have already explained, Hartmann is under arrest for suspicion of treason. This is a serious matter. Most serious. I'm afraid that there is nothing I can do."

"I need him, Herr Oberst. The success of this mission depends upon Hartmann being at my side."

"One sailor," Langsdorff said. "Surely one sailor more or less doesn't doom the mission, does it?"

"More or less? Is that how you think of men's lives, Herr Oberst? More or less?"

"I suggest," Langsdorff said, "that you get back to your boats, Kapitaenleutnant. You must have a great deal to do."

Kern watched Langsdorff fill his cup with tea. The man was the worst kind of fool. A fool with power. He was dangerous and not to be underestimated, but Kern knew that he had no choice. "Yes, Herr Oberst," he said. "I have a great deal to do."

* * *

Adolph Hitler smiled weakly and took Doenitz's hand.

"Welcome, Grand Admiral, welcome."

The fuehrer's appearance shocked Doenitz. His pale skin, hanging limply from his cheeks and jowls, was an unnatural gray. His dark eyes darted nervously about as he spoke, and a pathetic shuffle replaced his customary vibrant walk. There was no fire in the man, Doenitz thought as he shook the fuehrer's hand; a sick man was leading Germany. The fuehrer silently motioned Doenitz to a chair with a flick of trembling fingers. Hitler made his way to a large map table in the center of the room.

"We haven't seen you in a while, Grand Admiral," Hitler said, studying the map.

Doenitz glanced at Jodl, who stood unobtrusively in one corner of the conference room. "I was told that you were unavailable, Mien Fuehrer."

Hitler's head remained suspended over the table. "Unavailable? When have I ever been unavailable for my grand admiral?" Almost as an afterthought, he looked about the room for Jodl.

The general quickly stepped forward to supply the excuse. "Your duties, Mien Fuehrer. The invasion."

Hitler said to Doenitz, "There you are, Grand Admiral. Duties kept us apart. But isn't that the way of it?" He gestured to the map. "The Allies have landed in France. They have doomed themselves. We'll crush them, Grand Admiral. We'll let them come on, farther and farther. A rat sticking its head into a hole. Snap! We'll close the trap, and cut off their head. Isn't that right, Jodl?"

Jodl's voice came from the shadows. "Yes, Mien Fuehrer."

"Mien Fuehrer," Doenitz said. "We have a situation that you must resolve. Operation Griffin."

Hitler looked up. "There are thousands of situations that I must resolve, Grand Admiral. I would ask my generals to do so, but they have no daring, forever counseling caution. They hesitate, Grand Admiral. When I want them to be daring, when all of Germany needs them to be daring, they hesitate. So it is left to me! Me! Very well, I am daring. I will not hesitate. My attention is required everywhere. Speer cannot do his job—he calls upon me. Goring fails to keep the Allied aircraft at bay—he comes crying to me . . ." Hitler stopped, as if he had lost his train of thought. "So, you too have a situation that requires my attention. What is it?"

"Operation Griffin was taken from the Kriegsmarine and given to the SS. That is unacceptable, Mien Fuehrer. This is a Kriegsmarine operation."

Doenitz heard the soft click of a door opening behind him. He turned to see Reichsfuehrer Heinrich Himmler enter. The low light in the room gleamed off of the reichsfuehrer's glasses, hiding his eyes. As always, a day's growth of coarse beard darkened his sallow face, giving him a haunted appearance. He looked like a village tough.

Himmler stopped and clicked his heels in salute. "Mien Fuehrer." He turned to Doenitz. "Ah, Grand Admiral. A pleasant surprise to see you. Jodl and I wondered where you were."

Doenitz turned back to Hitler without a word to the reichsfuehrer. "To continue, Mien Fuehrer, Operation Griffin is a Kriegsmarine operation. In my opinion the SS has overstepped its authority. Not only have they taken over the project, but they have killed

a sailor and placed under arrest a Kriegsmarine officer."

"An unavoidable necessity," Himmler said, coming
forward. "The man is under suspicion in the plot
against your life, Mien Fuehrer."

Doenitz did not back down. "Those charges are ab-
surd, Mien Fuehrer. I know the officer personally. He
is a loyal German."

Hitler's fist crashed down on the table. "Must we
argue? Can we do nothing but argue. You are like
children, bickering. 'This is mine, I want it.' 'No, it's
mine, give it to me.'"

"It is a matter of proper authority, Mien Fuehrer,"
Doenitz said. "You yourself charged me with Operation Griffin. I undertook the mission faithfully, and to
the best of my abilities. Now I find the SS control the
project and my men."

"There is no reason for hysteria," Himmler said in
his smooth manner. "From my reports, the project appears to be proceeding well. We should be able to
launch our attack within thirty days."

"That is not the issue. The issue is one of authority.
This concerns SS control over Kriegsmarine material
and personnel and a Kriegsmarine mission. I respectfully request, Mien Fuehrer, that you countermand
the order placing this project under SS control, and
return the mission to the Kriegsmarine."

"The grand admiral exaggerates, Mien Fuehrer,"
Himmler said. "The SS is there only to assist the
Kriegsmarine. We have the necessary equipment to
safeguard the U-boats from air attack, and we have
the administrative capability to manage the project. It
is, of course, still a Kriegsmarine operation. The success of the mission lies solely with the navy."

The grand admiral spoke evenly. "Mien Fuehrer, I

have served you loyally from the beginning. I and my officers and men have done as you ordered. Many have died in service to you and the Fatherland. We ask only, what is the order? and we carry it out. It is with this spirit that I undertook Operation Griffin, handpicking the officers and men. Despite my personal attention to the project, and my years of loyal service, I find that my men and this important mission are no longer under my control. I can only conclude that I have failed you somehow, and that you no longer have confidence in me."

Hitler held up his hand to protest, but Doenitz continued.

"It is for that reason, Mien Fuehrer, that I respectfully submit my resignation." Doenitz pulled an envelope from his inside breast pocket and held it out to Jodl. The general came forward hesitantly and took the envelope.

"No. No, no," Hitler said. "Grand Admiral, now is not the time for this sort of thing. Germany needs you, I need you. I can't allow this."

"I have no other option available to me, Mien Fuehrer," Doenitz said.

"Mien Fuehrer," the reichsfuehrer said, "I'm sure that the grand admiral and I can resolve this amicably. His resignation is not necessary."

"Mien Fuehrer, nothing short of returning the project fully to the Kriegsmarine will satisfy me. All you need do, Mien Fuehrer, is give the order."

"Mien Fuehrer," Himmler said, "I've already gone to great lengths to move two antiaircraft companies to Evanger. It would seem such a waste to have them disengage and return to Germany."

Hitler made his way around the map table, thinking. Doenitz was prepared for an explosion. It was

Hitler's method. Surprisingly the fuehrer remained calm, almost indifferent, searching the map table for his answer. He finally turned to Doenitz.

"I cannot allow you to resign, Grand Admiral. Germany needs you. I cannot allow you to resign. Tear that up, Jodl. Let us speak of it no more. Reichsfuehrer Himmler, I order you to relinquish command of Operation Griffin. It belongs to the navy. Let them run it. Do it immediately. Your antiaircraft companies can stay there, but do not let them interfere with the navy. Their role is antiaircraft only. And support. Who is the SS officer in charge?"

"Langsdorff, Mien Fuehrer."

"Langsdorff? Well, leave him where he is. But the Kriegsmarine will be masters of Evanger."

"Yes, Mien Fuehrer," Himmler said.

"There," Hitler said sarcastically. "Does that please you now, Grand Admiral? Are you happy?"

"My officer?" Doenitz asked quickly. "Hartmann?"

"Let me remind you, Mien Fuehrer," Himmler said, "that you have charged me to root out the infamous plotters in the attempt on your life."

"Yes, this is true." Hitler waved agreement. "The SS, Grand Admiral, have jurisdiction in this matter. I can do nothing about that."

"Mien Fuehrer, I am to meet with Kapitaenleutnant Kern to discuss the mission. I respectfully request that you give further consideration—"

"No! These animals tried to kill me! Me, Grand Admiral!" Hitler thundered. He moved uncertainly toward Doenitz and held out his fists. "I will catch them and twist the life out of them. I'll feel their blood dripping through my fingers. They, they . . . they! They will know how it feels. The reichsfuehrer is authorized to stop at nothing. He must find and bring to justice all

182 Steven M. Wilson

those who have plotted against me. Me!" The fuehrer pounded his chest. "My own officers, Doenitz! In my map room! They tried to kill me. To kill Germany. They tried to kill the Reich." Hitler came within inches of Doenitz. "But they failed," he whispered menacingly. "Now they will pay. All of them will pay. You have your project, be satisfied with that."

"Mien Fuehrer?" Himmler said.

Hitler gave a quick nod for the reichsfuehrer to continue.

"How will we know if the U-boats succeed? Or even if they survive the voyage?"

Hitler considered the question under the harsh glare of the map light. His skin appeared translucent, beads of sweat glistening on his forehead. *He is a dead man,* Doenitz realized.

"Mien Fuehrer," Doenitz said, "I have given instruction to Kern that they maintain radio silence. It is apparent that the Allies can locate our vessels by following their radio transmissions. It is far too dangerous for them—"

"Surely," Himmler broke in, "the Kriegsmarine can spare one vessel to relay Kern's safe arrival off of the English coast."

"Mien Fuehrer, the risk is extreme—"

"Well then, halfway," Hitler said. "Place them at the halfway point and let them radio that Kern has gotten that far at least. I need to know, Grand Admiral. I must have information to make decisions." He clutched an imaginary feather in his fingertips. "See how elusive it is? How quickly I must snatch intelligence from the air? It is a fleeting thing and if I do not act decisively"—he opened his hand and blew across it—"the thing is gone forever." He shook his finger at Doenitz in a grandfatherly way. "You see how

I need information? You must always be careful to provide it for me."

"Mien Fuehrer—" Doenitz began.

Hitler waved him into silence. "Can we not agree on this one point?" he asked.

"What is one U-boat, Grand Admiral?" Himmler said. "Put a sentry at the halfway point so that we know that Kern is not dead."

"Can that not be done, Grand Admiral?" Hitler pleaded sarcastically.

"Yes, Mien Fuehrer."

"Good," the fuehrer said, satisfied. "My grand admirals argue with my reischfuerers, the Luftwaffe argues with the Wehrmacht . . . I am the only one who sees what must be done. Where would Germany be without me?"

Neither Himmler nor Doenitz replied.

Hitler answered his own question. "Germany would be ruined, that's all." And then, as if distracted by another thought, added: "Go, Grand Admiral, you have things to do."

Doenitz saluted, turned, and left the conference room. He had most of a victory, and yet he was deeply troubled. Perhaps it was the fuehrer's appearance. Perhaps he was simply tired from having to deal, however briefly, with idiots like Jodl or jackals like Himmler. Perhaps it was because he knew that the reichsfuehrer never gave up, that somehow he would extract his revenge from Doenitz for taking Operation Griffin. At least he could tell Kern that the SS was moving out, and the Kriegsmarine was moving back in. What he couldn't tell him, Doenitz realized, was what Kern wanted to hear most, what was going to happen to his executive officer? Maybe it was time for him to visit Norway. It wouldn't hurt for the men at

Trondheim to see him; at least they would not feel as if the Reich had forgotten them.

On the return, he could stop at Evanger and find out how close Guenter the Silent was to leading his U-boats against England. No, Hitler would be furious. Trondheim would have to be content with his messages of support. And he would see Kern soon enough. No, Hitler would never let him go. The fuehrer would demand that Doenitz stay close by. Kern would have to come to him.

Doenitz heard someone approach from behind. He turned to see Himmler.

"Congratulations, Herr Grand Admiral," the reichs-fuehrer said smoothly. "The Kriegsmarine is once more in the business of rockets."

"Thank you," Doenitz said, waiting for the real reason for the conversation.

"There is something that the fuehrer neglected to tell you."

"Yes?"

"There has been a change of plans. Shall we walk?" Himmler suggested, slipping his hand under the grand admiral's elbow and guiding him down the narrow corridor. "You see, the warheads severely restrict the range of the rockets. A ton, after all, is a considerable weight. And what damage could a ton of high explosive do, after all? It is a great waste to expend so much to deliver so little destruction."

"What are you getting at?"

"How would you, if you were limited as to means of attack, make the most effective use of such a weapon?" The reichsfuehrer let the question hang.

Doenitz stopped. "What are you talking about?"

Himmler smiled. "Biological warfare, Herr Grand Admiral. Death on a much broader scale. Terror and confusion to the enemy. Instead of explosives, the rockets will be filled with anthrax."

"Anthrax?"

"A most deadly virus. One that can wipe out thousands of lives in a fortnight. Cripple the English. Sicken thousands of American soldiers waiting to invade Germany. Render Liverpool a desert. Deny the allies their greatest port as an embarkation point. Turn the English coast into a wasteland."

Doenitz felt the blood drain from his face. "No."

"The fuehrer's orders, Herr Grand Admiral. Your rockets will be filled with a disease for which there is no cure."

"I will not be a part of—"

"Oh, please don't! Don't protest! Your sudden burst of righteousness disgusts me. You are a part of it. Just do as the fuehrer orders and all will be well." Himmler looked at him in pity. "Do you think this is the same war that we fought in 1941? You don't think things have changed? We're fighting for our lives against the Bolsheviks and the Jews, Herr Grand Admiral. Do you think that they would refrain from using this weapon if they had it? How many thousands of Germans must you see dead in the streets before you accept the fact that this war is to the death? Kill or be killed, Doenitz. The enemy is at the gates, we must fight with every weapon in our arsenal or die. For the Fatherland, Herr Grand Admiral. For the fuehrer."

Doenitz finally found his voice. "We have come to this?"

A look of disbelief crossed Himmler's face at Doenitz's innocence. "We are driven to this."

A hauptman walked passed them, his boot echoing on the marble floor. Both remained silent until he was out of earshot.

"You will have a U-boat rendezvous with Kern at the halfway point and report on his progress," Himmler said. "As the fuehrer wishes."

"You know that you have condemned the men of the rendezvous vessel to death, don't you? The Allies will find them from their radio transmissions. How long do you think that U-boat will survive?"

"Long enough to do its duty. After that, I don't care. This is your project now, Herr Grand Admiral." Himmler smiled benignly. "Those are your difficulties to deal with. Will you order it?"

There was one Type XIV Supply U-boat left. If she could make it around the British Isles, she could take up station and remain at a rendezvous point until they made contact with Kern. Or until tracked down by the Allies. He had no choice.

"All right," Doenitz said. "We can have a boat on station in seven to ten days."

Himmler smiled, his owlish eyes bright through the thick lenses of his glasses. "I was sure that you would find a means, Herr Grand Admiral. Oh, and I shouldn't worry about your Leutnant Hartmann. I'm sure that this matter will clear itself up in good time."

"In time for him to sail with his comrades?"

"That remains to be seen," Himmler said. "Good day, Herr Grand Admiral."

Doenitz watched Himmler walk down the corridor, his shoulders hunched, his rapid gait stilted.

"It has come to this," Doenitz said. He felt dirty as he watched Himmler disappear through a doorway. "Now we are the worst kind of butchers."

Chapter 16

Berlin, Germany

Berlin was destroyed. Buildings were nothing more than tombstones of blackened rubble, and smoke hung over the capital like a veil of death. The city stank of ruin. The streets were crowded with wreckage, leaving barely enough room for Kern's driver to maneuver between streams of refugees. They walked past Kern's window, heads down, defeated, pushing baby carriages and carts piled high with their belongings. Children walked beside them, their innocent faces streaked with dirt, haunted eyes searching for the life they once knew. A little blond girl, her thin arm locked in an older man's grip, her grandfather by his age, stared at Kern through the car window. Her hair was matted with filth, her thin face smudged with grime, except for tracks washed clean by her tears. Kern saw the look in her eyes. He recognized it. He had seen it before when sailors who were little more than boys looked at him after their comrades were sewn up in canvas bags and dropped into the sea. Why? Why did this have to happen? He had no answer to give them. To say that it was war was trite.

To mention duty and honor when the waves swallowed the lifeless bodies seemed pathetic. And if this

sounded so to men, what did you say to little girls
standing at piles of rubble that used to be their lives?
Kern looked away from the child, and closed his eyes.
Let the politicians tell the people why. He was too
tired to think of it anymore.

The car soon made its way out of Berlin into the
country. It was almost normal here. They passed
farms where cattle grazed quietly in fields as yet un-
scarred by bomb craters. The only time that the war
intruded was when the car had to pull off the road
and into a patch of woods as enemy fighters roared
overhead. Kern stood next to the car, watching them
through the lace of branches. They meandered about
the sky, unchallenged. Hawks searching the roads for
prey. Finally they tired of the game and roared away.
When the sound of their engines had faded, Kern ordered, "Let's go."

The car pulled into the Koralle about midnight,
and Kern was immediately shown into Godt's office.
He was tired, and the sight of the immaculately
dressed staff officers in pristine furnishings angered
him. He wished for an instant that they had seen the
little girl.

He found a large chair and sat, waiting.

"Kapitaenleutnant Kern?"

Kern awoke to see Godt standing before him.

"My apologies, Vice Admiral," he said, rising. "I fell
asleep."

Godt smiled but he looked weary, haggard. The big
man had lost weight. "Think nothing of it, Kapitaenleutnant. I'm sure that you are tired after your
journey. Did you have much difficulty?"

"Some, Herr Vice Admiral." Kern had made the
journey aboard E-boat and floatplane. They traveled
at night, all the time watching the skies for the enemy.

They raced for Germany like a frightened rabbit races for the sanctuary of its warren.

"Yes," Godt conceded, as if such a journey could contain little else. "The grand admiral will be with us shortly. He is very pleased with what you have been able to accomplish thus far. He realizes that it has not been without trial."

"Yes," Kern said.

"Would you like some tea?" Godt asked. "We can still provide you with tea here at Koralle."

"Yes, please," Kern said. He watched as Godt called for tea. It was delivered a few minutes later. It immediately refreshed Kern.

"How is the spirit of your men?"

"Well, Vice Admiral," Kern replied.

"Sufficiently trained, I presume?"

"Not as well as I would like, Vice Admiral." Kern took a sip of tea and set the cup on the saucer. "The crews were inexperienced, except for mine, of course. I could not train them as I wished. I divided my crew between the other two boats."

A troubled look crossed Godt's face. "Divided?"

"I kept a third. Each of the other boats got a third. My men are more experienced, better disciplined." Kern watched the dark liquid swirl in the delicate cup. "I felt it my only course of action."

"Of course," Godt said quietly.

But I loathe myself for destroying my crew, Kern thought. *Do you understand that, Vice Admiral? It was a hateful decision, and my men visit me each night and with their eyes they accuse me of murdering them. Is this true guilt? Is this how a man feels after betraying another?*

"Before the grand admiral arrives," the vice admiral said, breaking into Kern's thoughts, "you should know that he has been unable to convince the fuehrer to release Hartmann. Is he still at Evanger?"

"Yes," Kern said. "Oberst Langsdorff takes a perverse pleasure in keeping him under my nose. I was able to visit him; I took him some food and some books. He is in as good a spirit as can be expected, but I fear for his safety once we set sail. If we are unable to free him . . ."

"I understand."

"His arrest has nothing to do with treason."

"Yes," Godt said. "I read your report. You struck Oberst Langsdorff."

"That is why he arrested Teddy Hartmann. Hartmann has no more interest in politics than you or I. He is a loyal Kriegsmarine officer. I would trust my life to him. Langsdorff could not get to me, so he arrested Hartmann."

"So you see how the SS works," Doenitz said, closing the door behind him.

Kern snapped to attention.

"Be at ease, Kern. That is how Himmler and his men are," the grand admiral continued, pouring himself some tea from the setting on the desk. "They are cowards. They entertain themselves with vast ceremonies and the reichsfuehrer presents them silver daggers or some nonsense like that. He has convinced Hitler that they are a knightly order, Teutonic warriors pledged to serve the fuehrer and Germany. I have seen their work, Kern. They are the knights of the devil." When he had prepared his tea, he looked at the kapitaenleutnant. "All will be well for Germany when this is behind us."

Doenitz was uncharacteristically subdued, nearly to the point of lethargy. Dark circles ringed his eyes, and he moved slowly. Kern thought that the Lion looked old.

"Yes, Grand Admiral," Kern said.

"How is the SS treating you?"

"They keep to themselves now, Herr Grand Admiral," Kern said. "They man the antiaircraft guns and run drills. They guard the camp, but they have nothing to do with my men and we have nothing to do with them."

"Hartmann?"

Kern thought for a moment before answering.

"Well?"

"Hartmann is concerned, Herr Admiral," Kern said. "He thinks that if he is not released before we sail, he will never be released."

"He is perceptive. Or prophetic, I don't know which," Doenitz said. "And you, Kapitaenleutnant Kern, are you a prophet? Can you see what will become of you and your men?"

"Yawolh, Herr Grand Admiral. My men are ready. My boats are ready. All we need is your order."

"My order," Doenitz repeated grimly. "You know the likelihood of your returning is slim?"

"Yes, sir."

"You're aware of the risks that you must take before you get anywhere near your target?"

"Yes, Herr Grand Admiral," Kern said firmly. *Get on with it! Do you think I'm a child? Do you think that I haven't been out there before? I know the risks. Give me the order and send me away from this madness.*

"Good," Doenitz said. "I should hate to send someone on a mission like this who did not have conviction. Those rockets are ready then?"

"Yawolh, Grand Admiral. We have made both land and submerged dry-firing drills. We can surface and deploy the rockets into firing position manually in five minutes. We can submerge and fire the rockets electronically in three minutes."

"Eh, well, Godt assures me that the White Coats have that particular situation well in hand," Doenitz said. He tapped the table with his fingers, in thought. "I have sent Oberleutnant Seeckt on ahead. You know Seeckt?"

Kern remembered a slim autocratic man whose tailored uniforms never showed a spot of grease or smelled of mildew. He was very precise, a good oberleutnant.

"U-1027?" Kern asked.

"Yes," Doenitz said. "How he gets that big Milch Cow about without being sunk is beyond me. You will rendezvous with him so that he may inform us, specifically the fuehrer, of your progress. The rendezvous point is included with your sailing orders. This is critical, Kern. Firstly, you must meet Seeckt. Secondly, you must get to your launch point. You understand? It is imperative that you arrive on station and launch your attack."

Why involve Seeckt? Why not simply order me to surface and contact Goliath—the Kriegsmarine radio network? Was he the only one who could see this? Maybe the madness had eaten into the Lion's brain.

"Yes, Herr Grand Admiral," Kern said. The grand admiral had sent Seeckt and his men to their destruction. The supply U-boats were twice as big as the Type VIIs. They did not dive well, or maneuver worth a damn, and they were much easier for Allied planes to spot when they were on the surface.

Doenitz hesitated and then spoke. "Guenter, there is something else. Something that I was not aware of until just recently. It concerns the warheads."

Kern looked at Godt for a hint of what the grand admiral was going to say, but the big man dropped his head.

Doenitz finished off his tea and set the cup on the table. "The fuehrer, apparently, feels that the missiles would be more . . . effective, if the standard warheads were replaced."

"Replaced, Herr Grand Admiral?"

Doenitz looked at Kern and replied: "With a biological substance, Guenter."

"Anthrax, Kern," Godt said softly. "Reichsfuehrer Himmler has convinced the fuehrer that we should launch a biological attack against Liverpool."

Kern felt his heart hammering in his chest. His mouth was dry and suddenly he was alone, so terribly alone—there was no one to call upon. Not Godt. Not Doenitz. Not his long-dead friends. It could not be—what they were saying, what they contemplated could not be. Langsdorff had known about this abomination.

"I am not familiar . . ." Kern said in a voice that was barely audible.

"You needn't concern yourself with that, Kern," Godt said.

"Yes," Kern said quickly. "I would like to know, Admiral."

"It is an airborne substance, Kern," Doenitz said. "I don't know exactly how it works. I don't want to. It is to be inhaled by English and, hopefully, American soldiers. I am told that it is nearly always fatal. Death is excruciating."

Kern listened carefully to Doenitz. He could tell by the grand admiral's tone that he was deeply troubled but that meant nothing to Kern. Somehow, Doenitz and Godt would be clear of this while his hands would be forever filthy.

"Why are we doing this, Grand Admiral?" Kern asked.

Doenitz said, "There is nothing left for us to do. The Fatherland is dying, one soldier—one sailor at a time. Her cities are in ruin. Women and children suffer most horribly. Buried under rumble—burned alive—driven mad by it all. It is war. A new type of war. One that I cannot condone." Doenitz straightened and his voice became firm. "But I am not asked to condone it, Kern. I am ordered to do my duty. Now I am ordering you to do yours. Take your boats to their destination and make war on the enemy."

There was a deep silence in the room. Kern knew what was expected of him, but he could not bring himself to speak or to move. To make war on soldiers or sailors was one thing—now this disease that he was to carry to the enemy, this filth would be unleashed on civilians as well. Civilians die in war, but somehow what he was asked to do—what Doenitz had ordered him to do—made him feel sick inside as if the last vestige of civility was ripped from him. The last wooden sword in Germany's arsenal, Otto had said.

"Kern?" Doenitz said. "If you are incapable of completing your mission, tell me. I will replace you. I cannot have someone who is not committed to the mission lead it. Shall I replace you, Guenter?"

"Nein, Herr Grand Admiral," Kern said, stiffening to attention. "I will do as ordered. I can sail within twenty-four hours of returning to Evanger, Herr Grand Admiral."

"Twenty-four hours," Doenitz said. "That should satisfy the fuehrer, Godt. That means that with luck we will have our boats stationed off the coast of England within four days." He added, "With luck."

The kapitaenleutnant said nothing in reply.

"We German submariners make our own luck, don't we, Kern?" the grand admiral said, but the words were hollow. He picked up the envelope and held it out to Kern. "Your orders are specific. They give you the target and sailing instructions. Signal me when you leave Evanger. Otherwise, I do not expect to hear directly from you. You will not break radio silence for any reason, is that understood? You must rendezvous with U-1027 at coordinates detailed in your orders. They will inform me of your progress, or your failure to appear. With three boats, we can hope that at least two of you reach your destination. But I am counting on all three, Kern. Don't disappoint me. You must reach your destination and launch your attack. You came through Berlin?"

"Yawohl, Herr Grand Admiral," Kern said, taking the packet.

"You saw how things are. We are near the end. If your attack succeeds, we may be able to convince the Allies that we have hundreds of these rocket-carrying submarines capable of leveling English cities. It is a gamble, Kern, but a gamble that we must take. You must succeed. Do you understand me? Do not fail. All of Germany is counting on you."

"Yes, sir."

"What torpedoes do you carry?"

"Gnats, sir. Six."

"Escort killers? Good, Kern. I'm afraid you won't get a chance to go after tankers this time. Perhaps next time. Well, there are your orders. You sail in twenty-four hours. Any questions?"

Kern licked his lips. "Hartmann, sir."

"Hartmann. I'm afraid that there's nothing I can do for him. I've tried. The fuehrer is immovable. Himmler has him convinced that half of Germany was in on the plot. Hartmann has the bad luck to be the nephew of some petty official who looked suspicious."

"Yes, sir," Kern said. "Then I am left to my own devices?"

The grand admiral's eyebrow arched slightly, trying to read Kern's meaning. "Any questions?"

"I have no other questions, sir," Kern said.

"Then you are dismissed, Kapitaenleutnant Kern," Doenitz said. "Godspeed."

Godt watched Kern leave and then turned to Doenitz. The grand admiral shook his head.

"I don't know if he will succeed, Godt. That's your question, isn't it? Can he get those three whales out of Norway without getting killed? I don't know. No one knows but God."

"Yes, sir."

Doenitz exploded. "Say something, can't you? Don't just agree with me."

"I think," Godt said, "that we have sent Guenter the Silent on a hopeless mission. I think that no matter what, it will do no good. I am also ashamed of my role in this. I wonder if God will forgive us."

"We do not answer to God. Only to the fuehrer and the German people."

"Yes, Grand Admiral."

Doenitz walked to the large board on the wall and jerked the curtains back. Tiny black flags littered its surface. "Don't talk to me about hopeless missions. One must always have hope. Kern knows what he is up against. He knows what the stakes are. I told you, it is a gamble. We throw the die. How they land, no one knows. So it is luck after all. We send our young men out with nothing more than their own skills and a teacup full of luck. When the luck has run out, one hopes that their skills can save them."

"Yes, sir," Godt said.

Doenitz shook his head, defeated. "I know. I know, Godt. I can only pray that our young friend there can truly make his own luck and that God takes pity on Germany. Now I will get some sleep and then I will go and tell the fuehrer that his great plan is under way. He will be ecstatic, no doubt. He will dance about and belittle Goering and Model because the air force and the army can not do as he asks. He will see only what he wishes to see: a vast armada of U-boats sailing toward victory. God help our German submariners, Vice Admiral. God help Guenter Kern."

Chapter 17

Evanger, Norway

Kapitaenleutnant Guenter Kern waited as his officers seated themselves at the table in the Wreck's wardroom. Frick was the last in, of course, wiping the grease from his hands. Leutnant Mend, the navigation officer, took his place next to Leutnant Engle, the radio officer. The two had become fast friends over their length of tour about Kern's boat. They were both quiet, very competent, and veterans of the U-boat wars. Kern wondered how they would view his plan.

"Make sure that door is shut tight, Frick," Kern ordered. He waited until the chief engineer took his place before he began.

"We have our sailing orders," Kern said. He had decided not to tell them about the new payload. He was still not reconciled to it himself.

"And Leutnant Hartmann?" Frick asked.

"There's nothing that Headquarters can do. Doenitz was definite on that."

"The bastards," Frick said. "I should have ordered our guns to open up on the lot of them."

"I'n d that you didn't, Frick," Kern said. "I was standing directly in front of them."

The group gave the comment a muffled laugh. It seemed out of place—they had had so little to laugh about lately. Kern began speaking.

"We sail in twelve hours." He saw the men tense, their excitement barely contained. They were ready. They were tired of Evanger and of cloud-bound Norway and constant training and tired of the SS. They had become irritable and sullen and Kern knew that the only remedy was to get out of this hell and go to sea. "Report," he said.

The officers, beginning with Frick, quickly went over U-3535's condition.

"Your rockets, Frick?" Kern asked.

"Ready, Kaleu," the chief engineer said quickly. Hartmann, as torpedo and gunnery officer, should have reported on the weapons' readiness. Kern missed him.

"Good," Kern said. "I'll meet with Gorlitz and Hickman immediately after we're done. Now, what I have to say to you, remains with you. It concerns no one else. Understood?"

The officers nodded expectantly.

"I don't intend to leave my executive officer at the mercy of Langsdorff and his men. When we go, Teddy Hartmann goes with us. But I can't do it alone. If you agree to help me, you ought to know what you're in for."

Frick was the first to speak. "That doesn't make any difference, sir."

"It will if we're caught," Kern said. "It could mean prison, maybe even execution."

"We can't leave Leutnant Hartmann here, sir," Mend said.

"No, sir," Engle agreed. "I think that to leave Leutnant Hartmann here is to condemn him to death."

"He's right, Kaleu," Frick said. "I couldn't live with myself if we left him."

"All right," Kern said. "This is what I have planned."

It took little more than an hour to reveal what he intended to do. The others listened closely, saying nothing until he had finished. Then they asked questions, and made suggestions, both carefully considered.

"There is something else for us to consider," Kern said. "Something we had better think carefully about. When we return." The question of returning to Germany after the mission was one that Kern had considered from the beginning. He knew when he said it that it was truly a question of if, and not when. He had been at war long enough to know that nothing was certain. For that reason, he said, "When we return to Germany after the mission, we could face court-martial."

"Kaleu," Frick said. The others let him speak. "We know what you're saying. It's good of you to tell us what to expect. But Hartmann is one of us. When we go, he goes."

The other two officers nodded their agreement. *I should feel something*, Kern thought. *I should feel pride for these men, or love, or concern, or something. Something. But I feel nothing. Have I become dead inside? But you knew*—he answered his own question—*you knew that these men would not forget their comrade and you knew there was only one thing for them to do, and that they would do it.* Such feelings were not easily defined, and were therefore rarely shared. But they were real, precious, and known, in one form or another by each member of the crew of U-3535. You were ready to give your life for your shipmate, because he was your shipmate, and because too many times he stood with you, side by side, on the Devil's Shovel. Kern understood.

"Let's go then," he said. "We have a lot to do."

SS Corporal Hossbach poured coffee from the battered tin pot into a cracked porcelain cup he had found back in Evanger. Private Amann, sitting on a fallen tree trunk, watched him. It was a cold night, and the coffee's aroma beckoned him.

"Are you going to share that?" Amann asked hopefully.

"Not with you, Amann," Hossbach said, watching the steaming liquid fill the cup by the light of a small fire. "You should learn how to make your rations last, like a good soldier."

"I didn't know that we were going to get stuck out here until the end of the war."

Hossbach set the coffeepot down and picked up the hot cup gingerly. "Stop complaining and listen. That is what a listening post is supposed to do, listen."

"I have been listening," Amann said. "I haven't heard anything but birds and your farts."

"Tommy will come, never fear," the corporal said, blowing across the cup. "But you won't hear him unless you shut up."

Amann stared off into the blackness, toward the calm waters of the fiord. They had been fours days at this listening post, four miles from Evanger. He pulled his greatcoat over his shoulders and watched Hossbach sip his coffee. The man was a pig, but somehow he always managed to find food or wine, or like in one of the houses at Evanger, real coffee. The corporal smiled up at him and smacked his lips in delight. Amann turned his back on him. A pig.

Suddenly, Hossbach stopped drinking.

"What's that?"

Amann threw his greatcoat off and stood, listening. "What?"

"Shut up! Listen," he commanded, setting his coffee cup on the ground and standing.

Amann strained to hear something in the blackness. There! There it was! He turned expectantly to the corporal.

Hossbach shrugged and turned his attention back to the darkness. Finally, he whispered, "It sounds like engines."

Amann listened. It did sound like engines. Far away. He watched as Hossbach made his way to the field telephone. It could be airplanes. A night raid didn't make any sense, but it wasn't Amman's place to question enemy tactics. He watched as Hossbach crouched near the telephone, his head cocked toward the night sky. Airplanes, it had to be airplanes. It was hard to pinpoint the source, the sound came from every direction, bouncing off of the rock-face cliffs and the flat water of the fiord.

It grew distinct now, Amann thought, a low throaty roar. It seemed to come closer, and then remain constant. Hossbach shot Amann a questioning look. The noise was growing dimmer. Amann realized that he could no longer hear it.

"What happened?" he asked Hossbach, his voice breaking the silence.

Hossbach shook his head.

"Whoever they were, they didn't come here," Hossbach said. "I guess someone else is going to catch hell tonight." He settled back on his haunches and glanced at his feet. Damn!"

Amann followed Hossbach's gaze to the ground.

His coffee cup lay on its side, the contents glistening in the light of their campfire. The private turned away, hiding his smile. He silently thanked the distant, unseen aircraft, Tommy or not.

Chapter 18

Evanger, Norway

Langsdorff clapped his hands together and rubbed them heartily. "Ah, how I envy you," he said to Kern, as they stood on the rise above the three U-boats. The crews were busy loading the last of the supplies and checking the RGTs. The rockets sat awkwardly atop their rails on the backs of the big boats. Kern was offended by the way that they destroyed the sleek lines of the U-boats. They should not be forced to undergo this injustice before they even had a chance to prove themselves against the enemy, Kern thought. These were U-boats; let them behave as U-boats. He finally realized what Langsdorff had said.

"Envy?"

"Yes!" the SS oberst said. "You are given a great opportunity, Kapitaenleutnant Kern. Think of it; the first time that a missile attack was delivered against any enemy by submarine. And you shall sail"—he glanced at his wristwatch—"in less than four hours. A voyage of destiny—a journey of the first magnitude. This is exciting."

"Exciting," Kern said. "Yes."

"You know, Kapitaenleutnant Kern," Langsdorff said. "Such an undertaking will be closely watched by a number of high-ranking officials. I'm sure the fuehrer himself is deeply interested in this mission, since it is he who conceived it. The opportunities that lie before us are endless."

"Opportunities?" Kern said. Now it was "us." He and Langsdorff were friends again, comrades on a vital mission for the Fatherland.

"Yes, yes," the oberst said. "Careers are made in this manner, Kern. Don't you see it, man? Come now, Kern. I know we've had some difficulties in the past, but let us put that behind us. We have to think of the future, Kern. The future! There will be more than enough glory for both of us. That's what you have to think of, Kern. Not those differences. In the vast scheme of things, such clashes mean nothing. They are nothing. Don't tell me that you haven't thought about the possibilities for your career, Kapitaenleutnant? That can't be possible. You must have thought about the outcome of this mission?"

Kern smiled thinly at Langsdorff. "I've thought of the outcome. Quite a bit, in fact. It will certainly affect my career."

"Affect your career! Come, Kern. You're much too modest."

Kern watched some men move quickly from the Wreck down the spindly gangplank and onto one of the boats. They were loading what few luxuries that they could beg from the Wreck's crew. Candy perhaps, a few canned goods, cigarettes—things that would be crammed between pipes and over bunks. The voyage would not be long, but there was always the unexpected. Safer to carry too much than find yourself wanting.

"You knew about the new warheads?" Kern asked.

206 Steven M. Wilson

"Yes," Langsdorff said matter-of-factly. He did not bother looking at Kern. "What of it?"

"I am told those that fall to it will suffer a horrible death."

"I was told that as well. I was told that it will be most effective. Death is death, Kern. Does it matter how the enemy dies?" Langsdorff said.

Kern considered the question. "No," he said. "I suppose not."

"No, indeed," Langsdorff said. "Consider instead what it means to the Fatherland no matter how distasteful you find it personally. We all have those feelings at some point. Not every order issued is warranted or even well thought out, but every order must be accepted. You don't think that I agree with everything that I am told, do you?"

"No," Kern said.

"No, of course not. But an order is an order and I comply promptly, without hesitation, knowing full well that what I do I do for the fuehrer and Germany."

"I never doubted that for an instant," the kapitaenleutnant said. "I must see to my boats. Please excuse me, Oberst Langsdorff."

"Yes, yes," Langsdorff said. "See to your boats. We should have had a band for you, Kern. Unfortunately that is one of many luxuries denied us in Evanger. Perhaps a modest ceremony of some kind to send you off."

A tiny smile crept across Kern's face. "Perhaps we can manage a memorable sendoff," he said to Langsdorff. "I'll see about it." He walked down the hill toward his boats.

Langsdorff watched as the setting sun colored the tops of the mountains across the fiord. It would work, he told himself. The U-boats would sail right under

Tommy's nose! Himmler would be pleased, and the reichsfuehrer always rewards those who please him. Langsdorff crossed his arms in anticipation. *The Knights Cross of the Iron Cross will be mine. Himmler will probably bestow it on me.* He pictured the ceremony in his mind: standing at attention before Himmler and the fuehrer, surrounded by SS officers, the thunder of kettledrums as Himmler approached and slipped the ribboned medal over his head. It was his! He knew it! It didn't matter if Kern returned. Better that he didn't; no use complicating things. Langsdorff rubbed his jaw with a gloved hand. *Besides, he struck me. I won't forget that.* He watched as the crews swarmed over the boats, the RGTs nearly hidden in the black shadows of the tender.

Langsdorff noticed that the sun's deepening shadows completely swallowed the U-boats. Spot lamps suddenly sparked to life, bathing the boats in a field of somber light. The flashlight beams of the men inspecting the RGTs danced about the U-boats' decks. It would be much better if Kern did not return. Much better.

Frick listened patiently to Spengler and Mueller, wondering how the White Coats managed to feed and clothe themselves without assistance.

"The bands securing the rails to the deck should be checked periodically," Spengler said, hovering over a large diagram of the RGTs on a makeshift worktable in the rocket shed. "Undue stress might be put on the rails if the bands are not sufficiently tightened. Warping could occur."

"Remind Kapitaenleutnant Kern of this," Mueller said. "Should he take any actions that result in strain on the bands. Remind him that under no circumstances must he dive below two hundred meters. I recommend that he stay well above one hundred meters just to make sure."

"One hundred fifty meters should suffice," Spengler argued. "My calculations prove that the RGTs will survive the pressure of up to 150 meters in depth. I have them here should you wish to see them. Inspect the lift motors frequently—we've tested them many times."

"How about every five minutes?" Frick asked.

Spengler's eyes narrowed in confusion before he realized that it was a joke. He chuckled dryly.

"No. Of course not. They should function perfectly. No need for those hand cranks." He began picking through a pile of papers on the table. "I have the test results on the lift as well."

"No, thanks," Frick said quickly. "Look, we've been all through this. We already know what to do and what not to do."

"You must be sure," Mueller insisted. "These instruments are very fragile. We have overdesigned them. But sometimes complications arise."

"I understand that," Frick said. "Kapitaenleutnant Kern is very pleased with the work that you've done, and he appreciates the time that you've taken with the crews."

"If only we had a few more weeks with the crews—" Spengler said.

"Days," Mueller said.

"Think of how much more we would have accomplished," Spengler continued. "Your men were very attentive, Leutnant Frick, but I'm afraid much of what we told them was over their heads."

"They looked bored at times," Mueller said.

"Confused," Spengler said.

"Gentlemen!" Frick said in frustration. "We're ready. We're leaving shortly. Just give me the launch manuals and I'll be out of here."

"The launch manuals," Spengler said. "Of course! That's it. We didn't give them the manuals."

"You're absolutely right," Mueller said sheepishly.

Spengler signaled for a technician. "Please go into my office and get the launch manuals for the RGTs. There should be three sets, one for each U-boat." As the technician left, Spengler turned to Frick. "How silly of me to forget something as important as the launch manuals. I don't know what's become of my mind. I really must learn to be more careful about such things."

"We seldom forget anything," Mueller said. "But things have been frantic. And that unfortunate shooting."

"Indeed," Spengler agreed.

The technician returned with a stricken look on his face. "They aren't there," he said.

"Not there?" Spengler repeated, horrified. "But that's impossible."

"Professor Spengler . . ." Mueller began thoughtfully.

"We must conduct a search immediately," Spengler ordered the technician. "We must have the launch manuals."

"They have them!" Mueller said. "Don't you recall? We gave them to Leutnant Frick two days ago. I did, didn't I, Leutnant Frick? I'm sure of it."

Spengler and Mueller looked at Frick. The chief engineer snapped his fingers.

"You're right! You gave them to me two days ago. How silly of me to forget. I must learn to be careful."

Frick grasped each scientist's hand in turn. "Professor Spengler, Professor Mueller, thank you, gentlemen. Thank you for everything. We'll take care with your rockets. Never fear. Thank you again." He turned abruptly and left.

"What an extraordinary man," Spengler said. "I hope he knows what he's doing."

"Indeed," Mueller agreed.

Chief Petty Officer Kerrl leaned against the rocket shed, drawing on a cigarette, when the door opened quickly and Frick appeared. Kerrl watched Frick close the door.

"Well?" Frick said.

"All set," Kerrl said. "When the stern ropes are cast off: ka-boom."

"You're sure that it will work?" Frick questioned him.

Kerrl looked hurt. "Sure? What the hell kind of question is that to ask an arsonist?"

"You're not an arsonist," Frick reminded him. "You're a U-boatman, and it had better work. For Mr. Hartmann's sake. You'd better get to the boat."

Chapter 19

Evanger, Norway

Kapitaenleutnant Kern stood in the port watch station on the bridge of U-3535, waiting. Below him, Leutnant Mend stood ready at the surface control station in the forward part of the conning tower. He and one of Frick's mechanics would oversee the rudder station, the repeater compass, two engine telegraphs, two revolution indicators, and the rudder indicator. Kern knew that Mend would respond to his orders without hesitation. That was especially important tonight. Tonight they left on the most important mission that they had undertaken. And tonight they staged a jailbreak.

"How are you down there, Mend?" Kern called out.

"Very well, sir."

Kern nodded and looked over U-3712's bulk to U-3719. He could just make out Hickman's torso above the bridge recess. He would lead them, casting off first and moving out into the fiord. Gorlitz would follow at a safe distance, and then U-3535.

Kern had given Hickman specific orders as to speed and course once the boats were under way, and to both officers he reaffirmed: "No radio contact unless it's absolutely necessary. Do you understand that?

Tommy can locate us from our radio chatter, so you are not to break radio silence unless it is an emergency."

"But, sir," Gorlitz had said. "How are we to keep in touch once we reach the open sea?"

"You each have the course and time and point of rendezvous with the Milchkuh. If we become separated going across, and that is likelihood, we can meet there. Failing that, you have the target and launch location in your sealed orders. They specify the date and time at which we are to arrive at the launch locations. You must adhere to that schedule regardless of what happens on the way across. Remember that. Everything you need to know to complete your mission is in your orders."

"Not to be opened until under way," Hickman had said belligerently.

"As so ordered," Kern had reminded him. "Any other questions? No? Good. Hickman, you will cast off when I give the order. Gorlitz, allow three boat lengths, and then cast off. I will bring up the tail. Let me remind you that the importance of this mission cannot be overstated. Germany is counting on us to succeed. It will be difficult, and extremely dangerous, but our training has gone well, and I am convinced of our success."

Gorlitz seemed to brighten a bit. Hickman had said nothing.

Kern closed the meeting. "All right, if there's nothing else, you have your orders."

Now as he stood on the bridge of U-3535, Kern wondered what kind of a chance they really had. Between the Tommies and the Americans, there would probably be a hundred ships hunting each U-boat, never mind the aircraft. U-boat luck, Kern reminded himself, U-boatmen make their own luck. He looked at his watch, turning the face slightly to read the luminescent dial. Ten minutes. He hoped Frick and Engle were where they were supposed to be—making a U-boatman's luck for Hartmann.

Leutnant Engle joined Frick behind a fallen tree at the edge of the forest. The houses scattered before them were silent, the only signs of life a few lights that slit blackout curtains. An SS sentry walked his post without enthusiasm.

"The boat's ready," he said. "Anything going on at Hartmann's hut?"

Frick smiled to himself. That was how Hartmann himself had described the building just to the left, in which he was confined. "My little hut . . ." was his wry description of the small house in which he was kept, guarded only by a single SS trooper.

"Nothing," Frick said. "That soldier looks like he's ready to doze off. What time do you have?"

"Twenty after," Engle said. "Just a few minutes more."

Kern saw movement on U-3719. Men were casting off lines. He looked at his watch. Right on time. He pulled the cover off the voice tube and whistled into it. A muffled whistle answered him.

"Ready to get under way," he called down.

"Permission to report," Kerrl called back. "All hands present or accounted for. Engine room ready, upper and lower decks cleared for departure."

"Right," Kern said. He looked toward the bow, and then astern. His men were ready at their lines. He

watched as U-3719 slid slowly out into the fiord. Even
with Hickman at the helm the big boat looked dangerous. He caught a glimpse of the RGT astern of the
boat's conning tower. What could they do if his boats
were loaded with torpedoes instead of having those
monstrosities strapped to their backs? He shook the
thought from his head. There was no time for that.

U-3719 cleared the camouflage netting and sailed
out under the stars, her black wake rolling gently
against the hulls of the other boats and the Wreck.
The water slapped at the boats, beckoning them to
follow.

Kern heard Gorlitz give the order to let go the
lines. The engines of U-3712 began to throb as the
water swirled into eddies at her stern. The big screws
were biting into the waters of the fiord, easing the
boat out into the night, accompanied by the muffled
healthy roar of her diesel engines.

She was like a beast upon the water, Kern thought,
a strange, powerful, enormous beast that had no
equal in the seas.

They would be leaving soon, leaving Langsdorff
and his SS, leaving the politics of high command,
leaving this tattered little village of Evanger and the
countless hours of drill. Make-believe war, his veteran
crew named it derisively when they grew tired of the
drills. Pretend that Tommy is overhead; imagine that
there's a destroyer bearing down on you. This after
hundreds of drills that proved they were more than
ready to meet the enemy. They were ready, Kern
knew, he hoped the kapitaens and the crews of the
other two boats were. *The pride that I feel in my men,*
Kern thought, *I can not transfer to Hickman and Gorlitz.*
He thought of his men, those he had sent to Gorlitz
and Hickman. His men.

He had come to them after serving six months as an exec under that madman Popp. Then they were a new crew and U-686 was a new boat, and they came together uncertainly, like strangers on a dance floor. Kern was half convinced that the broad yellow band that was painted around U-686's conning tower was the Kriegsmarine's way of telling everyone to stay out of their way; they aren't really U-boatmen yet.

Kern had watched his crew, learned from them, and eventually unfamiliar faces became men. Each day had revealed more: Frick was a highly competent engineer whose ability with women soon became legendary; Hartmann was a good-natured officer, protective of his men; Kerrl said little and looked like a small-town farmer; and the others grew to be known by Kern as well. A bond had grown among them, binding them. The drills became a rhythm of sorts, a rhythm of actions. It came out of the constant training, diving, surfacing, torpedo, navigation, gunnery; each with its carefully crafted procedures—each man assigned, each man doing what had to be done, each, eventually, doing it well. From this had come a mutual trust, and the trust was cemented by combat.

They are truly my brothers, Kern had realized one day.

In front of him the curling waters of her wake followed U-3712 as she sailed out into the fiord. There was nothing else to mark where she had been—the waters of the fiord filled in her existence.

It was time to get under way.

Kern turned and ordered the deckhands, "Let go aft! Haul in the stern line!" He bent to the speaking tube. "Hard a-port. Starboard engine ahead one-third." He thrilled as the deck trembled beneath his feet the moment the boat's diesel engaged. He watched as the hull put some distance between itself and the Wreck. "Haul in the bow line!" he ordered.

The crew quickly complied, stored the line in its forward compartment, and waited expectantly for orders. If everything went as it should, the only order they would receive was to go below.

Kern gave the order to bring her clear of the Wreck and to engage the port engine. U-3535 responded beautifully. The excitement built in him as he glanced at his watch. He looked astern. Langsdorff had his men drawn up on the hill, in honor of their departure. They were a brown smudge on the beach. "Lookouts up!" Kern called down into the conning tower and stepped to one side. A seaman joined him in the cramped space of the port watch station, and two seamen appeared in the starboard watch station. There was very little room in these small spaces, much less than on the older boats. But then there would be; the Type XXIs were designed to remain underwater. He glanced at his watch. Any moment now.

Engle nodded to Frick. They both stood quietly. Suddenly, from the far side of the camp came a tremendous boom and a cloud of flame.

"Well, I'll be damned. Kerrl's bomb worked after all," Frick said.

The sentry in front of Hartmann's hut stopped and watched the ball of flame roll above the buildings and turn into black smoke. The rocket shed began to burn furiously.

Engle tapped Frick on the arm. "Let's go."

They moved out quickly, rapidly covering the distance to the sentry. The soldier turned to see Frick's fist coming straight for his nose.

* * *

Langsdorff ducked instinctively when the bomb went off. Somebody called, "Air raid!" and the oberst shouted: "To your posts! Sound the alarm!"

Men bounced off one another as the formation scattered. Langsdorff listened carefully through the shouts of his men. He heard no aircraft; there were no other explosions. Suddenly the two scientists were at his side.

"It's the rocket shed!" Spengler shouted. "It's on fire!"

"Did you get everything out?" Langsdorff asked. "Is there anything left inside?"

"No!" Mueller said as the air raid siren began to wail. "I mean there is nothing left inside." He grabbed Langsdorff's sleeve. "Where shall we go? Is there a shelter for us?"

"Let go of me, you imbecile! Go to one of the slit trenches." Suddenly one of the flak towers began firing, sending tracers flashing into the air.

Engle glanced up at the tracers and Frick bound and gagged the guard.

"They're shooting at ducks," he said as Frick produced the keys to the guardhouse.

"Here they are!" He held them up triumphantly. Engle snatched them from his hand and quickly unlocked the padlock holding the door beam in placed.

"Teddy?" he called out as loudly as he dared. "Wake up! It's time to leave."

Hartmann's face appeared at the small window in the door.

"What the hell are you doing here?" he asked. "What's going on? Is it an air raid?"

Frick darted to the edge of the building and kept watch as Engle fumbled with the beam.

"It's a rescue!" Engle said as he threw open the door. "Come!"

Hartmann stepped out tentatively and looked around. His face broke into a smile.

"It's good to see you, Leutnant Engle," he said, taking Engle's hand in his.

"It's good to see you, Exec," Engle said.

Frick joined them. "I'm sure that we're all very pleased, but now it's time to go see the Kaleu."

"Right!" Engle said. "Come on."

Langsdorff stood in front of the burning shed and his men tried to put out the fire with buckets of dirt. They had no firefighting equipment. He stood by, helplessly, as a mass of roaring flames consumed the building. The two scientists stood next to him.

"I'm certainly glad that there was nothing of consequence in the building," Spengler said.

"We're fortunate to have had everything packed on the trucks for transport," Mueller said.

Langsdorff ignored both of them. Hauptmann Lossow approached in the glare of the flames and saluted.

"They thought they saw an aircraft," he said to Langsdorff, referring to the flak tower's outburst.

"This is sabotage. I know it."

"Well," Lossow said, watching the building burn, "they didn't get anything. The building was empty."

"Who would blow up an empty building? Who knew it was empty?"

Lossow shrugged helplessly. Suddenly his eyes grew wide in understanding. He understood the moment that Oberst Langsdorff did.

"Sergeant!" Langsdorff shouted. "Bring a squad of men! Follow me! Now!"

"Come on, Exec!" Frick said, leading the others through the tangle of underbrush. "Speed up!"

"I'm going as fast as I can," Hartmann said.

"We've got five minutes to get to the boat and row out to meet the Kaleu," the chief engineer said.

Engle, at the rear, stopped and looked back toward the village. "Wait! Wait!"

The three remained frozen in the darkness, listening.

He turned back to them. "They're on to us! I heard them shouting!"

"Come on!" Frick said. They began to run as quickly as they could in the darkness, dodging broken limbs and piles of brush, climbing over fallen trees. Frick ran as fast as he could, knowing the others would match his pace. He saw the boulder jutting out of the ground. It marked where they were to turn and head straight for the fiord. "Follow me," he called back to his two companions. "Just a few minutes more." He offered a quick prayer to the Fellow Upstairs. He thought briefly about giving up women in a trade for a safe escape, but he quickly discounted that.

Langsdorff turned to Lossow, as Hartmann's sentry was untied. "Send to Kern immediately that he is to return to base. Tell him that if he does not do so, he shall be considered a criminal in flight and dealt with accordingly."

The sentry's gag was finally removed and he forced himself into attention in front of Langsdorff. The sergeant stood next to him, steadying the soldier.

"Well?" Langsdorff said.

"Several men attacked me, Herr Oberst. They released the prisoner."

"Which way did they go?"

"That way, Herr Oberst." The sentry pointed. "Through the forest."

"Sergeant, place this man under arrest," Langsdorff ordered, jerking his pistol from the holster. "Have your men follow me. Shoot to kill."

"Yawohl, Herr Oberst!"

Langsdorff waved his men on. "Follow me!"

Frick heard Engle cry out. He stopped and turned. Hartmann stopped at his side, panting.

"Engle? Are you all right?"

The leutnant's form rose off of the forest floor. He was hobbling. "Stay here," Frick ordered Hartmann.

"Don't worry," Hartmann gasped between gulps of air. "I can't move another step."

Frick made his way back to Engle, who was limping painfully. The leutnant waved him off. "Never mind me! Keep going."

Frick threw Engle's arm over his shoulder and, wrapping his arm around the leutnant's waist, said, "Don't be a hero." Using the engineer for support, Engle hobbled forward painfully, trying to keep his weight off of his injured leg.

"Keep going, Teddy," he called to the exec. "Just head straight."

Hartmann nodded and did as he was told, but he slowed his pace to match that of the other two. He heard a shout behind him. The SS was gaining.

"Leave me," Engle ordered Frick.

"With all due respect," Frick said, pulling him along, "shut up."

"I can see it!" Hartmann cried. "The fiord. Up there!"

"Keep going," Frick said. "Come on, Leutnant. We're almost there."

They kept moving as fast as they could, the sound of their pursuers growing louder. Frick could feel the leutnant's sweat through his uniform. He knew the man's pain was excruciating. Suddenly, they were there, on the rocky shore of the fiord, facing the vast, black expanse of water. Hartmann was already searching for the boat. He turned to Frick in alarm.

"Where is it?"

The engineer gently lowered Engle to a fallen log and looked around quickly. "This is it. This is the spot. It has to be around here some place."

"No," Engle gasped. "It's about twenty feet down that way. We're just above it."

Frick and Hartmann ran in the direction that Engle motioned. They found the boat, an upturned skiff, exactly where Engle said it was.

The engineer looked up the fiord. There was no moon and a thin layer of clouds dimmed the stars. Light was denied him. "I don't see the kaleu yet. Let's get it launched, and you row it down towards Engle. I'll get him up and load him in the boat."

They quickly turned the skiff over, threw in the oars, and pulled it into the frigid water. Hartmann jumped in and fit the oars in the oarlocks. Frick splashed back ashore and ran down to Engle.

"Christ, Frick," the leutnant said, gritting his teeth against the pain. "They're almost here."

Frick pulled Engle to his feet. "Here's Hartmann and the boat, Engle. Come on. Just a few feet more."

Engle cried out in pain as he stood, and almost tumbled out of Frick's arms. He looped his arm over the engineer's shoulder and nodded. They made their way down to the water's edge and into the fiord. Hartmann rowed up to meet them. Carefully, Frick lowered Engle into the skiff. He heard shouts and glanced up. He saw the flashlight beams searching through the gloom. They weren't going to make it.

The engineer hoisted himself into the boat and quickly grabbed the oars.

"Row!" he shouted, as his oars bit into the water. He and Hartmann pulled in unison, each stroke taking them farther from shore, farther from capture. Engle was twisted around in the stern, watching the shore.

"There they are," he said to his companions.

Frick looked up to see a dozen or so soldiers, in the soft glare thrown off by the lights, fill the tiny beach. Several flashlight beams searched the water and fell on them. The engineer squinted as a beam crossed his face.

"Stop!"

Frick recognized the voice. It was Langsdorff.

"Stop or I will order you shot!"

A single shot rang out and a bullet whined next to them.

"We'd better stop," Hartmann said. They shipped oars and Frick threw his hand up to shade his eyes from the glare of flashlights.

"What do you want?" the engineer called to the beach.

"You are fugitives from justice. Return to shore immediately or I'll have you executed in your boat."

Frick heard Hartmann say, "He'll have us executed anyway."

"You two could swim for it," Engle said. "The water's cold but you could make it."

"No," Frick said. "Let's go back. Maybe the Lion can get us out of this mess when he hears about it."

"If he doesn't hear about it after the fact," Hartmann said. "All right, Oberst," he shouted into the darkness. "Here we come. Don't shoot."

They turned the skiff around, and slowly began rowing back toward shore.

"When we get there," Frick said, pulling on his oars, "don't anyone say anything to anybody. Those bastards will twist our words around and hang us."

"Did you hear that?" Engle said, straightening.

"What?"

"I thought I heard something," the leutnant said, peering into the darkness.

"It's so damned dark out here I can barely see you two," Frick said.

Langsdorff watched as the rowboat, caught in the beams of the flashlights, slowly rowed toward him.

"When they get here," he ordered a sergeant. "I want them separated. Understood? I don't want them talking to one another."

"Yawohl, Herr Oberst."

Langsdorff watched the backs of the men at the oars, curving and straightening in a continuous rhythm. Now he would have three traitors to show for his troubles instead of one. This should make quite an impression on Himmler.

"Herr Oberst?" his sergeant said, looking past the rowboat. "I think there's something out there.

Suddenly the night exploded with a roar. The tops of the trees behind Langsdorff disintegrated in a blast of splinters as bullets ripped them apart, showering the soldiers with debris. Langsdorff and his men threw themselves to the ground. Langsdorff looked up to see tracers zipping angrily through the darkness. They all appeared to come directly at him. In the staccato flashes of the heavy machine guns, he could make out the partial shape of a U-boat's conning tower.

Suddenly the firing stopped, and silence fell on them. The only sound to disturb the night was the faint rustling of falling branches.

Langsdorff raised his head cautiously. He noticed some of his men still had their flashlights on.

"Turn out those lights!" he hissed angrily. They quickly winked out.

"Oberst Langsdorff?" a voice came out of the darkness. "Where are you going with my men?"

Langsdorff's head came up.

"Kern!"

Kapitaenleutnant Kern raised the speaking trumpet to his mouth. "Frick!" he called through the trumpet. "Turn your boat around and come here." He leaned over and spoke in the voice tube. "Turn on our running lights."

Small lights, green forward and red aft of the conning, snapped on.

"Kern!" he heard Langsdorff shout from the shore. "These men are fugitives. Release them to me or face the consequences."

"On the contrary, Oberst," Kern said through the trumpet. "Release them to me or we will lower our guns a few degrees and commence firing. This time it won't be the trees that suffer." He turned and called down the hatch: "Get some men on deck and give them a hand. Let me know the minute they're aboard."

Oberst Langsdorff stood slowly. The boat with the three men on board floated, barely visible, just twenty feet from him. Rage rushed over him. He could order his men to shoot; there would be little chance of the three surviving at this range. All he had to do was to give the order. He looked at the debris at his feet.

Kern shook his head and called into the speaking tube. "That idiot is taking too long. Give them another burst over their heads."

At either end of the conning tower, the machine-gun turrets blazed into life. Every fourth round was a tracer, arcing through the night. Kern stood with his hands over his ears, bathed in the harsh flash of the guns. The sharp clattering of the guns echoed across the fiord. Kern ordered cease fire. The guns stopped.

"All right! All right!" Langsdorff shouted. "I release those men to you. Nevertheless, I hold you responsible, Kern. There will be a reckoning when you return."

The kapitaenleutnant placed the speaking trumpet to his lips.

"Frick? Proceed to the U-boat. Get a move on. We haven't all night." He waited a few minutes, and heard the sound of the boat bouncing against the hull. The flare of the machine guns had destroyed his night vision.

"They're aboard, Kapitaen," Mend called up to him.

"Very well. Both ahead one-third. Let's catch up with the other two boats," he ordered.

The U-boat's engines throbbed into life as Kern guided her into the middle of the fiord. He ordered two-thirds ahead when he was convinced that he was well clear of the shore, and ordered his lookouts to keep a sharp eye out for the stern lights of the other two boats.

Twelve miles down the fiord, the crews of three Royal Navy Motor Torpedo Boats also kept a sharp lookout.

Lieutenant Beach, RN, felt Yeoman Crossfield close to him on the dark bridge of his tiny boat.

"It was gunfire all right, sir," Crossfield said. "Dutchy heard it too,"

"What the devil are those bloody Germans shooting at here?" Beach said.

"Captain?" Williams called up from the radio station just aft and below the bridge. "V for Victor just reported lights coming down the fiord. Two, he thinks, sir, but he can't tell for sure. Distance appears to be four thousand yards."

"Very good," Beach said. V for Victor was on his right, about fifty yards, and A for Adam was on his left, the same distance. His boat, M for Myrtle, was between them. "Signal to A for Adam, tell them lights approaching. Possibly two vessels. Tell them to hold their position until I give the signal." He leaned over the bridge spray shield and called down to the bow, "All right, chaps, Jerry is coming. Be ready with those flares the minute I give the order." He turned to Crossfield. "Yeoman. See to your torpedoes."

"It's V for Victor again, sir," Williams said. "He says definitely two boats. Two green running lights, about five hundred yards apart, closing."

"Right. All boats, start engines," Beach ordered.

The low roar of the three torpedo boats' engines

filled the darkness, as the strong smell of diesel enveloped them.

"Closing on three thousand yards, sir," Williams said.

"Very good," Beach said. He wanted to wait until the boats were abeam of them before he ordered an attack. Not only would that give them a larger target to shoot for, but also they would be attacking slightly astern of the U-boats, if they were as everyone guessed. He'd seen the photographs. His money was on U-boats hiding under that camouflage. Now all they had to do was catch them under the light of flares and sink them.

"V for Victor again, sir. He thinks they're U-boats running on the surface, closing at approximately eight knots."

"Right, Williams. Ask him how far out from us they will be."

The reply came back in a moment.

"V for Victor estimates two to three thousand yards, sir,"

That was farther than Beach wanted. He wanted to close to within five hundred yards of the boats, fire his flares, launch his torpedoes, and get the hell away. Jerry was staying well out in the fiord, which was to be expected.

"Make to both boats," Beach finally ordered. "Move out one thousand yards, slow ahead, maintain station. Execute now."

The engines of the three boats increased in pitch, and they moved out, nearly invisible in the darkness. At a thousand yards they cut back to dead slow, just keeping enough speed to maintain headway, creeping within attack distance. There they waited as the green lights drew closer. Minutes passed. Beach could see the lights now.

"Stand by," he said to Williams, his eyes on the lights. He watched them coming closer, growing larger. Then he saw them. The red stern lights. The U-boats were abreast of him.

"Flares!" he shouted, and quickly looked away. He heard the dull thud of the launcher, followed by the angry hiss of the flare arching its way into the sky. "Execute attack!" he shouted down to Williams.

Suddenly, there was a distant pop high overhead and the fiord was bathed in a sickly green light. Dead ahead were two of the biggest U-boats he had ever seen. He saw both ends of the conning tower begin to sparkle excitedly. Machine guns.

V for Victor and A for Adam roared in to attack, V for Victor slightly ahead to keep from colliding with A for Adam as they maneuvered wildly to avoid the probing fire of the U-boats. The torpedo boats churned the black waters into wide, white wakes, glistening with phosphorescence. Their own machine guns sprang into action, sending tracers floating gracefully at the U-boats.

Chapter 20

Kern saw the telltale spindly trail of the flare as it climbed into the night sky.

"Alarrrmmm!" he shouted into the voice tube. "Battle stations! Surface action. Both engines emergency ahead."

The flare deployed, bathing the distant boat in its harsh light. He saw the flashes of machine guns before he heard the report. Now they would have to fight it out on the surface.

"Kapitaen?" Mend called up through the hatch in alarm. "U-3712 and U-3719 report that they are being attacked by enemy torpedo boats."

"Tell them that we're coming and to take evasive action. Do not dive!"

Kern turned back to the action ahead. The flare was nearly to the water, and tracers flashed back and forth between attacker and attacked. The U-boats were fast enough to escape on the surface. They would be vulnerable to their attackers if they tried to dive now. The big boats simply hung too long on the surface, even at the hands of experienced crews. Speed was their biggest advantage.

The flare was snuffed out by the cold waters of the fiord. There remained only the flashes of the guns to tell where the boats were. Suddenly, Kern saw the thin trail of another flare clawing its way into the sky. It exploded, and its flickering light revealed the dim shapes of the U-boats, and the ragged wakes of their attackers. Tracers crisscrossed one another as the enemy boats fought to get into position to launch their torpedo. U-3535 was rapidly closing the distance when Kern saw the stern of one U-boat rise slightly.

"No! No!" he screamed, as if they could hear him.

He watched as two of the torpedo boats broke off action and headed toward the diving U-boat. To dive, the U-boat had to clear her bridge and gun turrets, cutting the group's defensive firepower by a third. Worse still, her kapitaen ignored the fact that the big boat took longer to dive than smaller U-boats. She had doomed both herself and her companions.

A motor torpedo boat came swerving in abeam of the diving U-boat. Two splashes appeared directly in front of her motor torpedo boat's bow, and she twisted away from her target. Kern knew that she had launched her torpedoes. He waited.

The water erupted alongside the U-boat with a dirty flash, and her stern whipped to one side. The dull crunch of the detonation reached Kern as the spray rained down on the boat's deck. In the light of the flare, he saw her bow jerked above the water, and then slide quickly into the darkness. Her stern tipped skyward and disappeared. She was gone

Kern shook the sight out of his mind and found his voice.

"Gunners! Surface targets dead ahead. Commence firing," he ordered and called down a course change to bring both turrets to bear on the torpedo boats.

U-3535's machine guns clattered into action, sending short bursts of fire toward the enemy boats. The jets of water danced around one torpedo boat, as the guns found their range. Pieces of the boat exploded into the air. Coming as she did across the action, U-3535 was able to rake the enemy boats before they knew she was there. One torpedo boat, twisting to get into position, suddenly settled into the water and stopped; her engines were dead. The torpedo boat that the gunners of U-3535 targeted burst into flame, slowed, and began to list to port.

Kern watched as her crew abandoned her. Some of them got off before the boat exploded in a mass of orange and yellow flames. One enemy boat destroyed, two damaged enough to break off the action.

Then the flare went out and they were in darkness pierced only by the licking flames of the burning boat.

Mend called up from the conning tower, "U-3712 reports, sir."

So it was Hickman, Kern thought. He fought to control his anger. Sooner or later, Hickman would have killed himself and his men with his arrogance. *But he killed my men as well. Or did I?*

"U-3712, sir?"

"Yes?" Kern said.

"Superficial damage to the tower caused by enemy fire. No other damage apparent. They're checking the RGTs."

"Acknowledge report received. Permission granted to remain surfaced. Tell them that U-3535 will take the lead. They are to follow at five hundred meters. Have Frick come topside and check our rockets as well."

"Kapitaenleutnant?" Mend said. "What about U-3719?"

Kern knew what Mend was asking: should they stay and look for survivors? And he knew what the answer was: there were no survivors. Her bridge had been cleared for diving, and her hatches sealed. She was already flooding her tanks when she was hit so that the hole that the torpedo blasted in her pressure hull had sealed her fate and those of the men who were entombed within her forever.

"Send to Evanger. U-3719 attacked and sunk by enemy torpedo boats. Request assistance. Give them the location, Mend."

Mend acknowledged the order. A few moments later, Kern heard the familiar voice of Teddy Hartmann. He moved to one side of the port watch station as the exec climbed up the aluminum ladder from the surface control station. In the pale light of the burning torpedo boat Kern could see that Hartmann was worn out, thinner by ten or fifteen pounds. He had paid a price for his confinement. But then Hartmann smiled.

"Permission to come aboard, Kaleu," he said.

"Kaleu? You've spent too much time with Frick," Kern said as he broke into a grin. "It's good to have you back aboard, Exec. But you might have been safer in the hands of the SS."

"I think it would have been unhealthy, sir. I belong here."

"It's good to have you back."

U-3535 continued down the fiord with her sister ship keeping station well aft of her. The RGTs of both boats survived the enemy attack, and Gorlitz reported only superficial damage to his boat after a quick inspection. The U-boats communicated by Varta-Lampe, the flashing lights piercing the darkness.

The boats neared the mouth of the fiord just as the dawn's weak light revealed the distant horizon. The black shapes of the mountains watched impassively as the two boats cleared the fiord and made for the open sea. When both boats had taken a land bearing, Kern gave the order, "Clear the bridge."

The bridge watch tumbled down the conning tower ladder, followed by Kern, who pulled the heavy hatch shut and locked it. A petty officer and seaman took up their positions at the hydroplanes and waited as each compartment reported ready to dive.

"Diesel engines, stop," Kern ordered. He heard the sound of the engine telegraph and knew that the order would be relayed in the engine room by hand signals. The response came back and Frick relayed it to him in an even tone.

"Fuel lever switched to zero, air intakes shut off, diesel engines unharnessed, Electric motors engaged," the engineer said, naming off the actions to switch from diesel to electric motor drive—to prepare U-3535 for her descent into the depths.

Kern said, "Diving stations."

Frick's eyes scanned the dials. "Ready to dive," he said calmly.

"Flood," Kern ordered.

"Flood," Frick repeated. Kern watched the men respond to his orders. They moved quickly, expertly, never wasting a movement. Normally Hartmann or the watch officer would dive the boat, but Kern preferred to do it. He wanted the practice, he told his officers, "I have to practice as much as you."

The emergency evacuation vents were quickly opened, and the flood valves activated. Air escaped from the tanks with a roar, and the boat began to creak from the weight of the seawater that rushed in. They were seeking to balance the boat by a combination of compressed air and seawater as ballast.

"Forward plane, hard down. Aft plane, down," Kern said. The order was repeated and executed. Kern looked up to see the indicator on the depth gauge move slowly across the dial.

"Tower down," Frick said as the water covered them. They could hear nothing but the creak of the boat and the murmur of water rushing into the buoyancy cells.

Kern watched the gauges. "Forward up ten, aft up fifteen," he commanded. Frick moved behind the hydroplane operators and rested his hands on their shoulders.

"Boat balanced, Kaleu."

"Close vents. Both ahead dead slow."

Frick watched the gauges as the U-boat settled into her depth. Now it was time to fine-tune her buoyancy. "Take on twenty-five gallons forward, trim eight gallons aft," he ordered. "Both planes to neutral. Ready to take soundings." He waited until the boat was absolutely horizontal before he picked up the microphone and announced: "Attention, zero!"

Now she held, a delicately balanced behemoth between ascent and descent—suspended in her element. He waited while soundings were taken of the diving cells and reported back to him. He quickly copied them in the diving log book.

"All in order, Kaleu," he finally reported.

"Take her to thirty meters. Both ahead one-third," Kern said. Hartmann was standing in one corner of the crowded control room. "Teddy? Come with me."

Kern and Hartmann made their way to the kapitanleutnant's tiny cabin. Kern closed the green curtains for privacy, and began dialing the combination of the small wall safe.

"What happened to U-3719?" Hartmann asked.

Kern guided the dial into place before answering. "Hickman hesitated," he said, and then jerked the handle down, opening the safe door. "He waited until Tommy was right on him before he dove." He pulled a sealed envelope from the safe, tore open the flap, and unfolded the orders. "He killed his boat and his crew. They didn't deserve to die like that."

"Two boats," the exec said. "Is that enough?"

Kern did not reply. His eyes ran quickly over the paper in his hand. Finally, he looked at Hartmann.

"That depends, Exec."

"On what?"

Kern handed the orders to him. "If you think that two U-boats are sufficient to attack Liverpool."

"Liverpool?" Hartmann said. He read the orders and looked up. "Christ! Liverpool! Through the Irish Sea?"

Kern smiled and pulled the address microphone from its holder on the bulkhead. He clicked it on.

"Attention! This is Kern," he said, his voice carrying to every part of U-3535. "You've all worked very hard to make this U-boat the finest such in the Kriegsmarine. Well, now you'll know the reason why. The fuehrer himself charged the Lion with this mission. We are to launch our rockets against the English city of Liverpool."

Kern and Hartmann heard the men cheering.

"The fuehrer is convinced that once the Allies realize that we can sail the Atlantic at will and launch rockets at their largest cities, they will think twice about invading the Fatherland. Our mission is one of the utmost importance. After the English perhaps we will have the opportunity to take on American cities. The fuehrer and Germany expect every man to do his duty and carry the war to England. That is all. Carry on."

Kern hung the microphone on its bracket and switched off the address system.

"Do you think it can be done, Kapitaenleutnant?" Hartmann asked.

"Yes," Kern said. "I don't know how many more Type XXI boats with RGTs will follow, but yes, it can be done. We've survived the war so far, Teddy. I believe it was for a reason. I believe this is the reason."

"England," Hartmann said. "I'd like to see the look on Churchill's face when rockets start exploding in Liverpool. Yes. It can be done."

"Teddy," Kern said. "The warheads aren't filled with high explosives."

Hartmann looked at him questioningly. "What . . ."

"It's a disease. Anthrax. We are taking disease to the enemy."

A look of disbelief swept Hartmann's face. "You must be joking. You can't be serious."

"It will kill more efficiently than high explosives," Kern said, echoing Doenitz's cold explanation. "It will kill thousands. It is carried on the wind and anyone who breathes it dies."

"But, Kaleu . . ."

"Welcome to a new war, Teddy."

Chapter 21

Off Rathlin Island, North Channel

Land approached Hardy on the bridge of HMS *Firedancer*, carrying a dispatch in his right hand. The destroyer rolled a bit to port in the moderate seas and Land steadied himself on the binnacle. Hardy glanced at Number One and then leaned over a brass voice tube.

"Engine Room!"

"Engine Room, aye."

"The seas are picking up a bit. Up twenty."

"Up twenty, aye."

Land handed Hardy the dispatch.

"Just came in, sir," Number One said. "Some of the motor torpedo boat boys had a run-in with some new German U-boats last night in Norway. They think they got one, but the others got away. Everyone's on alert."

Captain Hardy read the dispatch carefully. Then he folded it and put it in his pocket.

"Coming out of Norway," he said to no one in particular. "New boats. Doesn't say how many. They'll likely give the Shetlands a wide berth and pop up west of Ireland."

"If they were the old boats we could shoot up the Minches and catch them before they got too far,"

Land said. "But these new boats are supposed to be three times faster than the old ones. By the time we got there, they'd be gone."

"Here we sit between Inishtrahull and Tiree, looking for sea monsters. No bloody U-boat captain in his right mind is going to bring his boat into this straight," Hardy said. He walked to the windscreen and looked out over the gray waters of the Atlantic. Spray whipped past him in a fine mist as the wind pulled it from the tips of the waves. He slapped the top of the windscreen with his fist and turned.

"Brown! Make to Fleet Officer, Derby House."

The signalman quickly produced his dispatch pad and began to write.

"From *Firedancer*," Hardy said. "'Request permission, independent action against enemy U-boats leaving Norway. Suspect they will pass northeast of my position.' Sign it *Firedancer* and get it off immediately. Request priority response."

"What makes you think that they'll pass close enough to us to warrant independent action?" Land asked.

"I didn't say anything about them passing close to us, Number One," Hardy said brusquely. "I said they would pass northeast of us. Look here. We've got ships and airplanes close in from the Channel to the Outer Hebrides. Add to that every convoy that inbound or outbound carries its own defenses and in the middle of the Atlantic you've got Hunter-Killer groups ready to pounce at the first sign of a periscope. So, what does Jerry have to do to save his skin? Split the difference. Keep far enough west of the Isles so that he has deep water, but not so far out as to attract the wrong kind of attention. So my plan is to take my little flotilla straight out to bag him."

"Do you think Derby House will approve, sir?"

"That's the question, isn't it, Number One? We've spent our time in Purgatory. There's only so much pleasure a man can derive from the sight of Westray and Rousay off the starboard bow going up and off the port bow coming down. We need to get out of this and back to the open sea, or I'll get as rusty as old *Firedancer*'s scuppers. It's not natural to take a seaman and stake him out within sight of land. What Derby House will do is anyone's guess, but we'll wait for an answer."

Hardy's answer came four hours later. The W/T operator handed the message to Brown the moment it was recorded. Brown took a moment to read it.

"I don't fancy giving this to Old Georgie," he said.

"He won't get it if you stand there, now, will he?"

Brown fixed him with a cool look. "I'll be back up to Chief Yeoman of Signals in no time, so I'll thank you to keep a civil tongue in your head." He turned and left the W/T room and made his way to the bridge. Hardy was enjoying a cup of tea. Land was standing next to him, smoking a cigarette.

Brown announced, "Message from Derby House, sir."

Hardy glanced at Land, who took the flimsy, opened it, and began to read, " 'To *Firedancer* from F.O. Derby House. Suspicions unwarranted as regards U-boats. Permission denied independent action. Maintain assigned station.' "

Hardy looked up. Brown readied himself for the explosion. It did not come. Instead, Hardy slipped the dispatch into his pocket, continued to sip his tea, and watched *Fearless* and *Fury* as they cut through the waves off *Firedancer*'s starboard beam. *Punjabi* hung back a bit off the port beam, like a wearisome relative always late to reunions. Brown stood as immobile as possible, while Hardy finished his tea. Finally the captain spoke.

"Send to Derby House," he ordered, and then waited patiently as Brown fumbled for his pad. "'From *Firedancer* to F.O. Your eyes only. Remember Kate's knickers.' Signed, *Firedancer.*"

Brown's pencil stopped on the pad. He looked up. Hardy stood wedged in the corner of the bridge, looking at him with a kind expression.

"Did you get that, Brown?"

Signalman Brown finished writing. "Yes, sir."

"Good. Now go and send it off," Hardy said. He turned to Land. "I'll be in my sea cabin, Number One. Come and tell me when the fleet officer replies."

In less than an hour, there was a knock on Hardy's door.

"Come."

Land entered to see Hardy propped up in his bunk, sketching on a pad of paper. The captain looked up.

Land held up the flimsy. "It's from Derby House, sir. From the fleet officer. It says 'Independent action approved. Good hunting.'"

Hardy continued to sketch. "Very well, Number One. Please make course corrections to take us out and signal our new orders to the flotilla. I'll be up in a bit. I'm just finishing up a barn. On my grandfather's place in Surrey. Dreariest place on earth."

"Yes, sir," Land said, and started to leave. With his hand on the doorknob, he stopped and turned.

"You want to know about the message, don't you, Number One?" Hardy asked, shading an area with the edge of his pencil.

"Yes, sir," Land said. "I couldn't sleep if I didn't know."

"In due time, Number One. Tell the chief to light off number-three boiler. When she's right, we'll run her up to twenty-seven and put some spray over her forecastle."

"Right you are, sir," Land replied. He closed the door and stood in the narrow corridor. A rating squeezed by, begging Number One's pardon.

"That crafty old bastard," Land said under his breath, and headed for the bridge. "Damn his Hat and damn his story."

Godt entered Doenitz's office and found the grand admiral studying the large map board on the wall.

"Well?" Doenitz said without turning.

"U-3719 with Peter Hickman commanding was lost with all hands," Godt reported. "One British motor torpedo boat was sunk, one damaged, and one escaped. It appears that Kern and Gorlitz continued undamaged."

"But it is obvious that the British know of the existence of the boats."

"Possibly."

"It is likely, Godt. The British boat that escaped would certainly have reported the results of their attack. So the British know that there are two U-boats headed out into the Atlantic."

"Herr Grand Admiral," Godt said. "They cannot know the capabilities of these boats. That is in our favor. Kern is experienced. One of our best kapitaens."

"That is on our side," Doenitz agreed. "There is no reason to consider that the British suspect the target.

That is on our side as well. Kern will maintain radio silence. It will drive me insane not to have timely reports on his progress, but he will do as ordered; he will not break radio silence for any reason. That is on our side, I suppose—his silence."

"Yes, Grand Admiral."

"They will rendezvous with Seeckt and then we will know. That will be another four days. More if they run into difficulties."

"Yes, Grand Admiral."

"Has Himmler called again?"

Godt had trouble suppressing his smile. "No, Grand Admiral."

"Yes. Go on and smile, Godt. I had a good laugh out of it as well. I should have known that Kern gave in far too easily when I told him that there was nothing to be done. Himmler will take the matter of Hartmann to the fuehrer and I shall have to listen to our leader rant for an hour, but that is nothing new. Himmler and his men can go to the devil for all I care. But Kern." He turned back to the map. "We have asked him to do the impossible. He must sail the Verdamnt Atlantic and attack England's largest city with two U-boats. If he succeeds, he must return across hundreds of miles of hostile waters. I am glad that we have some things on our side, Godt. Now, if we just had luck on our side, it might tip the scales in our favor. It is about time that Germany had good fortune on her side, isn't it, Godt? Maybe we can pray for luck to befall our Fatherland, and a little for Guenter the Silent as well."

"I understand, Herr Grand Admiral," Godt said.

"From the beginning, this operation has been one of compromise. I promise Kern fifteen U-boats; I deliver four. I promise him RGTs that will work, and one in five does so in their tests."

"Herr Grand Admiral," Godt said. "You cannot give your men what you do not have."

Doenitz shrugged at the suggestion and locked his hands behind his back.

"I tell you truthfully, Godt. Many times—many times I have considered this mission a fool's errand. A waste of time, men, and U-boats, none of which are ours to squander. My resolve was strengthened each time by Kern's ability to overcome obstacles. I thought: perhaps there is a chance. Now that he is at sea, Kern is in his element. I can count on the fingers of one hand the kapitaens who are capable of doing what we ask of Guenter Kern. But you are right, Godt. I have no answer for you, old friend. We will not know until the moment of attack."

Chapter 22

Grid Coordinates BE-18 in the North Atlantic

Kern was out of his bunk and on the way to the control room before Hartmann's voice faded from the address system. The exec was waiting for him near the radio room, hovering over Reche, the diminutive radio/sound operator. The other men chided Reche for his innocent, beardless face. He was very quiet and very capable.

"What is it?" Kern asked, sliding in next to Hartmann.

Reche did not look up; he sat poised over a console crammed with dials, slowly twisting the indicator for the Nibelung—the device that picked up underwater noises.

"Funker"—Hartmann used U-boat slang for the radio/sound operator—"has picked up something on the S-Anlage. Pretty far out, eighteen to twenty miles. Perhaps more than that. It seems to come and go."

"Mahalla?" Kern asked, wondering if it was their luck to run into a convoy that they could not attack.

"No," Hartmann said. "He thinks—"

Reche's finger came up, silencing Hartmann. The exec and Kern waited.

When Reche spoke, it was in a calm and unhurried

tone, but it was barely above a whisper, as if the boy knew that the enemy would hear him.

"It's very faint. Several ships. High-speed screws. They just hang there."

Kern looked at Hartmann. "Hunter-Killer."

Hartmann shrugged. "Maybe. They never get close enough for Funker to get a fix. He's been at it for ten minutes. I thought you ought to know. It's logged in the KTB. Did you get any sleep?"

"Some," Kern said. "How is everything else?"

"Up here, fine. The men have finished servicing the eels. They're itching to try them on a escort."

"I bet they are, but we're not going to let Tommy or the Americans know we're down here. What else?"

"You'd better go back and see Frick. I don't think he's slept since we left. He won't leave his precious engines."

"I'll go talk to him. Who has the watch?"

"Mend."

"All right. You go and get some sleep. Tell Mend if Reche picks up anything closer, I want to know. I'll be aft with Frick."

Kern made his way toward the engine room, squeezing past the crew's quarters and diesel engine room, into the E-motor room. Foodstuffs were crammed into every unused corner. The freezer simply wasn't big enough for all the cuts of meat, loaves of bread, and wheels of cheese needed to feed the men over the length of the voyage. With those and the canned goods, U-3535 looked more like a floating store than a warship. Kern stopped in the tiny galley to pick up a cup of steaming tea from the cook. His assistant was preparing sandwiches for the men. Kern balanced the hot cup carefully in his hand as he ducked through the hatch and into the tight confines of the electric motor room. He was greeted by the hum of the Seimen's electric motors and the rush of air from the big air coolers above them. Mechanics stood guard over the gauges and dials of the starboard and port electric motor panels in the forward section of the room. Frick was at the motor control station talking with another mechanic. He didn't notice Kern's presence, but that hardly surprised the kapitaenleutnant; Frick seldom took notice of anything when he was with his engines and motors.

"Problems?" Kern asked, sipping his tea.

"Always when dealing with boats fresh from the yards," Frick said. He dismissed the mechanic and turned his attention to Kern. "What brings you back here, Kaleu?"

"When's the last time that you slept?"

Frick was disappointed. "I thought it was something important."

"It is. I can't have you falling asleep when we get to England."

"I'll be awake, don't worry about that."

Kern looked around. "How is everything back here?"

"Everything is working as it should. So far," Frick said.

"The Schnorchel mast still drags when we extend it," Kern said. "What can you do about it?"

"When can you give me four hours on the surface?"

Kern sipped his tea. "No. We stay submerged until we reach Seeckt. I'll learn to live with the mast. I was very pleased with the last test of the Silent-Running Motors."

Frick grinned broadly. "Aren't they a wonder? They did well enough in the fiord, but they do even better in the open sea. No American or Tommy asdic operator will be able to hear us when we go to silent running. My only concern with it is the wear on the V-belts. With twelve to each motor, one's bound to wear unevenly or break after a while."

"But you have replacements?"

"I got all Edland had, but that was only eight."

"Then you'd better make the original belts last a very long time. But you can do that, can't you, Frick?"

The speaker behind Kern's head crackled before the chief engineer could reply.

"Kapitaen to the control room." It was Mend.

"Get some sleep," Kern ordered Frick quickly. "Or I'll have you strapped to your bunk."

Frick's answer was a broad grin.

Hartmann was with Mend in the control room when Kern arrived.

"Reche continues to pick up those faint screws, but they're not getting any closer," Hartmann said. "It's like they're moving parallel to us. Not getting any closer, but not getting any farther away, either."

"Funker's not picking up Gorlitz by mistake, is he?" Kern replied. "He hasn't many hours training on this new system."

"We thought of that, Kaleu," Mend said. "So we had him break off contact and open a search. He found Gorlitz right off. He let me listen. Even I could tell the difference between U-3712 and the sound of those other screws."

"I've ordered him to keep you informed of any variations in the reports," Hartmann added.

"I thought you were sleeping," Kern said. "It doesn't speak well of a kapitaen when his officers refuse to follow his orders."

"I'm was on my way," the exec said, "when Reche

picked up a weather broadcast. We've got bad weather coming towards us."

"How bad?"

"A force-five to force-seven. We can expect to be in the middle of it in about twelve hours. That means we won't be able to run the Schnorchel."

"All right, we'll raise the Schnorchel now, and run on diesel as long as we can," Kern ordered.

"I wonder if Gorlitz picked up the broadcast?" Hartmann asked.

"Was it Goliath?" Kern asked Mend.

"Yes, sir."

"He was told to monitor Goliath," Kern said. "He picked it up if he was listening."

"Kaleu," Hartmann asked, "what about those screws Reche is tracking? They might be able to read our Schnorchel head on their radar."

Kern gave Hartmann's concern some thought.

"It's unlikely, Teddy. The head creates such a small image, it will probably be overlooked. And whoever it is, is too far away to see the Schnorchel's wake. Take the boat up to fourteen meters and raise the mast. Let's go to the diesels," he ordered Mend, and to his exec he said: "Go and get some sleep. I want my officers and men rested when the time comes to launch our rockets."

Land and Barton joined Hardy on the bridge. They found the captain looking over the choppy seas and into the dull gray sky. He did not look happy. "Two bloody days, Number One! We've not so much as gotten close to a U-boat. We've sailed back and forth so often, old *Firedancer*'s worn a furrow in the ocean. They're out there, by God! Derby House has been cheeping all along that we've missed them, but they're out there, by God. They want us back in shortly, 'with all dispatch,' they tell me. I've been begging off, trying to buy a bit of time. We won't go back in until we've had at them."

"We'll find them soon enough, sir," Land said.

"It'll have to be soon enough. We've got a round of dirty weather coming in on us. Could be a bit nasty all around but it can't be helped. We've had good weather for over a week now. Well, I don't suppose the Almighty is amiss for tossing in a gale now and then. How does that sound to you, Number One? Get your blood moving to hear that?"

"Indeed, sir," Land said with a smile. "But you know, sir, maybe the trouble's in your Hat. You're not wearing it, and whenever you do our luck seems to pick up."

"The Hat!" Hardy said. "That's it, Number One! I should have had it on all along. Go and fetch it from my harbor cabin," Hardy ordered a rating. "Look in the wardrobe. Top shelf."

Several minutes later, the seaman returned with a cheap cardboard hatbox.

"Ah," Hardy said. "There it comes now."

The rating handed the box to Hardy with supreme care, who removed the top. Barton looked to Land for some sign of explanation, but Number One stood with a half smile fixed to his face.

"Can't go into battle without my Hat, can we, Number One?" Hardy asked, as he handed the box top to the confused Barton. "That's what it was all along."

"No doubt about it, sir," Land said.

"Well, take it, Barton, blast you! It won't bite."

The sublieutenant took the hatbox lid.

"There it is!" Hardy said, his hands diving into the

box. Barton watched as he withdrew a black bowler. Hardy quickly snatched his cap from his head, threw it into the box, and placed the bowler on his own head as if it were a crown. He tilted it slightly to the left before looking at Land.

"How does she sit, Number One?" he asked.

"Splendidly, sir."

"All right, take it away," Hardy ordered the rating. "Well, Barton? What's your opinion?"

The sublieutenant's mouth opened but the words were a moment in coming.

"Very nice, sir."

"Very nice?" Hardy looked at Land. "He thinks it's very nice, Number One. Do you even know what it is, Barton?"

"A bowler, sir?"

"Of course it's a bowler. A blind man could tell that it's a bowler. I mean do you know the significance of it?"

"No, sir," Barton said. "I'm afraid not."

"Well, listen carefully. You're about to get a lesson in the history of the sea. In the old days, merchant captains used to wear bowlers such as this. It was a matter of pride, Barton, when a captain was awarded his bowler. When *Firedancer* began her service to the convoys, she earned quite a reputation for herself. Didn't she, Number One? We saved more than our share of merchantmen and tankers. After a particularly hot run, a group of captains came to *Firedancer* and awarded me this hat. It was their way of thanking me, of thanking the crew of *Firedancer*, for saving their lives and their ships. So whenever we go into action, I wear this hat. And I wear it with pride. Now do you see, Barton?"

"Yes, sir."

"Good. If you do your duty on this run, I may let you wear it."

"That would be lovely, sir," the sublieutenant said.

Hardy grimaced. "Lovely! Don't take what I said to heart, Barton. I was lying. My head is the only thing this bloody monstrosity sits on, and with good reason. It belongs to me."

A whistle came through on the voice tube, and a muffled voice said, "Bridge?"

Number One leaned over. "Bridge. Land here."

"This is Stackhouse, sir. The captain wanted to be informed if we run across anything."

"Go on," Land said. "The captain's listening."

"We've got a signal, sir. Very faint. It's rather difficult to keep it on-screen."

Hardy clapped his hands together. "There it is! By God, it was the Hat! Tell him I'm on my way."

"He'll just be down, Stackhouse."

"Right, sir."

Hardy left the bridge, and when he was safely gone, Barton whispered to Number One, "I didn't know what to say about the Hat, sir. Really, I didn't."

Land laughed. "Don't think a thing about it. I have to bite my tongue every time he puts it on. He loves it though, and he's right about the honor of the thing. Those merchant captains meant to honor Old Georgie when they gave it to him."

Number One instructed the engine room to increase speed by twenty revolutions. He had the signalman make the increase in speed to the other ships by Morse signal lamp.

"Captain Hardy and Stackhouse have been together for a number of years," Land told Barton as the signal lamp clicked out its message. "Longer than I've been with Captain Hardy. For my money, Stackhouse is the best senior yeoman asdic operator in the fleet. As solemn as a parson, but tenacious."

"He's the big man, isn't he? Square jawed?"

"That's him."

"Message acknowledged from all ships," the signal-man informed Land.

"Very well," Land replied, and then said to Barton, "He lost his wife in one of the early raids on Liverpool. Just two daughters remain, I believe. He has a score to settle with Jerry. I suppose we all do in a way, but for him it's personal."

Hardy leaned over the screen, next to Stackhouse. "Have you got on the bastards?"

"Pretty hard to tell, sir. The sea's working up to something," Stackhouse said, tapping the screen with his finger. "We're getting a lot of distortion here."

"Yes. Bad weather's coming in. What do you have?"

"Here," Stackhouse said. "I get just a wisp of an echo off the SL-3 radar. But it's very fine for picking up a Snort's head. We've got nothing on Huff-Duff, ground or sea wave, so Jerry's keeping his mouth shut for once."

"More's the pity," Hardy said. "If the U-boats aren't transmitting, it makes the bloody bastards harder to find."

"Nothing on asdic either," Stackhouse continued. "Maybe Jerry does have his boats covered in rubber skin, like they said."

"Uh," Hardy said, his eyes on the green field of the Plan Position Indicator screen. "Maybe the new ones do, but I doubt it. Keep after that, Stackhouse. There are several of Jerry's new boats out there and I want them. We'll try to get you close enough to pick up any kind of signal. Huff-Duff, radar, asdic—we'll get you close enough to send one of them off."

"How many boats, sir?"

"We're not sure, Stackhouse. It could be three or more. They may decide to run in a pack or split up. If I were Jerry out in the Atlantic in a brand-new U-boat, I'd keep everyone together. They could certainly raise bloody hell with the convoys that way."

"Can't picture you as a U-boat captain, sir."

"I wouldn't want to be one, Stackhouse, with you looking for me."

Stackhouse leaned forward slightly, squinting at the screen. "Thought I saw a Snort, sir. In a different location, though."

"Two boats."

"Two boats? Yes, sir, it could be two."

Hardy walked to the voice tube on the sound room wall and called up the bridge.

"Bridge, Land."

"Number One? Double the lookouts. Have the other ships do the same. We may have Snorts off our port beam at five to seven thousand yards. Stackhouse has something on his radar."

"Right, sir. I've rung up another twenty revolutions."

"Back her off, Number One. We can't have our own screws interfering with asdic. Ease us to port a bit. If it is Jerry over there, I don't want to scare him off. They might decide to lay doggo."

"Action Stations, sir?"

"Of course, Number One," Hardy said. "Why else do you think I'd wear this damned silly Hat on my head? I'll be up in a moment."

"Do they know who we're chasing, sir?" Stackhouse asked as Hardy moved next to the asdic operator.

"No. Not a clue. New class of U-boat is all that we

know. They'll have some of their best men at it
though. I'll send back to Derby House and inquire."
Hardy clapped the operator on the shoulder. "Keep
after them, Stackhouse."

"I will, sir. I'll start asdic as soon as we've slowed."

When Hardy got to the bridge he instructed Brown
to inquire of Derby House any additional information
on the U-boats they were chasing. Then he made
mention to Land of a band of dark clouds low on the
horizon.

"I've been watching them, sir," Land said. "Rough
weather ahead."

Hardy tugged his Hat farther down on his head.
"Keep an eye on the barometer, Number One. My old
bones tell me there's a drop coming in. How's young
Barton holding up?"

"Well, sir. Very well, in fact. He makes a fine gunnery officer. Spends a good deal of time with the
Hedge Hog and depth charge crews. His men pay attention to him; smart as paint."

Hardy looked up from under the rim of his bowler.

"Laying it on a bit thick, aren't you, Number One?"

"Perhaps. But he's a good man, you've got to give
him that."

"All right," Hardy growled. "Just don't make him a
candidate for the Posthumous V.C. Party yet."

"No, sir," Land said. There was a shrill whistle on
the voice tube.

"Bridge! Asdic! Possible Snort contact off the port
beam!"

"Dead slow," Land ordered the quartermaster.

"Dead slow," he echoed and then rang it up on the
engine enunciator. The answering ring came back,
"Dead slow, sir."

Hardy and Number One hurried to the port side of the bridge. Land handed a pair of binoculars to Hardy.

"Brown," Hardy called over his shoulder. "Make to the flotilla: 'Possible submarine contact off my port beam. Reduce speed to five knots.'"

"Yes, sir," Brown said, and hurried to break out the pennants.

"Anything?" Land asked Hardy.

The captain's answer seemed an eternity in coming. "Nothing. See how far out Stackhouse makes them."

Land called down to the asdic operator, "Stackhouse? How far away is the submarine?"

After a moment, Stackhouse replied: "Over ten thousand yards, sir. Signal is very weak. Very weak."

"We've dropped down to dead slow. What does your asdic say?"

"A moment, sir," Stackhouse replied. "Faint, sir. Could be anything."

Land looked at Hardy. "You don't suppose it's true? I mean about that rubber skin Jerry's putting on his boats."

"Wouldn't surprise me a bit," Hardy said, adjusting his binoculars. "If there are a couple of Snorts out there, I can't make them out. Tell the lookouts to keep a sharp eye out. Does Stackhouse have a course?"

"Stackhouse?" Land called down. "Do you have a course for us yet?"

"Three-oh-three, sir."

"Dead on with us, sir," Land said to Hardy.

"Who's shadowing who? Who's the hunter and who's the hare?"

Brown appeared on the bridge. "Message from Derby House, sir," he said, handing Land the flimsy. Number One read it quickly.

"Type XXI boats, sir. Three or four of them got

away from our chaps in Norway. Jesus." Land stopped. Hardy looked over in expectation.

"Twenty-five knots submerged, sir," Land continued. "Sixteen on the surface. Loaded to the gills with those damned Gnats. Destroyer-killers. Twenty of the bastards."

"Bloody hell!" Brown said aloud, forgetting himself. "Handle with care."

"Quite right, Brown," Hardy said dryly. "Pass that on to the other ships. "Port twenty, Quartermaster!"

"Port twenty," the helmsman replied. "Twenty of port, wheel on, sir."

Hardy turned to Land. "We've got to ease on to these chaps very carefully, Number One. I want to get behind them. We'll pull a Walker on them, creep right up their ass, and then unload on them. But it'll take a while until we're in position. Rudder amidships."

"The bad weather."

"Rudder amidships, sir."

"Right. It'll probably get to us before we get to them, but I'd rather be safe than sorry. If it hits before we zero in on them, there's nothing to do but ride it out and try to find them on the other side."

"Yes, sir," Land said, watching the dark clouds on the horizon suspended in a pale yellow sky. He glanced at the message again. "They think that one of the captains is a bloke named Kern."

"One of Doenitz's pets. Guenter 'the Silent.' He and Maus were friends."

"Maus?"

"The Americans have him. Kern is good. Anybody who has lasted this long is bound to have something on the ball. All right, Mr. Silent U-boat Kapitaen," Hardy said, putting the binoculars to his eyes, "let's find out who's the hound and who's the bloody hare."

Chapter 23

Grid Coordinates CC-03

Firedancer's bow fell down into a rising wave, shattering the iron-gray water with a crash. Spray exploded over the forecastle, burying the Hedge Hog emplacement before it dashed itself against the spray shield below B gun. What survived was snatched by the wind and whipped into the faces of the bridge watch, soaking them despite their oilskins. Land turned his back on the spray field just as it struck the bridge, pulling his head down in his shoulders to keep the ice-cold water from finding its way down his neck.

Even Hardy had replaced his bowler with a nor'easter, although this was the only concession that he made to the worsening weather. His spirits were up, Land knew, because they were always highest when the weather was bad. He looked at it as a personal contest: one man against the overwhelming power of the sea.

It was the talk of the wardroom how after especially dirty weather Old Georgie stayed on the bridge all through it, reveling in the storm's anger. The worse the weather got, the more invigorated the captain became. He stayed throughout the worst of the storm, with poor old *Firedancer* whipping and sawing across the waves, sometimes rolling thirty degrees so that the bridge watch was actually looking up at the mountainous waves. And there was Hardy, that inscrutable smile on his face, strengthened by the increasing power of the storm. Eccentric, it was said of Hardy. At times like these, Land thought, the man might be considered mad.

"Trust the North Atlantic to foul the best-laid plans of mice and men, Number One," Hardy shouted over the roar of the waves hitting *Firedancer*'s bow. "That close to them we are, when this bloody weather hits."

"Best-laid schemes, sir," Land corrected.

"Eh? Schemes, is it? Well, no matter, we can't pick up a blasted thing in these conditions, can we, Number One? Asdic and radar don't mean a thing when the sea's at you."

The deck dropped out from under Land as *Firedancer* fell into a trough and then pulled herself up again. They were still making headway but it was a laborious process, and they could not increase their speed for fear of the storm taking hold and tearing poor *Firedancer* apart. They could ride the sixty-foot waves, but they could not batter their way through them; the ship simply would not take the punishment.

The other three ships rode the waves as best they could, occasionally appearing at a crest, as looking hopefully for their companions. The sky was a dirty grayish-yellow, tinged with green. It was unnatural, and foreboding.

"We'll keep on this course until it blows past us," Hardy said. "Jerry was on the same course before this hit. He should be there on the other side when we get out. We'll find him, Number One. Don't worry. We'll get him."

Land had given up all thought of the U-boats that *Firedancer* was tracking. His mind was focused on surviving the storm. He had ordered lifelines strung and told Barton to put all of the depth charges on safety as a precaution against an accidental explosion. There was no doubt in his mind that if something did happen to put the men in the water, no one would survive. There would be no question of the other ships picking up survivors. It couldn't be done, the seas were too rough.

Still, in all of it, Hardy was nothing less than an eternal optimist. It was as if God had made some secret covenant with the captain, that Hardy and the Lord had agreed upon a certain place and time for his passing, and until that moment Hardy was invincible. Perhaps, Land rationalized, that was why Hardy never eased down and to lie to during a big blow: he knew that he had the Lord's assurances. The most that the captain would do during a gale, Land knew, was to grudgingly drop to eight knots. "That's enough!" he'd growl. "No sense in throwing in the towel over a bit of spray." Maybe he was a madman, Land thought, but he was mad only when it suited him.

"Number One?" Hardy shouted to him, although they were just a few feet apart on the bridge. "Any relation to Land? That poet chap?"

"No, sir," Land returned. Hardy had asked him the question at least four times before. "No relation, sir."

"Never read much of his stuff. Should have, I suppose, but never got around to it."

A wave exploded under B gun's shield, the water spray cascading over the bridge.

"Bit of a monster," Hardy observed casually. "Only bit of poetry that I recall was something about a gale off Iceland. Let's see. Oh yes. 'The ship goes wop with a wiggle between and the steward falls into the soup tureen.' How about that, Number One?"

"It certainly is appropriate, sir. Kipling, I believe," Land said, switching on the binnacle light. Its low glow seemed especially comforting in the darkness of the storm.

"Well, we've seen worse, haven't we, Number One? Bound to get worse before it gets better, eh? Course it could come right around and get us again."

"Yes, sir," Land agreed. They had seen worse, much worse. There had been times in force-six gales when the hogging and sagging of *Firedancer*'s hull in the thunderous seas had frightened Land nearly to distraction. Twice he thought that the ship would destroy herself, twisting her hull through the towering waves, her steel plates groaning as if in the grips of death itself. He had been frightened, terribly frightened, and only afterward in the bright calmness that followed, when the young officers had gathered in the wardroom to speak in awe of the storm, was Land able to manufacture nonchalance about the encounter. But it was well after the storm, when he had finally gotten a grip on his senses.

It was several minutes before Hardy spoke again.

"Jerry thinks that he is in the clear because of this weather," he said grimly. "He's probably sailing along below the surface, having a high old time of it. Well, he's got another thing coming, Number One. This weather will slow us up a bit, but it won't stop us. And when Jerry comes out of the other side of this, he's going to have company. He'll stick his periscope up and look around, and then up comes his Snort and he'll suck in fresh air, and all will be right with the world. But it won't be, Number One. *Firedancer* will be waiting for him, and we'll sail right up his ass and blow him to kingdom come."

It was then that Land saw his hands begin to glow. He held them up, transfixed. The storm was gone, so too was his fear of it. There was nothing in the world but his hand. He looked over Hardy's head. The mast just aft of the bridge began to glow as well, the assorted radar and radio apparatus seeming to come alive with a yellowish green glimmer.

"Well!" Hardy said, looking at Number One's hands and following his gaze to the mast. "*Firedancer*'s been smote by Saint Elmo's Fire. Look at it, Number One! What a wondrous trick of nature."

Hardy raised his own hand, spreading the gloved fingers. His hand was a shimmering outline. "How I long for some great literary passage to quote. I don't know any. All I can do is hang on to my ship and pray that God will spare us from the sea. That's Him talking to us, Land." Hardy stretched his fingers wide. "God come down during the tempest to tell all good seamen to have faith in the Almighty, and trust to a stout ship.

"A man needs to quote Shakespeare at a time like this, doesn't he, Number One? Or the Bible. There's a right handy book to have around when times are bad. It won't do me a bit of good, Number One. I'm not a well-read man or an educated man, and if I had to put more than two words together, I would be doomed. I'm not a religious man, either. No self-respecting church will have me, I'm sure of it. But by God I appreciate the Almighty and what He can do. I'll tell you this from what I've seen at sea: God's hand is in it. When I get to the Pearly Gates I'll give the Almighty a 'well done,'' and to hell with all the sanctimonious clergy. The sea is my church, Land.

Every wave a pew and every storm a sermon, and the screech of the wind a heavenly choir. When God delivers His sermon, He'll broach no sleeping." Hardy dropped his hand. "I'd give my left leg to quote scripture, but there's nothing for me to draw on." He looked out to sea and then added, "Except God help the seamen on the seas and under them."

Guenter Kern steadied himself against the periscope housing as U-3535 swung back and forth fifty meters below the surface. Even at this depth the storm's power could be felt.

Hartmann stood quietly behind the hydroplane operators, his eyes on the Papenberg gauge. He calmly gave his orders to the men at the hydroplanes, as he fought to keep the boat level, and at its prescribed depth. It was a difficult and delicate process.

If the boat was jerked toward the dangerous surface waters, the RGTs might be damaged by the thunderous wave. Or if she broached, it might be within sight of the enemy ships that Funker had discovered. To go deeper . . . To go deeper would take them farther away from the storm's fury, but Hartmann, Frick, and Kern all asked the same question: could the RGTs take the pressure of a hundred meters or more? The White Coats said 150, but keep it at a hundred to play it safe. Why not keep it at fifty and play it safer? Who was to say that the wondrous new weapons would survive the journey even at fifty meters below the sea's surface?

U-3535 jerked suddenly to starboard and heeled over twenty degrees. Debris went flying, and Kern heard the cries of pain and surprise from throughout the boat. She slowly righted. Kern looked up as the lights flickered momentarily and then strengthened.

"Kaleu, if we don't take her down we might lose our cargo," Hartmann said.

"All right," Kern said. "Take her down to seventy-five meters. Both ahead slow."

"Forward plane down fifteen degrees," Hartmann ordered. "After plane down fifteen. Dead slow."

U-3535 fell slowly. Kern glanced at the depth gauges, and felt the boat even out as Hartmann called for the planes to be returned to neutral.

The exec gave Kern a look of relief. "She feels better."

"Yes," was all that Kern said and made his way to the sound room.

Reche sat at his console, one earpiece of his headset on, and the other pulled back off his ear—listening.

"Anything, Funker?" Kern asked.

Reche looked up. His eyes were bloodshot and his chin was covered with a faint haze of blond stubble. At times such as these, even the young became old men.

"Nothing, sir," Reche said. "I thought that they were trying to find us with asdic, but I couldn't be sure. I heard the radar though, very faint chirps."

"Looking for our Schnorchel," Kern said. As the enemy radar searched for them, it emitted a strange birdlike sound on the FuMB 26 that changed to a series of low moans as the signal intensified. This advanced radar-detection unit was a long way from the crude Biscay Cross of the old boats, but accomplished the same thing: it told you that there were ships out there hunting you.

"I haven't heard anything since that," Reche said.

"You won't in this storm," Kern allowed. "Do you know how many there were?"

Reche nodded without looking up. He adjusted a dial, and pressed the earpiece tightly against his ear. "Four, sir. Destroyers or destroyer escorts."

The boat pitched slightly to one side and her nose dipped. She quickly righted herself.

"Right," Kern said. "This storm ought to blow over in six to eight hours. We'll send up the Schnorchel. If the Tommies are out there, we'll know."

The boat twisted again and shook. The storm was intensifying. The address system crackled into life.

"Kaleu to the engine room!" It was Frick. Something was wrong.

Kern dashed back through the control room, squeezing past seamen. "Make way!"

He quickly ducked through a bulkhead hatch and found the chief engineer standing in the center of the E-room, looking up. Frick's hand came out, stopping Kern, as the engineer's eyes searched the space above him. Kern remained motionless, silent. Every man at his station was like a statue, waiting.

Kern heard a sharp clank above him. He looked at Frick. It came again, louder—two reports this time, roughly corresponding to the motion of the boat.

"It's the RGT," the engineer whispered. "Something broke loose."

Kern licked his lips. "Are you sure?" He knew he needn't have asked the question. There was nothing on the deck about the E-room that would account for the noise.

Frick nodded. The noise came again, louder. "Part of the rail support, I think."

Kern waited for the noise. The clang of metal on metal filled the room. "How long?"

"It just started. Something's been torn loose by the storm." He looked at Kern for a solution.

"We can't surface. It's hell up there and the destroyers will be waiting for us."

"I don't know what it is, Kaleu. I don't know how serious it is. Can we get deeper? That might help keep it from tearing loose."

Kern felt sweat trickle down his back. It was warm in the boat. It would get warmer until they could surface and ventilate. His mouth was dry.

"We're at seventy-five now. I don't know about going any deeper. I know we can't surface."

A clang sounded loudly overhead, as if to remind Kern of the urgency of a decision.

"I don't know what it is," Frick said again.

Kern stepped to the address system and pushed the button. "Control Room!"

Mend answered.

"Take her down to one hundred meters, Mend. Very slowly. Something's come loose on one of the RGTs and it's banging around back here."

The noise sounded right over Kern's head, and he ducked instinctively. "Now, Mend. Very carefully."

He clicked off the address system. Frick stood next to him, listening. The engineer's pale skin looked sickly in the low light of the E-room. Sweat trickled down his face and disappeared in the thatch of curly, dark beard that covered his face. They waited for the sound again, as U-3535 groaned in protest at being driven deeper into the sea.

Land clutched his hat with one hand, and held on to the lifeline with the other. He felt his life belt tug reassuringly at his waist.

"That last one tore away your gig and one of the boats," he shouted at Hardy, barely two feet from him.

I've had the others tied down as well we could, but it's damned dangerous even with lifelines. I had the men stand down from action stations. If a U-boat appeared ten feet off our bow, we couldn't do a thing but look." The howling wind whistled past them, tearing at their clothes and words with equal determination.

Firedancer's bow crashed down in a rolling wave, sending spray up in the path of the wind. It was driven against the bridge like tiny bullets, stinging the men on watch again through their oilskins. The sky was black now, broken only by a glimpse of boiling clouds that churned overhead.

Hardy merely nodded at Land's report, keeping his face turned away from the wind.

"If this keeps up much longer, Number One," he shouted, "we'll have to lie to. She's blowing too hard for us to do much of anything. At least the bloody barometer has stopped falling. There's something. Anything from the others?"

"Nothing since this started. I hope they're holding their own."

Firedancer shuddered as she clawed her way up another wave. The crest exploded over her bow, drenching the bridge in spray.

"I hope you're right. God has to help them this night. There's not a damn thing I can do. As soon as we're out of it, I want to resume searching for Jerry. We're bound to have damage forward, especially the Hedge Hog. Have young Barton on it immediately when things clear."

Land heard a faint whistle and bent down, putting his ear to the voice tube.

"Engine Room," the strained voice stated. "We're taking water here. The pumps have got it under control."

"Right!" Land shouted back into the tube. He moved close to Hardy. "Engine Room, sir. They report they're taking water but they have it under control."

Hardy nodded. "The screws are coming clear as she tops the crest. That's what's shaking her, but it can't be helped. I've got to have steerage or we're done for."

"I hope those bloody bastards are catching some of this," Land said.

"Not likely, Number One," Hardy said, knowing exactly what Land was talking about. "They're well below all of this, as snug as a bug in a rug."

Kern looked up, waiting. Nobody in the E-room moved or made a sound. All they heard was the dull hum of the electric motors and the low whoosh of the blowers. So far. U-3535 slid sideways through the water, listing slightly. Kern tensed, waiting for the noise. There was a clatter overhead, but not the loud bang that he expected.

"Something's dragging across the deck," he said.

Frick nodded in confirmation. "Maybe it's whatever was clanging before."

"When this is over, we've got to surface and get it fixed. Quickly," Kern said. He allowed himself a sense of relief; the banging was gone. "If it continues to make a racket the Tommies will pick it up."

Frick's look told Kern that he understood the situation.

"How soon until we rendezvous with the Milchkuh?" Frick asked.

"Three days if the weather lets up. Four if we have to put up with this much longer. I want to get back up to fifty meters. I've got my doubts about those damned things in deep water."

"All right, Kaleu," Frick said. "I'll have a crew standing by. The minute that you give me the word, I'll take them up myself and fix those devilish rockets."

"Maybe we can wait until reaching Seeckt. If I can avoid surfacing twice, it cuts down the chance of being found."

Kern looked up, waiting. After a few minutes, the clatter came again. "We'll have to be satisfied with that. Let me know if you hear any more noises. I'll be in the control room."

"Kaleu?" Frick said as Kern began to duck through the bulkhead hatch. "You look tired. Maybe you ought to get some sleep."

Kern smiled at Frick's joke. "You'd better watch yourself, Engineer. I might just decide to take this beast down while you're on deck."

Chapter 24

The storm eased off a bit several hours later and Land had tea sent up to the bridge from the wardroom galley. A pale yellow sun shone thinly through breaks in the heavy cloud cover. The wind was constant, blowing from the northeast, but it lacked fury. All of the bridge watch had dispensed with their oilskins.

Now they drank their steaming tea gratefully, and scanned the horizon for signs of the other destroyers.

Able Seaman Payne spotted *Punjabi* steaming to take up formation as if the storm had been nothing more than a bit of unusual weather. *Fearless* and *Fury* reported in two hours later, both in reasonably good condition after the blow. Number One had *Firedancer's* damage report ready for Hardy to review when the captain called for his next cup of tea. Hardy studied the report's highlights as the brisk wind pulled thin clouds of steam off the cup.

"Hedge Hog's twisted on her base, is she? Well, that won't do. She can't be fired, can she?"

"No, sir," Land replied. "Some of the loads are jammed in place. I'm afraid it's out of action."

"Run of bloody bad luck," Hardy said, handing the report back to him. "Still, I suppose it's only fair. That's the only real damage any of us have to show for the storm."

"More bad weather to come," Land mused.

"Bound to be," Hardy said, studying the sky. "We're in the eye of it, all right."

Land lapsed into an inventory of the duties that were bound to befall him because of the storm. He'd get to them soon enough. Time for one more cup of tea. It arrived just as Hardy turned to him.

"You surprise me, Number One," Hardy said. "I would have thought you to want to question me over the message I sent the fleet officer. About Kate's knickers."

Land had forgotten all about it. "Well, sir. The thought had crossed my mind."

"Down twenty," Hardy said to the helmsman. "Starboard ten degrees. We'll bring her bow just off the wind a bit. No sense in punishing the old girl."

Number One nodded his agreement as the order was relayed back.

"Some years ago, before the war," Hardy began, "before I was married, the fleet officer and his wife and I used to socialize. His wife was a bit of a wet blanket, always ill about something or other. Still is, I'm sure. One summer an American film actress came to visit. It was a beautiful summer. The ship I was on was in for refit, so I had a lot of free time on my hand. Funny how the summers before the war seemed so idyllic, didn't they, Number One? Like it was another century. A peaceful time before the madness began. Well, to continue. Kate was some distant relative of the fleet officer's wife's family, some cousin or niece or something like that. A free spirit, Kate was. Bubbling over with good times, always fun around her, a party sprang up wherever she went. Lovely girl, very pretty, always laughing, witty, intelligent. The fleet officer and Kate hit it right off. He was a bit older than she, but they were natural together. All this unbeknownst to his wife. Things were going swimmingly between the two, without the wife knowing, until she, the wife, happened across a pair of Kate's knickers in their Bentley. She confronted her husband. The fleet officer was beside himself. A scandal would ruin his career and, of course, they were living off her family's money. You know how the navy pays, Number One.

"There was nothing for the fleet officer to do but concoct some outlandish yarn about me borrowing the car, and the knickers must have been the result of one of my nefarious adventures. The wife and I had never gotten along well and all, and she was more than willing to believe that I was the culprit in this little adventure. I don't think she would have been happier if the fleet officer could have linked me to some murder. Luckily, the poor man had time to ring me up and advise me of the story before the wife showed up at my digs to haul me over the coals. She liked doing that sort of thing in person, Number One, the smell of blood and all of that. Being a true friend, I corroborated the fleet officer's story, even throwing in a few ingredients of my own, spicing it up a bit. Of course the wife was absolutely horrified and told me so in no uncertain terms. I was henceforth banned from any and all association with the fleet officer and the family, and I probably would have been flogged if she had her way. The subject has never come up between the fleet officer and me since."

"What happened to—"

"Kate? Oh, she returned to Hollywood and to her career in film. I'm sure you've seen her films. She's played queens and socialites, that sort of thing. The fleet officer was in a blue funk over her for quite a while, but he got over it. There you have it."

"I had no idea," was all that Land could manage.

He walked back to check the barometer. It was falling. The storm would get worse. When he returned to his station on the bridge, Hardy hadn't moved.

"Let it not be said, Number One," the captain said, folding his arms over the windscreen, "that we sailors lack loyalty and passion."

"No, sir."

"Now all you have to do is decide whether the story is true."

"Sir?"

"What kind of subordinate would I be, passing on rumors about my superiors? Let it not be said that Firedancer was disloyal."

"No, sir."

"Bridge, asdic," came through the voice tube.

"Bridge here," Land said. "What is it, Stackhouse?"

"Picking up a faint echo off asdic, sir. Can't tell if it's a U-boat or some damage to the dome from the beating that we took. But there's something else, sir. Sort of a pounding, like metal on metal. It doesn't come often, erratic really, but it's distinct enough."

Hardy leaned over to the tube. "Stackhouse? Did you say we have damage to our asdic?"

"Looks like it, sir," Stackhouse replied. The asdic-hydrophone, suspended in water, was encased in a dome under the ship's hull. "I'm getting an unusual echo off the sound beam, but the noise is real enough. It's close enough for me to pick it up on my headphones."

Hardy turned to Number One. "Blast! Make to *Fury*. Tell her our asdic is out and she's to take the sweep ahead. Have *Punjabi* and *Fearless* take positions on either side of us. Stackhouse? Can you get us to that noise of yours?"

"Yes, sir."

"There you are, Number One."

"The U-boats."

"That, or old Triton at his forge. Or whatever the bloody hell he's got down there. Get the course, Number One, and let's go find our U-boats."

Brown approached Hardy. "Signal from *Fury*, sir. 'No contact. Request Sweep Plan Baker.'"

Hardy called down to Stackhouse, "Stackhouse. *Fury* doesn't pick up anything on asdic. Do you still have that noise?"

"No, sir. No noise and nothing shows on our asdic but a lot of snow. It's out, sir."

"Keep at it." Hardy turned to Brown. "All right, Brown. Make to *Fury,* Institute Baker. Tell *Punjabi* and *Fearless* to take the flanks. It's time to plow again."

It was several hours later that Stackhouse called up to tell them of the contact. The seas were moderate and *Firedancer*'s crew had been able to repair most of the damage done because of the storm. All except what had been carried away and the asdic doom mounted on the ship's hull. Barton had his men working on the damaged Hedge Hog immediately after the worst of the storm had passed.

First they carefully removed the depth charges, and with winches and brute strength, managed to level the thrower. After several dry runs, the gunnery officer pronounced it repaired and ready for combat. Everything was forgotten with the news of a contact.

Hardy joined Stackhouse in the dark confines of the sound room.

"It's a sky-wave transmission, sir," Stackhouse said apologetically. "That's all I've got, I'm afraid, sir. She's out at least a hundred miles. Maybe a bit more. Huff-Duff just picked it up."

"A U-boat," Hardy said.

"I'd say, sir. Can't tell what they're sending, but I don't think it's a message."

"How's that?"

"They're just running through the alphabet, sir."

"I see. Not our boats, eh, Stackhouse?"

"No, sir. Not the ones we've been chasing. This is another chap. Well ahead of us. Our U-boats are between him and us, sir."

Hardy called up to Land to increase speed and pass the information on to the other ships. He watched Stackhouse as the chief yeomen delicately turned the frequency knob, and the indicator crept slowly across the dial, searching for a strong signal.

"Very weak. Very weak, sir. It's strange, sir. The keying, I mean."

"What about it, Stackhouse?"

"He's using his transmitter as a homing beacon. It's like he's calling for someone."

Hardy straightened and thought for a moment.

"He's calling for our chaps. It's a rendezvous. Keep after it. Let me know if there's any change." He quickly made his way to the bridge. Barton had just relieved Land and the young gunnery officer stood to one side as Hardy arrived.

"Twenty-eight knots, Quartermaster," he ordered the helmsman. "Signals? Make to the flotilla. 'Possible U-boat rendezvous approximately one hundred miles due west of this position. Make all possible speed.' There it is, Barton, if we can't find the bloody bastards in the ocean, we'll get them when they resupply. That's what it is, I'm sure of it. There's one of those big supply boats out there, waiting on our chaps to come suckle. Are your lads up to it, Mr. Gunnery Officer? A whole bloody wolf pack?"

"Yes, sir," Barton returned. "Get us there, sir and we'll do our bit."

The speaker over their head crackled. "Kaleu to the radio room."

Hartmann followed Kern out of the small cabin and along the passageway.

They stopped at the entrance to the radio room and listened to intermittent buzzes coming over the loudspeaker.

"What the hell is he doing?" Kern asked. "He'll have every American ship within two hundred miles down on us."

Reche looked up at them helplessly. "I think it's a recognition signal, Herr Kapitaenleutnant. They just keep repeating it."

"Maybe he is afraid that we'll miss the rendezvous," Hartmann suggested.

"Seeckt has more sense than that," Kern said. "This is suicide. If he wants to kill himself, all well and good, but leave us out of it."

"What are we going to do?" Hartmann asked.

"We've got to rendezvous with him—those are our orders—but we won't surface until we know the area is clear."

"What about those signals Funker picked up before the storm?"

"Reche," Kern said. "Have you picked up those destroyers since we came out of the storm?"

"No, sir," Reche said.

"They must have given up on us," the exec said.

"Or they're still looking for us and just haven't found us yet."

The buzzing continued, short, angry bursts of electricity filling the tiny room. "Shut that off!" Kern ordered

Reche. "Put somebody else on the radio and get back to your sound equipment. I don't want those bastards sneaking up on us when we get to Seeckt."

"Maybe there's been a change in orders," Hartmann said.

"No. The Lion would have sent out something on Goliath. He wouldn't have sent it to Seeckt to pass on to us. Mend?" he called back into the control room. "How much longer until we rendezvous?"

Mend quickly glanced at his charts. "Just over six hours, Herr Kaleu."

Kern bit his lip in thought. "Are the batteries fully charged?"

"Yes, Kaleu. We've just finished an hour ago. The exec said to leave the Schnorchel up to air out the boat."

Kern looked at Hartmann.

"I thought the men could use some air."

"The more that the Schnorchel is up, the more chances we give Tommy to find us. It leaves a wake, Teddy. It's a small wake, but it's still visible. Maybe they can pick it up on radar. Even with rough seas. We don't know."

"You're right."

"Take it down, Teddy."

"Herr Kaleu?" Reche looked up from his sound equipment. "I think the Tommies are back." He turned up the volume for Kern. They heard an almost imperceptible ping, coming at regular intervals. It was asdic, searching for them.

"Time to outrun those bastards," Kern said. "Teddy, both ahead full. I want to make a high-speed run to the rendezvous and get that over with. From there to our station is less than a hundred miles. Tell Frick I may want his V-belt drive sooner than we expected."

"Yes, Kaleu," Hartmann said.

Kern turned back to Reche. "Whoever that is, he doesn't want to give up. Does he, boy?"

Reche managed a smile. "No, sir. I guess what they say about the English being stubborn is true."

"Well, we'll show him something about being stubborn, won't we?"

"Yes, Kaleu."

"Keep at it," Kern ordered Reche. "Let me know if there is any change."

"Message from *Fury*, sir!" Brown called to Hardy. The signalman read the Morse message through his binoculars. "Possible contact U-boat dead ahead. Request permission increase speed to target."

Brown looked to Hardy for his reply. The captain had his bowler on, and the short brim was pulled well down over his head. "He looks like a peeler," Brown mentioned to the helmsman in passing.

"You ought to know," the helmsman said. "You've had your run-in with the law, haven't you?"

"Make to *Fury*," Hardy said. "Permission granted; lead on. Action Stations."

The clanging alarm bell brought seamen to their stations in a rush. Men flew to the Hedge Hog and gun mounts; Barton dashed off the bridge and down toward his station with the aft depth-charge throwers. The fire party took their station just aft of the funnel, and the cooks cleared the galley tables, getting ready for the wounded. The men were at their stations when Land suddenly appeared on the bridge, hastily pulling his duffel coat on—his fingers fumbling for the buttons.

"*Fury* has scared up a contact, Number One," Hardy said calmly. "We're just after it to see what it's about."

"Our Norway boats?"

"Yes, yes. They're being called in by Mother, I suspect.

That's the signal that Stackhouse came across. Mother calling her children."

"Yes, sir."

"Well, Mother had better set the table; she's got company coming."

"*Fury* again, sir," Brown said. "Target speed increased. Estimate target speed twelve knots."

Land let out a low whistle. "She's really flying, sir."

"One of their new boats," Hardy agreed. "Enough to make your mouth water, isn't it, Number One? Just think of bagging one of them, or two or three, however many are out there. Brown? Make to *Fury*—increase speed to twenty-seven. Copy, *Fearless* and *Punjabi*."

The Morse lamp quickly began clicking out the message, as Hardy explained to Land: "They're closer to that supply ship than we are, Number One. So we'll go twice as fast and catch Admiral Doenitz's new U-boats sunning themselves."

"We'll have a bit of luck, sir." Land looked up and was greeted by a clear afternoon sky. "The storm's gone around us. But Jerry can see us coming."

"Yes. I expect they'll scatter when we fly in to them, Number One, but that can't be helped. There's no sneaking up on them while they're on the surface, and we've little enough luck while they're submerged. The nearest Hunter-Killer Group is still well out of range, so I can't count on their aircraft."

"What about the VLR chaps?"

"Socked in, I'm afraid. I could use some Very Long-Range aircraft right now, but they can't get to us. No. It's up to us."

Land said nothing. It was the way that Hardy wanted it, a private contest of speed and skill. A bit eccentric, Land thought. But in war, eccentricities can be dangerous.

Chapter 25

Kern slowly swung the periscope around. Hartmann stood near him, waiting expectantly. The other men in the control room were silent; the only sounds that could be heard were the soft hum of equipment and the faint swish of the periscope in its bushings as Kern traversed the horizon. The sea was an endless plain of gentle green swells, and the sky a chalky white haze of undistinguished clouds, with the sun a soft glare in the west.

"Down," Kern ordered, stepping back. He looked at Hartmann. "It's clear. Prepare to surface."

"E-motors, three times ahead."

The increased speed would put more water over the hydroplanes, making them more responsive and allowing the boat to surface quickly.

"Engineer reports diesels are ready," Mend called.

"Open main air pressure valves," Hartmann ordered. Sailors frantically opened valves and spun hand wheels; green lights blinked on across the board as compressed air filled the buoyancy tanks.

"Bridge watch, stand by."

"Fifty meters," Mend called, his eyes on the depth gauges. "Forty meters. Twenty. Tower comes free."

Frick and his engineers waited near the galley hatch. The moment the boat surfaced, they were to inspect and repair the RGT rails. They had five minutes, Kern told them.

"Engage diesels," Hartmann called back as Kern, standing on the aluminum ladder leading to the bridge, spun the wheel and pushed open the hatch. Air rushed through the hatch as the U-boat's pressure equalized. The diesel motors kicked in, pumping exhaust into the buoyancy tanks to drive out any remaining seawater.

Kern scrambled up the ladder, quickly took his place on the port bridge station, and scanned the horizon with his binoculars. Behind him came the other members of the watch. They took their stations, looking for enemy surface vessels or aircraft. The anti-aircraft gun turrets at both ends of the conning tower swung to life, their guns pointing like fingers into the sky.

"U-boat surfacing to starboard," the petty officer behind Kern said. The kapitaenleutnant quickly found the U-boat's conning tower as it broke the surface of the water. U-1027 slowly rose into view.

"It's Seeckt," Kern said, as water streamed from the big Milchkuh.

"U-boat off the starboard bow," a lookout said.

"We've made contact with Seeckt and Gorlitz," Kern called down into the surface running station. "Pass it on."

The Milchkuh crept closer to U-3535 as U-3712 maintained her position, rolling gently in the low swells. Kern saw several figures on the bridge of the Milchkuh. As the U-boat crept closer, he could make out the slender form of Oberleutnant Seeckt.

"Greetings, Herr Kapitaenleutnant Kern," Seeckt

shouted across the narrow band of water that separated the two boats. "How was your voyage?"

"Uneventful," Kern returned. "Why were you signaling?"

"The fuehrer's orders," Seeckt said. "He did not want his hero to miss the rendezvous. "Now that I see that two of you have arrived, I'm to radio Goliath."

"There are enemy ships on my tail," Kern shouted. "They should be just behind me. You'd better wait until we're well clear of you."

"I can't," Seeckt said. "Orders are orders. I'm to report the minute that you dive. So those are the new boats?" He saw Frick and his crew inspecting the RGTs. "What have you on your backs?"

Kern looked aft. "Have you found it?" he called to Frick. The engineer waved.

"A cross brace buckled and tore lose. I can't repair it but I don't think it would harm anything to take it off. Everything else seems to be all right."

"Three minutes," Kern shouted back. He turned to Seeckt. "Any news of home?"

There was a moment's hesitation before the commander of U-1027 spoke. "Not good news."

"It never is anymore. Rockets," he said in answer to Seeckt's question. "Haven't you heard? U-boats carry rockets now."

"What do you hope to do with those things? Win the war single-handed?"

Kern did not bother to respond. Instead, he ordered Mend to give him the portable Varta Lampe. He signaled to U-3712, asking their condition. Gorlitz signaled back that the Schnorchel was not working properly and the batteries were low. Kern ordered him to begin a high-speed surface run immediately, hoping that it would reduce the time necessary to recharge the batteries. Kern cautioned him to keep a sharp eye out for enemy aircraft, and urged him to repair the Schnorchel as quickly as possible. He handed the lamp to a petty officer and scanned the sky. The sky was hazy. The glare hurt his eyes. He lowered his binoculars and spoke to Seeckt again.

"You had better be very careful. The enemy must know that you're here," Kern said. He knew how stupid the advice was. Seeckt knew that. He also knew how little chance he had of seeing Germany again.

"All finished, Kaleu," Frick called from the deck.

Kern saw U-3712 heading west at three times emergency speed, her deck awash, nearly lost save for the square tower that jutted from the rolling waves. She looked insignificant in the vastness of the sea, an inconsequential flotsam on the waves. Frick and his party were below when Kern turned to Seeckt.

"Take care, Oberleutnant Seeckt. Good luck."

"Good luck to you, Kapitaen Kern," Seeckt shouted across the water. "Make those things count for something, won't you? We could all use some good news."

There was nothing else for either one of them to say. Whatever happened now would happen.

"Watch below," Kern ordered. "Prepare to dive."

"Bridge? Stackhouse, sir."

Hardy leaned over the voice tube. "Bridge. Captain," he responded.

"Huff-Duff reading, sir. Ground-wave transmission. Estimate fifteen to eighteen miles dead ahead, sir."

"Right. Brown, make to the flotilla. Enemy U-boat dead ahead, fifteen to eighteen miles distance. Action Plan Hercules, repeat: Action Plan Hercules."

Hardy leaned over the voice tube, but before he

could say anything, the sighting bell rang on the bridge, and Stackhouse's excited voice came out of the tube.

"Bridge? Radar sighting. Possible U-boat, fifteen miles. Strong signal. U-boat on surface run, six to eight knots, bearing 230."

Land took his place next to the helmsman. It was his duty to maneuver the ship as the U-boat's bearing and range changed, but all of that would depend on how well Stackhouse could track the enemy.

"U-boat ten miles ahead," Stackhouse said. "Signal strong. Bearing 230."

Hardy leaned over. "Just one, Stackhouse?"

"Yes, sir. One only. A big boat, sir. Possibly a supply boat. Huff-Duff is still picking up her signal, and I've got her on radar."

Firedancer knifed through the water, *Fearless* and *Fury* keeping pace. *Punjabi* brought up the rear, but kept a good station off *Firedancer*'s stern.

"Brown?" Hardy said. "*Fury* and *Fearless* pennants. Execute Hercules."

The signal pennants were quickly run up the yard. They snapped excitedly in the brisk wind as *Firedancer* surged ahead. *Fury* and *Fearless* swung to starboard, their bows beating the water to a white froth as they heeled over. They were like hounds that caught the scent, straining to be unleashed. The tiny flotilla narrowed the distance between themselves and their target.

"Bridge? Stackhouse. She's diving, sir."

"To *Firedancer* from *Fury*," Brown said to Hardy. "'Asdic contact firm—classified submarine, range fifteen thousand yards—inclination opening. Tallyho!'"

Hardy reacted as if Brown had just announced that tea was served. "Port fifteen."

"Port fifteen," the helmsman returned.

"*Fury* and *Fearless* are flying the contact flag, sir," Land noted as the two destroyers ran well forward of *Firedancer* and *Punjabi*. A few minutes later he said: "*Fury*'s got her attacking flag out. *Fearless* is standing by."

Suddenly Land heard a dull report and watched as twenty-four depth bombs arched out from *Fury*'s bow to land in a rough diamond pattern in the water. The destroyer quickly rolled over the spot and when she was well ahead of it, the water exploded in a phosphorescent column with a low boom. It hung in the air before falling gracefully back into the sea. Almost immediately, larger depth charges were flung from either side of *Fury* by her Y-throwers. The throwing arm separated from the charge and they both fell into the sea. Several seconds later there was a huge explosion that lit the base of a column of water as it rose over *Fury*.

"*Fearless* is attacking, sir," Brown notified Hardy as the other destroyer moved in. She repeated the same process as her sister, tearing the water to foam with her depth charges. They took turns for the next twenty minutes, racing back and forth over the submerged U-boat, while *Punjabi* and *Firedancer* remained at a distance in case the U-boat should slip past the other two. After a pass that saw *Fearless* drop depth charges from her stern rails, a black stain appeared on the water. It began to grow and spread over waves. Hardy picked up a pair of binoculars and trained them on the spot.

"It's oil," he said. "Bits of debris as well." He said nothing for several moments. "There's a body." There was no excitement in his voice. "Make to *Fearless* and *Fury*, Brown. Cease operations. Form up."

"*Fury* reports, sir," Brown said. "Contact eliminated."

"Right. Brown," Hardy said. "To *Fury* and *Fearless*: well done." He turned to Land. "I'll give them a minute to fall in behind us, and then we're off again. That's the Mother, I'm sure of it, but her children are out there some place and I want them as well."

"It'll be dark in several hours, sir," Land said.

"Yes, I know, Number One, but we're close to Guenter Kern."

"I mention that only because it'll make hunting a bit dicey, sir. We ought to let *Fury* and *Fearless* take the lead, sir. Their asdic works and they've got several knots on the Tribal."

"You're right, Number One. Tell them to lead off and we'll follow."

"Yes, sir."

"What do you think, Number One?" Hardy asked after the message was sent. "Do you think the Hat has brought us more good luck?"

"Yes, sir. I don't think that there's anything like it in the Royal Navy, sir."

Hardy pulled it from his head and studied it in the setting sun. "By God, I believe you're right, Number One. And there's certainly no one as likely to wear such a device as myself."

Funker looked up at Kern and Hartmann to speak, but instead pressed the earphone against his ear. He listened intently, nervously licking his lips. He was still a boy, Kern knew, but he was one of the best soundmen that the kapitaen had ever seen in action.

Funker slowly twisted the direction wheel, listening carefully. Finally, he announced without taking his eyes off the dial, "It's Seeckt, sir. Sounds like two or three destroyers. The depth charge patterns are very tight. Well timed." He looked up. "Tommy."

"You're sure?"

Funker nodded.

Kern pulled Hartmann to one side. "What the hell is Tommy doing way out here?"

"Hunter-Killer."

"Without bees? No. They would never fail to call in at least one carrier. What size ships, Funker?"

"Destroyers, sir. Fast screws."

"Nothing larger?"

Funker shook his head, threading the knob a fraction of an inch to the right. His hand flew up for attention. He clamped the headset against his ear. "Something is breaking up. A U-boat, Kaleu. She's gone."

Kern leaned against the bulkhead. "Have Frick engage the V-belt drive," he ordered Hartmann. "Pass on to the crew that I don't want to hear so much as a fart from any of them. Whoever those Tommies are, they aren't amateurs. I don't want to end up like Seeckt."

"Should I tell them?" the exec asked.

"What?"

"About Seeckt," Hartmann said.

Kern looked around the control room. He saw men trying to look as if they didn't know what was going on between the officers and Funker.

"There's no need to," Kern answered. "They already know."

A knock at the door awoke Doenitz from a restless sleep on the couch in his office. He sat up immediately and reached over to the lamp behind the couch. The light flooded the room, stabbing into his eyes.

Doenitz saw the shadowy bulk of Godt standing in the doorway. His features were obscured by the harsh light that flooded around him from the room beyond. The figure of the vice admiral was spectral, like a ghost come to call in the night.

"What is it, Godt?"

"The report has just come in Herr Grand Admiral, from U-1027."

"Well? Is it good or bad?"

"U-3712 and U-3535 have reached the rendezvous."

"But not U-3719. This confirms the report we got from Norway then. Two U-boats left, Godt."

"Perhaps they will get through."

"To do what? To annoy the English? At best to alarm or alert them?"

"Sometimes, Herr Grand Admiral," Godt began slowly, "a few men can accomplish a great deal."

"Has it come to this, Godt? Are we reduced to clutching at hope as it floats above us, just out of reach?"

"Where there is life, Herr Grand Admiral, there is hope."

"Do you really think that? Can you say with certainty what will happen to those young men that we have sent out into the Atlantic?"

"With certainty, Grand Admiral? No. But I know that if God wishes it to happen, it will happen."

"And if our fuehrer commands that it will be done? In whose authority do we put our trust?"

"We put our faith in God, Herr Grand Admiral, and out trust in German sailors."

"Seeckt? What has become of our young aristo-crat?"

"We lost the signal."

"Yes, of course we would. God's will, Godt?"

The vice admiral did not reply.

"Go and get some rest, old friend," Doenitz said. "Pay no attention to me. I am tired."

"Grand Admiral? We have both seen bad times for Germany. You and I were in the Kriegsmarine between the wars. We had no money, no ships. Nothing. We went from that to chasing the Tommies and the Americans from the seas. I do not say that this mission will save Germany. I do say it is entirely possible for Kern to reach England and launch his rockets. With God's help."

Doenitz reached over the back of the couch and turned off the light. "God help German sailors," he said to Godt.

The vice admiral turned and pulled the door closed behind him. Blackness swarmed into the room to cover the grand admiral as he lay back down on the couch.

"God forgive me for what I have done," he whispered in the darkness.

Chapter 26

Land shook Hardy gently. Number One knew not to turn on the overhead light in the captain's sea cabin to awaken him, the glare robbed Hardy of night vision and he would spend the first ten minutes awake dressing down Land. Hardy kept a small lamp on his desk burning when he retired. The light provided some illumination but it was too faint to interfere with the captain's night vision.

"Sir? You'll want to know this, sir."

Even in the darkness, Land could see Hardy's eyes blink open. He knew that the captain would need a moment to get oriented. Land stood back from the bunk, well clear of Hardy's legs when he slung them over the bed rail and put his feet flat on the cold deck. It was one of Hardy's rituals. Never go to sleep with your shoes on, Hardy informed him one morning over tea, it causes irregularity.

"I'm up, blast you, Number One. Quit badgering me. That's what you solicitors do, isn't it? Badger witnesses?" Hardy ran his hands over his face roughly. "What is it?"

"We've lost the Jerries, sir."

Hardy looked up in surprise. "Lost them? What the bloody hell do you mean that we've lost them?"

"*Fury* thought that they had picked them up when

we were done with that U-boat but now they say that they can't find the signal."

"They *did* pick them up. Don't give me any non-sense about *Fury* losing those U-boats."

"Yes, sir," Number One said. "But it's true."

"What course?"

Land gave him the course and speed and waited patiently while Hardy thought it over.

The captain shook his head in bewilderment and slipped on his shoes. He stood quickly, not bothering to tie them. "Come on, Number One. Move along. Let's get to Stackhouse and see what this is all about."

"Fifty feet, Kaleu," Mend called back to Kern.

"All right, Funker," Kern said, from the control room. "See what you can find out."

He didn't like this, putting only fifty feet of water between U-3535 and the enemy, but he wanted information, and this was the only way to get it short of surfacing and sending a radio message. To do that was to commit suicide. Kern knew the Tommies were still out there. He felt a sudden pang of regard for his new boat. Silent running really meant silent running with the V-belt drive. A high-speed dash, once capable only on the surface with the Type VIIs, now was an opportunity for U-3535 to clip through the depths like a shark. What a wondrous machine. If only they had had them in the beginning.

Kern watched Frick as the engineer stood behind the two hydroplane stations supervising the boat's trim. Three years with Frick, Kern realized. A little more than two with Teddy. Kern looked back to the sound room. Teddy was listening to the radio with an extra pair of Funker's headsets. He knew nearly as

much about the radio as Funker. The exec tapped
Funker on the shoulder and motioned for another
frequency. Engle and Mend. Months? No, nearly a
year. They were a strange pair, very smart. He judged
them both brilliant after several training runs with
them on U-686—but sensible. Kern saw the fresh
faces of Mend and Engle as the two stood wide-eyed
before him their first day aboard.

Mendle. Someone in the crew combined the two
names. Not out of derision, more to identify that they
behaved alike, thought alike, apparently liked the
same things. It might have been Frick who first
named them—Kern couldn't remember.

Hartmann looked at him and shook his head.
Nothing on the radio yet. Kern wasn't surprised. They
were on their own, expected to run silent until they
reached the launch coordinates. And then? Surface
and hope the other U-3712 was waiting. Double-check
their position, submerge, and fire. All very simple.
Nothing to it. Nothing to it.

And the run home?

And the run home, Kern thought, would be the
most dangerous that he had undertaken. The Tommies who had been following them, the ones that they
had escaped, at least for a while, would be waiting for
them.

Two boats, four rockets, a handful of men. It was a
long way from Lake Constance, lying back along the
boat's tiller when the wind was even and losing himself in the pure blue canopy overhead.

Kern looked at Hartmann. The exec shrugged an answer. Nothing out there yet. *What did I expect?* Kern
questioned himself. An order recalling them? A message
telling them the war was over and the Kriegsmarine was
to stand down?

Perhaps the news that a hundred more Type XXI boats were on their way to attack the English and, far from being on the brink of disaster, Germany was poised for victory. *Now you sound like that idiot Goebbels,* Kern admonished himself. *Everything is fine.* Germany's cities weren't piles of rubble, the Russian winter had not killed off the German army, U-boats were not being sunk faster than they could be built— or young men could be trained.

"Watch the Papenberg," Frick directed one of the hydroplane men. "Compensate to keep her steady, but don't overreact. She's a big boat."

Died for the Fatherland, Kern thought. *How many of my friends?* He tried to bring their faces to mind. They came slowly and with each came a name—a roll call of the dead.

Stop it, you maudlin bastard! Get your mind out of the past and down to business. You're alive. Stay that way.

"Well?" Kern said to Hartmann.

"Nothing, sir," Hartman said.

"All right. Keep Funker on it, Teddy. Plot out a course and time for a high-speed run to the launch point."

Hartmann handed the earphones back to the radio operator/sound man.

"At what speed, Kaleu?"

"Fourteen knots," Kern answered, then noticed Frick smiling at him. "Something funny, Engineer?"

"No, Kapitaenluetnent. Just watching you get ready for a fight."

"Can you disengage the V-belt drive up here, Frick?" Kern asked. "Shouldn't you be back with your precious engines?"

"Yawohl, Mien Kapitaenleutnant."

The engineer brushed by Hartmann, who was at

the chart table, doing his computations. Kern looked around the control room. Almost in an instant his crew seemed to have sparked into life, filling the room with energy, a quiet excitement that was revealed in how crisply the men moved to their duties. It was because he reminded them of their purpose, Kern knew. Even after the bread was moldy and the cheese was covered with a green fuzz and the water tasted of diesel fuel, and the air in the boat clung to everyone, heavy with the odor of unwashed bodies; even after they had the hell knocked out of them by Tommy—they did their duty. He was proud of them.

"What did that idiot on *Fury* say?" Hardy snapped at Land as Stackhouse peered at the radar screen. The sound room was barely large enough for the operators and one other person: Land was forced to stand face-to-face with the enraged captain.

"Just that they lost him, sir. They had a strong signal one moment, and the next it was gone."

Hardy turned on the asdic operator. "Well, Stackhouse?"

"We're not picking up a thing, sir. Nothing on the radar, but we might be too far back to read a snort's shadow. We haven't picked a thing on Huff-Duff. All that's left is asdic, sir. *Fury* says that hers is operating. Fields is over there, sir. He's very competent. If he lost them, sir, he'll find them again."

"Well, your confidence in your fellow asdic operators aside, Stackhouse," Hardy said, "I'm tempted to rig up a bo'swain's chair and send you over there myself."

"If we could run up on them, sir, maybe there's a

chance I could pick up their snort on radar," Stack-house said. "It leaves a distinctive signature."

Land saw his chance. "The seas are a bit rough, sir. They'd be running with their snorkels well above the water."

"You think they would, do you?" Hardy said. "These kapitaens didn't last this long making mistakes, Number One. I'd bet just the opposite is true, but we'll give your theory a chance. Keep at it, Stackhouse. I don't know why *Fury* lost the asdic signal. Maybe Jerry just shut everything off and is laying doggo out there some place. He's got to have air, and that's where I'm counting on you. Find that snort's shadow." To Land he said, "Increase speed five knots. We'll be running too fast to pick up anything on asdic, so tell the others to use their radar. Tell them to keep a sharp eye, Number One."

"Yes, sir," Land said. Their only chance lay with finding the faint signature.

"And, Number One?" Hardy called as Land stepped out into the gangway. "Tell them the first operator who finds the snort gets one of my paintings as a reward. Signed, mind you."

"Yes, sir," Land said. He didn't have to imagine what the response to that message would be.

Chapter 27

Aboard U-3535 in the Irish Sea

Kern waited patiently as Hartmann checked his figures for the second time.

He looked at Kern, expectation in his eyes. "We're here."

"Both back, dead slow," Kern ordered immediately. "Balance the boat." He was dressed in bulky foul-weather gear. The control room was silent, except for a seaman calling out the decreasing depth. Just past Funker's cramped quarters, Frick and six seamen, dressed in foul-weather gear as well, stood ready. Just in case.

Kern waited until Kerrl reported.

"Attention, Zero. Boat is balanced."

"All right, Frick. Let's see if your lift motors work."

"Right, Kaleu," Frick said. He clicked on the intercom. "Kerrl, engage the lift motors."

They looked up, waiting for the telltale whirring of the motors. They had heard it a dozen times before, a soft, effortless humming. The motors had worked perfectly in the fiord. Perfectly.

"This is Kerrl, we have a problem."

Kern rubbed his face.

"What is it?" Frick said into the intercom.

"The motors aren't engaging. They're dead."

"Shut it down and start over," Frick said.

"Nothing's showing on the board, Frick. It's dead."

"Never mind," Kern said.

"This is a bad place to surface," Hartmann said.

"We don't have a choice."

"Kaleu,"Frick said, "give us a moment. We'll get it."

"Increase E-motors to both ahead emergency," Kern said. "No, Frick. We'll use muscle."

"Kaleu—"

"Take her to periscope depth and hold," Kern said. "No. There is no discussion. I want to see if Tommy has any surprises waiting for us."

"Fourteen meters," a seaman at the Papenberg called back to Kern.

"Battle stations," Kern called. "Prepare for surfacing. Have diesels ready for immediate high speed. Funker?"

The soundman, clamping both earpieces tightly to his ears, glanced at Kern and shook his head. They were alone. Except for the possibility of bees.

"Periscope," Kern commanded, and waited as the eyepiece came level with his eyes.

He quickly snapped the handles down and pushed his forehead against the foam rubber rest, twisting his head until the position was comfortable. He was assured of the fit by the way the eyepieces fit around his eyes. It was a familiar feeling, and oddly, with it came a sense of calm. It was quiet on the boat. The crewmen knew that the time was near for action; each one was lost to his own thoughts, about home, about loved ones, about the job that they all had to do.

Kern looked back to Hartmann. "All clear. Scope down. Schnorchel down."

"Ready to surface," Hartmann said. Two men began

spinning the multiple hand wheels and valves on the Christmas Tree to free the passage of air to the buoyancy cells.

"All green," one of the seamen called back.

Frick had a forlorn look on his face. He always had that look when his machines failed him. Kern ignored him. He knew the engines would fail. All this time underwater—he knew they would fail. He quickly made his way to the aluminum ladder, climbed two rungs, and locked his hands into the spokes of the hatch wheel, ready to spin it.

"Tower clear. Hatch clear," the seaman at the Papenberg said.

Kern spun the hatch wheel with all of his strength as the deck crew moved to the ladder. He pitched open the hatch, ducking at the same time so that the frigid cascade of water trapped near the hatch bounced off his hat and shoulders. It was a trick that he learned as an ensign, a hundred years ago.

"Lookouts," Kern said as he scrambled up the ladder and took his place on the port bridge station. He quickly threw up the armored panels and pulled the tampons from the speaking tubes. He hastily blew into the tube.

"All right, Teddy," he said. "Time?"

"Clock's running," Hartmann replied. "Four minutes, thirty seconds."

Kern heard the hatch at the base of the tower clang open. A seaman squeezed in behind him and immediately began scanning the night sky with binoculars. Two seamen took position at the starboard bridge station. Kern watched as Frick led his team across the deck to the missiles. Five minutes was all they had to deploy and lock the platforms into place and replace the radio-controlled firing mechanisms. If the lift motors were out, then the firing mechanisms were probably bad as well. They would be replaced as a precaution. Frick had tested the replacement controls dozens of time on the voyage. It was the controls that he was most concerned with, he told Kern. He did not mention the lift motors.

It was very simple: a panel would be removed from each rocket, the old controls removed, and the new mechanisms installed that were to receive the firing signal from the U-boat. Very simple, the White Coats had told Kern, an elementary piece of equipment.

"Teddy?" Kern called into the voice tube. "The Hohentweil is not up. What's the problem?" The radar transmitter/receiver had to be extended to work properly. It lay dormant in its recess behind the port watch station, unusable. Without it, U-3535 could not see enemy aircraft or ships approaching. She was doubly blind in the darkness.

Hartmann's muffled voice came back through the voice tube. "Trying to fix it, Kaleu."

"Get it done but don't lose track of the time," Kern replied. He turned to the lookouts. "Keep your eyes open. The radar's out." The seas were moderate, swells rolling lazily under U-3535. That was their only bit of luck, Kern thought.

She was big enough to ride out these low seas well and give the men at the deck crew time enough to deploy the rails. He studied Frick and his men as they swarmed over the rails and rockets, working frantically to raise them into position. They reminded him of a child's story. Which one? Devils . . . demons, dancing in a clear black night under the faint light of a million stars. Which one was it? There was a poem . . . a chant of some kind, no, an incantation, his father called it.

Demons dancing in the night, below the stars' indifferent light.

Kern leaned to the voice tube. "Teddy? Where's my Hohentweil?"

"Working on it, Kaleu."

"Work faster. We're blind up here. What's the time?"

"Three minutes, twenty-three seconds."

"Three minutes," Kern called to Frick. He didn't expect an answer. Frick had sense enough to concentrate on the duty at hand, but Kern wanted the engineer to know how much time remained. I'll give you just five minutes on the surface, Kern had informed Frick. Five minutes to get those rails up and locked into position. If you take any longer than that, Kern added, I'll dive out from under you.

Kern wasn't serious, but if need be, he would do it. If need be, he had to do it rather than risk the boat, the crew, and the mission. Frick knew it.

Kern rubbed his forearms briskly to keep warm, a habit he had picked up from somewhere. He looked into the darkness. Gorlitz should be out there somewhere, getting ready to launch his rockets.

No, Kern told himself, Gorlitz would never be first at anything—not even with Kern's men aboard.

A shriek cut through the night from astern, running through Kern's bones like a saw.

"What in the hell are you doing back there?" he shouted to Frick.

"One of the rails is twisted," the engineer's voice returned. "It's binding against the support." There was another shriek as the protesting aluminum pieces ground against one another. Metal on metal, slicing into the night—like torpedoed ships that scream out in horror. It was those shrieks that knifed through the water and into the hulls of the U-boats that had killed them. No silent death, but plaintive cries from dying ships, masking the sounds of dying sailors.

The rail squealed once more and Kern saw the shape move in the darkness as if it were transforming itself without the aid of men. One of the rails was slowly being raised into position. The other remained in place.

"Teddy? Time?"

No answer.

"Teddy!"

"Three-oh-seven."

"Get that *Verdamnt* radar fixed!"

Kern fought back the urge to drop through the hatch and fix it himself. Kerrl would be working on it, and Hartmann as well. Another man would just be in the way.

Calm yourself. Let the men do their job.

"One side, Kaleu! Coming up!" Teddy shouted from below. Kern squeezed himself back against the armored panels as Hartmann suddenly appeared through the hatch, followed by a sailor. They quickly climbed out of the watch station onto the tower, making their way to the Hohentweil. They moved carefully on the slick surface; one misstep and they would slide off the tower's rounded top.

"Two minutes, twenty seconds." Engle's voice came through the tube.

"Two minutes, Frick," Kern shouted.

"The motor is burned out," Hartmann said as he and the seaman began jerking at the Hohentweil's mast, trying to pull it into position. "We had to disengage it." The two men grunted as they tried to free the radar. "Try it from there," Hartmann instructed the sailor.

Three minutes on the surface and no enemy ship or airplane in flight, Kern thought. Maybe it worked. Maybe whatever was supposed to happen happened, and the enemy was as blind as U-3535. The irony of the situation struck Kern: both sides blinded at once.

"There!" Hartmann said as he and the seaman pulled the Hohentweil mast into position.

"Can you extend it?" Kern asked. The mast was upright but not deployed, leaving the radar dome just two or three feet above the tower, severely restricting its range.

"We'll try," Hartmann grunted, as he tugged at the mast.

"Kaleu?" It was Engle calling through the voice tube.

"Yes?"

"Funker just told me he's picking up all manner of radio activity from the Tommies."

"What activity?"

"A lot of traffic. It's all code, of course, but from the tone of it Funker thinks they have problems."

"*They* have problems?" Hartmann threw in. "No good, Kaleu," the executive officer said, backing away from the Hohentweil. "I don't want to damage the dome."

"That's better than nothing," Kern replied. "Engle? The radar mast is up, but it won't extend. Tell Funker we can give him a mile or so and to keep his eyes open. Put someone else on the radio. And let me know the instant that the situation changes."

Kern heard the sound of the other rocket being slowly raised. "When we get back let's have a meeting with those White Coats. I don't like the idea of sitting on the surface while our men try to raise those things by hand," he said to Hartmann.

"I could go help them," Hartmann replied.

"No. Get below and keep an eye on the radar. I don't want to be surprised when the English wake up and find us at their doorstep. The sky will be swarming with bees."

"More targets to shoot at, Kaleu," Hartmann said with a smile.

"Get below, Teddy," Kern replied. "Let me know the minute your targets show up."

"One minute!" Engle called out.

Kern turned to Frick. The second rail stopped moving. It was only just off the deck. He could see the chief engineer and his men tugging at if frantically. One of the dark forms detached itself from the group and ran forward, toward the hatch.

"One minute, Frick," Kern shouted across the deck.

"This one's warped badly, Kaleu."

Kern cursed under his breath and for an instant wanted to turn his anger on Frick. *Why hadn't you prepared for this? We ran through every conceivable problem in Evanger and now you tell me this?* But Kern said nothing. He was almost mad with anger, but he said nothing because he knew that you prepared for every eventuality except the one you can't conceive of.

"The whole damned assembly is warped, Kaleu," Frick continued. "We're going to cut part of it away, otherwise we can't get it up."

Kern read the frustration in the engineer's voice clearly enough.

"Do anything that you need to, Chief Engineer," Kern said, making certain that his voice was calm. "Just do it in thirty seconds or less."

There was no answer from the deck. Now it was up to Frick to make things work. A seaman raced back to the rockets with a torch and tanks. Moments later

Kern heard the soft sound of the torch being lit and saw a pointed blue flame appear, bathing the men and rockets in an unnatural light. With their half features and hunched bodies straining against the malfunctioning rail, the men looked like gnomes. Demons, Kern thought again.

Maybe we are on the Devil's Shovel after all.

Land had the binoculars pressed tightly to his eyes, fixing on the tiny dot of light flashing out of the darkness.

"It's the Tribal, sir," he said, reading the Morse lamp.

"What has *Punjabi* to say that interests me?" Hardy said, looking cold and miserable with the bowler jammed down on his head.

"'Strong—signal—'"

Suddenly a whistle came through the voice tube.

"Bridge, Sound Room." It was Stackhouse and he was clearly excited

"' . . . On—surface—approximately—'" Land continued to read.

Hardy leaned over the tube. "Bridge, Hardy. What is it, Stackhouse?"

"'Appears—to—be—'"

"I've got an image on radar, sir. Not much of one, but it's bigger than a conning tower. It's not a Snort. Approximately fifteen miles out south-southwest."

"Number One!" Hardy said. "For God's sake be quiet, will you? I can't hear the man. Go on, Stackhouse."

"Could be a U-boat on the surface, sir. One of those big ones. Doesn't look like they're making more than five knots or so."

Hardy gave the speaking tube a troubled expression. "Now, why would Mr. U-boat be riding on the surface at five knots?"

"Tracking a convoy, sir?" Land ventured.

"We've been told of no convoy," Hardy said. "Stackhouse? Are you picking up anything else?"

"No, sir. Not a thing."

"Action Stations, Number One," Hardy ordered. He stepped back from the tube and looked out over the dark sea as the trumpet sounded for Action Stations. "This is a strange turn of events."

"Maybe she's riding on the surface because she's damaged," Land said.

"Quite possible, Number One. Then again she could be a bloody decoy and there are more of those bastards waiting for us to take the bait. Oh, what did the Tribal want?"

"She was reporting contact, sir."

"Nonsense! Nobody beats Stackhouse at this game."

"It looks as if they did, sir."

"They did, did they? Must have been a freak of nature, that's all I can say. Very well, Land. They get the painting, but I choose it. Never saw an intelligent face aboard a Tribal yet. Not a one of them would know bullocks about art."

"Yes, sir. All stations have reported, sir. Ships on Action Stations."

"Speed?"

"Twenty-eight knots, sir. I'm afraid that we've topped out on our revolutions. The old girl is feeling her age."

Hardy removed the bowler and rubbed his head vigorously. "Damned thing's gotten a size too small on me. Must be the humidity. Feeling her age, is she? Well, I am too, Number One. I think I'll stand down when we get back. Find a nice warm office to watch the war from."

"I can't see you sailing a desk, sir."

"I can," Hardy said. "No more freezing nights on the bridge. No more forty-hour days. No more having my brains beat out in dirty weather."

"No more thrill of the chase, sir?"

Hardy slapped the bowler on his head and tapped it down, low on his forehead. He threw his elbows back and leaned against the windscreen. He paused in thought before answering Land. "It's all coming to an end, Number One. Germany's on her last legs and Japan isn't far behind. The war long ago became too big for simple captains and single ships. Now we all dash about in squadrons with aircraft carriers and electronic wizardry."

"It's the nature of war, sir."

"Oh, I know that. Bound to happen. I begin to wonder what kind of world will come out of all of this."

"Kind of world, sir?"

"What will we leave our children and grandchildren?"

"I should hope a kinder world, sir."

"Perhaps," Hardy said.

"Perhaps indeed, sir."

"Well, enough of that nonsense," Hardy said. "Talking doesn't pay the butcher, does it, Number One? The U-boat will pick us up soon enough, and when it does it'll pull the waves over her head and disappear. When she does that, we'll go to Action Plan Zulu. The Tribal reported the contact first, so she goes it first. Never thought I'd say that, Number One. It's a dark day indeed when a Tribal beats out this ship."

Chapter 28

Aboard HMS Firedancer *in the Irish Sea*

Hardy leaned over the voice tube and pushed the bowler back on his head. "Stackhouse? What do you show now?"

"No change in speed or course, sir. Contact is still bearing south-southwest."

"Distance?"

"Just under three miles, sir."

Hardy grunted. "It's a mystery, Number One. Maybe Jerry thinks just because it's night he can't be found."

"He's wrong, sir."

"Wrong as can be, Number One. Dead wrong at that. Make the signal to the others, execute Zulu."

"Right," Land said. "Yeoman, make to the other ships, execute Plan Zulu."

The lamp shutters fluttered softly behind Number One as the signalman sent out the message. This was when Land became excited, during the chase. To him it was everything. Nothing thrilled him so much as the sound of the bell from the Huff-Duff room or the pinging of an asdic reading over the loudspeaker that told him that Stackhouse had the target on the plan-position indicator. Number One knew that it was the opposite with the captain: Hardy seemed to explode when they came in for the attack, the battle being between him and the U-boat and everyone else just staying out of the way. Perhaps that was why they made such a good team—they were opposite in nearly everything.

"Bridge. Stackhouse."

"Yes?" Hardy said.

"Target bearing 146 degrees, range two miles. No change in course."

"Right," Hardy said. "Keep after it, Stackhouse." He turned to Land. "We're after him, Number One. We'll come up behind him and boom!" His fist struck his open palm. "Send our friend to the bottom."

"What about the others, sir?"

"Others? Oh, you mean his chums. We shan't worry about them, Number One. My theory is there is something wrong with this boat and he was forced to the surface. Stackhouse tells me that Jerry's creeping along at five knots. Well then, we'll spark along at twenty-eight knots until we're a mile out from him. Drop it down to fifteen at one mile and fix on his stern. At a thousand yards it's seven knots and then we've got him."

"And then do we go after the others?"

"Yes."

"Bridge. Stackhouse."

"Bridge, aye," Hardy said.

"Contact firm—classified submarine. Range eight thousand yards—inclination opening. Still bearing 146 degrees."

"Right," Hardy said. "There you have it, Number One. Close enough. Drop us down to fifteen and bring us astern of Mr. U-boat."

"Who do you want to lead the attack, sir?"

"Lead? *Firedancer*, who else . . ." Hardy remembered. "Oh. The asdic. Bloody hell!"

"What about *Punjabi*? She found the boat, after all."

"Oh, very well. Give it to the Tribal. We'll position ourselves in the rear."

"Yes, sir," Land said and gave the necessary orders to the quartermaster and yeoman. He watched the dim shape of *Punjabi* in the distance as she acknowledged the signal. The Tribal jumped ahead excitedly as she increased her speed to take position, her wake churning nearly white in the darkness.

Hardy seldom shared an opportunity to lead the attack if he could help it. Morrison on *Punjabi*, a taciturn man with a limp and perpetual scowl, must be almost happy at the turn of events. *Fearless* and *Fury* would follow the Tribal, with *Firedancer* last.

"That bloody asdic!" Hardy growled.

"It's given us good service until now, sir," Land said.

"Well, now is exactly when I need it most, Number One. Bringing up the rear!"

"Signal from *Punjabi*, sir," the yeoman of signals announced, intent on the distant light flashing in the darkness. "'Contact firm—classified U-boat—'"

"Hell," Hardy grumbled to Land. "We already knew that."

". . . Range . . . 4,100 yards. Taking . . . position . . . astern. Speed . . . seven . . . knots."

"Seven knots, Number One," Hardy ordered.

"Stream the CATS, sir?"

"Yes, yes. It would be just our luck to have a torpedo run up our ass."

Land gave the order to reduce speed. He opened a small cabinet underneath the spray shield, pulled out a telephone, and switched a black button on.

"Torpedoman Anders—Depth Charge C," the reply crackled with static.

"Bridge—Land. Deploy the CATS."

"Deploy the CATS. Aye, sir."

Anders was very good. Just the right sort to have with Barton back there, Land thought.

Duty on the stern depth-charge station became much more dangerous with the enemy's acoustic torpedo. Once fired by the U-boat, they sought out the loudest sound in the ocean, homing relentlessly on that noise until they struck. Land had seen the results of an acoustic torpedo striking a destroyer in the stern. One of the E-class ships—*Encounter*. Her stern was sheered off; all that was left was a mass of curled, blackened metal and smoking wreckage where her engine room had been. She rolled helplessly about in moderate seas, struggling to keep afloat. She became a pathetic cripple whose deformities caused Land to want to look away.

That was the theory behind dropping to seven knots and streaming the CATS. It was thought, but never proven to Land's satisfaction, that reducing speed to seven knots reduced the target sound of the escort. The CATS were an added precaution. Trailing far behind the ships, they made enough noise to draw in the acoustic torpedoes. Sometimes, Land knew, those damned Jerry torpedoes would circle around and strike the U-boat. Sometimes, but never enough to suit Land. He never forgot *Encounter*.

"There we are," Hardy said as *Fury* and *Fearless* slid easily into line. "Good handling, those two. Smartly done. Very competent all. We need to get you off old *Firedancer*, Number One. Get a command of your own."

"I've thought of it, sir."

"Thought of it? There's much more than thinking about it, Number One. You have to act."

"Message relayed from *Punjabi*, sir," the yeoman signalman called out.

"Yes?"

"'Yellow Warning.'"

"She's going in," Number One said. "Good luck, *Punjabi*."

"Message relayed from *Punjabi*, sir. 'Attack flag.'"

Hardy brought a pair of long-range binoculars to his eye. "Haven't got a pagan's chance in heaven of seeing that U-boat," he said to no one in particular. "Still, it would make my day." Land produced binoculars and watched as well.

"What do you see, Number One?" Hardy asked.

"I imagine the same as you, sir. Little enough."

Hardy whistled into the voice tube. "Stackhouse. We can't see a bloody thing up here except black sky and blacker sea. Keep us posted."

"Aye, sir. The U-boat's still on the surface. A thousand yards between *Punjabi* and the target. She is a big boat, sir. Bigger than anything I've seen."

"The Tribal will make short work of her," Hardy said, straining to see the action through the binoculars.

"Nine hundred yards now. I believe *Punjabi*'s dropped to five knots, sir," Stackhouse said.

"Can you see anything, Number One?" Hardy asked.

"I can just make out the Tribal's wake, sir," Land returned. "I can see her shape as she blots out the stars." *She moves through the night like a phantom,* Land thought, and for an instant he wanted to say that. But he withheld comment. Hardy would not like talk about phantoms in the night.

"Eight hundred yards, sir," Stackhouse said. "*Punjabi*'s steady."

Land admired the senior asdic rating's calm manner. He could have been describing tugs docking a cruiser, instead of the last minutes of men's lives.

"U-boat diving, sir!" Stackhouse said, betraying little excitement. "U-boat submerged."

"Get them, *Punjabi!*" Hardy growled behind his binoculars. "Smash them up! Smash them up!"

Yellow-green towers flashed in the darkness—the depth charges churning the sea. Moments later the dull boom of explosions reached Land's ears. It was all very innocuous, Land thought, light and noise and nothing to say that it was a battle. Several more flashes tore the night, followed by the kettledrum-like explosions.

"Lovely pattern, Number One," Hardy commented casually. "Those are the Hedge Hogs, I believe."

"*Fearless* moving up, sir." Stackhouse's voice came out of the darkness. "*Punjabi* pulling off to starboard. *Fearless* attacking."

Land watched as the unnatural light erupted out of the black sea. It shimmered in a mound that rose slowly off the surface and then exploded in a tower of water.

As the column began falling, the noise reached them— rumbling out of the darkness like an unseen train.

"Smartly done," Hardy observed. "There go the Y-mounts now. Make sure our chaps are ready, Number One. Can't have the others outdoing us, now, can we?"

"*Fearless* signaling, sir," the chief yeoman of signals sang out. "'*Fearless* to *Firedancer*,'" he began, reading the Morse code of the distant light. "'Secondary explosions . . . confirm . . . U-boat . . . destroyed . . . some debris . . . visible . . . suggest . . . attack . . . continue . . .'"

A huge flash filled the night sky, blinding Land. As he jerked his eyes away from the binoculars, the sound of an explosion rumbled over them like a wave.

"Damn!" Hardy shouted.

"Message interrupted, sir," Signals called out.

A sharp whistle from the voice tube pierced the night. "Bridge! Wireless/Telegrapher! *Fearless* has been struck, sir! Believe acoustic torpedo."

Land saw the flames of the damaged ship lick hungrily through the night. He picked up the bridge microphone and quickly pressed the talk button as the captain began issuing orders to the helmsman. "Supply party," Land announced. "Prepare to fight off-board fire." His eyes were drawn to the bright fire that illuminated the damaged ship's superstructure amidships. Poor *Fearless*, struck in the stern—dying. God help her. The bridge buzzed in activity.

"Bridge? Stackhouse."

"Bridge," Land quickly replied.

"Contact lost. Nothing on sonar. They got off a message before they were destroyed. We picked it up on Huff-Duff."

That was it. The U-boat was dead, but Hardy was concerned about the signal. "Calling for their chums."

"Maybe," Land answered.

"Well," Hardy said, "their friends can't help them now."

"Signal from *Fearless*, sir," the duty signalman called out. "'Am taking . . . on . . . water . . . aft. Severe damage . . . request . . . assistance.'"

"Make to *Fearless*," Hardy replied. "'Message received. Hold on, I'm coming.'" He spun to the voice tube. "W/T? Bridge!"

"W/T. Aye, sir."

"Make to *Fury* and *Punjabi*. 'Approach *Fearless* with extreme caution. Stand by to take off crew if necessary. Report any U-boat contacts immediately.'" He turned to the duty signalman. "Make to *Fearless*. 'Can you remain afloat?'" Back to W/T, "'Repeat. Watch out for U-boats.'"

"Taking her in, sir," Land said, moving *Firedancer* closer to the stricken vessel.

"Message from *Fearless*, sir. 'Engine . . . room . . . destroyed. For . . . God's . . . sake . . . stand by . . . to . . . take . . . us . . . in . . . tow.' End."

"What the devil does he think I'm going to do?" Hardy said. "Run off?"

"Message from *Fearless*, sir. 'Many casualties . . . engine . . . room . . . sealed. I'm all right now, Jack.'"

Hardy looked at the duty signalman. "'I'm all right now, Jack'? What does that mean?"

"Begging your pardon, sir," the flustered signalman returned. "It's a little levity on the operator's part. It's a saying they use in the music halls. Comedians, sir."

"Well," Hardy said, satisfied. "If *Fearless* can laugh a bit, everything will be fine. Carry on."

"Yes, sir."

"Bridge? W/T."

"Yes?" Land said, forgetting to identify himself.

"Message from *Fury*. 'Request permission take *Fearless* in tow. Proceed to port. End.'"

Land looked to Hardy for a reply.

"I suppose we haven't much of a choice, have we, Number One?"

"Make to *Fury*," Land said back into the voice tube. "'Permission granted, tow. Proceed to any port at your desecration. End.' Anything else, sir?"

Hardy did not reply. He walked to the far side of the bridge, turned, and walked back.

"Sir?"

Hardy shook his head, but in such a distracted manner that Land was unsure if it was in response to his question. He knew better than to ask a second time.

"Make to the Tribal," Hardy said to the duty signalman. "'Take up lead on original course. Look for targets.'" The only sound on *Firedancer*'s bridge was the soft sound of the Morse lamps' shutters, opening and closing. "'Proceed with caution. *Firedancer* will follow. End.'" He looked at Land and nodded. "He's out there, Number One. Our friend Kern."

"You don't think that was him," Land said.

"Our late U-boat? No. Not at all. Bad boat handling. A rank amateur. They sat on the surface too long, it wasn't him. I feel it for certain. Do you understand that?"

"Feeling? Intuition?"

"That's it. Intuition. Maybe I've gone mad after being out here for so long, but I know that wasn't Kern. If that wasn't Kern and he didn't expire along the way somewhere, then Guenter the Silent is still on course. So are we, Number One."

"Yes, sir," Land said with a smile. This was vintage Hardy—the sort of story that passes round the fleet from the mouths of seamen and officers until the truth is so misshapen that the only thing of it that remains accurate is that it was said on *Firedancer*. Hardy stood on the bridge and read the U-boat captain's mind. One more legend to add.

"There's only one thing that galls me, Number One."

"What is that, sir?"

"*Firedancer* has to be led into battle by a Tribal."

"Can't be helped, sir. Their asdic works."

"I know that," Hardy growled. "First time that Stackhouse ever let me down. Put us in *Punjabi*'s wake, Number One. Our friend Guenter is still out there."

Chapter 29

Aboard U-3535

Frick's five minutes were long gone. That wasn't what concerned Kern now; it was the flash of lights that they saw on the horizon. They sputtered out, replaced by darkness. There was finality to the night consuming the light, the last act of an unseen play. Hartmann, standing on the conning tower roof, lowered his binoculars.

"I couldn't see anything," he told Kern.

No one on the bridge spoke. They knew what it was that remained invisible below the horizon. They knew that the same thing awaited them in all likelihood.

Kern realized that Engle was calling through the voice tube.

"Yes, Engle?"

"Eight minutes now, sir."

Anger instantly flared through Kern and he jumped up onto the roof of the conning tower.

"Frick?" he shouted. "I said five minutes, not twenty! What the devil are you doing back there?"

The chief engineer's voice came out of the darkness. "Almost got it, Kaleu."

"Do you want to spend the rest of your life on the

bottom?" Kern asked. "Get that thing up and locked into place."

"Kaleu?" Hartmann said.

"What?"

"Funker just told me that he picked up a distress signal from U-3712."

Kern waited for Hartmann to finish.

"They reported that they were being attacked," the executive officer continued soberly. "That's all."

"Got it, Kaleu," Frick shouted from the stern. "Ready to go!"

Kern watched as the deck party scurried back to the conning tower. He felt empty, used up, and for a moment he was not even sure that he could turn and make his way back to the bridge station. His strength was gone, his will was gone, and nothing recognizable remained of him. He felt that if he did not move he would be paralyzed atop the conning tower. More of his men dead.

He knew what it was; it was shame, deeper than he had ever felt in his life. He wanted to scream. He wanted to shout at the heavens to God and to the idiots who sent him on this suicide mission. He wanted to be away from the madness, away from the guilt that ate at him, back on Lake Constance. His eyes sought out the crisp light of the million stars in the blackness above him. He was a boy, lying with his arms thrust behind his head aboard his tiny craft, floating on the soft waters of the lake, comforted by the stars above.

"Kaleu?"

He felt Hartmann's hand on his shoulder. Kern nodded without looking at the officer. He was afraid to speak, for fear that his emotions would be betrayed in his voice. Finally he said, "All right, Teddy," in little more than a whisper. The sight of the other men watching snapped Kern to.

"Diving stations!" Kern shouted. "Clear the bridge!" One by one, the lookouts dropped through the hatch and into the conning tower. Two men stayed to try to return the stubborn Hohentweil to its housing. "Leave it," Kern commanded.

The men did as they were told and slipped through the hatch. Kern turned to Hartmann, but his executive officer spoke first.

"It wasn't your fault, Kaleu. I think you sometimes forget that it is the war."

There was nothing for Kern to say, no way for him to explain how he felt and what he knew was waiting on all of them. No words existed for a moment such as this.

"You first, Teddy," Kern said.

The executive officer pulled down the splash guards and disappeared down the hatch. Kern took one more look into the black sky. The stars shimmered in reply. They were friends to Kern; he knew them as a boy and felt comfort at their presence.

"Good-bye, old friends," he whispered and then descended into the conning tower, pulling the hatch behind him. It shut with a clang, and there was a faint whir as the wheel was spun to seal it against the water pressure. U-3535, the undersea rockets strapped to her back, blew air from her ballast tanks and shuddered as the diesel engines shut off and the electric motors took over. Slowly, by the bow, the gray shape began to slide into the black water, churning the sea white with her attempt to return to the safety of the depths. Her forward deck disappeared first, then the water raced greedily to consume the conning tower, and when the tower was gone, all that remained were the rockets, and in an instant they too were gone. All that existed of U-3535 was a faint swell with a white top, running to mark where the U-boat had gone. That did not last. The sea disavowed any knowledge of the boat and the men.

"I knew it, Stackhouse!" Hardy shouted, clapping the sailor on the back. "I knew you'd find him. Didn't I say that, Number One? Didn't I say that there wasn't a Jerry alive that could elude Stackhouse?"

"No, sir. I don't believe you did."

"Well," Hardy said, looking over the senior asdic rating's shoulder at the radar screen. "If I didn't say it, I should have. Now, boy, show me what I'm looking at."

"Just there, sir." Stackhouse pointed on the screen. "Sometimes if the seas are up, I'll get ghosts thrown back at me. The impulses, I mean, like shadows."

"Yes. Go on, go on."

"Well, normally I'd say that the signal we just saw was that. But after getting a look at the signal from the other U-boat, I don't think that it's a ghost."

"No ghost, eh?"

"No, sir. Here's the strange part of it. She didn't disappear all at once, sir, like a ghost would do with the rise and fall of the seas. It was gradual. Like she was shrinking."

"Or she was U-boat diving," Land said.

Stackhouse looked up at Number One from his station. "Yes, sir. That's what I thought too."

"If we picked it up, then the Tribal picked it up," Hardy said. "Possibly. Stackhouse, you've restored my faith in you and your kind. Not that I lost it for any length of time, you understand. Just a temporary condition."

"Yes, sir," Stackhouse said, as Hardy and Land made for the bridge. Chief Yeoman of Signals Stapleton was just finishing a steaming hot cup of tea when Hardy passed him. Stapleton quickly handed the cup off to Brown.

"Signals? Make to the Tribal."

"Message just coming from *Punjabi* now, sir," the duty signalman called.

"I knew it!" Hardy said.

"'*Punjabi* to *Firedancer* . . . strong signal . . . ten miles . . . ahead.'"

"Trust that inconsiderate oaf to get out his B-bar before I could," Hardy said to Land, referring to the opening Morse signal for U-boat.

"' . . . Contact firm . . . classified . . . U-boat . . .'"

"All right! All right," Hardy snapped. "Acknowledge the message and let's get on with it. '*Firedancer* to *Punjabi*. Well done. Proceed at best speed to target. *Firedancer* will back you up.' There! I've said it, Number One. Care to stand down from Action Stations now?"

"Wouldn't hear of it, sir,"

"Good. Now listen to me. I want that U-boat for *Firedancer*. She's ours, make no mistake about that, and if we get her I'll sign every officer's wine chit twice over. Pass that along, Number One, and let's make a good showing for *Firedancer*.

Funker looked up. "Two. High-speed screws. Destroyers. Bearing three-oh-oh to three-six-oh."

"How far?" Kern asked. "Speed?"

"A little less than ten miles, Kaleu. Close to thirty knots."

Hartmann waited for his question at the plotting table.

"How far to the launch point, Teddy?"

"Three miles. If we want to be exact."

Kern knew that the crew was waiting on his reply. They would do anything he asked, he knew that. But they wanted something in return, something that only he could give them. That was the way it always was, the crew would give him their support and loyalty without question, but in return they wanted to be treated like U-boatmen. Like a covenant, Kern once tried to explain to a photographer in the calm darkness of her bedroom. She had listened, running her fingers through his short beard. They had just made love and he thought it important that she understand something about himself. Perhaps because he knew that he would never live to have children and therefore the knowledge would die with him. Perhaps partly because it meant a great deal to Kern and he wanted to share it with her.

On the truest level, Kern said, it is trust. We learn to trust each other without question because our lives are at stake. Then there is respect. For ourselves and again for each other.

A brotherhood, she said, kissing his forehead, her warm breasts pressing against his arm, which ends only in death. Yes, he agreed, I guess you can call it that. She looked at him and said, I envy you. I have never been that close with anyone in my life. It is the war, Kern said. Everything is the war, she said, kissing him hungrily.

She was killed in an air raid on Dresden.

Kern looked around at the expectant faces in the control room. A brotherhood of mariners.

"No, Teddy," Kern said. "We don't want to be exact

today. Let's get those bastards off our back and go
find the English."

The crew cheered and immediately turned to their
stations. Teddy grinned broadly, his white teeth flashing against his sparse beard. Frick appeared, wiping
grease from his hands with a worn rag.

"What is this?" the engineer asked.

"Prepare to launch your rockets, Chief Engineer,"
Teddy said. The executive officer gave orders to turn
the boat stern-first toward land—pointing the rockets'
blunt snouts to Liverpool.

Frick looked at Kern for confirmation. Kern smiled
in return and nodded.

The engineer threw the rag to the deck. "High
time, I say!"

Kern pulled the address microphone from its
mount and pushed the talk button. "Attention! We
have reached the launch site. We will launch the rockets, then turn and deal with the English destroyers
that have been following us. They are unwelcome
guests in our waters and we shall ask them to remove
themselves." He clicked the microphone button off.
"Teddy, this is what you and Frick have been waiting
and training for. Get those rockets off the deck immediately."

"Yes, Kaleu. I hope the firing mechanism works."

"If it doesn't, Teddy Hartmann, I will send you out
on deck to fire them manually. And the chief engineer with you. Get to your firing stations."

Hartmann and Frick had command of the boat
for the period that it took them to align and fire the
rockets.

Kern squeezed by a seaman to Funker's tiny room.
The serious young man slowly twisted dials, listened
in the earphones, and watched his instruments. He

was following the Tommies carefully, Kern knew. He would not lose sight of them.

"Just the two, Kaleu," Funker said without looking up.

"There were four at one time," Kern said. "Are you sure there are just two now? Could this be another group?"

"No," Funker said, his face a mask of concentration. "The sound pattern is very distinct. Maybe U-3712 gave a good accounting of herself."

"We'll do better," Kern said. This time, the young man looked up and smiled.

"Yes, sir."

Kern rejoined Hartmann in the control room. Teddy had a microphone in his hand, held tightly to his chest. It was very quiet with only the soft click of relays and whispered orders from a chief to the hydroplane operators.

"Port motor half ahead," Hartmann ordered. "Set course one-eight-oh." To Kern he said, "I shot the stars when we were surfaced. I'll get us turned into position."

"What a way to fight a war," Kern said, "ass-end to the enemy."

"Course one-eight-oh," the helmsman confirmed.

"Port motor back," Hartmann said. "Depth?"

"Tower is twelve meters."

The rockets were positioned so that the tips of their noses, when the rails were extended, were the same height as the roof of the conning tower.

"Take us up two meters."

Kern smiled at Hartmann's calm manner. He would make an excellent U-boat kapitaen.

"Do you know what the crew has named the RGTs, Kaleu?" he asked Kern. "'Rarely Get There.'"

"We have a very creative crew, Teddy."

"Ten meters, tower to surface, sir."

"All ready, Chief Engineer?" Hartmann asked into the microphone.

"Yes, sir," the reply came.

"You've got your men on station?" Hartmann asked.

"If the rockets cause a leak, I'll be the first to know," the chief engineer answered. The railings were attached to the deck, not the boat's pressure hull, so that the likelihood of damage to the pressure hull was slim. No one knew for sure what would happen when the rockets ignited.

"I'd better be the first to know," Hartmann said. "I'm the one who can get us to the surface. Remove safeties. Stand by to launch." Kern knew that Frick was opening two tiny doors that covered the fire buttons. He simply had to push them when ordered, sending a signal to the ignition system in the belly of the rockets. They would fly from the submerged deck, shooting above the stern, and disappear into the night. All that would remain was the glowing stars of the rocket engines.

If, Kern knew, everything worked as it should. And it would, he knew. The best of German engineering, like this wonderful boat. He looked around. The best of Germany's sailors. Kern's mouth was dry. He tried swallowing, but it didn't help. He had not felt this way since his first war cruise as an ensign. When was that? Late in '39, wasn't it? It must have been because of the Fellow Upstairs that he survived—it couldn't have been from his own skill, not as many mistakes as he made on his first voyage. Where were those men now, the crew of his first boat?

Why should it not be the case? Kern asked himself. Why send men to die when all you need do is send

their machines out to do battle? Let the machines
rust on the sea floor without the bones of poor sailors
to accompany them. He looked at the bearded faces
of the men in the control room. There was Hartmann, whose kind eyes held his men in the highest
esteem and whose sense of humor rounded the sharp
edges of difficulty.

Kerrl, who would never be the engineer that Frick
was and who was entirely content with that destiny.
His strength lay in his unshakable ability to persevere.
Funker, quiet, young, dedicated Funker, his submariner's beard nothing more than light fuzz around
a boyish chin. The look in his eyes, they were an old
man's eyes. He had seen too much for his years.

Kern straightened, removed his battered cap, and
ran his fingers through his oily hair. And what were they
now? he thought. What was he now? To fire disease into
civilians—to bring war to women and children. Godt
and Doenitz ordered it easily enough and Langsdorff
accepted it without question. But was this how it was
done now? Most of his crew was dead, buried in the
black sea in splendid coffins, because the mission was
all that he ever contemplated. He never lost sight of it,
not even when Langsdorff and his bullies took over the
camp, not when Gorlitz and Hickman showed up—not
when he was told that he was to have three boats, not
fifteen. When does a warrior become a murderer?
When does a U-boatman give up all that makes him
what he is? "I'm responsible for my share of destruction
in this war," he remembered telling Langsdorff. Could
not dignity be one of the few things that survive this
war? He slipped his cap back onto his head and tugged
it into position.

His father's face came to mind—the words coming
softly out of the past: because it was the right thing to

do. *How could I live with myself if I had done anything else? Is that such a false notion—is it unrealistic to think that way and behave that way? What did my father give away?* Kern asked himself, and now, for the first time in the many years that had passed, he had the answer. Nothing. He saved the most important part of who he was and how he lived—his integrity.

"Teddy," Kern said softly. "Bring us about."

Hartmann looked up. "Kaleu?"

"Bring us about, Teddy," Kern ordered again. "Point our ass out to sea."

"But, Kaleu—"

"We are warriors, Teddy. Not butchers. Bring us about."

Hartmann exchanged glances with Mend. "Yes, Kaleu," he said. He turned to the helmsman and gave the order. "You heard the kapitaen, bring this big boat about. Ahead one-third, hard right rudder." He turned back to Kern and nodded.

The men braced themselves as U-3535 surged ahead and then began to turn slowly.

Frick's voice crackled over the intercom. "What are you madmen doing up there?"

Kern picked up the microphone. "Relax, Frick. We know what we're doing."

"Are you trying to put those goddamned things in the Irish Sea?"

Kern smiled at Hartmann. "Yes, old friend. That's the idea."

There was silence on the other end of the speaker until Frick's voice came through in a barely audible "Oh." And then he caught himself. "Well, this is a fine time to tell me, Kaleu," he said gruffly.

"We're in position, Kaleu," Hartmann announced.

"Proceed," Kern said.

"Ready for rocket one?" Hartmann called into the microphone. "On my mark at five . . ."

So we have come full circle, Kern thought. No diabolical weapons, no murderous disease flung at innocent women and children. He thought of the little girl in Berlin. No festering sores or whatever this hateful payload produced.

". . . Four . . ."

Kern wondered if this was the way that submariners would fight wars in the future, hidden from each other by the sea. *The depths are our protection, let them be our sanctuary.* Unseen men in wonderful boats that did everything. No, not everything. It was the men who sailed them and fought them and it was men to whom the homecoming was so joyous. There could never be boats without men; the thought was too obscene for consideration.

". . . three . . ."

Now we will unload these things and go and fight as we should. Ship against U-boat, sailor against sailor—our battlefield the green sea.

". . . Two . . ."

"Propeller noise, getting louder fast!" Funker called out. "Estimate distance at four miles. Speed thirty knots."

"Contact type?" Kern asked quickly.

"Destroyer, sir. Wait . . . two, sir. Two."

". . . One . . ."

Perhaps it is best that I do not see the future, Kern thought. *I would not want to captain a boat without men such as this to crew her.*

"Fire!"

There was a loud rush and the boat pitched wildly to one side. Men grabbed on to what they could to keep themselves from falling. Kern heard loose objects throughout the boat clatter to the deck.

"All stations report!" Hartmann ordered.

"Flood cells three and four," Kern ordered. This was expected. The boat needed to compensate for the weight of the remaining rocket. They did the same things for torpedoes, when one was loosed they immediately trimmed the boat.

It was an elementary procedure. "Bring the boat back to zero." Even a machine would know to do it.

All stations reported in except the engine room. No damage.

Kern hit the talk button on the loudspeaker. "Frick? Are you asleep back there?"

The chief engineer's excited voice came over the speaker. "Frick here. One away and no leaks. It's as dry as the desert here."

"Don't get too excited. We don't know if the damn thing cleared the surface."

"I heard it go, Kaleu! It was wonderful. Whoosh! And she was off the deck!"

"Get rid of the other one, Frick," Kern ordered calmly. "The English are coming for tea." He glanced at Teddy.

Hartmann nodded quickly and pressed the talk button. "Ready for two! Remove safety. Stand by to launch. On my mark . . ."

"Two miles, sir!" Funker sang out, his voice tight with excitement. He gave Kern an embarrassed glance. "Sorry, Kaleu." The boy never liked to show his excitement. He felt that was unseemly.

"Keep tracking them, Funker."

"Five . . ."

"Right, Kaleu."

"Four . . ."

"Funker, give me the range at half-mile increments."

"Three . . ."

"Kerrl, I want the attack periscope up the second that rocket is fired. Get the boat back to zero immediately. I can't shoot uphill. Be ready to dive to 170 and secure the boat for a wabo attack. We may have to take our punishment before we can welcome Tommy."

"Two . . ."

Kern positioned himself in front of the shaft for the attack periscope, his hands ready to grasp and deploy the range-and-sight handles the moment the instrument slid into position. His eyes were on Hartmann, and Hartmann's were on the stopwatch cupped in his hand.

"One . . . Fire!"

Nothing happened.

Hartmann shot Kern a terrified glance. "Frick!" the executive officer shouted into the microphone. "What the hell is going on back there? Didn't you hear me? Get that damned thing off my boat!"

There was no reply.

Kern moved instantly. "Hartmann! Go!" he commanded. The exec sprinted toward the engine room. Kern picked up the microphone dangling by its cord and clicked the talk button. "Attention. This is Kern. The second rocket misfired. Tommy has two destroyers coming, so be prepared for wabos." He released the button and waited. They couldn't dive deep enough to escape the English depth bombs with that damned thing on their back and they couldn't maneuver worth a damn with the extra weight and bulk.

They were trapped near the surface. Within easy reach of even the most incompetent destroyer captain. Kern felt beads of sweat run down his neck. Nothing moved. No one talked. *Hurry, Teddy! For God's sake, hurry!*

There was a whoosh, and the boat shuddered, rolling to one side. Men who had forgotten the experience of the first rocket tumbled across the deck. Several cried out in pain as they struck pipes, wheels, and levers.

"Prepare for diving maneuver," Kern ordered into the microphone. "All men to the bow room. Now!" The sudden rush of weight would tip the boat's nose down and make U-3535 dive faster. "Both engines emergency ahead. Hard right rudder. Flood tanks one and two." Kern continued giving orders as the men rushed past him and toward the forward torpedo room. Those who remained on station frantically pulled levers and rotated hand wheels to increase the speed of the air exiting, and the water entering the tanks. "Down twenty on the forward hydroplanes. Dive to 170."

Kern heard the roar of the water rushing into the buoyancy tanks accompanied by the hiss of the air being ejected. His eyes darted to the Papenberg. Fifty meters.

The U-boat groaned as she clawed for the safety of the depths. She was a remarkable lady, but she was big and she protested such treatment. Loose tools slid down the deck and bounced off table legs, stools, and instrument panels.

"One point five miles, Kaleu," Funker said. "Speed thirty knots. Two destroyers only. No other contacts."

The angle of U-3535's dive deepened but not enough to satisfy Kern. Her stern was still too close to the surface—still vulnerable to wabos.

"Flood trim cells one through four," Kern ordered.

It was risky, for with the trim cells flooded, only her speed kept her from plummeting to the bottom. If the engines gave out now, they would sink until the pressure destroyed U-3535. "Left standard rudder. Give me depth readings every twenty-five meters. Bring us about. I need sea room to maneuver."

Hartmann appeared in the control room. "Sorry," he said but Kern didn't know if he was apologizing for being off station or the failure of the rocket to fire when ordered. It was not important. Keeping away from the wabos was.

"Teddy, get ready to deploy the Pillenwerfer," Kern said. The Pillenwerfer was a chemical device that when released would provide a false signal for the enemy's asdic.

"Seventy-five meters," the hydroplane man said.

"One mile, Kaleu. Speed still thirty knots."

"They must want to meet us very badly," Hartmann said under his breath.

"We're heroes, Teddy," Kern allowed wryly. "We're the first U-boat to launch rockets at the enemy."

"I wonder where in the hell they landed."

"One hundred meters, Kaleu!"

"I don't, Teddy. I'm just happy to be rid of them," Kern said, picking up the microphone. "All men back to your stations. Close and secure all watertight doors. Engine room?"

"This is Frick," the voice crackled over the intercom system.

"Stand by for V-belt drive," Kern said. "Silent running. Turn off all unnecessary machinery. Go to emergency lighting." He hung the microphone on its hook and said to Hartmann: "Let's make it as difficult as possible for our English friend to find us."

"Yes. Let's," Hartmann replied as the men rushed

back to their stations. From throughout the boat came the clang and whir of watertight doors being closed and sealed.

"One hundred twenty-five meters on the Papenberg."

"One half mile, Kaleu," Funker said. "Targets reducing speed. Down to twenty knots. One has dropped back a bit. Something's in the water . . . antitorpedo devices. Ten knots. Now less . . . probably five knots."

"One hundred fifty meters, Kaleu."

Kern nodded. "Up ten degrees on the forward hydroplanes. Teddy, bring the boat to zero. Have Frick start the V-belt drive, speed five knots. I don't want the English to hear us or see us, so now we need a little luck."

"We can go deeper," Teddy said. "The boat is built for it."

Kern smiled in reply. "Yes, I know we can, Teddy," he said gently. "But first I want to bloody Tommy's nose. With our V-belt, they can't hear us. We will sneak up on them and give them an eel or two. All right?"

Hartmann understood. There had been enough running on this trip—now it was time to fight. "Right," he said.

"Lost them!" Hardy shouted. "How the devil could the Tribal lose them?"

"I don't know, sir," Land returned as Signal finished reading off the message flashing over the Morse lamp.

Signals looked at Land helplessly. "That's it, sir. Nothing else."

Hardy shook his fist skyward. "I vow to the Almighty above that if I ever get out of this, I will never take a

Tribal to sea with me again. Have we the rat hole that
Jerry slipped into? We've got that at least, haven't
we?"

"His last location? Yes, sir."

"Well, by God! Tell *Punjabi* to head for that."

"Aye-aye, sir," Land said and gave the order to Signals to make to the Tribal.

"I swear to God, Number One, our ships might not
frighten the enemy, but by God, sir, they frighten
me!"

"Message sent, sir," Land said. "CATS are streaming."

"*Punjabi* signals yellow flag, sir," Signals called out.

"Well, at least they have the good sense not to fly
the contact flag," Hardy growled. "That would certainly add insult to injury."

Land watched as *Punjabi* adjusted her course, edg-
ing up to seven knots, the maximum speed that was
reported safe from the acoustic torpedoes.

"Signal is attacking, sir," Number One reported.
"She's at them, sir. In fine form, too."

Hardy leaned on the windscreen and watched the
Tribal at work. "Yes, well, we'll see about that. Veer
well off to starboard, Number One. We'll come back
around to launch our attack."

"Yes, sir."

Firedancer rolled heavily, her stern swinging to port
and her knife-edged bow to starboard. She churned up
a lane of white water that glowed fluorescent in the
darkness, marking her passage. She was anxious to be
at the enemy. *Punjabi* kept steady on her course. Suddenly the Y-mount launchers on either side exploded
with a puff of white smoke and a flash in the darkness.
The charges threw the thousand-pound depth charges
high into the air. In slow motion the Y-mounts sepa-

rated from the depth charge, invisible in the darkness, and they fell into the sea. At her stern, the depth charge bell rang and her crew began rolling depth charges out of their rails every fifteen seconds. More Y-mounts were blown out to port and starboard, with dull booms and quick flashes of greenish light. Anxious not to be excluded, the Hedge Hogs shot from their mount on the bow, arching graceful into the darkness so that the only evidence that they existed was the twenty-four simultaneous splashes 250 yards in front of the Tribal.

"Good pattern," Hardy commented. "Good show." He knew that all they could do was wait, as the depth charges sank to their prescribed depth before exploding.

Land had a stopwatch in his hand, holding it close to the faint light of the binnacle so that he could see to count off the seconds. It was not an exact science, trying to kill an enemy with barrels of high explosives. The underwater explosions would not be lethal unless they were within thirty feet of their target.

"Now," Hardy heard Land say.

The black water exploded with a great rumble and tower of white water that rushed into the air. Charge after charge exploded, tearing at the sea in an effort to get the enemy.

Kern gripped the attack periscope housing to keep from being thrown to the deck as U-3535 jerked from the nearby explosions. The big boat danced sideways through the water before finding a quiet patch in which to settle.

"Report!" Kern commanded. The damage reports came back negative and Kern gave Hartmann a smile.

"Take her up to periscope depth, Exec," he said. "Now it's our turn."

Kern watched the Papenberg as U-3535 slowly moved upward. He silently planned the method of attack, and wondered if it would be possible to position the U-boat directly between the two enemy destroyers. He knew it was unlikely, but the thought thrilled him just the same.

"Depth?"

"Twenty-one meters," Kerrl said.

"Hold us there," Kern ordered. "Periscope." He swung around the housing as the rising periscope cleared the deck and stopped just below eye level. His hands gripped the handles securely, and he flipped through the lenses, trying to find the right power to locate the destroyers. Waves washed over the small head of the attack periscope, blurring the images that were already difficult to see in the darkness, but Kern would take the periscope no higher. Much smaller than the cruising periscope it still left a wake that was visible even at night.

"Got it," Kern said as his eyes picked out a shadow in the darkness. He leaned past Hartmann to Kerrl. "Forward Torpedo Room," he ordered. "Tubes one and two ready for submerged attack. T-11. Torpedo depth seven . . . open tube doors. Stand by for angle. Speed five knots. Range one thousand yards." He knew what the Tommies wanted to do, they wanted to sneak up behind him. He pressed his head against the foam rubber mount, blocking out even the faint light and images that surrounded him. He was alone with his target and his U-boat. "Target angle fifty left."

"Tubes one through four ready," Hartmann reported.

"New impulse bearing 140," Funker said.

"Chief, hold our exact depth!"

"Forward zero, aft ten," Kerrl ordered the hydroplane operators.

"Hold zero bearing," Kern said. And then to Funker: "Well?"

"New impulse still 140. Speed five knots."

"Let me know if they increase speed." To Hartmann: "Course and speed plotted?"

"Yes, sir."

"Fire tubes one and two on my mark. Ready? Three, two, one . . . Mark."

The boat pitched slightly as the torpedo left the tube with a whoosh of escaping air.

"One fired, sir," Teddy reported, stopwatch in hand.

"Ready? Three . . . two . . . one . . . Mark!" The second torpedo was on its way. Kern slapped the handles back into their recesses and ordered: "Down scope!" He moved out of the way and the periscope descended. "Close tube doors one and two. Time?"

Teddy's eyes never left the watch. "Ten seconds . . . nine . . . eight . . . seven . . ."

"Take us deep, Kerrl, 250."

He saw Teddy smile at the order, his eyes on the hand sweeping around the watch face.

"Okay, Exec?" Kern asked.

Teddy nodded. "Three . . . two . . . one . . . Contact."

There was nothing but silence.

"Missed!" someone said in disgust.

"Number two?" Kern said.

Teddy kept counting. "In three . . . two . . . one . . ."

"Kaleu!" Funker shouted. "I think it's turned on us!"

"What?"

"Oh, God," Kerrl said.

"Quiet!" Kern barked. "Are you sure, Funker? Be

sure about that." He waited as the soundman frantically twisted knobs and sealed the earphones against
his ears with his hands. He looked at Kern in horror,
his eyes searching for an answer.

"I don't know, Kaleu . . . I can't tell."

"Be sure, Funker," Kern said calmly. "You can do it."

Funker's trembling hand played over the black
knobs, his unwavering eyes fixed on the thin needles
that danced across the face of the dials. He looked at
Kern and nodded.

"All stop!" Kern shouted. He flicked on the intercom. "Frick? Shut everything down. Everything!" He
looked around the control room. "Not a sound. Do
you hear me?"

"Killed by our own torpedoes," Hartmann whispered as the sound in the boat died. Emergency lights
sparked to life, bathing the men in red.

Kern turned to the soundman. "Funker?" he whispered.

"It's looking for a target."

No one moved or spoke—the ship was dead, floating lifelessly in the cold sea.

Kern could feel his heart thundering in his chest and
he knew that the others must hear it as well. He found
himself breathing softly as if to draw a deep breath
would betray the boat to the torpedo. It was a mindless
weapon that saw only a target, any target, and finding a
target it drove in relentlessly until it made contact—
until it destroyed the thing that it was after.

Sweat trickled down Kern's forehead from under
his cap and he thought of scratching it but he dared
not move. His nerves were strung so tightly that he
was frozen in place. Every faint noise was a shout,
every breath a scream, every tiny crack of the boat set-

tling a cannon shot. And out there, unseen, was the hunter.

Funker adjusted a knob, grimacing as if the motion itself would draw the T-11 to them. He bit his lip, listening. The others waited, watching him.

One of the young helmsmen began to cough. The others shot him a look that silenced him.

"Funker?" Kern whispered and then damned himself for speaking. But it must be safe now. The thing must have sped off in search of other targets, to run out of fuel and sink harmlessly to the ocean floor. It must be safe now.

The young soundman removed one earphone and looked at Kern with relief. "She's gone."

Kern held up his hand for silence before anyone spoke. "You're sure?"

"Gone," Funker said.

"Power up," Kern ordered Hartmann as the men relaxed. "Let's get back at it. Tubes three and four, prepare to fire. Periscope depth. Take me up so that I can find those bastards." He smiled at Funker and clapped him on the back. "You had me worried."

Funker nodded, slipping his earphones back on. "I was worried too, Kaleu," he said weakly.

Kern moved to the attack periscope as it slid up. He unfolded the handles and wrapped his arms around the shaft and pushed his eye into the eyepiece. He swung it around. "I have them." He called out the coordinates to Hartmann, who plotted the angle and speed. "Scope down," Kern ordered as he stood back. "Ready?" he said to Hartmann.

"Yes, Kaleu."

"Teddy," Kern said. "Sink them. Not us."

"I'll do my best, Kaleu."

"On my mark. Three . . . two . . . one . . . Mark."

There was a heavy whoosh and the boat pitched slightly as number three was fired.

"On my mark. Three . . . two . . . one . . . Mark."

The second T-11 left the boat and Kern ordered: "Close outer doors. Time to impact, Teddy?"

Hartmann frowned as he studied the watch. "Ten . . . nine . . . eight . . . seven . . ." he counted down, the others watching him. "Three . . . two . . . one . . . Contact."

Silence followed his words.

The men groaned and cursed.

"Silence!" Kern snapped.

"Three . . . two . . . one . . . Contact."

They heard a dull rumble above them.

Kern clapped Hartmann on the shoulder as the control room erupted with cheers.

Punjabi's stern shot out of the water and her bow was thrust down into the sea. She whipped to starboard, shaking herself free of the blow. She righted herself and then slowly listed to starboard.

Land spun around to stare into hell. What was left of *Punjabi*'s stern was ablaze, yellow flames licking around the aft gun mounts and into the night sky. The fire was reflected off billowing clouds of smoke that rolled out of what had once been the engine room and the aft depth-charge station. There was no doubt that the engine room was gone and a good thirty feet of the stern. They had their supply party, but there wasn't much that could be done because there would be no power for the water hose pumps. *Punjabi* was a powerless hulk, blazing on the open sea.

"How dare they do that to the Tribal!" Hardy

roared. "Cut the CATS," he shouted to Land. "Get them off my ship and give me full speed!"

Land picked up the bridge telephone and shouted: "Aft Station, release the CATS." And without waiting for an acknowledgment he said: "Engine Room, Bridge. All speed. Everything, do you hear?"

"Helm," Hardy ordered. "Starboard, thirty."

Firedancer kicked forward and twisted starboard, shuddering as her screws bit into the sea. She beat the water into a white froth and raced past *Punjabi*, a mother rushing to the aid of her endangered child. *Firedancer* rolled sharply to starboard as she turned to put herself between the U-boat and the stricken vessel. She was running close to twenty knots, all caution forgotten.

"Smash them up, *Firedancer!* Smash them up, girl!" Hardy shouted as the destroyer raced into the darkness. A ragged cheer rose in the darkness from *Punjabi*'s beleaguered crew.

"Contact!" Funker said, clapping his earphones tightly to his head. "Enemy destroyer. Fast, sir. Twenty to twenty-five knots."

Kern was ready for the onslaught. "Emergency power, nonessential lights out. Everybody quiet. They can't get us if they can't find us."

No one moved. The lights dimmed, making the U-boat crew shadows of men.

"Bearing's getting louder."

Kern rubbed his hands together. His palms were sweating. They always did when it got like this, when the devil was about to descend on them.

"Sound bearing's getting louder. Sound bearing 210 degrees . . . getting louder . . ."

Kern waited. Funker would tell them when. Kern saw the soundman's arm inch up toward the headset. He would fling them off at the last moment, before the explosions ruptured his eardrums. His small hands poised near the headset, waiting . . . waiting. "Wabos in the water," he announced calmly. "Arming." He jerked the earphones off his head and threw them on the tiny table.

Dull explosions pitched the boat to port. The lights flickered.

"This fellow knows what he's doing," Hartmann said to no one in particular.

Three explosions quickly followed one another. The deck dropped out from under Kern's feet as the force of the simultaneous explosions drove U-3535 deeper.

"Leakage at tubes!"

"Leakage above exhaust valves!" someone shouted.

"Gentlemen," Kern said calmly, "you can report without becoming excited."

"When do we have your permission to become excited, Kaleu?" Hartmann whispered.

"When the water gets up to your waist."

A wabo exploded with a crash overhead, jarring the boat viciously.

"That's getting close," a seaman said.

"I hope we're not trailing oil."

Kern looked at the boy who was worried about oil. He was a child and surely this was his first war cruise. "It's night above us," Kern said. "No reason to worry about a trail of oil."

Suddenly Kern heard something clatter above his head. He knew what it was.

"Jesus!" someone whispered. "It's stuck on the deck." It was an unexploded wabo, rolling along the boat's outer hull. Everyone's eyes were on the unseen wabo as it slowly made its way across the deck and bounced off the tower. They could hear it now, rolling down the outer hull, dropping below them. Kern prayed silently—*let it drop, dear God, let it drop*. If it exploded now, they would die. He tensed, waiting . . . waiting. The 250-pound wabo exploded, throwing U-3535 upward. He heard several of the crew cry out and a dazed crewman, his face covered in blood, brushed past him. The lights flickered and went out.

Kern heard a crewman gasp in terror. "Keep calm now, boys," he said. The lightbulbs began to glow faintly, struggling to spring to life.

"Leak in the engine room."

"Leak in torpedo room."

"Kaleu? Frick's been injured."

It was a young chief from the engine room. His eyes were wide with terror and his face had taken on a deathly sheen in the poor light.

"He'll have to wait," Kern replied. "We can't do anything now."

The chief nodded and turned to go back to his station.

Hartmann stopped him. "How is Frick?"

"We think his neck is broken. He can't breathe very well."

Hardy ordered *Firedancer* back for another depth charge pattern as the sea churned phosphorescent in their wake. Land and the lookouts searched the waters for signs of debris or the telltale tracks of torpedoes.

"We won't give them time to set up for another shot, Number One," Hardy shouted over the continuous booms of the exploding depth charges. "They'll be so busy dodging about they won't have time to set up."

"And then what?" Land said as the ship shook under the onslaught of her own explosions.

Hardy drove his fist into his palm. "I'll smash the bloody bastards in the water, and if they surface I'll blow them to hell with my guns."

"Message from *Punjabi*, sir," the duty signalman said. "Morse lamp. 'Many dead. No power. Flooding under control. Kill the bastard.' End of message."

"Make to *Punjabi*," Hardy said. "'Consider it done.' End of message."

"Bridge, Stackhouse."

"Bridge here," Land said into the voice tube.

"I'm getting something odd about thirteen hundred yards off the port beam."

Hardy exchanged glances with Land. "How is that bloody fool getting anything in this mess?" He pushed Land to one side. "What is it, Stackhouse?"

"It's metal banging against metal, sir. It's a god-awful racket."

Hardy grinned madly at Land. "We've got him, Number One! By heavens we've got him! Get us over there."

Three more explosions came in rapid succession, shaking U-3535 brutally. Kern was thrown back against the periscope mount, striking his head. He saw flashes of light and then a black cloud. He heard voices, but they were too far away to concern him. His vision began to clear and he felt hands drag him to his feet. He was dazed and something was running down his face, but he couldn't think of what it might be. *It can't be water; if there were water in the boat, we'd all be dead*. He realized that he was thinking nonsensically and he forced himself to concentrate. There was Hartmann's face. And there, Kerrl, and Funker.

Then he heard it—everyone did. A sharp clanging sound, echoing throughout the pressure hull.

"The rails," Hartmann said. "They've broken lose again."

Kern gave a sharp nod and turned to Kerrl. "Take us up, periscope depth."

"Kaleu . . ." Hartman began.

"Up," Kern ordered again.

"We won't have a chance," Hartman said as Kerrl gave the orders.

"Give me my attack periscope, Teddy. I'll give us a chance."

U-3535 rolled as water was forced from her tanks with a roar. The attack periscope slid into Kern's hands. He slapped the handles down and quickly scanned the horizon, searching for the enemy that was trying to kill them.

Firedancer's bow filled the lens.

Kern jumped back and slammed the handles into position. "Scope down! Now! All dive!"

U-3535 groaned as air was expelled from her tanks.

"Everyone forward!" Kern ordered. "Both ahead full."

The men who could be spared dashed through the hatches like madmen, scrambling toward the forward torpedo room. The boat's bow dipped slowly as the men rushed wildly through the control room. Kern slapped them on the back as they passed him, shouting: "Faster. Faster."

"Kaleu!" Funker shouted and then U-3535 was struck by a mountain. She heeled over roughly, throwing shouting men against the bulkhead in a jumble of arms and legs.

Kern pushed himself away from the plotting table as the boat's emergency lights flickered madly. Suddenly ice-cold water began to pour over him.

The tortured screech of tearing metal filled the air around *Firedancer* as the destroyer shuddered from the impact. She hesitated and then broke free, her twisted screws shaking the ship like a terrier shakes a rat.

"All slow," Hardy shouted, picking himself up off the deck. "Goddamn it, Number One, I didn't say ram the bastards!"

"Aft Depth Charge Station," Land called into the telephone. "Barton? Give them everything! Do you hear? Bring them up."

Chapter 30

Aboard U-3535

He knew these men; these men were his crew. Everything was all right. Everything would be just fine now. Turn U-3535 around and head for home. Not that stinking little town in Norway, but home: Germany. *Wit, we'll go to Wit.*

"Kaleu!" Hartmann shouted. "Are you all right? Guenter?"

Kern rubbed his hand over his forehead and felt blood. "Yes. Yes." His men were frantically trying to stop a dozen leaks in the control room. He looked down. Water was up to his shoe tops.

"She hit us," Hartmann said. "Everything up top is sheared off. We've got leaks everywhere. We're taking water forward and aft. The pressure hull is sprung."

"Yes," Kern said dully. He coughed and wiped more blood from his eyes. "Take her up, Teddy. Prepare to abandon ship. Get the codebooks and log. Get everyone ready."

Hartmann nodded and flipped the intercom switch on the bulkhead. "Prepare to abandon ship. Gather the wounded and move to your stations." He switched off the intercom and looked at Kern. "Frick can't be moved. He screams every time someone touches him."

"Get everyone out Teddy," Kern said. "Now."

* * *

Land rushed to the port windscreen as *Firedancer* staggered forward, the vibrating screws beating a staccato rhythm through her plates.

"Lookout reports something on the port bow," he said to Hardy.

Firedancer's captain joined him, pushing his derby free of his forehead to accommodate binoculars.

"Yes, by God!" Hardy said, slapping the windscreen. "She's coming up! Prepare to board, Number One. Have a boat crew stand by. Turn us bow-on to her. I don't want to show her our beam."

"We can't, sir," Land said. "The rudder's jammed as well."

Hardy dropped his binoculars and looked at Land. "Jammed?"

"Everything is a mess underneath. Rudder, screws, shafts."

Hardy growled under his breath and shook his head. "She's too damned dangerous and we're too damned weak to do much about it."

"She's coming up, sir," a lookout shouted.

Hardy and Land watched as the gray bulk of U-3535 broke the surface in a mass of churning water. Its conning tower was reduced to a mangled, twisted wreck.

"There's where we popped her, Number One," Hardy said. "She's a bloody big bastard, all right."

Number One pressed a pair of binocular against his eyes. "Hatches are coming open, sir. She's abandoning ship."

"They'll flood her, by God, they will," Hardy said. "We can't let that happen." He studied the sea momentarily. "Prepare a boarding party, Number One.

Have Signals make to the U-boat in straight Morse code: 'Do not attempt to maneuver.'"

Kern made his way to the torpedo room hatch and clapped a young sailor on the back. The man turned, his face contorted in terror.

"Just climb the ladder, boy," Kern said. "Get up there and wave your hands to Tommy. Nothing to worry about." He waited until the ladder was clear, looked aft for any sign of others, and then climbed quickly through the hatch. His men were huddled in dark clumps along the narrow deck. In the distance he saw the gray shadow of an enemy destroyer slowly making its way toward U-3535. Beyond he saw the bright glare and oily black smoke of the destroyer that they had torpedoed. Kern felt a glimmer of satisfaction at the sight.

"Kaleu?"

He turned at the shout. It was Hartmann, making his way along the rolling deck, a canvas satchel clutched in his arms.

"Here is everything. Codebooks, log, everything."

Kern took the heavy bag from Hartmann and weighed it momentarily in his hands. It was heavy with failure and reminded Kern that he had lost his boat. He flung it as far as he could manage. It hit the water with a silent splash and disappeared.

A shout went up from the men on the deck and Kern turned to see the British destroyer launching lifeboats and a cutter.

"They're coming to rescue us!" a seaman said.

Kern looked at Hartmann. "They're coming to board us, Teddy. They want our U-boat."

"They won't get her," Hartmann said. "She's taking too much water."

"We can't take that chance. See to the men, Teddy," Kern said as he started for the hatch.

Hartmann stopped him. "Where are you going, Kaleu?"

"I'll set the charges. I'll be back up in time to thumb my nose at that Tommy captain."

"It's too dangerous, Kaleu. She's going. You'll be trapped."

Kern put his hand on Hartmann's shoulder and squeezed it. "See to the men, Teddy. We'll toast each other with English tea in a few minutes."

Hartmann nodded and said nothing.

Kern quickly made his watch to the torpedo room hatch and started down the ladder. He stopped just long enough to pull the hatch shut with a loud clang and dog it tight. The boat shifted heavily throwing him to one side. Perhaps Hartmann was right; the old girl wouldn't last much longer. He looked down to see water swirling angrily around his shoes. He wouldn't need the charges after all. U-3535 had her own ideas about capture.

Kern made his way to the engine room as U-3535 rolled heavily. He found Frick lying in a foot of water, shivering. Two other seamen, dead, lay near him.

"Hello, old friend," Kern said, kneeling next to the engineer.

Frick struggled to talk, his haunted eyes searching for an answer from Kern.

"Don't worry. We're going up. You'll be in a nice soft English bed in no time."

"You're a liar," Frick whispered.

Kern smiled. "You know I can have you demoted for that."

Frick grimaced as a wave of pain rolled over him. His face was pale and his eyes were taking on that glassy, far-away look of dying men. "Who will run your stinking boat if you do?" he finally managed.

Kern sat down next to him and took off his cap. He looked at it absentmindedly and threw it atop a control panel. "I suppose you're right." He took Frick's hand in his. He felt the boat shudder as more water poured in. She was settling by the bow; she had more leaks than she had let on.

"Get out of here, you damned fool," Frick whispered.

"Soon," Kern said.

"You ignorant bastard! She's sinking. Get out now."

"The Tommies want her. They're sending a boarding party over."

"She won't let their rotten filthy hands touch her. She's a lady."

Kern leaned against a pump housing.

"Kaleu?" Frick said, his voice weak and ragged. "She's a fine boat, isn't she?"

Kern smiled. "A fine boat, old friend. A fine crew. They both deserved better." He felt the boat slide and knew that she would be gone any moment now. "Have you ever been to Lake Constance?"

Frick breathed raggedly and whispered, "No."

Kern closed his eyes and thought of sailing. He saw the clear blue sky and the crisp white sail fat with wind. He felt the smoothness of the tiller with his hand as the water tugged playfully at the rudder, trying to snatch it away from his grip. He heard the soft rush of the lake beneath him and felt the spray tickle his face. He laid his head back on his neck and looked up at the stately shimmering clouds, and knew that nothing in his life gave him as much pleasure as to know that they smiled down on him.

U-3535 trembled and then lurched and the deck slid out from under him. His eyes met Frick's, and in an instant they both knew. Then the sea devoured them.

Chapter 31

Holy Island, the Irish Sea, October 1978

Cole sat back in his chair and closed the notebook. Land was at the liquor cabinet. He turned with a bottle in his hand. "Care for another spot?"

Cole examined his glass but thought better of it. "No, thanks. But don't let me stop you."

"No danger in that," Land said, pouring himself a healthy measure. The sun was just rising, its warmth filling the horizon and broad sea, the sky above it electric with orange, blue, yellow, and red hues. The light poked its head inquisitively through half-closed curtains, drawn late last night to keep the cold sea air out.

Cole watched it brazenly reclaim its rightful place above the earth. Suddenly a blast of light flooded the room, startling him.

"Sorry, old boy," Land said, stepping away from the open curtains. "I don't see as well as I used to."

"I wonder why he did it," Cole said.

"How's that?"

"Why the U-boat captain sent those missiles out to sea? To come all that way—to travel that far and not complete his mission."

"Would you rather he had?" Land said, but the

question was only a reaction. "No, of course not. Forgive me."

"But it's an interesting question."

"We shall never know," Land said. "A case of taking one's secret to one's grave."

"It was just one less abomination unleashed on the world. We can thank God for that."

"God, or one man's conscience," Land said. "In any case it would have been horrible if the missiles had reached land. But they didn't, of course. Some Coastal Command chaps were tracking them on radar and they fell into the sea. Lucky for us. Lucky for Liverpool, I mean. I wonder if that chap was so different from us."

"I make it a habit of avoiding philosophical questions," Cole said. "In war, they could prove to be very dangerous."

"You mean the enemy is always the enemy. Nothing more, nothing less?"

Cole nodded. "If you want to sleep at night."

"Did you know that Churchill authorized biological warfare? When things were going badly for us, there was talk of using that hideous stuff against the Germans. Desperate measures. So the question still stands, Cole: was he so different from us?"

"Read my book and find out," Cole said. There were no answers to questions such as that. It did no good to suppose or guess or play games of hindsight after men had died. It did nothing but build guilt and uncertainty and increase the almost intolerable burden that one carried. *That I once carried*, Cole corrected himself. *That I carry*.

"It's the old man coming out in me," Land said. "My musings, I call them." He waved the mood away.

"Ah, it's all nonsense anyway. If old Georgie were here he'd set me straight in an instant."

Cole sighed deeply. "War makes people and nations do terrible things." He watched Land set his glass on the end table and he noticed the look of a man whose memories were wrapping themselves around him like a veil.

"You're getting tired, aren't you? I shouldn't have taken so much of your time."

"I'm afraid so," Land said, easing himself out of his chair. He extended his hand. "I'm getting along in years. Sometimes I forget myself. It was very nice of you to come by. Do come again."

"I'd like that, Land. And I'll bring a bottle to replace yours."

Land laughed and walked Cole to the door and watched as he climbed into a tiny sports car and drove off. He looked at his hands. They were wrinkled and covered with spots and the fingers were twisted with arthritis. Land closed the door slowly and made his way back into the den. A hideous painting of a country barn hung on the wall next to the fireplace, and on the opposite wall was a faded photograph of a group of young naval officers gathered around an aged man wearing a derby. The derby itself hung beside it.

He walked to the window and gazed out over the cliff to the pale blue sea beyond, watching the endless waves roll placidly toward him. There was no horizon, just the ocean and a misty sky.